THE TAKEOVER

Don Moggs

Pen Press Publishers Ltd

Published in Great Britain by
Pen Press Publishers Ltd
39–41, North Road
Islington
London N7 9DP

ISBN 1-905203-10-1

Cover design Jacqueline Abromeit

About the author

Don Moggs was born in London's East End, the son of an engine driver on the L.N.E.R. After early schooling in the West Ham and Dagenham, he won a scholarship to Romford Royal Liberty School, later moving to the grammar school in Enfield.

Pre-war, he worked as an office clerk and during the war served in the RAF as a pilot and an accountant Officer. After the war he qualified as an accountant, going on to become Financial Director of a public company. He has also worked as a consultant in industry and as administrator to an international firm of architects and consulting engineers.

Don Moggs currently lives in Surrey, where well in his eighties he continues to write. Previous publications include; *Dad's War*, an account of his wartime experiences, *The Moscow Contract*, and *The Takeover, first published in 2000*; this is a revised edition. Also published by Pen Press: *The Adventures of Diana and Harry, Incident 1986 and The Turin Contract*.

To my wife, Diana.

CONTENTS

take over *vb (adv)* **1** to assume the control or management of. **2**. *Printing.* To move (copy) to the next line.
◆*n* **takeover. 3a** the act of seizing power, control, etc. **3b** *(as modifier): takeover bid.*

PROLOGUE

JULIUS STEINBERG had come to the end of the road, a very long road with many casualties on the way. Although he was not a criminal in the accepted sense – indeed he was regarded with respect and admiration by many – he was viewed by some as a villain who had ruined lives, caused death and inflicted suffering on innocents. He would of course be mourned but there were many who, had they noticed the announcement of his demise, would shed no tears.

The circumstances of his death aroused no comment, he was after all almost ninety years of age and even though his health had been good throughout his life, a sudden heart attack and a fall from a balcony came as no surprise. The doctor certified natural death caused by a sudden heart attack and the matter was closed.

The local police chief of the small New Hampshire town had visited the house to see the corpse more as a matter of routine than trying to find any cause of foul play: after all, their small town had for two decades benefited from tourists who wanted to see the home of Julius Steinberg, who all said was the true example of the American dream.

The police chief had met Mayor John O'Reilly on his way out of the house. "Bad business, John," he said.

"Yeah, it's going to affect the whole community – my business sure will suffer."

Mayor O'Reilly, up from Boston some thirty years back, stepped and looked out across the vast lawns towards the huge ornamental gates just visible from where he stood.

"Maybe we can still get them to come, maybe we gotta do something to make them wanna come, yeah, that's it, we gotta make them remember him – maybe a museum – yeah that's it, a museum… and a carousel or two for the kids. That oughta do it – what do yet say, Rube?"

Rube nodded. "Guess you sure gotta do something, this town'll die – he was a big man, we even got those Limeys coming here to see his place, he sure must have made an impression in Europe – two of them guys came just yesterday, beats me what sort of kick they get out of it. Jake at the hotel will sure be sorry to lose all that business – maybe you should talk to him, John."

Jake's hotel had prospered since Julius Steinberg had moved close by. The six bedrooms had for some years past been nearly always full through spring and summer, in fact right through to fall. There were those of course who regularly came to get a break from the city and to spend time in the beautiful New England countryside or by the lake from which the town got its name, Primrose; but then there were those who came to buy souvenirs, see the house and perhaps even a sight of Julius himself walking downtown. Jake would certainly notice the difference, pondered the mayor.

Back at the hotel the guests were entering the dining hall as John O'Reilly came through past the small reception area. Jake was hovering nearby. "Howdy, Jake, like to have a word with you when you got time."

Jake nodded and made a gesture indicating that at that moment he was quite busy. Just then two casually dressed middle-aged gentlemen walked past and into the dining room. Jake smiled at them and turned towards O'Reilly. "Them's two Limeys come all the way from England to see the town," he said. "They act for a travel company and come to see what places to recommend their customers visit. I guess without Julius around they could mark Primrose down, even though folks seldom saw him."

"That's what I want to talk to you about, Jake. Guess you gonna miss out on that kinda business from now."

2

"Yeah, we've had a number come over the last few years – these came over once before. Reckon it ain't going to be too easy from now on – folks are sure going to be sorry."

Jake Ramsden had bought the small hotel many years back after being left money by an old aunt who died in Portland – he had never liked his forestry work and resolved to change his way of life. Work in the hotel was pretty hard in the summer months but he could take it easy in the winter. Since Steinberg had set up in town, his work had certainly increased but so had the money and he was now able to employ a manager to take the main chores of running the business in the season. Jake had spent much in improving the place but he was still comfortably off for even if his rooms were not full there was always the dining room, which was nearly always full from the many new people who had "followed" Julius and bought or built holiday homes around the town.

In the dining room the two Limeys sat at a small table near a window and ordered the meal recommended by the waiter. At an adjoining table sat a man and a lady also of middle years – the lady spoke. "You're English, aren't you? I simply love your accent, my husband and I were in Europe only last year and we visited London, Cambridge, Oxford and of course Stratford. Don't you just love Stratford, dear?" She turned to her husband who embarrassingly nodded assent. She continued. "What part of England are you from?"

The darker of the two men replied, "I come from London but my friend is from Yorkshire."

"Is that near Stratford?"

"Well, no, not really although of course distances are never very great in England."

"What brings you to this part of the world, I guess it must have been something to do with Julius, did you know him?"

The man from Yorkshire answered, "Yes, in a way we knew him – we work for a travel company and it seems people, even in Europe, want to see where Mr Steinberg lives."

At that moment the waiter arrived with drinks and the first course for the man and lady.

"Are you staying long in Primrose?" the lady asked.

"No, we are going home tomorrow – we are flying from Boston in the afternoon."

* * *

The next morning the two Limeys paid their bills at reception and drove their hired car to Boston. Some eight hours later they were aboard a 737 bound for London. They sat back and fastened their seat belts and soon the plane taxied onto the runway and, with the noise of its engines rising to a crescendo, moved forward and gathering speed shot up into air at what seemed a near-vertical angle. Ten minutes later they were served with dinner and a drink after which they settled back to pass the next seven hours or so dozing or sleeping; they would arrive at Heathrow at six thirty next morning.

Their trip had been worthwhile, it had been a long time in coming but at last it was over, what they had set out to do had been done.

Many years had passed and some old friends were no longer with them, it had cost them a lot, not just money but time and unnecessary anger – it had taken over their lives. Was it worth it? How had it all begun?

There is nothing like not being able to sleep to make one think and even though the lights on the plane had been dimmed, one of the two Limeys could not sleep, he wanted to talk but his companion was out, dead to the world.

He recalled when it had all begun – yes, that was it – it was summer 1968 or was it '69, but not a good summer for him – not like that summer a short while ago when he had been called back from his holiday in Dorset in order to help

4

conclude an important contract with the Russians, which earlier that year he had negotiated in Moscow… all had been golden then and it was at that meeting, near to midnight, when the MD had pulled him aside to tell him he would be the next Group Chief Executive. He had truly hit the heights then and the following year his wife had been introduced at a special cocktail party as the wife of the next top man – but sadly later that year following an operation she became depressed and was sent to a mental hospital for treatment. Yes, it was the summer of '69 when it all began. Their American associates, who had licensed their products to his company in the early fifties due entirely, he understood, to a very astute John Good, managing director of a major subsidiary in the Group, had asked whether the Board objected to them buying a small stake in the company. A reasonable request since they had granted the British company licences for the whole of Europe and indeed anywhere else in the British Commonwealth, except of course Canada, due to its proximity to their own country. John Good's company had certainly not sat still and over the years had built a thriving export business largely based on these licences. He remembered the Board had agreed in principle to the request but before anything could be finalised the Americans had been taken completely by surprise when they found themselves the victims of takeover by a much larger American company, The Broadside Chemical Corporation, which very soon sent their boss over to England to carry on negotiations with the Board of the British company.

This man wanted not just a share but the whole company. Our traveller hesitated in his thoughts – what was this man's name?

His companion moved and opened his eyes. "What time is it?"

"I set my watch to UK time, so it says one thirty. Now you're awake you can help me – what was the name of the boss of the takeover that never was?"

"What on earth are you worrying about that for, can't you sleep?"

"No I can't, everything keeps running through my mind, sorry but if I don't get his name it'll only be worse."

"Joe Miller," his companion said sleepily.

"Of course it was – now you can go back to sleep."

Yes that was it, Joe Miller – he was probably all right but you can never be sure – I wonder what happened to him after he bowed out – looked as if he could have been a real high flyer; retired now, I shouldn't wonder.

Now I remember, he thought, I was called back off my holiday for a second year running to attend an extraordinary board meeting to discuss the possible sale of shares. That must have been when old John Good gave that impassioned speech for sticking to as many shares as possible to thwart any foreign takeover. If a Union Jack had popped up out of the table I think we would have all stood up and sung Land of Dope and Glory. He smiled to himself – old John was dead now, I went to his funeral on the South Coast somewhere, he was a good man.

For a time his mind wandered back to when John had taken him on as his accountant – that was about twenty-five years ago – he could remember the office and the man's red hair already beginning to thin. He remembered that it was a bright sunny day – how could it have been otherwise, surely all days were sunny then and the big country house in which he was temporarily in digs was like a mansion in the middle of a beautiful forest full of strange birds as if in a foreign land.

His mind wandered over the years and slowly he too fell asleep.

* * *

When war was declared in 1939 many companies with offices or factories in London moved out, often into country mansions, to safer areas such as Bedfordshire or Oxfordshire, some fifty or sixty miles out of town, taking most of their staff with them and building living accommodation in the grounds. Others decided to stay closer in but generally beyond or in the Green Belt. Thus parts of West Surrey became attractive and the company in our story moved to two such houses. One was made the headquarters whilst the other housed the kitchens, dining rooms and accommodation for casual visitors. The grounds extended for several acres and amongst the rhododendrons they built huts for offices and laboratories.

A few years after the war the company, The Weyford Engineering and Chemical Company (WECO) had so expanded that new premises and factory space was sought and the moves began in the late fifties to the outskirts of a larger town – by the middle sixties the company had a number of factories and office blocks in the area with warehouses and distribution centres in Manchester, Birmingham, Glasgow and Sheffield. The Group employed some 1500 people and work was provided throughout the UK for scores of sub-contractors until it was possible to say that the livelihood of several thousand people depended on the company.

As has been said before, a good proportion of the work in which the company was involved was derived from American know-how, but the remainder was British inventiveness and large sums had been brought into the UK by the sale to Germany, France and Japan of certain aspects of this know-how.

The company had gone public in the early fifties with a substantial number of shares in the hands of "families" with their respective directors representing them on the Boards of the various companies which formed the Group. The main board in the late sixties had lost two of the men who had started the company but now their sons were there with successors to the main jobs brought in some years earlier – there was also one new director, Ray Holmes, who had worked his way through from accountant to one of the subsidiaries – he had been told by the two senior MDs and the chairman that he was the next Group chief executive.

The company being export orientated, many of its employees spent a great deal of time overseas, mostly in Europe but also much further afield. There were frequent visitors entertained in the UK offices from overseas countries as far afield as China, Japan, Australia, India and Israel and more recently the USSR. One of the subsidiary companies' engineering directors turned salesman, Tony Bentley, had taken a Land Rover, specially fitted out to demonstrate what the company could do, and driven across Europe and into Russia, which was then very much more difficult to enter than it is today and a closed book to much of the West. His visit had eventually paid off and a couple of years later contracts in the millions had been or were being negotiated.

Thus in 1969 the company was prosperous with averagely good profits but equally important bringing much needed finance into the UK and providing a living for thousands.

Not all members were present at the extraordinary meeting of the WECO Board, called to discuss the proposal put forward by Joe Miller and his American colleagues. The company secretary opened the meeting on a nod from the chairman and reiterated the reason for the meeting being called and set the proposal on the table.

The meeting, which had followed a good lunch in the directors' dining room, started quietly enough with the chairman and managing director making points on what the procedure would be if the Board agreed to the sale. It became obvious that certain members were not so interested in the welfare of employees or that the company remain British but were more concerned with whether the price offer would be sufficient to make it worthwhile selling their shares. Most of the Board were in their sixties and either nearing retirement or if in ordinary employment would have already retired – thus their own personal prospects would most likely be concerned with how much their settlement would be to get out and what price they would get for their shares. However, one of the senior directors, John Good, made an impassioned speech on keeping the company British and establishing that whatever was done assurances should be obtained to ensure the company remained more or less as it was. Ray Holmes endorsed these remarks but did not involve himself too deeply less his colleagues would think he was only concerned with his position as Group MD elect. The meeting was adjourned when the discussion became somewhat heated and it was resolved that a committee of the two senior executive directors go away and return with counter proposals to put to the Americans.

The meeting reconvened later that evening and new proposals were agreed. The following day an arranged meeting was held with the Americans and terms and conditions were provisionally agreed for the takeover. Loose assurances were given that the company would remain generally as it was but not finalised, as the meeting was interrupted by an urgent call from America which Joe Miller, the president of the American corporation, took.

He returned to the meeting and reported that a company called Arkansas Oil had bid for his company and that he therefore could not continue the negotiations as he had to return immediately to corporation headquarters in Pittsburgh.

The unbelievable had happened, for the second time in a matter of months American companies involved in negotiations with the British company had themselves become subjects of a takeover.

The chairman duly closed the meeting with a request that the secretary find out all he could about Arkansas Oil and report back to the Board as soon as possible. He requested all be prepared to meet at short notice should a further approach be made by the Americans.

* * *

The boss and majority shareholder of Arkansas Oil was one Julius Steinberg. Steinberg had come up the hard way; he was a true entrepreneur, not always successful in his early days but always looking for opportunities to build his companies. He had operated overseas in various fields taking risks, cutting corners and making himself known to many in powerful positions in third world countries and in the USSR. His parents had emigrated to America from Poland towards the end of the last century and as their ship had arrived in New York that is where they stayed. Steinberg's father eventually found work as a labourer on the construction of the Brooklyn Bridge. Julius never forgot this and would often trot it out in speeches, adding in later life that he had enough money now to buy the goddam bridge if it were up for sale.

He built a reputation as a hard man to work for and was known by his employees to be ruthless, but somehow all his enterprises in later years seemed to prosper. Staff, however, were frequently changed and it used to be said that any employee who remained for three years got a gold watch but staff seldom remained to find out if this were true.

Arkansas Oil in the late fifties had been a small private company owned by an erstwhile prospector who having been in the oil business since the early part of the century thought it was now time to get out. Steinberg, on the other hand, although retired, was itching to get back in business and had by chance met the owner, Jan Larsen, in a bar of an hotel in Banff, Canada, where they were both on holiday.

Within two or three hours of their meeting and after having disposed of two bottles of the best whisky, Arkansas Oil had virtually passed on the shake of hands over to Julius Steinberg, who meanwhile had called his lawyer from

Chicago to come out to Banff right away. The lawyer, on a big retainer, had reluctantly left Chicago on the first plane available flying via Winnipeg to Calgary and then by hired car to Banff. The documents for transfer were produced the following day with the aid of hotel typists and signed with witnesses by both Larsen and Steinberg.

Two weeks later Steinberg was pulling strings in Middle East countries and within two months had been granted concessions to look for oil alongside some of the big boys. Whether it was the money paid over to help things along or whether it was the staff he gathered around him who were paid local money and cash into numbered Swiss accounts, no one really knows but whatever it was he struck it rich – so rich that in order to use his surplus funds he was forced to invest elsewhere when he found there were no longer any easy pickings in the oil game.

Several acquisitions and ten years later he was in a position to buy out the big American chemical corporation, Broadside Chemical, whose president was Joe Miller.

The offer made for the shares was something the Board of the chemical corporation could only recommend their shareholders accept and thus two months later the company became part of Arkansas Oil.

Joe Miller remained for a time as president and then was promoted upwards to personally assist Steinberg run his Group. Less than a year later Miller was left out and new people chosen by Steinberg had taken over all the senior posts in the chemical company. The move of promoting and then pushing someone out was not invented by Steinberg but in his career he made good use of this manoeuvre.

Julius Steinberg, having accomplished his acquisition of the giant chemical corporation, turned his attention to the proposed acquisition by that company of the British company with which their subsidiary had a licensing arrangement. His interest had been aroused when he learnt of that company's export achievement throughout the world and particularly in

Eastern Europe, his parents' homeland. He sent Joe Miller back to the UK to conclude the negotiations started a few months earlier. The senior directors of the British Group having previously reached conclusions with Miller were allowed by their Board to conclude negotiations but obtained nothing in writing to safeguard the interests of employees but simply concentrated on the share price to be offered. The share price finally agreed was very fair and sufficiently attractive to warrant shareholders selling.

Within two months the offer was made and accepted with the shares duly passing to the Americans. However, the British company, far from being left alone to carry on, as had verbally been agreed, was straightway told to report to a little Swiss company a subsidiary of a New York company, part of the Steinberg empire.

The persons running the Swiss operation would not, with perhaps one exception, have advanced above junior management in the British company, which they were now to control, and understandably this was resented in WECO. However, the reason for the Swiss company being involved was that they were the key to the tax operation set up in Europe, a fact revealed to senior staff of WECO in the first meeting held following the takeover.

A representative of the Swiss company, Raoul Mitterand, took the meeting and, with the aid of a chart, explained the benefits of triangular invoicing when a company is heavy into exports and controlled by a multi-national company.

The idea is this: the Americans set up a company in Switzerland or wherever they want to accumulate capital and where company tax rates are relatively low and get the exporting company to send the goods direct to the importing country but to invoice the company in Switzerland. However, instead of invoicing at the proper rate, the invoice is made out for a much reduced amount sufficient barely to cover the cost of production. The Swiss company then invoices the importing company at the full rate and thus the profits of the

UK company are syphoned off to Switzerland, the UK Revenue losing tax it would otherwise collect.

Before the takeover it had been necessary for Arkansas Oil to seek approval of the Bank of England to purchase. The bank had given approval, no doubt with an eye to the dollars which would come into the country but it is suspected, in view of what subsequently happened, without giving any consideration as to what might happen to that company thereafter.

Immediately following the triangular invoice meeting the representatives of the American/Swiss company were presented to the senior staff of WECO at a lunch held in the senior staff dining room. The representatives were only two in number and most of the meeting were pleased there were not more, particularly if there were any more like Abe Slyberger, a New Yorker and president of the corporation. The other representative was Raoul Mitterand, a French citizen living in Switzerland, educated at the Sorbonne and the Harvard Business School.

Slyberger was an unscrupulous individual in the Steinberg mould but more than this he was objectionably crude and enjoyed trying to belittle people using foul language – he certainly could not have fitted into the Board of the British company with over half its members from public schools. He was instantly disliked, whilst his French sidekick running the European operation for Slyberger was not at first so easy to fathom.

There must have been some apprehension among those present at the lunch and who were to remain working in the company after the crude exhibition of this objectionable individual. However, since this individual was likely to be based in the States not too much was said at the time.

As to their intentions now the takeover was complete, it was difficult to know except it was now obvious they were looking to strip the company of its profits and the Revenue of tax. That was their intention but this was temporarily thwarted by the WECO financial director, Ray Holmes, pointing out that this was contrary to the Companies Act and therefore should not be done; not a very wise thing to say to the new bosses which was not to be forgotten. In spite of this hiccup they subsequently overcame it by getting the UK company to deliver all goods to Switzerland and invoice there, the goods then being transhipped to the original destination. As regards what were their intentions other than stripping profits and cheating the Revenue, their stock answer was, "We don't know yet, we haven't opened the package."

It comes as no surprise to those who have been victims of a takeover that pacifying statements made by the aggressor are generally worthless. However, unless you have previously been the victim of a takeover it is most likely you will believe what you are told if the takeover company know their job. There is generally a period when the aggressor company dare not rock the boat until they have a feel for the new victim – of course, they will rid themselves of the fat at the top such as non-executive directors and others who are there only because they are family of the original owners – but they will be sure to keep key personnel until they have had time to bleed their brains and then put in their own men.

It was thus with WECO and many others taken into the Steinberg empire. Generally, main Board directors, except any very key ones, retired, were bought out or employed on a consultancy basis. In WECO, the finance man was the only main Board director held over with certain senior executive directors of subsidiary companies. The next move is to introduce one or two of their own men into the upper strata of the company and then gradually push out those who are no longer required. Sometimes it takes time but mostly within two to three years or less it should all be over.

Since the old MD had been "retired", as had the other senior executive directors on the main Board, there was a vacancy for the Group MD or chief executive post but instead of giving the job to the old regime's choice, the financial director, which would naturally have frustrated the plans for their own man, they decided on a committee of four to run the operation.

Committees are seldom able to run an operation efficiently and to run a group of companies is suicidal and the persons arranging this must have known, particularly as one of the four appointed was their own man, Maurice Schmidt, although to the other three of the committee it was not then so obvious. The financial director and pre-acquisition choice for chief executive was given the job of "chairman" of the committee with a grandiose typical American title for the job. It was a thankless task and it was not surprising with each committee member wanting to do as he pleased that Ray Holmes soon told Raoul Mitterand that he would have to find an MD or ruin the business.

Over the next two weeks a charade was played when the committee were sent to Switzerland ostensibly to decide who would be this MD and Raoul Mitterand was naturally to make the choice, and it became obvious he had been briefed to pick their man. Various activities and open sessions of trying to get each of the aspiring candidates to tear each other to pieces, the choice was made after a day when they had been asked to come down the mountain on ski bicycles (ski-bobs). Ray Holmes, the financial or numbers man, laughingly said he had blown his chances when he not only kept up with Mitterand, a man used to the mountains and skiing, but landed on top of him in the snow when Raoul had fallen.

That night the Arkansas Oil protégé was duly picked as the man but Mitterand was completely taken by surprise when the three others told him they were not prepared to work with his choice. A half hour or so later, after what was assumed to be a call to the States, he returned to say that he would appoint Tony Bentley as the new MD and make Maurice Schmidt, their man, the deputy.

The appointments were made but this situation did not last long, as soon after Tony Bentley was promoted to European manager in Geneva and those who knew the Steinberg tactics would have smiled to themselves as clearly the writing was on the wall. Schmidt was of course made MD and Steinberg had the set-up he wanted, albeit a few months late.

Johnny Thostedt the other member of the committee had been allowed, albeit temporarily, to carry on looking after his side of the business, as too was Ray Holmes, the numbers man, whose first task was to introduce a system of detailed financial reporting for the parent company in the States. The information required made it necessary to increase staff in the accounts department and for all to work much overtime before the new procedures were in place. Each month a telex message had to be sent to New York detailing the results of the month's trading so that these figures could be incorporated in the total figures presented to Steinberg in his Group report – the telex was consistently twelve feet long.

The procedures took several months to set up at a considerable cost. Meanwhile, steps were being taken to move the manufacture of certain products away from the UK and into Europe. In particular, the profitable chemical manufacture was split up and distributed around the European agents so that the agents no longer bought in from England but they were now able to manufacture in their own right and sell to their customers. Of course they too were being bought out by the American company and they too would have to invoice Geneva with their sales, allowing Geneva to invoice their customers.

The UK company was destined to contract on the chemical side and as soon as arrangements could be made the engineering side of the business would be moved to Europe. However, by 1971 the company was still managing to keep well over a thousand people employed but, although not known to other than perhaps the Steinberg men, the end of WECO was fast approaching.

The first senior man to go was Ray Holmes, the one remaining pre-acquisition main Board director.

Ray had been with WECO for nearly fifteen years, having started as an assistant accountant and worked his way through to be chief executive elect of the Group prior to the takeover. Now having worked with the Americans for two years and been through the trauma of the fixed MD selection, Ray had settled down and worked conscientiously. Before the takeover he had been approached by various consultants to see if he wanted to leave – head-hunters they called them – and indeed since the takeover he had considered moving, but having a sick wife he knew a change of job and perhaps an enforced move would in the circumstances not be sensible. He thus carried on.

Towards the end of summer 1971 he was asked to meet Steinberg in a well known London hotel where this man kept a suite. Not knowing what the meeting was about but assuming it to be a meeting to discuss the latest position of WECO, he arrived at the meeting armed with documents with which he would be able to detail progress.

Reception guided him to the penthouse suite where he was met by a secretary, who introduced him to Steinberg sitting in an easy chair near what in winter would have been a log fire, used to give a homely atmosphere to an otherwise centrally heated building. The secretary retired to another room and Steinberg, a small man, who in spite of his known age looked at least ten years younger, eyed Holmes, then forty-nine years of age, a little uneasily.

"What do you know about this guy, Dailey?" he said, shifting around to face Holmes, who was still standing.

Holmes hesitated for a moment. He had been taken by surprise; it was certainly not the question he had been expecting. "I assume you mean Fred Dailey, the ex-Group MD."

"Yeah, that's the guy."

"Exactly what is it you want to know, I can only tell you how I found him at Board meetings before you took over. I really hardly knew him as a person, I worked mostly with John Good who you may have heard of."

"What do you think of the company's performance?" Steinberg interjected.

Holmes guessed from the way Steinberg asked the question that he felt things were not as he expected and chose his words carefully.

"Well, I realise the profit does not match what we had prior to the takeover but you have to remember that some of our profits have been moving to the Continent – we have lost overseas markets and on your instructions have been sending chemicals to Switzerland invoiced at much lower mark-ups."

Steinberg shuffled uneasily in his chair and told Holmes to sit down. "I've already discounted that, I'm concerned with your engineering business, which hasn't been changed by us – your profits are nowhere near what we projected when we examined the numbers given to us by Dailey."

Holmes knew a little of Dailey, enough to know he was no fool and was very used to the Steinberg type of operator. Dailey had been responsible to shareholders of WECO for a number of years and they had never complained, he knew it was necessary for them to always have confidence in the company and its management and occasionally it was necessary to value work-in-progress a little higher some years than others. Perhaps old Dailey had had an optimistic valuation placed on the WIP when he dealt with such a character as Steinberg. Within reason the accountants had to be guided on work-in-progress valuations by the engineers who knew the jobs, and past history had shown little to be complained about.

"I am told the engineering business is pretty healthy – yes, the profits are not wonderful but we have had a takeover and there must always be some effect on work when there are staff worries. We have had a few good men leave too as result of the takeover." Holmes knew this was probably not what Steinberg wanted to hear and he judged by the expression on the old man's face that he was not impressed.

"Do you realise we paid twenty million dollars for your corporation and what 'ave we got? – an engineering section that is giving us peanuts. Dailey's numbers don't add up – what sort of a guy is he?"

Holmes could see Steinberg was angry – not that what he had expected from the takeover and what he had so far got would make any marked difference to his total wealth, it was simply that Steinberg was supposed to be the sharp character and perhaps, just perhaps, this crummy Limey had taken him for a ride.

The meeting continued, with Steinberg at every opportunity trying to get something on Dailey. However, he failed and no doubt in a fit of pique said he was going to have his lunch and that the meeting should continue at two o'clock when his lawyer would be present. He never suggested Holmes should join him or was in the least bothered where Holmes would eat. It was this lack of common concern that settled in Holmes' mind that this man had the manners of an arrogant ignorant bastard.

Not quite sure what was happening and feeling very angry within, Holmes left the hotel and walked towards nearby Green Park passing a sandwich bar on the way and buying his lunch. Inside the park he sat on the grass in the bright June sunlight and watched the little children playing close by their mothers. He had time to think and try to guess what he would next be asked. He knew they were after old Dailey and he resolved that he would do his best to tip him off. Near to the appointed time he reluctantly walked back to the hotel.

Back at the hotel Holmes was introduced to the lawyer and the discussion continued – the lawyer asked many awkward questions that were strictly below the belt and without the opportunity to object to a judge Holmes had to take great care as to how he answered. This man was obviously a sharp character and tried every trick to get

Holmes to say something that might give them a lead into pinning something on Dailey. Holmes had nothing to give away and certainly was not going to give any hint of agreeing with their conclusions – he was particularly concerned that he knew that his old MD, John Good, was the other one who undertook the negotiations and no way would he have dropped this man in trouble.

The meeting came to end at four o'clock and the lawyer said he wanted to talk to Holmes again. A meeting was arranged when Holmes would bring along the accountant directly responsible for the particular side of the business that Steinberg was concerned about.

The following Monday, the meeting was duly held at the offices of the lawyer and the accountant did his best to explain away the forecast made which had not been achieved. The lawyer gave nothing away but from the questioning it became clear that it would be very difficult, if not impossible, to prove that the figures had been falsified in any way. However, Steinberg could, without a doubt, still try and take some action, after all money was really no object to him.

Holmes returned to his office and for the next two or three weeks carried on working as usual. It was on a Friday afternoon in the first week in October that Schmidt poked his head round the door of Holmes' office and said, "Can you come and see me about four this afternoon?"

Holmes looked up from the work he was doing and replied that he would.

Holmes entered the new MD's office at about four that afternoon. Schmidt was sitting at his desk but as the numbers man entered he got out of his seat and walked towards his drinks cabinet, speaking as he did so. "Ray, I expect you've heard about the reshuffle being planned." He hesitated as if expecting a reply.

"Yes, I heard something but guessed it didn't affect me."

"Well, that's quite true," he paused and then, "You know we haven't got a job for you… would you like a drink?"

Holmes was taken completely by surprise and could feel his anger rising. "What the bloody hell do you mean, we haven't got a job for you?"

Maurice Schmidt looked slightly embarrassed but ignored the question. "We're giving you a year's salary, and your car. Now come on, have a drink."

"You can stuff your drink – when do I leave?"

"When you like."

"Right. I'll be in Monday morning to collect my cheque and you won't see me again – you can sort out any paperwork – goodbye."

Holmes walked back to his office, picked up a few papers and went straight to his car and drove home.

As he drove home he thought of his past fifteen years with the company, his promotion through to the main Board and then being told he was to be the next Group MD, or chief executive as they had then decided to call it.

What would his sick wife have to say – he was forty-nine and it probably would not be all that easy to find another job – it was something he had never expected.

He drove his car into the short drive and sat there for a moment, collecting his thoughts and deciding the best way he would tell his wife.

Sylvia, his wife, greeted him at the door. "Anything the matter, Ray? You look worried."

"I have lost my job."

"Lost your job? I don't believe it – you're pulling my leg."

"No, I'm sorry, I'm not – Schmidt called me in this afternoon and said they haven't got a job for me – I didn't stop to ask any more, they, whoever they are, have decided to get rid of me and I'm out. They've given me a year's salary and my car – but of course I've got to sign papers that I resign or I won't be able to collect my cheque."

Sylvia put her arms round him and gave him a squeeze. "Don't worry, Ray, you'll soon find another position – go and sit down and I'll make a cup of tea."

She returned whilst waiting for the kettle to boil and put on a Chopin record, one of her husband's favourites, which she sometimes did to help him unwind when he came in from work after a stressful day.

"What are they going to do without you?" she said.

"Oh, I expect they've got it all worked out, or they think they have. Anyway that's their problem – I'm going in Monday to collect a few papers and that'll be it."

When his fifteen-year-old son came in from school, he told him what had happened and assured him there was nothing to worry about but for a few days Dad wouldn't be going to work.

* * *

Phil Johnson had worked in the accounts department in the WECO group for nearly fifteen years. She had known Ray Holmes since he first employed her as a copy typist, and over the years she had learnt all there was to know in the routine work of an accounts department and had received recognition by becoming chief clerk. She had, in the last few years, become somewhat remote from her old boss since he had been promoted to the main Board but was very sorry and shocked to learn of Ray Holmes' departure. In fact, it was hard for those who had known him and known how highly regarded the previous directors and senior employees had held him to understand why he had been pushed out.

"If they get rid of someone like Ray Holmes, what chance have we got?" she remarked to others in the accounts department who on the Monday morning were busily discussing his downfall.

This was the first real indication since the takeover that things were going to change and at least it made all in employment down South in WECO aware that jobs were no longer secure. It was about this time that staff in depots in the Midlands and North were also alerted to the new situation when Ted Wilson in the Sheffield depot was suddenly sacked. From now on the atmosphere in the company changed. Work carried on as hitherto but most people were on their guard and extra effort was made to look busy. The friendliness of the Group was gradually being lost and over the next two years would almost disappear, as indeed would the company.

Ray Holmes was the first but a few months later his redundancy had been followed by other senior employees, both directors of subsidiaries and staff, until just over two years later the company, to all intents and purposes, no longer existed.

The 1500 employees were no more and the many companies who had obtained work from the Group would now be hard pressed to find alternative orders for their factories. The UK had lost substantial export business, the Revenue had lost tax, and thousands who were directly or indirectly employed were going to find it hard to pick up the pieces.

The few million dollars brought into the country on the approval of the Bank of England had been lost many times over to the country by this one takeover which was not reported in the press and did not merit any mention whatsoever except to the many who had suffered as a consequence.

Unemployment in 1971/72 had been rising and for many ex-WECO employees there would be difficulty in finding new positions, particularly if they were of a certain age and had been employed in a senior position.

There was much bitterness and some levelled this at the ones who had "sold them out" but others who knew more cursed the day the Americans had taken over their company – if this was progress then they could have it. The circumstances of leaving and how the many ex-employees dealt with their own situation is of considerable interest when looking into how and why Primrose, New Hampshire, was to become so important.

* * *

Ted Wilson was among the first of the many redundancies which took place in 1971/72 and of course at that time the full impact of what would happen to those redundant persons had not then been realised. Anger there would most certainly be, but how deep and lasting that anger would be could only be measured by what happened to them as individuals in the months to come.

The redundancy of Ted Wilson, a storekeeper in the Sheffield depot, was typical of many.

It was on the last Friday in October that he was called to the manager's office after the latter had received a call from head office. Barely two minutes later Ted left the office and after speaking briefly to the two young ladies in the outer office, one of who handed him an envelope, he left the building as if in a daze.

Ted Wilson walked slowly down Queen Street and stopped before pushing the iron gate of No. 59 open and looked back up the road almost as if he had changed his mind about entering. He hesitated again before walking the two steps to the door and fishing inside the letterbox for the piece of string to which the key was attached. He opened the door and walked into the small kitchen at the end of the passage where his wife, Joan, was washing up.

"You're early tonight, Ted. I haven't even started getting your tea – don't remember you ever coming in at this time."

"Hello, love, yes I am early, got something to tell you – could we have a cup of tea?"

"I'll put the kettle on, it won't take long – you go in the front room and put your feet up, you don't look too good – I'll be in, in a minute – Joey's not back from school yet."

Ted Wilson went into the front room, sat in his usual armchair and waited.

"There you are, that'll make you feel better. Got a headache, have you?"

"No, it's not that… I've been given the push."

"Oh no, Ted, why, what's happened? I can't believe it."

"They say I'm redundant… that's a nice word for saying I'm sacked. They've given me a week's pay and said goodbye – after twenty bloody years all they could say was sorry and goodbye. I don't know what we're going to do, Joan. I couldn't get things straight in my mind after I left the depot – I walked home."

"You walked all that way, what made you do that – it's nearly four miles, you must be worn out."

"I wanted to think… I don't know what to do – I thought they liked me there. Old Fred said he couldn't say much but he'd been told to get rid of me. It's those bloody people down in London or somewhere. Fred said things were changing since those Americans took the company. Don't know how they expect to distribute all over the north if they sack the only man who works in the warehouse. The girls in the office who gave me my money said they were sorry to see me go."

"Oh, Ted, I'm so sorry. You must feel awful. You mustn't worry, we'll manage. You'll find another job, I know you will."

"I wish I felt so sure, there is nothing round here and unemployment is on the increase – I know several lads I went to school with who are on the dole – it's not easy and what do I know anyway? What I have got to offer?"

"Don't let me hear you say that, you've got a lot to offer, you're honest, you work hard and—"

Ted interrupted, "Ay, but what else – I've got nowt else."

When Joey came home from school they at first didn't tell him but later that evening they thought it best that he should know his dad was out of work and they told him. He didn't seem to mind, as he said he knew a lot of his mates whose dads were on the dole.

"I heard before I left the depot that some others down south had got the push too – I reckon the Yanks are having a shake-out as my namesake Harold called it."

Ted did not sleep too well that night and next day he went down to the Labour Exchange and signed on – he would have to wait a week before they would give him any money but at least now he knew what to do. He never ever had expected to be unemployed, he knew the company was doing well and there had been no warning or indeed any rumours... what was it all about?

* * *

Don Wilson a respected buyer in one of the major subsidiaries of the Group was the next to go – in fact in the week following the Ray Holmes' departure. Wilson was a truly long-serving employee, having joined the company in its pre-war days. What exactly would happen to his previous function in the company he did not wait to find out.

He signed on at the Labour Exchange and was not surprised to meet Ray Holmes, who had signed on a week earlier. They decided to call into a local and chew the fat over a glass of beer. But what could be said? Here they were – two men, one forty-nine and the other fifty-one, it would not be easy for them.

They met regularly while collecting their money but gradually the conversation changed from WECO and discussion of the good times and the bad, to job applications, interviews and the frustrations of seeking new employment.

Some months later Ray Holmes found himself alone when collecting his money. Don Wilson had found a job – but Ray knew how bitter Don was and for the record he noted his address and telephone number.

Don's new employment meant that he now had to travel to South East London to a company in Eltham – it took him two hours by public transport and an hour and a half by car when he could afford the petrol. He was not a happy man, he had been given a paid-up pension which would not be payable until he was sixty-five but if the value of money changed for the worse his pension would reduce. At the time of these dismissals inflation was virtually unknown, but only a year or so later it hit the country and with inflation rising to well over twenty per cent per annum for two or three years and then staying above ten per cent for some time, the paid-up pensions became worthless. Don Wilson would become even more bitter.

STEINBERG

I

THE PREREQUISITE of being a successful entrepreneur must, it seems, include being a hard man, even some would say ruthless. Of course there may be exceptions but these must be few and far between. Julius Steinberg was a hard man and indeed ruthless and yet to the great American public and to influential people throughout the world he was a philanthropist giving money to art galleries and other charitable causes. There was no doubt, however, that this was the thin veneer he used to further his ends in obtaining contracts and gaining respectability and influence with those who, as a child, he had never dreamed he could ever meet. From this point of view the reader might have some sympathy with the man; he had after all made it, and made it big from quite humble beginnings. However, scattered on the way he had left a trail of hundreds of battered lives of which he seemed to have no regard whatsoever. Some will say if he had not done it then someone else would – but is this an excuse? Can we excuse a man who has caused so much misery, and fête him as a successful businessman? The question should be put to those who suffered and see their response. We know what the answer would be but what can they do about it, what indeed would they be prepared to do about it?

In 1971/72 when many redundancies were taking place in WECO, the full impact of what would happen to those redundant persons had not yet been realised. After all, it depends on what happens thereafter which determines the lasting anger, if any, and thus time only will tell the true depth of anger.

Steinberg had met his London lawyer following the meeting the latter had had with Ray Holmes and the other accountant. The lawyer advised Steinberg that as far as he could see there was nothing for the WECO Board to answer and he would be wasting his money to take them to court. Steinberg was not happy but agreed he would follow the advice given although inwardly he was convinced he had been taken for a ride.

He was driven straight from the lawyer's office to Heathrow and was soon on Concorde flying to New York where he arrived early that evening.

Steinberg had two offices in New York, one in the Wall Street area which was used for meeting and entertaining prospective customers, civil dignitaries, and anyone who needed to be impressed. His second office, where most of the staff supporting the whole of the Arkansas Oil Corporation worked, was across the river in Brooklyn. Not only was office space less expensive but he had always felt more at home in Brooklyn, where he had been brought up as a young man. Although not now often in the Brooklyn office he always looked forward to a visit there and enjoyed hearing the true Brooklyn accent of many of the staff, and in any case from his office at the top of the building he could see the Brooklyn Bridge, which somehow he felt was a part of his family.

He was met at the airport by a chauffeur, who stood close to the entrance to the arrival hall with a placard on which was written "Ark Oil".

"Take me to Brooklyn I need a rest."

"They got problems with the elevators when I left but I figure they should he fixed by the time we get there, the traffic at this time is somethin'."

Steinberg said nothing and forty-five minutes later they arrived to find the elevators repaired. Steinberg, in fact, had his own elevator which other persons could not use unless they had a key. It went straight to his twelfth floor office.

"Nice to see you, Mr Steinberg – have a good trip?"

"Well no – I got some thinking to do, get hold of MacDonald. I want him here in half an hour."

The secretary knew Mac was on his way home but she also knew her boss and when he wanted to see someone he meant it, no matter where they were. She therefore hurriedly bleeped Mac and before long he had returned her call and turned his car around and was on his way back through the rush hour traffic, cursing to himself at every hold-up.

His journey back to the office took the best part of an hour and when he got there he found the elevators were again not working so he had to walk up to the twelfth floor.

"Where the hell you been, Mac? Goddam it, I been sitting here waiting for you."

"Sorry, Julius, I was on my way home and had just got on the freeway when Julie buzzed me – and the traffic, and then those f****** elevators. Ain't it about time we got out of this building? Those elevators must have been around when you were a kid."

Steinberg flushed but ignored the last remark; no he wasn't going to move, this was where he liked to be.

"You knew I was coming back from London today, you should have waited, all some of you guys think about is getting home – why, when I was your age I seldom saw my home, out on the road all day and sometimes most of the night too – we used to work in those days."

MacDonald could see it was not worth arguing and sat down.

"OK, so I was late – I'm sorry. Now what is it you want, Julius?"

Steinberg got up from his chair and walked to the window and gazed at the lights on the Brooklyn Bridge – he was put out, they knew he liked everyone to be on hand when he returned and yet this guy had gone home.

"What do you think of Limeys, Mac?"

"Can't say I've thought much about it – been there once, quaint place, my pa was there during the war – seems to have liked the girls – but they don't mean much to me. Why? What is it, Julius?"

Steinberg turned from the window and walked over to a cabinet, opened the top drawer and took out a folder.

"Do you remember that Limey company that Burnside was interested in?"

MacDonald nodded. "Sure I remember, that's why you went to London, I know that – but I didn't know what it was all about – you kept this one much to yourself. What's the problem?"

"For once I think I might have paid a little too much – now, you know, Mac, I don't take kindly to doing that – in the old days I'd have called in some of the boys – but today you gotta act differently, those measures are not liked."

"Hell, Julius, I was looking at the numbers the other day, they ain't half bad, what makes you think you got a bum deal?"

"I don't like the engineering numbers and that Limey bastard, president or something, I'm sure gave me a bum steer – but I can't prove it."

"Jesus, Julius, what more do you want – what about all those dollars going into those Swiss accounts – it's one of the best things you done – don't knock it."

"Yeah, I know, but I got this feeling and no one beats Julius Steinberg and gets away with it, no one."

"Well, what do you want me to do?"

"I want you to run it down. I want you to get all their work taken out of England and moved to Europe – we've already started on the chemical side but now I want you to get the engineering moved – OK we were going to do it anyway but I want it speeded up – goddam it, Mac, no one beats Julius Steinberg.

"There's a numbers man over there who could make trouble, he's a straight guy but clever and he could cause trouble with the British authorities if he were there when we start the big run down – I want him out – now. Abe Slyberger knows how to do it – I don't want any connection with me. It'll just be Slyberger with his own man in England who will handle the job, Abe'll know how to do it."

"OK boss, I'll get in touch with Abe tomorrow. Now, there's a guy who I know don't like Limeys, but I guess they wouldn't go much on him either, come to think of it. How do you put up with that sonofabitch, Julius?"

"He has his uses."

MacDonald got out of his seat and moved towards the door.

"OK if I go now – what you going to do tonight if the elevators aren't operating?"

"I'll stay here overnight. I got Julie to make up my bed before she left. Now don't forget what I said."

MacDonald left the office and started his walk down the twelve floors. He wondered why Julius had been so keen to tell him tonight, why couldn't the man have waited until the morning? Well that was Steinberg, he thought, little thought for others, except his family, or unless it was to make more dollars or push him up towards high society.

II

Tony Bentley's promotion to European manager meant he had to operate for much of his time from an office in Geneva. He found that in the job there was really no meat – sure he visited the various agents in Europe and got agreements to the transfer of business from the UK to them but once that was under way he began to miss the work he had done in the UK where he had been of value and where he had made his mark. True, his salary was good but there was little job satisfaction. This was a man who had mixed with ambassadors and was well known in London amongst the right people. He had been instrumental in raising the flag behind the iron curtain and was liked and respected both at the Polish embassy and at the USSR Commercial Section at Highgate. The work he was now given offered no challenge. What was he doing sitting in a small office in Geneva, living away from home and doing very little?

In a way it came as a relief when the Steinberg machine decided it was time for him to go – there were no excuses made, just some cash and a goodbye. No "sorry to have mucked up your life" or "hope you find another position soon" – just "we have no job for you".

When he had got over the shock, for he had no idea he would be for the chop, he picked up the telephone and rang his old friend, Ray Holmes.

"I've been given the push, Ray – you're a man who's been through it – what does one do now?"

This was a telephone call Ray was to have repeated time and time again over the next several months as one after another of his ex-colleagues were dismissed.

Ray became the focal point for knowledge on the dole, tax refunds, references, CVs and job applications. It reminded him of the calls he would get in WECO the day after Budget Day – all seemed to think that either he had formulated the budget or that at least he had a secret line to the Chancellor of the Exchequer – when in reality he had to read the papers the same as them. He was sure he helped but as for getting a job he hadn't found one himself, so how could he help?

Tony Bentley was a very self-sufficient person and having got the basic information on the dole and the tax position, set about thinking what to do. He was not about to seek work from anyone else; he would work for himself.

Together with a friend he set up a small engineering company in Brentwood, Essex. It prospered at first but one of its main customers decided it would take a long time to pay what it owed and the lack of further working capital was its final undoing. Tony tried several other ways of making money, including setting himself up as a consultant to companies wanting to know how to enter the export market. For a time it worked but after a year or so clients dried up and he once again was fighting to survive.

III

Redundancy affects us in different ways and there are some who will openly admit it was the best thing that ever happened to them. Of course, these are the few and the vast majority will tell you it was one of the most traumatic times of their lives.

Tom Delaney was one of the few. For nearly thirty years he had worked in the WECO labs – he was never a likely candidate for promotion but he was a good, solid and reliable employee. Although born in London he had moved out to Surrey when the then small WECO had left Victoria Street in 1939 – he fell in love with the country as it was then and began studying birds, plants and the whole countryside and of a weekend he could be found walking the Surrey hills carrying a book, making notes and stopping to read.

He had married a young "country" girl soon after the war and they lived in a small terraced house in Woking – he had no children.

Tom, who hardly knew the Americans had taken the company, was taken completely by surprise when his boss told him he would have to leave. He was a timid man and did not even ask why but picked up the reference books he would read at every lunchtime and went home. He somehow was not very sad, for the following day he and his wife were going on a coach trip to the New Forest. He had been looking forward to this trip for weeks. The coach from Woking would take them through the forest, stopping at an hotel for lunch and then allow them two hours to do what they liked. Tom knew what he and his wife would do – they would walk in the forest and study the flora and fauna. He would say nothing to his wife about losing his job until after the outing was over – he thought it might spoil her enjoyment.

Tom had no car, although he could drive, and he and his wife caught the early bus into Woking and were on the coach by 8 a.m. and soon after, it left. Tom was like a schoolboy going on holiday – if only it could be like this every day, he thought, as the coach made its way up past Guildford Cathedral and on to the Hogs Back. One could see the countryside for miles on both sides and the weather was beautiful.

It was then the seed was sown – all these people were going to the forest but how many of them really knew anything about the country? How many of them would find it interesting to be taken round by someone who knew the forest? Well, not necessarily the New Forest but any forest, how many would know a beech tree from an ash or an oak, or would know a mushroom from a toadstool? Who would know a kingfisher, a hawk, a greenfinch?

"I wonder how many," he said aloud.

"What was that, dear, what did you say?"

"Oh, sorry, I was thinking and by mistake spoke out loud – do you know how many of these people on the coach really know anything about the country?"

"What a funny question, how would I know unless I asked them? Don't be silly, Tom."

"No, I'm serious, Jill – take a guess."

"Oh I've no idea but I reckon very few would know as much as you and perhaps only less than half would be interested in the countryside as such – most are on a day out and are looking forward to walking round Lymington and having a good lunch."

"Yes, I know but I bet there are three or four who would be interested in looking at the forest with an expert who could make it interesting for them."

"Yes, you're probably right."

"That's what I'm going to do – I'm going to be a forest guide – not just in the New Forest but all over the country – it'll be wonderful."

"Oh come on, Tom, when would you find time to do that?"

"I've got all the time in the world – I've left my job. We're going to move to the country – how about it, Jill?"

Tom Delaney withdrew his savings and, using public transport and cheap bed and breakfasts, was soon learning all he could about the popular places in Cumbria and the Peak District – reading guidebooks and studying maps – and wandering in the New Forest and reading up about Snowdonia. They sold their house and moved to a residential caravan site near the New Forest and made their plans.

He bought a good second-hand minibus and in the early spring of the following year advertised in two dailies for his guided tours of the New Forest. The response was surprisingly very good and in May he took his first party on their two-day tour of the forest. It was a complete success and soon he was having great difficulty in fitting in all those who wanted to go. Redundancy had made this man a new life – he was happy.

IV

MacDonald was an exception. He had actually worked with Julius Steinberg for nearly 20 years… and he didn't have a gold watch! It was difficult to define his position, he did anything he was asked to do – he was of course on first name terms with his boss but as most know this was not at all unusual in the States. No, he was closer than that – he was the nearest Steinberg had to a friend, not that Steinberg recognised him as a friend but he was someone to confide in and be reasonably sure that Mac would be able to come up with something that would help or make him feel better. Mac was no great brain but he understood people and was a person capable of saying the right thing at the right time. He too had come up the hard way – not that he had come up very far but enough to get out of Brooklyn and live in reasonable comfort with his wife and two children out on Long Island. He was not of Scottish ancestry, as his name suggested, indeed his grandfather was a Polish Jew who had come through Ellis Island in the early part of the twentieth century. The grandfather's name was unpronounceable to the average-speaking American so as soon as it could be arranged he had changed it to a name he had once read in a book he had borrowed from the library to improve his English. Some years later his son married a blonde, non-Jewish girl, a shicksa, and their son, our Mac, could with a bit of imagination have passed himself off as of Scottish ancestry if he had ever wanted, but Mac never did. In fact he was proud of being half Jewish and Steinberg knew this.

Mac duly went to see Slyberger and told him what Steinberg had wanted concerning the British company.

"Julius don't want nothing in writing – you gotta spell it out to them – he don't want no comebacks so be sure your guys know what they're doing."

"What's he take me for – he knows me better than that. I can fix it for him so's you never knew there was a Limey set-up."

Slyberger acted his part well and within a few days the first steps to the elimination of WECO had been taken.

Mac had met Joe Miller, the president of the Burnside Chemical Corporation and in a way felt sorry for the guy. Why he should feel sorry for someone earning the sort of salary he was getting was not so easy to understand, but then, you see, he knew Steinberg's tactics – he knew that although Miller had been made deputy in Arkansas Oil he wasn't going to last, they never did. Like him Joe Miller had had it tough when young, only he had roughed it in Chicago whilst Mac's education had been Brooklyn.

Mac could walk in street markets in Brooklyn and know most of the stall-holders who happily engaged in banter as he passed – many were school friends or old neighbours and amongst them were some who knew the inside of Sing Sing prison and others who had been lucky. Mac knew them all and if he wanted help he knew where to come, most of these people were the salt of the earth.

"Hey there, Mac, what do yet know? I seen Abe last week, he's out and he asked after you."

"What do yer know, Mac? How's it going out in the sticks?"

"How's old Steinberg? Never see him round here now – hear he's moved up State somewhere – guess we'll never see him round here again."

"Hi Mac – going to see yet ma?"

It would take Mac all morning to walk through the market if he stopped to talk to all who shouted out to him – he was very popular and always felt at home in these poor but happy surroundings. Each week he would try and get round to see his widowed mother, who still lived in the same tenement that Mac had grown up in as a child. Mind you, it was different then, he had tried to persuade his mother to move but she was adamant that she would stay so Mac had spent thousands of dollars making the apartment the grandest in the block.

No one still working for Steinberg knew him better than Mac – he knew his strengths and his weaknesses – he knew that above all the man wanted to be respected, he knew also that this man found it difficult to trust anyone. He could not believe that there were many honest people in business, probably because in his young days it seemed that all those who made money were less than honest. Steinberg as a young man had seen many of his age and neighbourhood make money after the introduction of Prohibition in the twenties – some joining the mobs which were formed to sell beer or liquor and others eager not to be left without dollars setting up gangs to "protect" shopkeepers. It was as a young man with one of his early companies that he first ran into Slyberger, who barely fifteen years of age was chasing all over New York City delivering bottles of liquor which he carried hidden in a basket beneath two or three joints of meat, the basket fitting above the small front wheel of his butcher's bicycle with the name Abe Brookman, Butcher, blazoned on the side. When I say ran into him I mean it literally, Steinberg, driving his new T Ford, knocked him off his bicycle in 34th Street with dire consequences – all the bottles were broken. Luckily for the young Slyberger, who was quite uninjured, Steinberg, with the help of a few dollars, was able to persuade the officer of the law, who was quickly on the scene; that the brown liquid was purely for medicinal purposes. Young Slyberger, terrified of reprisals from the liquor "factory" owners, was also put at ease when Steinberg gave him dollars equivalent to that which he would have collected from his deliveries. Steinberg made the lad give him his name and address and told him to call round to his office the next day where he would find him some work in return for some information on the people who were getting him to make deliveries.

Steinberg used this "introduction" to get business in supplying bottles to the "factory" and glasses for the speakeasies. He thus grew with the mobs but within the law.

Steinberg had once or twice told Mac this story and each time Mac had said, "Jesus, how the hell that young kid you knocked off his bicycle ever come to be that crude old bastard, Abe Slyberger, I'll never know – you say he was different then. Maybe you were too then, Julius."

Slyberger over the years had with the help of Steinberg built up his own business in costume jewellery but of course there was a price – there was always a price where Steinberg was concerned. Slyberger had to pay what in effect amounted to a royalty on all his sales which under normal trading conditions was really no problem but was nevertheless always something Slyberger resented as he had been paying over considerable sums for twenty-five years. Then came a slump in his business as competition suddenly got keener and he found himself in difficulties – he looked to Steinberg for help and help came by Steinberg buying out two of his major competitors and taking a controlling interest in his company – he now effectively worked for Steinberg and he resented this.

Mac, aware of this underlying animosity, was always wary of Slyberger, knowing him to be a distasteful individual – he hinted to Julius the problem but to the latter he was small fry and anyway Slyberger was a useful man to have to do any dirty work for him.

V

Ray Holmes after three months of unemployment was beginning to despair. He tried not to show it to his wife but it kept him awake at night. He had written for many jobs since he left and so far had not succeeded in getting an interview. It seemed that age was against him plus the fact that he was unemployed. He did from time to time find a job which advertised for someone nearer his age, but these were few and far between and the upper limit of forty-two meant he was eight years over, or now nearly nine. But of course he would write, even though he would have no chance but he had been told that he must keep making applications as something was bound to turn up one day. In any case how many jobs advertised for a man of fifty – most of them seemed to want around the age of thirty. Why was it, he asked himself, that so many companies had adopted the cult of the young? He certainly had not noticed many exceptional young men in his company. Of course there were bright ones but their lack of experience stood out a mile to the discerning senior, just the same as he and his friends must have done in their earlier days. No, you could not get the sort of experience necessary from schools or from books. The only advantage the younger men had to gain experience as compared with his generation was their ability to change jobs without anyone questioning whether anything was wrong with them. In fact it was beginning to seem to him that you only had a chance of getting a job if you were under thirty and could show you had been around a bit... in fact if you could show you were unable to settle in any job for more than a year, you were in!

It was all so frustrating; you never had a chance. Why should the fact that you had lived longer than others go so much against you? Here he was, caught in a current fashion he had recognised a few years earlier and written an article about – fashions in business management.

Friday was pay-day, he always disliked going to the "Labour" but unlike some he had swallowed his pride and joined. He was now getting used to it and knew the drill, so much so that a few weeks earlier he had all but advised the manager how to overcome the staff problems he appeared to have. There were certainly better ways of paying out and the general appearance and atmosphere left much to be desired. The feeling of degradation was paramount.

It seemed strange to him that not very long ago he was on top of the world. Here he was with time dragging and yet how quickly time had passed at work, there were never enough hours in the day. What a waste it all was... rushing around, worrying, losing one's temper and coming home absolutely drained of energy. Of course he wasn't alone in this, nearly every senior person in industry had similar pressures, he told himself. It's a crazy world, he thought, only three years ago his wife had been introduced at a cocktail party as the wife of the next managing director. Had he changed so much in that time? How could he communicate to others that he was the same man, had the same experience, could do the job standing on his head and...? It was hopeless. He remembered being told on one occasion, "For goodness sake, don't leave us, the company will fall to bits." Now he had left and so far it had not fallen to bits... well not quite, but at least he had heard things were beginning to happen and he could not help but inwardly feel his job had been justified.

VI

Julius Steinberg, having passed his orders via Mac to Abe Slyberger, put this small episode to the back of his mind. He now had a vast corporation and great wealth but although he had over the past few years gained a reputation in business he was as yet hardly known elsewhere – he meant to put this right, for the one thing the man desired besides power was the adulation of high society. In his search for oil he had already made himself known to many highly ranked politicians and dignitaries overseas – even royalty in some smaller countries with oil potential.

To move closer to the high society he so envied he planned to make generous charitable contributions and to build an art gallery, which he would fill with valuable works of art, many of which he had already acquired.

He had only a few years earlier moved out of New York to a new house he had built in New England where he intended to reside for much of the year whilst still retaining his apartment on 72nd Street close to Park Avenue. The new house was just outside the New Hampshire town of Primrose, close to where a number of old respected families had had their country homes for over a century. The house, although new with every modern convenience, was built in the old colonial style but nowhere ostentatious. The grounds of some hundred acres were partly wooded with boundary walls some ten feet high.

Steinberg when in residence would occasionally be driven into town and leaving his driver by the car would take a walk along Main Street to a small well-tended park by the side of the lake. For an hour or so, he would sit on a wooden bench seat and look out across the lake – it was a routine he followed often when the weather was clement. He became a familiar figure to the locals, who at first eyed him with suspicion but eventually ended in a nodding acquaintance. What he was thinking whilst looking across the lake they never knew but amongst themselves they considered him to be a sad man.

Steinberg knew he had arrived and been recognised when the nodding turned to friendly smiles and when one day he gave generously to an appeal for war veterans of the county he had certainly been accepted. He wondered when he might be able to entertain local dignitaries in his new home. He was not married although it did not take long for the more imaginative townsfolk to begin guessing and before long he had had a wife many years ago but had been single for over fifty years. But really no one knew and he was not the sort of man one could ask, he just had to be accepted as he was – a man without a history.

The face Julius Steinberg presented to Primrose was completely different from that which he presented to business people in New York and indeed throughout the world. In Primrose he was a quiet, somewhat sad and lonely man who kept himself to himself but was prepared to pass the time of day when anyone spoke to him. Primrose was initially quite unaware of his business activities and even when over the months they began to know more of these there was nothing to show the quite ruthless streak in the man. A rural community would find it hard to understand the pain and hardship caused to many when power-seeking men in business take over companies. Those not affected see only the wealth and success of the man and credit is given where perhaps credit is not due. Julius Steinberg had caused much anguish and suffering in his many years in business but it just did not bother him, or at least no one who knew him closely, such as MacDonald, ever saw any remorse or concern.

However, he was by no means a stupid man and he surely must have known that his activities in growing a multinational company had not happened without causing pain to some. He, no doubt, despised those who thought they had been treated badly, after all he had had it rough in his early life and he had fought his way through, no, he had no compassion in business – he always had to win.

The first person in Primrose to really talk to Steinberg was Jake Ramsden, who owned the town's one hotel; he too had been a stranger to this town some ten years earlier when his old aunt had died. He had always been a small-town man working in forestry and knew the difficulties of being accepted in a new town. The hotel business in Primrose was seasonal and in early spring he had few guests and time on his hands. It was thus on a beautiful day in April that Jake took himself down Main Street to the park by the lake. The grass under the trees was a sea of small daffodils and near the lake some rhododendron bushes were in bloom. On the wooden bench by the lake sat Steinberg, and Jake feeling in a friendly mood and full of the joys of spring decided to go over and speak to him.

"Good morning, Mr Steinberg, it's a lovely day – good day for taking a boat out on the lake."

"Good morning – sorry I don't know your name – how do you know mine?"

"Well, this is a small town, we know everything and everybody – I know how you feel, I was new here once. Then I grew up in a small town and knew the score – you're not from round here but people soon find out. No harm meant though. My name's Jake Ramsden, I own the small hotel in town – but business is mighty quiet right now."

"Have you got a boat on the lake?" Steinberg said, with obvious interest.

"No I ain't got one but plenty in town have – I could get one for you if you wanted."

"No, that's OK – I might like to go across one day, I guess."

"I hope you don't mind me asking but I seen you sitting here many times before and you always seem to be looking across to the other side – it ain't none of my business but you seem as if you know what's over there – have you ever been?"

Steinberg hesitated before answering. Who was this man that he should tell him? He wanted to tell someone but this was a small town and tell one and everyone would know. "Yeah, I knew this place fifty years ago – came here in 1917, was in the army then and we came to a camp near here before we shipped out to Europe. See that hill over there – well, we were camped just over the other side – I came across the lake once and saw this little town, it ain't changed much – knew a girl here."

"That's a long while ago, Mr Steinberg, I could barely walk then. So you came back to live here all those years later – she must have been some gal! Sorry, Mr Steinberg, just my joke, why don't I keep my big mouth shut?"

"No, that's OK – sure she was somethin'. I came here once after the war but she'd married – I always liked this place and figured that if I ever got enough money I'd like to live here. I seem to be a different person when I'm here. Gotta go now, guess my housekeeper will soon have lunch ready."

"Nice to talk to you, Mr Steinberg, come in and see us at the hotel and we'll have a drink."

Jake Ramsden walked slowly back to his hotel, so this was the big city tycoon who many believed unapproachable – he wasn't so difficult, Jake pondered.

VII

The redundancies at WECO continued and the manager of one of the divisions, Henry Turner, who had under licence manufactured products through an American company not in the Steinberg Group, decided he would consult a solicitor when he was suddenly told he was no longer needed. The American company backed him in this and with their help he was able to get a better settlement – he was also able to stop WECO from continuing an association with the American company, Dentrich, since they had only granted the licence as long as Henry Turner managed the division. He intended setting up a company on his own.

This, however, was the exception and most of those leaving were having great difficulty in finding alternative employment. For many who had purposely moved home near to WECO it would almost certainly mean, assuming a job were found, either moving home or travelling longer distances to work. The local town had only one other business of comparable size to WECO and not many other factories from which employment might be forthcoming.

For many living on the local council estate the problem of moving was often a nightmare, and then there was the cost which for some was just something they could not contemplate.

In WECO there had been chemists, laboratory assistants, engineers, draughtsmen, buyers, sales representatives, mechanics, skilled factory workers, erection engineers, works managers, drivers, general office staff, shipping clerks, accounts staff, storekeepers and of course office and factory cleaners. A formidable group of people for a moderate-size town to absorb.

This substantial group of people for the most part were well aware of what had caused the wiping out of the company – some simply knew it to be an American company which had caused the problem, some knew more precisely the details of that company and some knew the name of the head of that company, whom they held responsible. Some, however, blamed the major shareholders of the original WECO for allowing the takeover to happen. Whatever or whoever was blamed, the name which most frequently was heard was that of Julius Steinberg, a name which was becoming known to many in the UK not for his wiping out of WECO but because he headed a consortium searching for oil in the North Sea and had recently bought some valuable paintings at Sotheby's. Steinberg was beginning to get his wish, he was becoming known throughout the world and must surely soon be accepted amongst American society. He was also building a formidable array of enemies in both the USA and it would seem in the United Kingdom – somehow it never entered his mind, he had grown up in the tough business world in America in the twenties and thirties and it never really occurred to him that what he had been doing was causing misery to a high proportion of those in both countries who had lost their jobs as a result of his activities. Even had he realised, it was most unlikely it would have disturbed him.

VIII

It was just after Christmas, the second Christmas after being made redundant, that Ray Holmes received a welcome telephone call. His wife had been sick for almost four years now and was from time to time accepted into hospital where she underwent electro-convulsive therapy – her doctor in the hospital had learnt of her husband's difficulty in finding work and talked to her husband who was a consultant to industry. The telephone call was from him asking if Ray could do some work for him. Ray accepted the call almost in tears and, thanking the man, assured him he could do the job and would be most happy to take on this small assignment.

Ray was over the moon. He had made over a hundred applications for work in the period since redundancy and although he had succeeded in getting a few interviews and being short-listed on three or four he had not yet been offered any employment. Inwardly he had given up, resigned to the fact that he was unlikely to get employment again – he had even worked out how they might manage by selling their house, moving to a smaller one, and together with the small amount of savings might live off the proceeds for a few years. It was of course ridiculous really but it was an exercise he felt he had to do. Now this lifeline had been thrown to him and he was again a happy man.

The assignment was at a factory in Portsmouth, initially for a trial period of a week where upon the issue of a satisfactory report he would be hopefully offered some further work.

He could not afford the convenience of driving down by car so used the early morning stopping train leaving his local station at 6 a.m. returning home at 8.30 in the evening. His week at work was a special tonic to him and his report, carefully compiled at home, was accepted and he was given an extra four weeks' work.

The money he earned was a great boost to his morale but the end of the assignment left him feeling restless. He contemplated doing further consultancy but where to get the work since in those days advertising was taboo. A neighbour, an accountant, kindly got him an interview at a client's factory and he was promised work with them but they were not yet ready to undertake the work in question but they would get in touch later.

Two months later just after having an article published in a professional magazine he was given an interview for a full-time job – it seems that the interviewer had read the article and hence the interview. After a further interview with the partners of the firm he was offered the job. He started with them in April travelling up to town and getting back at about seven in the evening. Early in July he returned home from work, opened the door and called out to his wife that he was home – getting no reply and not finding her in the kitchen he went upstairs and into their bedroom. His wife was in bed asleep and next to the bed was a note and an empty bottle. He straightway called an ambulance and followed it to the hospital but she died the next morning.

The worry of her husband's unemployment and now in effect losing him for a long day after having had him around so much while unemployed had been too much for this sick lady to cope with and she had taken her own life.

Ray was devastated and took a long while to get over the blow – he knew his wife had been ill before he had been made redundant but he was sure her illness had been aggravated by his seemingly hopeless plight which had worried her. He had gained employment but at a very much lower salary than he had been receiving two years earlier and now he was away from home all day whereas in his previous employment he could sometimes pop in at lunchtime and, in any case, she knew he worked almost only round the corner. He fixed firmly in his mind that redundancy had been the cause of her death and the person who was ultimately responsible for this was Steinberg.

IX

Joe Miller as the president of the Burnside Chemical Corporation was an important person, at least Joe thought so and who was to say he was wrong. Any man who has the responsibility of over 5,000 employees has a right to think his job important.

Joe had entered the corporation as a young man of twenty-four after he was demobbed from the army at the end of 1946. In the intervening years he had worked hard and been rewarded accordingly until in 1967 he had been made president. A remarkable record of achievement marking this man out as someone special. Being an accountant he had for some time been very aware of the cash build-up in the corporation and had pressed many times for the Board to use it before they became a victim of a predator. In the short time as president he had managed to acquire one other company and was in the process of acquiring another when Arkansas Oil had come on the scene.

Joe could do nothing to avoid the takeover and trauma that would follow but was somewhat flattered when Steinberg said he wanted him as his deputy. Joe did not have to think too long before accepting, the salary offered was good and knowing Steinberg's age he could see himself in the not too distant future as head of this vast multi-national oil company. Of course Joe Miller really knew little of Steinberg, in fact until you worked for him or had been the victim of one of his schemes you could not be expected to know him – few people really knew the man and only Mac was anywhere near being close.

Steinberg had wanted to put his own man into Burnside and hence his approach to Miller – the one thing Steinberg did not like was employing someone who might know more than he did. He knew he could get sound men who would work under his direction and he was suspicious of any he did not know and who might one day prove to be smarter than him. Miller was suspected of being such a man and Steinberg had no room for him in his organisation.

Miller was given the run-around for just over a year and finally after a big argument with Steinberg over the work he was being allowed to do they agreed to part company. Miller was given $100,000 and signed a document drawn up by one of Steinberg's sharp attorneys which gave him no further right of redress against Arkansas Oil or against Steinberg as an individual.

Miller expected to find no difficulty in getting another senior post as he had in earlier years been approached by several large corporations. Alas although he knew nothing of Ray Holmes and his situation after leaving WECO, he was to find himself in a similar position – plenty of experience but out of a job and on the wrong side of forty.

He and his wife were not without some money but he knew that if they were to maintain the style of living to which they had became accustomed, he would have to find work soon.

Reading the morning paper some six months after he left Arkansas Oil he saw a picture of Steinberg presenting a painting to the municipal art gallery in Winnipeg, Manitoba, from which province he had managed to get an agreement to search for oil up near Hudson's Bay. Joe threw the paper to the floor and muttered to himself.

His wife sitting opposite to him at the table looked across and, seeing him angry, reached out and touched his hand. "Nothing in the paper can be worth getting so angry over. What was it, Joe? Has the market fallen again?" she said.

"No, I just saw a picture of Steinberg and I can't help getting angry. Everyone will think what a nice guy – it makes my blood boil – someone ought to tell 'em."

X

Simon Boyes and Joe Tooley had been assistant accountants in WECO for some years; the former was in fact deputy to the fairly newly-appointed Jerry Jameson and had been assistant to Ray Holmes many years earlier when Ray had been chief accountant. The former had married a young clerk in the department and had two children – not being qualified, although having a wealth of experience, he knew it was not going to be easy for him when the axe fell. He was in fact unemployed for nearly six months before he finally landed a job in Cornwall, some three hundred miles away. It was not a highly paid job but property was much cheaper down there than in Surrey so they were able to make the move and put some money in the bank. They both knew that unless Simon was able to increase his income very considerably they would never again be able to live in Surrey, their home county.

Joe Tooley was married but without a family, and thus his situation was not so desperate particularly as his wife was at work as an occupational therapist. Joe eventually found himself a job which lasted six months and then he faced another several months on the dole until he was offered a job at London Airport (Heathrow) with one of the smaller airlines. The salary was not good but as he said to Ray when by chance he met him at a football match, it was a job and he felt he could not continue relying on his wife to provide for him.

Both of the above had always been close to Ray Holmes, their ex-boss and they were well aware of what Steinberg had done to the company.

Then there were the chemists and lab assistants – some of whom were not too long unemployed but senior chemists and a few lab assistants had a very hard time finding jobs. One David Tibble who had been a director of one of the major subsidiary companies was particularly hard hit and in the end resorted to taking a smallholding in Hampshire, changing his lifestyle completely. In two years he was at his wits' end as his crops had not given him the income expected. He once again started to apply for positions as a chemist but it seemed his particular experience was not in demand and he too was on the wrong side of forty.

The list continues. John Jenning a chemist by profession but a training officer for some four years past had to forget looking for further work as he was already in his late fifties and as he said, "no one wants you at that age." Tom Wright, also a brilliant chemist and local lay preacher, gave up trying for a job as a chemist and ended up working for a charity. Mike Johnson, a sales director and engineer of some repute, also took early retirement when after two years he had not succeeded in getting any employment. Then there was Fred Green, who had worked as a storeman and as he was nearing sixty just could not find anyone to employ him and drove his car into the Thames at Walton.

It was when this shocking news was printed in the local press that Tony Bentley telephoned Ray Holmes and suggested they have a drink together to talk over old times.

Tony also rang around to others he knew who had had difficulties and six said they would turn up – others had said they would love to come but the date and time did not suit, they would come if there were another get-together.

Ray was the first to arrive, followed shortly by Tony.

"Glad you could make it, Ray – I thought it would be good to have a talk. I think most of us have not found it easy and it will be good to let off steam."

"Yes, a good idea – nice to see old friends."

"I've managed to get one or two others to come along, I expect they'll be here soon."

No sooner had he said this than two other faces they knew entered the bar.

"Well, I'll be damned," Ray said holding out his hand. "How's Jake?" he continued, shaking the hand of one of the new entrants, "and you too, Bob, this is a surprise."

Jake Wint and Bob Smart shook hands and the former walked to the bar. "What are you all drinking?"

"We're drinking double Scotches," shouted Tony, laughing.

"Well, you can buy your bloody own – I haven't had a double since I left WECO – I think I'll get meself a pint and make it last."

The good-humoured banter continued and in the middle of this came two other ex-colleagues – Jim Johnson, an engineer/draughtsman, and Charles Mortimer, an original main Board director whose father had been one of the company's founders.

"We met outside – I was surprised to see old Jim – how are you, Tony?" said Charles, walking across to Tony Bentley and shaking his hand – he nodded to the others present and sat down.

Jim Johnson, after saying hello to the others, made his way to the bar where Jake was just taking his drinks from the counter. "Hi yer, Jake, we've got a right mixture here tonight – surprised to see Charles here – what's it all about?"

Jake rested his glass on the bar. "I don't know, Tony rang me and wondered if I'd like to have a drink and talk over old times – that's all I know but it is a bit of a mixture, maybe Tony is going to try and start the old company up again," he said with a grin.

The six men continued a light-hearted conversation and shortly all of them were telling of what had happened to them since they had been made redundant, that is all except Charles Mortimer who had received a settlement from Arkansas Oil to leave at the time of the takeover. He also had had a substantial shareholding so it was unlikely he had suffered any hardship.

Jake was a happy-go-lucky individual, liked by almost everybody – he was an engineer who latterly had become an engineering buyer, a very good one. He had been unemployed for only two months when he found another job, but he said he had to travel some distance to work and the pay was not so good. Jake had worked for WECO for twenty-five years.

Bob Smart had been a director of one of the subsidiary companies; engineering was his background and when he left he certainly had difficulty in finding comparable work and finally set up a small engineering business of his own. He said he was making a go of it but it was hard work, which at his age was not what he had wanted – he was then fifty-two and had been a serving officer in the RAF until joining WECO some ten years back.

Jim Johnson, the oldest of those present, he was over sixty but exactly how old he never let on, said he had given up trying for work and was living, "if that's what you call it," off the dole. He was a bitter man; he had been with WECO since, the mid thirties.

Charles Mortimer once or twice was obviously uncomfortable but Tony Bentley assured him that was not why he had asked him along. "I wanted to see how we had all fared – I knew you would not have been in financial trouble but I reckon you missed being at work and thought you'd like to meet up with some of us again."

At about nine thirty Charles bought one final round and said he would have to go. "I'm glad I came. I am so sorry it has been so tough for some of you – if I'd known what it was going to be like, I would never have sold my shares."

Charles Mortimer left the pub and the others agreed that he was not such a bad sort.

Jake Wint looked around at the four others and said, "I reckon you got us here for more than a chat, Tony, what's on your mind?"

Tony hesitated before speaking and put down his glass.

"Well I don't know about you fellows but I was bloody angry at the way we were treated and I thought it would help all of us to have an opportunity to talk to each other and get the things that bother us off our chests. No, I had no other real intention, nothing planned. I just thought it might do all of us good. I hope I wasn't wrong."

"We thought perhaps you were going to try and start the old company up again."

"No, nothing like that, Bob, it's too late now anyway – we haven't got the rights to manufacture half the chemicals. Even if we have the know-how they'd sue us. And as for the engineering, well it never made big profits and as so many once said, at least part of the engineering was a bit like the razor and the razor blade – I'm an engineer but I recognised that there was some truth in our side of engineering."

"But why do the authorities allow this sort of thing to happen – twenty million dollars in the country and exports of at least five million a year lost and 1500 jobs lost in WECO alone – it's crazy."

"Yes I know – I agree – but what can we do about it?"

"I know what I'd like to do to that bastard, Steinberg – he's the real culprit – I've since heard that he did a similar thing in Canada. But even they haven't caught on, he's now got a concession to prospect for oil up near Hudson's Bay – the authorities never seem to look further than their noses." Ray Holmes had said very little in the evening but before he went he wanted to make sure that all present had it clear in their minds who was the real villain.

"Do any of you feel we should meet again, or do we now close a chapter on this part of our lives – what do you say? Shall we meet in six months and see if things are any better? One or two others I telephoned said they'd have come if they had had more notice. Shall we fix a date now and circulate it to a few others and we'll all meet on 15th September, if it's a week day?"

"My diary says it's a Thursday… and I think it's a good idea," Jim added.

XI

Steinberg over the next two years continued to build his reputation, his consortium had struck it rich in the North Sea and were now close to another bonanza in the far north. He had continued to diversify in the States and had taken over a sugar company in Atlanta, a timber company in Denver, a plastics company in Philadelphia and an electronics company in Los Angeles. The above still only represented ten per cent of the Group's turnover and Steinberg wanted this increased to at least thirty per cent – the trouble was that as fast as he acquired new companies his oil business was growing just as fast. However, he was determined not to be too dependent on oil and continued to look for other acquisitions. He of course only got involved in the niceties of takeover when the company had been thoroughly investigated after having been "found" by his many scouts whose job in life was to search for possible companies worth being drawn into the Steinberg net.

His name was now regularly appearing in newspapers in America and always as the great businessman – the Americans of course always have admired people who make it on their own. Thus people in Primrose, not usually too concerned with big business, could not help but notice that Steinberg was an important man.

Therefore, some seven years after moving to his new house in Primrose he was invited to a dinner at a nearby house owned by the most respected family in the area – a family who years back had made their money in railways. Present at the dinner were four or five representatives of other important families in the county. Steinberg was treated as one of them although his accent betrayed a man who had not been brought up in the Ivy League. He knew now that he had arrived.

It was about this time that Jake Ramsden noticed that his hotel bookings were becoming better. He did not at first realise what had caused the change until one day he was asked by some guests where the Steinberg house was situated.

"Are you a friend of Mr Steinberg?" he asked.

"Oh no. As we were touring New England we thought we would look into Primrose, having read that article in a magazine about Mr Steinberg and his chosen home in New Hampshire – it is a nice little town, I can see what made him want to live here. Ma and me come from Jersey City, not a bit like round here."

Following this revelation, Jake from time to time would ask why guests had chosen to come to Primrose and he soon found that a good number were coming out of curiosity due to Steinberg living there.

XII

People who had met Abe Slyberger were generally soon made aware of the man's apparent inability to converse without resorting to words that in a reasonable civilised society of the time were just not acceptable. Perhaps he was ahead of his time for today words then frowned upon are now regularly heard both in films and on television. However, Slyberger managed to use these words in such a way, generally associated with some crude assertion that made the listener aware that this man was not the sort of person one would like to take home to meet the family or indeed anyone of one's friends. He was a small man, overweight, bald and sported a grey moustache. He had been born on the East Side in 1911 and had had a tough childhood. His father was a Jewish immigrant who only a few years earlier had found it difficult to get work and even more difficult to learn to speak English. Abe soon got mixed up with local gangs but being small was often the butt of others but soon learnt that if he swore and behaved in an outrageous way these erstwhile tormentors began to accept him. At the age of thirteen he had started making deliveries of liquor to various parts of the city from an old warehouse on the East River where one day he had been caught breaking in by two men who told him they would let him go if he made some deliveries for them. He duly made the deliveries and when asked if he would like to carry on working for them, he agreed. Everyone knew that the making of liquor and its distribution was against the law but at that time many people still looked upon those who flouted this law as anything but criminals – at least in the early years of Prohibition this was the case.

It was in his early days with these employers that he had met Steinberg and introduced him to them. Steinberg gave him odd jobs to do and soon Abe had enough money to buy into a costume jewellery business owned by an old man to whom he had delivered liquor. The man was looking for someone to help him out and as he knew Slyberger delivered all over New York he had asked him to take some of the jewellery around with him to see if he could interest some of his customers. Slyberger had found it a useful cover for his deliveries and also found that he was a good salesman and hence he had been invited to put up some money and buy into the business. The old man had died in the early thirties and Abe, with the help of Steinberg money, had taken on the whole business which had grown considerably since he had first acquired a share. In return for his help Steinberg required a royalty payment on all turnover of the business.

Many years later when the business had run into difficulties Abe had again been forced to seek help and the only man he could think of with money enough to be of any use was Steinberg. As mentioned earlier, Steinberg had come to the rescue by buying out the competitors and taking a controlling interest in the Slyberger business. Although Steinberg had saved Slyberger's business from collapse the latter never liked virtually working for Steinberg and paying out for all time a share of the business which had grown even more after the competitors had been removed. He could never accept this had all been due to the help he had been given and thus always held a grudge against Steinberg and thought from time to time how he could be rid of the man and his agreement. The agreement it should be said was with Steinberg himself and not with Arkansas Oil.

Steinberg had run down the small companies which had previously been competitors of Slyberger but had then used them to set up a branch in Switzerland and invited Slyberger to run it for him – that had been in 1967 and it was thus that when Steinberg got involved in the WECO takeover he used the Swiss company to control his operations in Europe and at the same time let loose this obnoxious character into a field in which he was totally unsuited. Instead of inspiring confidence he was only able to make the victims of the takeover really wonder what sort of people they were dealing with. Both he and Steinberg invariably employed those of the Jewish faith in all senior positions in their companies – this was not unusual, after all there are few who would dispute that in relation to their numbers the Jewish people have been the most successful in making money in the business world. What was not acceptable was the way that these two individuals were prepared to operate in order to achieve their ends – they would, if questioned, not have seen anything unjust in what they were doing as they themselves would point to history and say how things had been made difficult for their fathers to find work both in the States and in their old countries simply because they were Jewish.

Abe Slyberger managed to close down WECO as required by Steinberg and continued to run the Swiss operation with the help of Raoul Mitterand. He received his salary regularly from Switzerland and his wealth in his jewellery business prospered – he also received a bonus on the European results and in the first year or so this was very good but things began to change after the closure of the British company, the annual profits were not nearly as great as had been forecast and Slyberger found that Steinberg had began to apportion the blame for this fall his way. In truth the management set up in Switzerland was not capable of managing the agents, now mostly subsidiaries, having over the past few years been acquired for the multi-national, neither did they have the laboratory facilities; chemists, engineers and top sales staff to run the operation. Steinberg's obsession with getting his own back on Fred Dailey was now coming home to roost. People in power will seldom admit to mistakes and Steinberg was convincing himself that it was Slyberger who was the cause of the downturn – he would have to get rid of him.

XIII

Although Steinberg's empire continued to grow he was now spending much less time travelling abroad and more time at his home in Primrose, that is all except for part of the winter months when he moved down to Miami.

In spite of his desire to be accepted among those he considered mattered, he had done nothing to return the hospitality shown to him by the Malloy family. It was not that he was ungrateful but simply that as he lived on his own, except for a housekeeper and servants, he was unsure as to how to entertain adequately – but it bothered him and whilst in his Brooklyn office one day talking to MacDonald about the new company they had acquired in Denver, he raised the subject with him.

"By the way, Mac, did you know I went to the Malloys for dinner a while back?"

"Mixing with high society, eh Julius? You'll be at the White House for dinner soon."

"This was bigger than the White House, Mac, these people are the real McCoy. Only the very best get to go to their place."

Mac did not follow up the line of conversation and was surprised when Steinberg carried on. "You should have seen the layout in that joint, real class – better than I've seen anywhere – it's what I like. But I wouldn't know how I could possibly return the hospitality – I wouldn't know how."

"That don't sound like you, Julius – you always say you can do anything. I don't see why you worry about it, you got a swell joint – what's your problem?"

"Come on, Mac, they got flunkies and swell waiters who know what they are doing. I got the housekeeper, Molly; I got a cook, what's her name … oh Jennifer, and three local gardeners – and of course the regular cleaners from that agency."

"You got Ruby your secretary – sure she could help."

"Yeah, yeah and I got Joe my chauffeur – come on Mac that's hardly a set-up to give a big party."

"But how do you know those flunkies and waiters weren't just brought in for the occasion – you can hire those guys from New York – mind you, it'll cost but why should you worry? If you really want to put on a show I can get someone to fix it for you."

Julius said nothing at first and then, "OK – why not – if you say it can he arranged let's do it."

"It'll take a while to fix up but when I got the right set-up organised you gotta tell me a date."

"Well let us fix a date right now – let's say in two months – say 23rd April – that's a date I like."

Steinberg didn't tell Mac why he had decided on 23rd April – Mac wouldn't understand and was just as likely to ask, "Who's dis guy Shakespeare?" Mind you, it was not that Julius was a Shakespeare fan, it was just something he had once read in a book and then there was that short tour he made when he was over in England when they took him to a place called Stratford. He thought he might let it slip out in conversation at the dinner that would be sure to impress.

XIV

Joe Thomas was one of the early people to be let go at WECO – not long after Ray Holmes. Joe was not, however, a high flyer – he was a factory worker employed in the chemical factory. He was known by nearly everyone and liked by many, including some of the WECO directors and managers. This in spite of him being a strong union man and perhaps some may consider a troublemaker. Actually he was a committed communist and made no secret of it – however, he did a good day's work and only fell foul of management when he brought men out on strike for some irregularity. No strike lasted more than a day but it was an irritant and when it was learnt that another communist had joined the factory, the MD had decided to recruit someone to advise the company what to do. The new man had not been brought in by Joe, in fact some of the men later said that Joe didn't want someone creeping into his job, but at the time management was worried as to how this had happened.

It's funny what people will do for money. The MD had heard of a well-known trade union man who had appeared in the news and on television many times who in his spare time was available to advise bosses of companies on what to do when unions were becoming a problem. To do the man justice he gave good advice and strictly the information was not really anti-union as much as anti-Communist – I suppose it could be argued that the infiltration of the very left wing elements into the union movement were doing the union members more harm than good.

His advice was to shut down the machine shop from which most of the trouble was emanating and where the new communist was employed and use outside contractors. This was a drastic step for the union man to recommend but it was implemented and only Joe, a harmless known communist remained. The MD was also given a telephone number to ring when new employees were being recruited so that he could be sure that no party members were joining the company.

This of course all happened before WECO was taken over but it was undoubtedly a success and there was no more serious trouble, just one or two minor stoppages called by Joe Thomas who was invariably found to be right.

Joe of course knew nothing of the number that the MD and his confidant, Ray Holmes, had been given and indeed used, but conceivably other companies' management had been made aware of this number and were using it, for after three years Joe had not found any employment. Joe was then in his fifties and a pretty bitter man – now more pro-Soviet and more anti-American.

Ray who when a young man had flirted with joining the Young Communist League liked talking to Joe and when he met up with him one Saturday when out shopping, he asked him if he would like to come to the pub meeting to be held the following week when he would be able to meet up with some of the people he knew when at WECO.

"I haven't got money to spend on a round of drinks, I don't think I'd better come, Ray."

"Don't be stupid, many of us are in the same boat and we have an understanding we buy our own – unless of course someone is feeling rich and insists on setting them up for us all."

"All right, I'll come but I've got no transport."

"I'll pick you up, don't worry."

XV

Ted Wilson had known what losing his job at the Sheffield Depot might mean, but in his wildest dreams he had not really envisaged three years of unemployment. He had gone through various stages of despair but his wife had been a great support to him and he was surviving. Young Joey had got used to their frugal style of living and his grandfather had made sure that at Christmas and on his birthday he would get a good present.

Ted had been a member of the union but had not in any way been active, although once he had met Joe Thomas the shop steward down in Surrey when he had been invited at the firm's expense to a firm's party one Christmas. Joe had looked after the Yorkshireman at the party and they had exchanged addresses. "I wonder what has happened to Joe Thomas," he said at breakfast one day.

"Who is Joe Thomas, Ted?"

"You remember, the man who looked after me at that party I went to some years back – he must have been sacked too because I heard that the company had closed."

"Well, if you want to know about him you'll have to write – I seem to remember he gave you his address."

Ted was not a good letter-writer but he was curious to know and at the same time wondered whether Joe might be able to help him find a job – so he wrote.

A week or so later he got a reply from Joe and found that both of them were in the same boat. Joe mentioned that he was going to a pub get-together with several of his old colleagues. He had said that he was angry as to how the American company had caused WECO to fold; he had then gone in to a tirade on multi-national companies. Ted, who had never thought much about the rights and wrongs of multi-nationals – in fact he wasn't too sure what constituted a multi-national – began to see what Joe was talking about.

"Joe thinks that multi-national companies should be more closely controlled by law and that all such takeovers should be monitored to make sure that British industry is not destroyed or moved out of the country."

His wife carried on ironing but appeared to be unmoved. "I don't know much about what should be done but, whatever, it is too late to help you – it doesn't help much to know who is at fault when you can't do anything about it."

"Joe says he is going to meet up with some of the other fellows he used to work with – maybe they will be able to do something."

"Oh come on, Ted, it's three years since you left – what do you think they are going to do? They'll just talk. But I suppose it helps get it off their chests."

"I know they can't do anything to help us but maybe if they feel strongly enough they could try and publicise what has happened – I never saw anything in the papers about our company being closed. I blame whoever is the boss of the company who took us over – I'd like to get my hands on him."

"That's not like you, Ted, you shouldn't talk like that."

"No, you're right but when you're treated like that it makes you angry, especially when you know there's nowt you can do."

XVI

Jake Ramsden was standing near the reception desk in his hotel when in came Slim Waters, the owner of a small shop which sold postcards and small items bought by tourists passing through whilst on holiday in New England. "How are you, Jake, how's business?"

"Not bad at all, had a few tourists staying over in the last week. What makes you leave your store on a Saturday?" Jake enquired.

"Oh I got Julie looking after it, I needed a break – getting too old to keep at it all the time – have yer heard about old Steinberg going to the Malloys – ain't that something? I never thought to see the day."

"He don't seem such a bad guy and anyway the Malloys may think they've always been what they are, but a hundred years back they weren't much different from Steinberg – my old grandma when she was alive said she knew Sean Malloy, the one who made all the dollars, and used to be pestered by his youngest son, George. I remember her telling Ma that old man Malloy was a rough and tough man who had got into railroads after the Civil War. Won some shares in a poker game down south in '65. Some say he got them from a reb in Richmond but I guess it doesn't matter now – anyways that was how he started."

"I heard you talked to Steinberg a while back – what's he got to say for himself?"

Jake took on an air of importance but rather wished there were more around to hear him say how he went up to Steinberg and talked to him.

"Sure I talked with him, he don't seem a bad guy – a bit sad I thought. Came to Primrose when in the army in '17 – knew some local gal and came back after the war but she'd got herself married. Never said whether he had ever been married – I told him to come and have a drink here one day – but after going to the Malloys I wonder if he'll ever come now."

"This girl he knew, any idea who it was?"

"No, I never asked, anyways that was fifty years back."

XVII

It was April 1974 and Julius Steinberg was in a nostalgic mood, it was fifty years since he last saw her. He remembered how when he returned from France in 1920 he had gone straight to Primrose on his disembarkation leave and tried to find her – he knew her name but not her address. After asking around he soon learnt that she had married and lived just outside Primrose. He had plucked up courage to find her house but lost his nerve when it came to calling at the door. He had waited nearby and after about an hour he saw her walking along the road from the town – she was by herself and he had surprised her.

"My goodness, it's you. I never expected to see you again," she said with obvious embarrassment. "I thought you must be dead or had forgotten me. What are you doing here?" she asked rather stupidly.

"You know why I'm here; have you forgotten? I never had your address but I told you I would come back after the war." He looked straight at her but she lowered her eyes... yes, she was just as beautiful as he had remembered.

"I'm married – I did wait for you but as time went by I thought you must have been killed. The war ended a year and a half ago. Why didn't you come sooner?" she asked.

"Yeah, I heard you were married... I got wounded and taken prisoner and ended up in a German hospital for many months. I only got back a week ago."

"I'm sorry, Julius, but you're too late, I'm married."

They had talked for some time and finally Julius said, "It's April 1920, supposing we meet in say four years from now and see how we feel then – maybe we will both be married by then – we could exchange notes – what do you say?" After some persuasion she had agreed but in order to avoid talk from others in the small town she said they should meet on the other side of the lake, where they had first met in

1917. They agreed to meet at two o'clock in the afternoon on the 23rd April, 1924.

In the four years that passed, Julius had already started to build his business but he never forgot Zoë. Two years later he married a Jewish girl he met in a dime-a-dance hall in Asbury Park, New Jersey. His marriage was not unsuccessful but he always remembered the girl he had met in Primrose and near to the arranged date in April 1924 he had made a "business" trip up to New Hampshire to keep the appointment. He somehow never imagined that she would forget or that any circumstances would stop her from turning up and he was right. Her marriage had not produced a family but in their way they were content – the physical attraction they had had for each other had waned but she hoped that their impending move to Bridport would give them a new start.

Julius had arrived at the appointed spot well before two o'clock, having driven in his Ford straight up from New York on the unmade roads. It was about three miles round the lake from where his friend lived and she had to walk the whole way but nevertheless arrived more or less on time.

She was obviously very pleased to see him but disappointed in a way to find he too was married. They talked in the car for a while and then as the weather was so beautiful decided they would go and sit on the grass away from the car. The spark of love was still there and, although not admitting it, Zoë regretted her past haste in getting married... this was the man she really wanted and she did not resist his advances. They were there until the sun began to sink behind the hill.

They did not make any arrangements to meet again, both now being frightened as to where it might lead. It had been a brief wartime romance, carried forward some years but like wartime romances had to end and both were now sensible enough to call it a day.

Julius had never forgotten her and was tempted after his wife died some years later to try to find her again but did not.

Now he was old but inside he was still young and the romance had grown with his years and hence he was drawn to Primrose.

Now fifty years on from their last meeting he once more made his pilgrimage to the spot across the lake where they had met.

XVIII

They say lightning never strikes twice but as far as takeovers are concerned this does not apply. The chances of it happening to an individual are not too high but it does happen. However, to be the victim of the same predator is obviously much less likely and then to lose your job twice through such takeovers would seem most unlikely and you would not be blamed in thinking that someone up there had something to say or that someone down here did not like you.

Joe Miller had at last found a position in an American company up in Canada. He had no real desire to leave his home in Pennsylvania but when you have been unemployed for over two years you get desperate. It obviously meant a big move and his wife was not at all happy at the prospect. Joe, however, would go up to Canada and work before the big decision was taken for the family to move.

The company concerned was associated with the oil industry and had opened an office in the nearest big town, Winnipeg, to the fields of exploration further north in Manitoba on Hudson Bay. The head office was in Chicago and their connection with the oil industry was the manufacture and erection of oil rigs. The office was situated on Portage Avenue.

Miller reported on a cold January morning in 1975, the temperature was fifteen degrees below zero. He entered the warm building and soon forgot the cold outside and the fact that he had decided that this job in Canada could not last as he had reasoned his wife would never be happy with the climate.

He was introduced to a number of the staff and then was informed of the work required which primarily was liaison with the prospecting area up north. It was then that he learnt that the company with whom he would be dealing was one owned by Steinberg. As soon as he heard the name his blood began to boil and he wished he had never heard of the job he had now undertaken. However, the weeks went by and the weather improved and no further mention was made of Steinberg – things were looking better. His wife came up to Winnipeg in the spring and seemed to be quietly impressed with the city and its surrounds. Perhaps after all, Miller thought, they would be able to settle up here for the few years necessary to give them enough money to retire down south.

It therefore came as a shock when he learnt that Steinberg had bought the company in Chicago and just four weeks later he was told that the Winnipeg office was to close, as all operations were to be dealt with from head office. The American staff who had moved up to Winnipeg were told to report back to Chicago, the local Canadian staff were given notice to leave and Miller who had been employed direct to Winnipeg was treated in the same way. It was doubtful whether Steinberg ever knew that one of his employees in Winnipeg had been Miller but to the latter that did not matter, he had lost his job twice through this individual and he was angry. Once again he would have to start the job-searching routine over again.

REVELATIONS

XIX

JULIUS STEINBERG was driven by his chauffeur north out of Primrose and round the lake to the spot where he had last seen Zoë fifty years ago. The chauffeur, Joe Mancini, stopped the car when Steinberg told him and the old man got out and walked towards the lake, almost in a trance. "You all right, boss?" Joe called after him – but the old man never replied. Joe, not wishing to interfere and seeing Steinberg stop and turn round, sat back in his seat and picked up his newspaper from the passenger seat. Once again 23rd April was a nice day and Joe guessed the old man wanted to get the feel of being outside and away from the hurly burly of his New York offices.

Julius stayed looking around for about ten minutes then slowly walked back to the car. "Just drive round the hill and then turn back and take me home. It's nice out here, don't you think, Joe?"

Joe, who had never thought much about the country, nodded agreement but thought – the old man's going soft. Steinberg was in a nostalgic mood and wanted to talk.

"You know I came here first during the war – not the last war, the 17–18 war – I was stationed for a while on the other side of the hill. Climbed over once and met this girl." Julius saw Joe look at him in his driving mirror – a quizzical look. "Yeah, I was young once and not a bad looking guy too," Steinberg added.

Joe Mancini was not sure what to say. He had been with Steinberg for nearly ten years but he had never heard him speak like this – the guy was human after all. However, his curiosity was aroused, "What happened, boss – did you see her after the war?"

Steinberg could not understand why he should tell his chauffeur his story but somehow he felt he would like to – after all no one else knew anything about it and it's sometimes good to share something with another. He thus related the story of their meeting after the war and even told him about their subsequent meeting four years later. "… in fact fifty years ago today," Julius finished.

"What happened to the dame, boss, have you ever tried to find her?"

Julius thought for a moment and looked disturbed, "No, I never did, guess after my wife died I never found time – I was too busy building an empire. It's only when I came out to Primrose that I really wish I had tried to see where she was – she could be dead now, there are not too many left as old as me."

Steinberg was driven back to his home and lunch. Mac had been true to his word and arranged for all the trappings necessary for Julius to have his guests to dinner that night. As he went to get out of his car, a flunkey opened the door and accompanying him into the house took his hat. Lunch was served to him and Mac, who was there to see all went well, by the temporary staff working for the New York agency that Mac had employed. Steinberg was impressed by the efficiency of the company and from what he had seen was sure the Malloys and their friends would be suitably impressed.

XX

On 15th September the few who had been at the previous meeting had grown threefold. Tony had done some good work in telephoning around and even he was surprised at the turnout. Obviously there still remained a deal of camaraderie but most had been spurred on to attend because they had suffered or were still suffering and hoped there might be a solution to their problems. When it seemed the whole party had assembled and the initial renewal of friendships had taken place, Tony, who had arranged to have the meeting in a small private room off the saloon bar, banged the table to get attention. Tony had always been good at making speeches and this night he once again was able to catch the mood of the meeting by giving a few words of welcome to all and particularly, as he said, those who did not attend the last gathering. He ended his short speech by relating a story he had recently heard concerning a man who had been made redundant and when the laughter had subsided he asked that all those who were willing should relate their story of redundancy and indeed that of any others who were not present where they felt it worth telling.

The stories carried a familiar ring to Ray Holmes – oh yes, they were all different and yet the same. A few after three years were still unemployed and no one present who had a job was earning as much as previously, whilst those who had left with paid-up pensions had found that the high inflation of the past two years had made the pensions they would draw at the age of sixty-five practically worthless – they were not a happy bunch of men.

"It makes one feel a little better to know that one is not alone and that others have suffered the same indignities and frustrations – I for one am pleased Tony called these meetings but it is even more frustrating to hear what has and is still happening and yet there is no one who knows how to stop it. Why should everyone accept that takeovers as they presently exist should be allowed to continue? Is this what democracy is all about? Surely it is up to those who have been victims of a takeover to make themselves heard in some way – we can't just have meetings telling ourselves how hard done by we have been and then go away and do nothing," Ray said.

"That's all very well but what can we do?"

Ray continued, "I'm not suggesting I know what to do but I just think it wrong that we do nothing – we ought to make ourselves heard, have a protest march," he said smiling, "write to our MPs, write letters to newspapers, let the country know what happens when such takeovers occur – I'm sure not too many know. Oh, of course they know that takeovers take place but no one seems to bother what happens after the takeover, whether it concerns the individuals or the products of the company. Of course if it is a vast company there are mild protests about foreigners taking over our industry but no one does anything and when there is finally news of a company's demise it is rarely if ever blamed on the takeover that occurred earlier. You know there are many men who it seems are held in respect who are there because they have headed up a programme of takeovers, men who have asset stripped, or who have sacked countless persons, or defrauded the Revenue, but are measured as successful because in doing these things they have made money for themselves. We should make it known that far from being respected citizens these men should be despised as being no more than criminals. Most takeovers result from someone's personal greed or ambition and these people should be known. Do we all know who caused the downfall of WECO?" Ray, who by now was really fired up, looked around at the others. "Well, just in case you don't know – oh yes, I know some of the old main Board should not have sold their shares, but I firmly believe that the Burnside Chemical Company, with whom there were most of the negotiations, would not have wrapped WECO up. No it was Arkansas Oil who were the culprits and the man who runs that company, Julius Steinberg, was the real man behind its final demise – it is he who is the criminal."

The assembled company remained quiet for a few seconds as if taking it all in. "Should we let this man know how we feel?" one of the company asked.

"What good will that do?" said another.

"He wants teaching a lesson – who the hell does he think he is?" was heard.

"Steady on lads," said Tony, interrupting the general clamour to get at Steinberg which had obviously been heightened by the few drinks the party had consumed "This guy is a million miles from here and his type would take no notice of some whinging Limeys – as he would put it – it would not concern him in the least," Tony added.

"Tony's right – he wouldn't turn a hair – I met the man, I think I'm the only one here who did meet him." Ray Holmes paused and the others did not interrupt, expecting Ray to say more. "He's a smooth character who's been around a bit, I understand – he's still building his empire and I hear he is still taking on other companies in the States – I'm sure we are not the only ones who have reason to wish him some harm."

"Are you suggesting we contact others in the States and try and work something out together?" one of the party said.

"No, I wasn't exactly thinking that way – but that's not a bad idea – it would be a job tracing people and anyway people in the USA may be more used to being treated in this way, expectations of job security in the States is not so well engrained as in this country – but it's an idea."

XXI

Jake's hotel in Primrose had the only bar in town and Joe Mancini, Steinberg's chauffeur, was a frequent visitor when his boss was at home in Primrose. Most locals who visited the bar at first paid no attention to the newcomer from New York but the ice was broken when Jake himself was seen to ask Joe questions about his boss. From then on others who had kept away from Joe in the past now passed the time of day.

It was exactly a week after Steinberg's party and Joe and John Butler were the only two in the bar, each sitting at opposite ends of the small bar. "Can I buy you a drink?" Joe called down to John Butler. John hesitated but remembering that Jake had talked to Joe only a few weeks back he felt it would be OK to accept.

"That's mighty nice Mr... I'll have the same as you," he said, moving along the bar and closer to Mancini. "Your boss staying around these parts for a while?"

"Yeah, he seems to kinda like it round here and does a lot of his work now from the office he had set up on the first floor of his house."

"What's he like to work for?"

"Well I guess he's OK up here but he's different in New York or Chicago He's a tough old sonofabitch and don't say much to those who work for him. I suppose some think he's OK but most are wary of him – I've known him ten years and until last week I would not have thought he had an ounce of feeling in him – in my time I've seen many men lose their jobs and come back looking for help but never seen him give any sympathy or offer any help."

"What made you change your mind about his feelings?" Joe had already had two Scotch on the rocks and was feeling in a particularly friendly mood. He looked around the room as if he didn't want anyone other than the questioner to hear what he was about to say.

"The old guy told me he knew a girl from around these parts."

"The sly old goat – that sure surprises me," John Butler said, giving a knowing smile.

"No, you got it wrong – he ain't seeing no dame now, this was years back during the 17–18 war. As he said to me she'd be pretty old now or dead."

"What was her name, Joe?" Butler asked.

"Oh, I don't know, he never said."

John Butler swallowed his whisky and licked his lips. "Sure would like to know who it was – my folks been round these parts for as long as anyone can remember, reckon we'd soon know who it was if you got a name."

Joe Mancini said nothing but could see how he might gain favour with the boss if he could find out for him where the dame was. He said, "Yeah, perhaps I'll get the boss to tell me her name, you never know she might still be around," he hesitated and took another drink. "But perhaps the boss doesn't want her found – if he did I'm sure he would have got something going before now. Guess I should have kept my big mouth shut."

Joe Butler nodded agreement and added, "Well, anyways, if you should get her name I could quietly find out whether she was still around. It might do the lady a good turn, old Steinberg is plenty rich."

By this time one or two others had entered the bar and the conversation changed. Joe left and whilst walking back to the house began to think of how he might get the girl's name. Before he reached the gates he had what he thought was a good idea.

XXII

Joe Miller returned to his home from Winnipeg and began again the routine of searching for work. He was now nearly fifty-five years of age and it seemed no one wanted him. He tried all the so-called friends he had made during his working life but although they appeared friendly enough no one put themselves out to help find him something to do. He began to get very depressed and saw his doctor who prescribed some anti-depressant tablets that Joe would not take. He was advised to see someone to talk with him and help him but as he said to his wife, "There's nothing wrong with me except I can't get work – a goddam shrink sure can't help me find a job." His wife pleaded with him to go and try what the doctor had ordered but he was adamant.

He found he kept having dreams which were nearly always the same. He kept seeing Steinberg and he was chasing him with a gun in his hand. Sometimes he would wake up sweating, believing he had killed the man, and his wife would have to assure him he had only been dreaming.

He started the routine of visiting the local library regularly where he would read through the daily papers and search for jobs for which he felt he was eligible to apply. Of course none of them wanted a man of fifty-five but he would convince himself that they would know this time that he was the man for the job.

This went on for some time and his letters of rejection were piled high. He at last realised that it was hopeless and unless he took on some job such as shelf filling at the local supermarkets he would not have any money coming in to the home. He could not bring himself to go along and apply for one of the vacancies which were often shown on notice boards around the store. All the time he kept thinking of Steinberg and how this man had ruined his life – something had to be done about it, how could he go on letting this man go on ruining others in the world, someone had to stop him.

Joe Miller next became devoted to finding out all he could about Steinberg, where he was now living, what offices he mostly used and who were those closest to him. His line of action was through his old company, the Burnside Chemical Corporation. Strangely he became more content than he had been for a very long time – he was doing something positive and he was determined to do it well. He did not tell his wife what he was doing although she noticed he was more relaxed and seemed to be less concerned with the fact that he had no job. She for her part was pleased as she thought that her husband had at last accepted his position, little did she know he had quietly decided that some action had to be taken against Steinberg and that he had better be the one to do it.

XXIII

Steinberg's party had been a huge success and he was obviously now accepted as a respected citizen of his adopted state of New Hampshire. His visits to New York and other cities became less frequent and it had been over a year since he had travelled outside of North America – in fact most of his moves outside of Primrose had been up to Canada and on the shores of Hudson Bay.

On one of these trips he had taken along his chauffeur, Joe Mancini. It was not often that he took his own chauffeur but he did not like long flights in light aircraft as he was prone to air sickness and thus he decided he would get his chauffeur to drive him up north from Winnipeg. He had been advised not to go by road as the journey of nearly a thousand miles would not be at all pleasant with few places to put up for the night – but he was adamant that he would not fly. Associates in Winnipeg planned the route for them and made sure they stocked up with plenty of food and spare fuel and two spare wheels. Joe who had been driving for years never imagined he would feel so tired as he did on this journey. The route given them took them northwest and into Saskatchewan to Canora via Kamsack where they spent the first night and then on north back into Manitoba to The Pas. It was here that Steinberg decided they would go no further by car and spending the night in the town's hotel he called for a plane to take them on the remainder of the journey.

Joe Mancini sat with his boss at the meal provided by the hotel proprietor and probably because they were miles away from anywhere and almost as if they were comrades on a long overland journey. Steinberg became talkative; Joe was told about his boss's early days at work – his time in the army and about how his father worked on the Brooklyn Bridge. Joe said little and allowed Steinberg to talk but at the mention of Primrose he asked, "You told me about a dame you met near Primrose many years back – did you ever remember her name?" Joe was surprised at his own boldness and the clumsy way he had asked – after all he had worked out a perfectly good plan to find out the name. He was equally surprised by the way his boss answered.

"Yeah, I remember her first name but not her second name," he said. The look of disappointment on Joe's face was not noticed by Steinberg as he went on, "Difficult to forget her name really, not too many girls are called Zoë."

XXIV

Following the meeting with ex-WECO employees, Ray Holmes regularly met up with Tony Bentley and one or two of those who had seemed particularly angry at the way the company had been destroyed. They met to determine what if anything they could do to stop this kind of takeover ruining lives and, as they saw it, British Industry. At the first meeting they all agreed that a letter should be sent to their local MP explaining what had happened and how they felt it necessary for Government to introduce legislation to control takeovers as they considered the Monopolies and Mergers Committee only took interest in shareholders, no consideration being given to employees and certainly no measures taken to control the effect of the takeover on the company's operation in the UK and exports by that company.

Although they got an early reply stating that the matter would be raised with others it was some months later that they were told that it would be too difficult for adequate measures to be taken and that since British companies were able to institute takeovers elsewhere in the world it would not be in the interests of the British economy to legislate.

The reply was no more than they had expected but nevertheless they were angry that nothing at all was to be done. It was decided they would meet one more time to see whether anyone in the meantime had any further ideas of what to do.

Meanwhile Joe Thomas, since he had written to Ted Wilson about the meeting he was attending with others from the old WECO group, thought he would keep Ted informed and duly wrote him a letter. He reported on what Ray Holmes had said at the meeting but said that although some of them would meet again he did not think there was a great deal that could be done. He also said he had applied for many vacancies in the area but had still been unsuccessful in finding a job.

"What has that Cockney got to say in your letter?" his wife asked at breakfast.

"How did you know it was from Joe Thomas?" Ted asked.

"Not very difficult, you don't get many letters and one from the south could only be from one person – unless you've got a girl down there you never told me about," she said with a smile.

"A chance would be a fine thing!" he replied. "No, not much to report except it seems this man Ray Holmes got really fired up at the meeting – they all seem convinced that Steinberg – you know the one who was in the paper last week – was the cause of WECO being closed and it seems he's done it many times before and since – not in England though."

"What are they going to do about it?" she asked.

"I don't see there is much they can do but someone ought to sort him out. He could ruin many peoples' lives and all that happens to him is that he gets rich and becomes famous – he ought to be stopped."

"If I were you, Ted, I would forget it – it's no good you getting angry again there's nowt you can do."

"Yes, I suppose you're right."

Ted Wilson had no intention of letting it rest; perhaps there was something he could do. At least he would write to Joe and offer his services although he knew it was most unlikely they could give him anything to do.

* * *

Ray Holmes took Joe to another of their meetings, only Tony Bentley and two others were present – the hardcore of disenchanted redundants as Tony called them.

"There is one other who we can count on to help," Joe said. "Do you remember a chap called Ted Wilson who worked up at the Sheffield depot?"

"I remember the one we asked you to look after at a party a few years back – a red-headed chap," Tony added.

"Well he wants me to tell you that he would be willing to help if there is anything he could do."

"That's good to know but we really don't know anything we can ourselves do let alone give something for him to do."

"How angry are any of you? Supposing we don't get anywhere, as seems likely, how far would you be prepared to go, writing letters and protesting, to stop this from happening again?" Tony said and, looking around at those present, waited for an answer.

"I guess when angry I could do just about anything," Ray replied, "but I wonder myself what I would be prepared to do now a lot of the anger has subsided."

"Has it subsided, Ray, or are you just holding it within?"

"I really don't know – I know I am very angry about my wife and at the time could have easily killed the man."

"What about you, Joe – are you angry enough to do almost anything?" Tony asked Joe Thomas, a staunch Communist since his youth who had led strikes and been in the forefront of protestations about workers' rights and indeed in many confrontations with the police at such gatherings. Joe remained silent for a while as if choosing his words with care – yes, he was angry, who wouldn't be? Most of those present had found some sort of work whilst he had nothing – of course he did not relate it to the fact that he was a known Communist – and none of those present had actually worked inside the factory works, they were all as far as he was concerned "white collar workers". Why should he stick his neck out for them?

"If I'm honest I came along to these meetings really hoping that someone might help me find work – I have always been against the bosses who do not treat their workers fairly, in fact as you all know I don't agree with our system of running the country. How far I would go to get what I believe to be right I have never tested – came close to it once or twice," he said with a grin. "I look upon this man Steinberg as being no different to scores of other men who think they have the right to exploit people for their own ends – sure I hate him but it's the system that produces these individuals that I hate more – give me a fair chance of changing that and I would do almost anything."

"Well, we're not planning on changing the system, Joe," Bentley added.

Tony Bentley looked at the other two who had not yet contributed their thoughts. "What about you Jake and you John – what do you think of all this – any ideas?"

Jake Wint spoke first, he had found work but would much sooner have still been at WECO – he had come along to the meeting as much to meet old friends as do anything positive which he really believed would never happen.

"I've not given it much thought, sure the man should be stopped but I have no idea of how this could be done, short of killing him," he said smiling, "and no one I'm sure is going to suggest that."

"I wouldn't be so sure," interrupted Bob Smart, " I get the feeling that one or two here are thinking just that –- am I right, Tony?"

Tony hesitated before speaking in a subdued voice. "Let me ask you all a question – what would be your reaction if you heard Julius Steinberg was no longer alive? I bet most of you would say good riddance – no one here would feel sorry, now would they?"

There was general agreement by nodding of heads and muttering. "What we are really saying is that this man does not deserve to carry on living and ruining peoples lives – it would be nice if he wasn't around. But how can this be done?"

"I'm sure none of us here have ever or could ever take a man's life, we're not killers and yet this man caused Fred Green to drive his car into the Thames and you know that Ray blames him for his own wife dying – and we're not through yet. We know some of our old friends have not yet found work, how do we know the killing has yet ended?"

There was silence for a while which was broken by Ray asking if anyone would like another drink. "I think we need one after that." Drinks all round and a change of conversation made everyone feel more comfortable. Nothing further was said or asked about Tony's statement, it was almost as if he had not said it. The party broke up, agreeing that Tony would give them a call when they could have another get-together.

Although nothing was said Tony knew that each of those present at that meeting would be turning over in their minds what he had said. Joe Thomas driving home with Ray sat for a while and then said, "Tony's going a bit far thinking along those lines don't you think, Ray?"

"Well I suppose he is really but I suspect none of us would go to the police if we happened to hear someone was trying to polish Steinberg off – it's just the fear of getting caught or not having the guts to do it that really concerns us, isn't it?"

Joe sat back and thought. "I suppose you're right," he said.

XXV

Joe Mancini returned to Primrose with Steinberg after the Hudson Bay visit. He was sure that after the last experience he would never be asked to drive up there again and he imagined that Steinberg himself would avoid any further visits as his flight from The Pas up to the prospecting area and then back to Winnipeg in a light plane was not exactly enjoyed by his boss.

A couple of nights after his return Joe happened to meet John Butler in the hotel. Actually although it seemed a chance meeting, Joe had gone along especially to see if he could meet the man.

Joe talked casually to John Butler but since there were two or three others present he did not at first mention what he had found out. Later in the evening just when John Butler had indicated he was about to leave, Joe said he had something to tell him – Butler's two friends said they would be going and left him alone with Joe.

"You remember how you said you thought that you or your family would almost certainly be able to find out if the lady Steinberg knew was still around? Well, I got a name – not a second name though but a first name that ain't that usual. But you know, John, I don't want you to let anyone else know about this or else I could lose my job – so we got to keep it dark – at least for the time being."

John Butler showed interest and said, "Sure, I understand – but only having a first name is going make it more difficult to trace. What was the name anyway?"

"Zoë – mean anything to you?"

"No, it don't – but I'll find the answer from my ma, she's sure to know if the girl was from these parts."

XXVI

Joe Miller told his wife that he had an interview for a post in Albany and that he would go up there by car, stay overnight and have the interview the next day and then providing the interview was not too long he would drive back that day. However, if it were late he would stay over a second night. He did not reveal that there was no interview and that he intended getting away from the hotel early the next day and driving on into New Hampshire and to the town of Primrose.

He wasn't sure what he would do when he got to Primrose but he guessed he would find the house that Steinberg lived in and try to see if it were possible to get inside without being seen. He wanted to learn all he could about Steinberg's movements.

XXVII

Joe Miller had an early call in the hotel he had stayed overnight in Albany, and before leaving he rang his wife. He was in fact just leaving the hotel but did not tell his wife, instead he gave her the impression that he had just got out of bed and had yet to have his breakfast; he told her his interview was at eleven and that he would ring her later if it seemed better that he stay over another night.

Immediately after the phone call he drove off and headed for New Hampshire and Primrose.

The countryside was very green and the roads deserted. He was enjoying the drive but every so often he would have a nasty feeling in his stomach as he remembered why he was driving north – he knew he was driving with a purpose in mind but his intention was to him unreal – could he seriously be thinking of doing harm to another human being? The thought bothered him and he switched on his radio where a local station was just giving a news bulletin and weather. He listened to what was clearly purely local news with a local weather forecast for the day. For a time his mind cleared and he smiled as he heard how local farmers were objecting to proposals for a new freeway in the area. He was suddenly brought back to the reason for his visit when the announcer said that Jake Ramsden, the proprietor of the Lake Hotel in Primrose, had told the local reporter that due to an increase in tourists he was contemplating increasing the size of his hotel. "Listeners will remember that Primrose is the town that Julius Steinberg, the well-known industrialist from New York, had long since made his home…"

Joe Miller punched the radio control button to off and tightly gripped the steering column of his car. Why was it he could get so uptight at the mere mention of this man's name? He would have to get a grip on himself, he thought, because otherwise he would give himself away when he started asking questions in Primrose about the man.

He had been driving for about four hours since leaving Albany when he saw the first sign indicating Primrose. He turned the car into the small twisting road which made its way alongside a fast flowing stream. Five miles along this road with trees and hills on the other side of the stream, he passed his first habitation on the right – a big iron gate between brick pillars announced a probable house of substance. From there, on the opposite side to the stream there followed other houses until about a mile further on a sign board announced Primrose – elevation 720 feet, population 520. A short distance on and round yet another bend he suddenly found himself in Main Street, a wide roadway with two or three shops on either side with cars parked at angles with plenty of space for driving past in both directions. Outside the building on the left from which hung a board in the ancient inn tradition announcing Lake Hotel, he pulled up and parked his car. It was lunchtime and as he made his way into the hotel he saw numerous guests making their way to what he assumed was the dining room.

"Can I help you, sir?" Jake Ramsden was standing next to the reception desk as he usually did when it was time for his guests to pass by on their way to the dining room.

"Yes, I would like some lunch – have you room for another?"

"Yes, sir – I guess we can find room for you. Not everyone in the hotel stays in for lunch. You come far?"

"I've driven up from Albany this morning."

"Follow me, sir," Jake said entering the dining room. "You touring or on business?" Jake was getting adept at questioning visitors when they arrived – after all it was a big decision to build an extension and he still could not be sure he was doing the right thing.

"A bit of both actually – thought I would see what sort of place Primrose was – heard it mentioned once or twice."

"I guess you've heard it in connection with our Julius."

"You mean Julius Steinberg, I guess – well I suppose it must have been, I can't really remember – I did hear he lived here."

"He sure does – built himself a mansion outside of town – comes into town quite often – lots of people come here from all over. Get people over from Europe and California – he sure is a celebrity."

"I guess your business is helped through him."

"There we are, sir, you can have this table by the window Yes, business has sure perked up in the last couple of years – thinking of adding more rooms and a bigger dining room."

Jake motioned to a waiter to come over. "Here we are, sir. Armand here will look after you – will you be staying?"

"No, not this time, got some business to do – but I'll be back."

After his meal Joe took a stroll along Main Street and passing a shop front advertising property in the area went inside.

"Nice day… what can I do for you?"

"I saw the houses in your window and I wondered if you know anyone around here who could design a house for me. It's only a thought I have but I am looking for some place in New England to set up home for my family – it's not at all definite but I have some money and want to put it in property." Joe Miller had not really thought it out but seeing the houses had given him an idea – somehow he would have to find out a little about the Steinberg house.

"Well I guess we could easily arrange to accommodate you, sir. We have many contacts in the area and build homes for newcomers. What sought of money have you in mind to spend?"

"I've been told you have a Julius Steinberg living around here – I guess he has a swell house – how about something like his."

"Oh my goodness, sir, we are talking rich. Pardon me for saying but that's rich, I might say obscenely rich," the young man said with a smile.

"Well, that's it – I got it. Now what can you offer?"

The young man reached for a pile of drawings under a desk, laid them on the table and thumbing through them withdrew one.

"You say you would like something like the Steinberg home. Well here it is." He turned the sheet round to face Miller. On it was a side and front elevation and a plan of each floor.

Miller looked at the plan carefully whilst making a mental note of the main features.

"This sure is some home," he said.

"None better around these parts. Of course something like this would cost a small fortune. We do all the work in the area. Mr Steinberg wanted to employ New York architects and builders but when he found out that most of the new homes for the wealthy moving up from the big city are in fact designed and built by local craftsmen, he changed his mind. I think if we can satisfy Mr Steinberg, we can satisfy most anyone."

"Very impressive. So if I decide to set up a home in the area, you are the man I come to see. I assume you have access to building land?" The young man assured him he had some very good sites available and would be most happy to take him around to see them.

"Not this time," Miller said," but I'll be back. Thanks for your help."

XXVII

John Butler visited his mother in her small house in Second Avenue most Tuesdays but so interested was he in the name Joe Mancini had given him that he called round the next day after he had closed the store. His mother was in her eighties but was a very fit lady with a good memory; she had lived all her life in Primrose.

"Hullo, Ma, how are you?"

His mother looked up over her glasses and put down the paper she was reading. "This ain't Tuesday, what brings you round to see me? I ain't got any money to give you," she said with a smile.

"No, I don't want yer money this time – I want you to try to remember something. Fella I met in Jake's place was asking about a girl he knew once many years ago. I thought you might know her and perhaps be able to tell me what happened to her."

"Reckon I knows most people in this town, that is except the foreigners who have moved up in the last few years – spoiling the place they are, didn't ought to be allowed, too many boats on the lake now." John knew how his mother viewed the newcomers and had heard all this many times before, but it didn't do to interrupt as she liked to get it off her chest.

"Yeah, I know what you mean, Ma, but it's good for the store and I really can't complain."

"You and your store, there's more important things than making money, why I remember when there were none of them new houses by the lake – it's all been spoilt and oughta be stopped."

"Ma, did you ever know a girl called Zoë from around these parts?"

His mother looked thoughtful for a moment and then said, "The only girl I knew of that name was way back when we were young – we both went to school together – a nice young

92

girl she was, Zoë Rochester was her name, they said her
parents had come from Europe before she was born –
Switzerland, I think – her father mended watches so I guess
he must have come from Switzerland, that's where they make
them, ain't it?"

"What happened to her, Ma?"

Ma looked out of the window as if trying to recall a
memory of long ago. Her son waited, allowing her to think.

"I remember my old man telling me that Zoë's proper
name was not Rochester but some French name which no one
ever pronounced correctly so her father had changed it – it
was Rochat or something."

John listened intently, he enjoyed hearing Ma's tales of
years ago, same as he knew his own family could trace their
ancestry back almost to the Pilgrim Fathers, or at least that's
what his pa had told him when he was young. Ma continued,
"Zoë Rochester got married soon after the war against the
Germans – not the war when you were young, the 17–18 war.
She lived just down the road for a few years but later moved
away, I remember she was with child at the time – her first.
Her husband, I heard, left her soon after they moved – to
Bridport, I think. Rumour had it that the child was not his."

"Any idea what happened to her after that, Ma?"

"Don't rightly know, son, but she had a boy, reckon he'd
be about fifty now, – Peter I think they called him – yeah,
that's it, Peter Bronson. He got himself in trouble with the
law – probably something to do with him not having a pa. I
reckon his ma had a rough time with him as a youngster."

"How come you know all about the son but not what
happened to his ma?"

Mrs Butler went over to an old case she kept under a
small table at the side of the fireplace. "I think I got
something in here." She dragged out the case and opened it.
Inside were papers and photographs; she started turning them
over onto the floor. "I was sure I had an old newspaper with
something about Peter Bronson but I guess I was mistaken. It

happened a long while ago, about the time of Pearl Harbour – it was the only time until this man Steinberg came to live round here that I remember Primrose coming into the news. This young man whose mother had come from Primrose came back here and with two other older men robbed our bank. They were all caught and they all went to jail – yeah, that's your Peter Bronson. I felt sorry for his ma."

John Butler was intrigued with the information given to him by his mother but was disappointed that she had no information as to what happened to Zoë. "Do you remember, Ma, if the boy was still living in Bridport at that time?"

"I'm sure they was still living in Bridport, cos cousin Amos who lived in Bridport wrote and said he know'd the family. Amos died ten years back so I guess you can't ask him where they are now," she said with a twinkle in her eye.

"Well thanks anyway, Ma – my friend will be interested in what you say. I'll be round to see you on Tuesday."

John Butler, who did not make a habit of going to the hotel bar more than one night a week, his wife nagged him if he went too often, determined he would go again this week to see if he could pass on his information to Joe Mancini.

XXIX

Talking about what to do accomplished nothing except, as far as Ray Holmes was concerned, to heighten the frustration and make him more angry over what had happened. He knew Tony felt much the same and he was fairly confident that there were one or two others who felt sufficiently strongly to try and do something about it. Letters to MPs and newspapers had brought nothing – no one seemed interested. But they would be interested if they believed there were people who felt strongly that if no lawful action could be taken then it might be necessary to resort to unlawful action. The trick would be how to let the media know something was being planned and yet not divulge what or who were involved. In any case, what sort of action was to be planned? Ray Holmes knew that unless the act to be undertaken was sufficiently unlawful no one would be interested – how far were they themselves prepared to go?

Ray telephoned Tony and said they should meet to discuss an idea he had. Two evenings later they met in the Queen's in Weybridge. Ray revealed his idea to Tony and they agreed to write anonymously to a number of the big dailies giving a prepared statement. The idea was for a seed to be sown, which indicated that certain groups of people who had suffered redundancy and who had not obtained any satisfaction to their requests for a review of the law relating to redundancy were considering taking the law into their own hands. Exactly what was being proposed they would not reveal but the statement was meant to be a warning to those responsible for takeovers which had caused suffering to many individuals and a detrimental affect on the UK economy.

Ray and Tony agreed that the statement which they hoped would be published would not be linked to them in any way and that in no way would they inform their ex-colleagues from WECO of what they were doing. Whether anything would actually be printed they did not know but on the assumption that at least one of the newspapers would see fit to find space they would call a meeting of those ex-colleagues who had expressed a wish at the last meeting that some action should be taken.

XXX

The comparative failure of Steinberg's European operation outside the oil industry was evidenced in the monthly figures that Steinberg received and perused either at his New York offices or at his home in Primrose. He still would not admit that the failure had been brought about largely through his desire to hastily close the UK company, WECO. The figures, or numbers as Americans prefer to call them, were getting no better, in fact the reverse was true. The Geneva operation run by Abe Slyberger on a part-time basis from the States muddled along seeming to be most concerned with completing the monthly return on time than bothering what was happening to the numbers in that return and certainly in Steinberg's estimation doing nothing to find out what was happening to various branch establishments throughout Europe whose operations were being reported.

"Christ, Mac, have you seen these goddam numbers from Europe this month? What's that sonofabitch Slyberger doing? This is the only operation we've got that ain't giving good numbers. What salary we paying that bum?"

Mac who had the inside on much of what Julius Steinberg was doing had been expecting this outburst to ring out one day; he knew that Steinberg was not happy about the Swiss operation.

"I somehow knew you would be unhappy about this month's numbers – Abe ain't doing so good. Maybe you need someone over there all the time to sort this lot out. You got Abe to wrap up the Limey operation who ran the European set-up – maybe you need a Limey to run it instead of Abe."

Steinberg looked thoughtful, maybe, just maybe, he thought old Mac had got a point – sure the Limeys had been running it before but the last thing he would do would be to start up that WECO operation. Fred Dailey was still very much in his mind and the mere mention of Limeys made his blood boil. "Yeah, I know, but whether a Limey could run it from outside England I am not so sure – but I suppose I could give it a go. The main thing is to get Slyberger out."

"That's easy, boss – you want I should tell him he's out?"

"Sure, why not – pay the bum off."

XXXI

The bar in the Lake Hotel had just two or three men drinking when John Butler entered. He looked at the three and was disappointed to see that Joe Mancini was not one of them – they were all strangers, tourists no doubt.

"Howdy, Jake." John Butler moved towards the proprietor who had just entered. "Seen anything of Steinberg's chauffeur tonight?"

"No, I'm pretty certain he ain't been in tonight. I don't even know if his boss is still up at the house – could have been driven down to New York. Don't tell me, John, you due to go up to the big house for dinner," Jake said and looked at the bartender as being the only one who might understand and laugh at his little joke.

"No, I wanted to see Joe on a personal matter. He asked me to find something out for him." Butler hesitated a moment as if wondering whether he could tell Jake about the girl. "Jake," he said, "you been living round here a lot of your life, did you ever hear of a Peter Bronson?"

"Peter Bronson, why sure I remember the guy. He's the one who robbed the bank way back; he was only a kid – served time in the Pen. Came out and the last I heard he was in the big time in New York – runs a couple of gaming joints in Vegas. He's a hard man, no one messes with Peter Bronson."

"That's funny, Jake, I've lived here all my life too but I never heard of him until tonight – how come you know and I don't?"

"That's easy, I guess it's your age – I'm seven or eight years older and I saw the robbery. Got meself called in to give evidence of what I saw – mind you, I was only a young kid at the time, visiting relations in Primrose, and being called in I suppose I took an interest as to what happened to the men caught. I read about Bronson about five years later in a local paper when he came out of Sing Sing and then when I

was down in New York visiting a couple of years back, I met
this guy in a bar and we talked. When I said where I was
from he said he knew it and gave me his card and said if I
was ever in Vegas to look him up. When I looked at the card
I remembered the name and knew who he was. But I'm sure
glad he didn't know I was the kid who helped put him in the
Pen, as I heard from another guy in the bar after Bronson had
left that he was a big shot gangster who kept just inside the
law by paying off local lawmen wherever he operated. A nice
guy to have on your side but not against you."

"I'm told his folks came from Primrose – I suppose you
knew that," John Butler interjected.

"Yeah, he lived down at Bridport at the time but they said
his ma came from Primrose – in fact part of the defence was
that he did the robbery for his ma. It seems her old man had
left her before the boy was born and she had had a very hard
life since then – she died whilst he was in prison. Bronson
said at his trial that he never knew who his father was, his ma
wasn't going to tell him until he was twenty-one and of
course she was dead before he reached that age. Knowing the
man I think it was a good job he was never told."

"That's most interesting, Jake – will you tell Joe Mancini
when you see him that I have got some information for him?"

"I wonder why Joe Mancini wants to know about Peter
Bronson – perhaps Steinberg wants a job done for him – do
you know, John?"

"No, he never told me – don't forget if you see him, I got
something to tell him – goodnight, Jake and thanks."

XXXII

Joe Miller returned to Albany after his visit to Primrose and
the following morning drove home. On the way he tried to
remember what he had learnt. He had taken the opportunity,
since the hotel proprietor had raised the subject of Steinberg,
of finding out where Julius Steinberg lived – how often he

generally appeared in town and what were his movements. He had also sketched from memory the layout of the house he had seen when discussing property He believed he had learnt these things without arousing suspicion, in fact Jake Ramsden and indeed the home salesman were only too pleased to give as much information as they could. Jake in particular understood now only too well that his trade was very much linked to Steinberg.

On arriving home he had to tell his wife that he had been unsuccessful in his interview but she was pleased to see that it did not appear to worry him unduly. Next day he went down to the library partly to think and partly to plan in the quiet what his next move would be. He knew he had to do something but how he was to accomplish his task he was still not sure. It was certainly a challenge and he liked a challenge.

XXXIII

Steinberg usually relied on someone else to do his dirty work for him. He always wished to appear the boss who was himself a victim of events. Thus when he told Mac to pay the bum off – he meant just that. There would be no discussion and somehow Mac would have to think up some excuse for it happening and he knew only too well that if he put the blame squarely on his boss's shoulder and was found out he would himself soon be looking elsewhere for work. Mac knew he would have to be careful. However, he had never liked Slyberger and inwardly he knew he was going to get some pleasure out of giving this man the chop.

He arranged with the payroll people to work out pay for Slyberger and to give him a cheque, which he could hand to the man with his notice to leave. Mac had previously asked Personnel to check how much would be due to Slyberger under the minimum terms of termination of his employment. Thus armed with a cheque and a standard form for him to sign, a form Mac would require him to sign before releasing the cheque, he went to Slyberger's office on 65th Street.

Luckily Slyberger was in this day and after saying who he was the man's secretary arranged for him to go in to see her boss.

"What brings you over here, Mac? Ain't they got something better for you to do than riding cabs across town to see me? What the f*** is up?"

Mac thought to himself, Slyberger is slipping up, only one swear word in a whole sentence. "I came over to say goodbye Abe, you're out – we ain't got a job for you – not any more. The numbers from Europe have been getting worse and the Board reckon we should have a change – perhaps employ someone who operates from Europe the whole time."

"You f***ing bastards, Christ, I know that sonofabitch Steinberg is behind this – he f***ing won't get away with it – he's dead."

This was more like the Abe Slyberger he knew, he certainly hadn't lost his gift with words. Mac allowed him to continue and found himself counting the swear words – Abe was now on his true form.

"Before you go out and kill him, Abe, we would like your signature on this and then I'll hand over a cheque." Mac presented Slyberger with the prepared document which said he resigned from his vice presidency in the European operation.

"I'm not f***ing signing anything," he said, throwing the paper back to Mac.

"Well, that's up to you, Abe, but I can't hand over the cheque until you do, that's my instructions." Mac picked up the paper from the floor and began to retreat to the door.

"OK, let me have it. I ain't got time to waste arguing with f***ing Steinberg. I'll get even with him – he ain't heard the last of Abe Slyberger. I know a few things about him, he'll be f***ing sorry he crossed me."

The paper signed and the cheque handed over, Mac left the premises.

XXXIV

The meeting suggested by the two Englishmen was duly arranged following the printing in two of the popular dailies of an anonymous letter, warning would-be takeover predators that they risked personal injury if it were found that they had acted other than fairly to staff or caused unnecessary hardship to individuals or had had a detrimental affect on the UK economy. Both papers added that the letters had been passed to the police who were investigating to find who had sent the letter which it stated had been signed by "Redundants Revenge".

On the last Thursday in October 1975 Tony and Ray met with the other ex-WECO redundants.

Tony said he had something to tell the meeting before they started. "I think you are going to be surprised at what I am going to say. I have been offered a job by Steinberg!" he said. There was a stunned silence as if no one knew how quite to answer. Ray, who looked more surprised than most, replied, "Well, that's a turn-up for the book, when did this happen?"

"I got a letter today – here it is – what do you think I should do about it, fellows?" Ray took the letter and with the others looking over his shoulder, read it aloud to the meeting.

The letter required Tony, if he accepted, to take over the running of the Steinberg European operation, excluding oil. He would be expected to spend much of his time in Geneva, the base for the operation, and he would have a two-year contract and a free hand to get the operation onto a more profitable basis. The salary would be $100,000 per annum, plus a share of any increase in profits, the terms of which would be negotiated on his visit to the States, should he decide to accept. An open return ticket on Concorde was enclosed.

"This is going to be hard to turn down, Tony – they must have got themselves into a hell of a mess and are hoping you can pull them out. What a nerve Steinberg has. What do you want to do, Tony?"

"Well, I've earned very little since I was pushed out of WECO and it's very tempting – especially as it is only for two years."

"But what about all our anger and what we thought we ought to do – you've been one of the strongest advocates of action and now this – still I wouldn't blame you for taking it – ours was all a lot of talk anyway," Don Wilson added.

Tony Bentley listened and waited to hear if there were any further comments but none came, Don Wilson had really said everything.

"What better way to get at Steinberg than to be employed by him – sure I could use the money, it would set me up for my retirement – I've no illusions he'd only keep me until the business had been turned around and I'm not sure anyway if I could do it now they've taken over all the agencies. I'd probably be out at the end of the two years so it seems a good idea to take from them what I can get and remember I get to go to the States and maybe meet Steinberg himself. Now, how could we have managed to get over there and sort him out? That's what we wanted to do, isn't it?"

"Looks as if someone might try and sort out him and his kind anyway – did you read that bit in the Mail signed 'Redundants Revenge'? Looks as if we're not the only ones getting fed up with these criminals," another added.

"Well I reckon you should take the job – and good luck to you – if you still think you'd be prepared to help any of us who would like to get back at the man, then that's fine but don't feel obliged to get involved – sometimes one has to think of oneself," Ray Holmes offered.

"One thing I can assure you is that this offer has not changed my mind about Steinberg, he's still a bastard in my book and I shall take what I can get, do my job and if I can get at him in any way for the sake of WECO, I will."

The meeting, seemingly having not much else to discuss, gradually broke up. It seemed to most that this was perhaps the end – it sounded fine that Tony would help but although they all liked Tony and felt sure his intentions were honourable, no one really believed it could last if he were so involved in the Steinberg set-up.

XXXV

Abe Slyberger's jewellery business gave him a very good living even after paying Steinberg the "royalties" which had been set up when the latter helped with finance in the beginning and later increased when he bailed Abe out of trouble. As has been said before, Abe hated these and had given a lot of thought as to how he could get rid of this burden – after all, he reasoned, I'm the one who has made this corporation what it is today, all Steinberg did was to buy out those two small companies which had been making it difficult for a time. Short of Steinberg dying, when he knew the royalties would cease, he was unable to think of how he could stop paying them. Now there was this other matter of the European operation.

In a way Abe was not too bothered with losing the job with Steinberg – at least now he would have more time to give to his own business and would not be expected to travel to Europe from time to time. Of course the money was useful but he already had his New York apartment and his house on Long Island and the amount of tax taken by the Government knocked a big slice off of it. No, he figured, he would hardly notice the difference. However, his pride was hurt and no one upset Abe Slyberger and got away with it, he said to himself – he'd come a long way since the days when he was, as a boy, the butt of the local bullies, if he couldn't manage a job himself he knew plenty who would do it for him. First, however, he would give it a bit of thought – it might be best out of town, he reasoned, and didn't old Steinberg have a place up in New England?

It was now November and getting mighty cold in New York and Abe knew that Steinberg usually spent a fair amount of his time down in Miami at this time of the year – sure he came back to New York from time to time and probably went up to New England but he knew he sure didn't like the cold.

It was near Thanksgiving Day when Abe called his secretary into his office. "I got a job for you – a poysonsal job, Judy," he said almost in a whisper. "Can you find out from Mac or someone where Steinberg lives in New England? I never did find out."

Steinberg kept his home in Primrose to himself and although calls could be made to him when he was up there, they were always redirected from his Manhattan offices. "I don't want Julius to know but I want to give him a surprise for Thanksgiving, so don't let whoever gives you the address know who it is enquiring – play dumb – think about it before you ring."

"If you want to keep it under wraps I don't think it's a good idea to ring their head office – I think it better to try outside. I remember I saw an article on Arkansas Oil in a magazine recently and I'm sure they mentioned the town he was now living – I'll make enquiries that way." Judy might occasionally appear to be the dumb blonde but she was not so stupid as she sometimes sounded to strangers.

Her enquiries met with almost immediate success and she was able to tell Abe that the town was Primrose. "I don't have the address but I looked up the town in a gazetteer in the library on 44th street and it is so small that I'm sure anyone there could give you the address – would you like me to try ringing the town?"

Slyberger did not want anyone in the town to know someone was enquiring after the address of Steinberg so he quickly put a stop to this line of enquiry. "You done fine, Judy. No, I don't want that you go any further I can soon sort that out now you've got the town."

Slyberger had married some years back but his wife had left him after less than a year – he lived on his own so he had no one who bothered about him not coming home – that is except his housekeeper on Long Island who generally expected him home on Friday evenings. This Friday he rang and told her he would be off on a business trip and would probably not be able to get home until Sunday.

XXXVI

Joe Mancini brought Julius Steinberg up to Primrose from New York in time for Thanksgiving. His boss liked to spend Thanksgiving at his home even though it was November and mighty cold up in Primrose – after the holiday he would get Mancini to drive him down to New York, assuming the roads were passable; it was not unusual to have a lot of snow about at this time, and then he would fly down to his hotel in Miami.

Thus the night before Thanksgiving Joe was able once again to get down to the bar in Primrose. One or two locals were in the bar but, not surprisingly, no tourists. Joe got talking to the bartender and asked if John Butler had been in – the bartender said he hadn't seen John all this week. Joe stayed a while but being on his own he decided he would go back to the house and was just about to leave when Jake came into the bar and seeing Joe walked over to him.

"Not many in here tonight, Jake – I was just about to go."

"No, I don't expect too many this time of the year – it's a dirty night out there. John Butler was asking after you the other evening, said to tell you he has something to tell you.

He asked me about a man called Peter Bronson, what's old Steinberg want with him, Joe?"

"Peter Bronson? I've never heard of him – nothing to do with Steinberg. That ain't what I asked John about. Did he say he wanted to tell me about this Peter Bronson?"

"Well, no – no, come to think of it he didn't – he said he had something to tell you and then straightway asked me if I knew a Peter Bronson – no, I guess one was nothing to do with the other. Old John said he'd be in on Friday night at about nine – why that's tonight – reckon he will be in any time now – you'd better stay if you want to see him."

Joe waited and had another drink, buying one for Jake at the same time. At just after nine thirty when Mancini had decided once again to go, John Butler entered the bar and seeing Joe acknowledged that he had seen him and walked to the bar and called over to Joe, who was now on his own. "Buy you a drink, Joe?"

"No, I've had a couple and I'm fine."

John Butler came over to Joe's table and seated himself opposite. "I got something to tell you. I was right when I said my ma would know about everyone who has lived around these parts. She know'd your boss's Zoë – Zoë Rochester she said – went to school with Ma, she did."

Mancini eager to know more interrupted John Butler. "Is she still alive?"

"Ma didn't know, as the lady moved out to Bridport but Jake reckons he knows."

"Oh now I know why Jake was trying to find out what I asked you about."

"No, you got me wrong I didn't tell Jake – I asked him about a Peter Bronson."

"Yeah, I know, Jake asked me why my boss wanted this man – what's this all about? I've never heard of the guy before tonight."

"I didn't know nothing about him either until my ma told me and then I happened to ask Jake if he knew of this man and much to my surprise he said he did. Peter Bronson is Zoë's son and according to Jake his mother died many years back whilst her boy was in the Pen. It seems he'd robbed a bank in Primrose. Jake said the father left her before the boy was born and rumour has it that it was because the boy was not his. The mother, Jake says, must have had a very rough time bringing up the boy and without a father he got in with the wrong people. Anyway he's still alive and would seem to have made it, albeit by dubious means. To put it bluntly, he's what in the old days we would have called a gangster."

Joe Mancini was disappointed. He had wanted to be able to find the girl for his boss; he reckoned it would have made the boss pleased with him. "You sure the dame is dead, John?"

"Well that's what Jake said and he seemed to know all about the Bronson kid – in fact he said he met him quite by chance when down in New York sometime back – he's in the big time now. If you're thinking of contacting the man, my advice would be to forget it – you never know with these guys what they might do if you bring up their past."

Joe Mancini left the bar after thanking John Butler for his help and was walking across the car park to his car, when getting out of a car nearby was someone who looked familiar. Joe was about to speak when the man accompanied by another looked the other way and, walking into the dark, disappeared. Joe thought about it for a moment and dismissed it from his mind as being ridiculous – he must have been mistaken, Abe Slyberger would never come to Primrose, his boss told only one or two people where he lived and he certainly would never have invited Slyberger out to see him – Joe knew he hated his guts.

XXXVII

Tony Bentley acknowledged the offer made to him by Arkansas Oil and replied saying he would come over to the

States to finalise the matter if they would telephone the date and place of the meeting.

A few days later he received a call from New York and advised that he should take the evening Concorde on Friday, 30th November and he would be met at the airport by Steinberg's driver, Joe Mancini – Arkansas Oil would arrange hotel accommodation.

At about six thirty on the designated Friday, Tony Bentley passed through customs and at Arrivals soon found Joe Mancini holding a board on which was written "Arkansas Oil".

"I'm to take you to your hotel and Julius will see you tomorrow at his Brooklyn office – I'll collect you at ten tomorrow morning." Joe Mancini imparted this information but said nearly nothing more and Tony sensed that this man did not want to speak. If Tony had known Mancini he would have understood why Joe was not happy with Limeys, especially if they acted as some had and treated him as a servant. Whatever employees thought of Steinberg, the man had generally treated him fairly.

The following morning Tony was met as arranged by the chauffeur and twenty minutes later he was making his way up in one of the old elevators to Steinberg's office. The meeting with Steinberg was brief and to the point, he wanted an improvement in the way the European business had operated and it was agreed that a bonus related to the increase in profits would be paid into a Swiss account in Tony's name. No mention was made of the old WECO company although Tony did say that he considered the closing of the UK operation and buying out the European agents by Slyberger had been the root cause of the failure to meet targets. Steinberg gave no indication that he had in fact ordered the closing of WECO and allowed the Englishman to believe Slyberger had himself taken this action. At the end of the meeting Steinberg called in Mac and gave him instructions to take Bentley along to the administrator to complete paperwork necessary before the Englishman returned to Europe. Tony found MacDonald most amicable, more so than anyone yet he had met in Arkansas Oil... he even offered to accompany Tony that evening and show him around town if he wanted a night out – Tony accepted.

Mac met Tony Bentley at his hotel and took him by cab to Greenwich Village to a favourite nightspot where they had a meal and a good conversation. Tony carefully pumped Mac about Arkansas Oil and Steinberg. Mac, after a few drinks, was most forthcoming but never ran his boss down. He admitted that he was ruthless and had done a few things Mac found hard to stomach but as he said it's a tough world out there and there is no room in big business for weaklings.

"He's getting on a bit now though, isn't he, Mac?" Tony said. "Don't you think he will want to pack up soon – I understand he already lives out of town which is often the beginning of leaving it all behind."

"Sure the old man is an old man in years but he's still young at heart and works long hours – yeah he moved out up into New England – got a swell joint up there, uses it as an office too, got all the latest in communications and is joined up to both New York and Chicago offices from there – it's quite a set-up," Mac said enthusiastically.

"Exactly where is he up there?" Tony asked.

"Well, I ain't supposed to tell, but I guess it won't make much difference you knowing when you are off back to Europe – I suppose he really only wants to stop a lot of business calls going direct without first being filtered out by his offices."

"No, don't tell me if you're not supposed – I was just interested as I once drove through part of that lovely country one autumn – the colours were out of this world," Tony interjected in an effort to make sure Mac could see it was only a passing interest.

"Ever heard of a place called Primrose?" Mac asked.

"No, I've not, where's that?"

"That's where the boss has got his mansion – Primrose, New Hampshire. Of course a lot of guys know now all about Primrose – Julius had an article about him in a magazine a year or so back and the town was mentioned. All sorts of people go up there to look at the town – he's become quite famous as you no doubt know – met royalty and everything. Of course he had very humble beginnings..." Mac continued to relate all he knew about Steinberg's upbringing in Brooklyn but Tony apart from nodding now and again was not really interested, his mind was ticking over as to what possibilities there were to get someone up to this New England town – the boys should be interested in this bit of information. Primrose, he repeated to himself.

XXXVIII

Joe Mancini, driving his boss back to New York after Thanksgiving, was in a quiet mood, he was thinking, should he tell him what he had found out or should he forget it. The snow had been quite heavy and before they left they were told the roads to the north were blocked and that for fifty or so miles the road south would be difficult. Joe had hardly noticed the snow and had driven almost in a dream but perfectly safely; Julius was sleeping in the back.

Joe suddenly had a thought – why hadn't he thought it before? It was, he supposed, possible – oh but it couldn't be – but supposing it was. It had suddenly dawned on him, supposing this Peter Bronson was Julius' son – if there were a chance should he say anything. No, how could he? But somehow he seemed to know that this dame Zoë had meant a lot to his boss and who knows what may have happened. Perhaps he could talk it over with someone and they could help him make up his mind. Yes, that's what he would do. But who?

XXXIX

Ted Wilson read his letter from Joe Thomas. "Joe says he's been to another meeting and, do you know what? one of the old WECO boss men has been offered a job back with Arkansas Oil – a chap called Tony Bentley; I never met him but I remember the name. I wonder if they're going to start up again – perhaps they can't do without us, eh?"

"You'll be lucky, nowt'll come of that for you – it's about time you got it into your head that WECO is finished and you're just wasting your time thinking about it."

Ted and his wife frequently had arguments over him still thinking about WECO when she was sure nothing would ever be done. She also felt it quite wrong that her man should after all this time still be so concerned with what happened to others who had been made redundant from WECO. "You've got your own life to lead, Ted – you're up here and they're down there – except for Joe writing, and once he gets a job you'll never hear again, I'm sure none of them know you exist."

"That's not quite true, Joe says he told them I would be willing to help."

"And what do you think you could do?" she said angrily.

"The way I feel right now, l could kill him – that bastard Steinberg."

"You know you don't mean it, Ted, you mustn't talk like that."

XL

Joe Mancini knew that Mac had been with the corporation longer than he had and he knew that Julius used Mac a lot and Mac seemed to be respected by him – or at least as anyone could be respected by the man. He would find a suitable opportunity to raise the matter with Mac.

Steinberg had flown down to Miami and Joe was now expected to do odd jobs as required by other senior members in the corporation. He knew that when the boss was away many of these seniors suddenly found a use for him and he found he was usually busier than when Steinberg was in New York.

Sure enough the time came when Mac wanted Joe to drive him down to Atlantic City with an important overseas customer who wanted to see some boxing and visit a relative from the old country. Having deposited the customer at the home of his relative and arranged tickets for the fights the following night, Mac told Joe to drive back to New York. Mac moved up to sit next to Joe and they fell into conversation. On his way down to Atlantic City with the two passengers seated behind the passenger screen, Joe had decided his plan of action if he could get Mac on his own.

The conversation on the way back was first about the customer and then changed to boxing.

"Julius has always said Dempsey was the best heavyweight – bit before my time though – Louis was the best when I was a kid," Mac said.

"Well, no one beat Marciano and in my book he must have been some guy." Joe Mancini added, "The boss and you were brought up in a tough district he tells me, did you do any fighting?"

"Well not boxing, fighting yes – you had to, to survive." Mac smiled.

"Bit different now for the boss living up there in New England – quite a change. I expect you know why he went up there, Mac."

"No, as a matter of fact I don't really know why he chose where he is, I think he once said he was up that way in his war – can't imagine Julius as a soldier." Mac hesitated as if thinking of what Joe had just said.

"Why, do you know why he went up there?" Mac continued.

"Well I might not be right and I really don't know if I should say anything, sure he was in the Army and stationed near to Primrose but there was, I think, another reason why he became attached to the place – I bet you can now guess," he said, looking at Mac expectantly.

"Goddam it, are you telling me it was a dame?" Mac almost exploded.

"Well, he never said as much but we went for a drive and we stopped at a place on the other side of the lake at Primrose and he told me he once knew a dame from there when he was in the Army."

"Has he seen the dame since he's been up there?"

"No. I'm sure he hasn't even tried – it was too many years ago. Anyway, wouldn't have done him any good – she's been dead since before the last world war."

"How do you know so much?" Mac asked.

"Well I know it was no business of mine but the boss was quite different when he spoke about this dame and I thought it would be nice if they could meet up once again, so I made some enquiries. Kept it quiet though."

They were now crossing the Hudson River and Mac was silently looking across towards the downtown lights. They were getting near to the East River to cross to Brooklyn before Mac spoke.

"Are you going to tell him?" Mac asked. Joe, who had begun to wonder in the silence following his statement whether he had been right to mention the dame to Mac, took his time to answer.

"I don't know what to do – I got some more dope and I ain't sure what to do."

"What kinda dope you got?" Mac asked.

"Well, I ain't at all sure I should say any more – the dope I got could be bad news and maybe not true anyways."

"What are you trying to tell me, Joe, why don't you come clean and get it off your chest – you ain't fooling me, I can see you wanta tell me."

For a moment Joe felt like a schoolboy caught with his hand in the cookie jar.

"The guy that told me about the dame said she had a son, a guy by the name of Peter Bronson – spent some time in the state pen. It seems the husband deserted his wife before the baby was born which he reckoned was not his but the mother would not tell her son who his real father was, instead she said she would tell him when he was twenty-one – unfortunately she died before she told him."

"What are you trying to tell me, you saying Julius is the father?"

"Well, no – not exactly – I was just thinking."

"Just thinking – Christ, you know what you are saying – who told you anyways?"

"No one told me, Mac, it's just what I figured could be – no, I ain't got no proof but it could be, you see Julius told me about how they arranged to meet five years after he had last met her when he returned from the war; we drove to the place they met and from what I gather the husband left her soon after they moved to Bridport, Connecticut. It could not have been long after Julius met her. What do yet think, Mac?"

"Yeah, you could be right but you're guessing – where's the boy anyway?"

"Not quite a boy now, Mac – goddam it, he must be fifty years old!"

PLOTS and VISITS

XLI

ABE SLYBERGER was a disappointed man, at least what he had wanted had not happened and it had cost him – but he consoled himself that he would get even.

After getting the name of the town where Steinberg was now living Abe had acted promptly – he made his way over to Brooklyn and to the neighbourhood where he had grown up. There were many in that neighbourhood who operated outside the law but he knew only one who had, it was said, taken on contracts for some of the big boys in Chicago and L.A. – this was one Pepe Galento who went under several aliases. Abe had gone to school and knocked around in his early days with Pepe's elder brother and remembered Pepe as a tough little boy who liked to be on his own – what he got up to when he went off as a young lad over to Manhattan no one knew or indeed saw fit to ask, but he came back with money and in a few years Pepe was the smartest dressed guy in the neighbourhood even though he never had a job that anyone knew about.

Abe walked from the subway round to where he knew the Galentos had lived. He climbed the stairs to the second floor and went along to apartment 1100 and rang the doorbell. A woman's voice behind the door called out in an unmistakeable Italian American accent which Abe was sure he recognised. "It's Abe Slyberger, Mrs Galento – I came to see if Pepe was around."

A lock was drawn and a key turned and the door opened as far as the security chain would allow and a woman's face appeared in the opening.

"You donta look like Abe to me – he ainta been seen in this neighbourhood for years."

"It is me, Mrs Galento – sure you know me, I went to school with Bruno and I used to come round here – Mrs Lavinsky was one of your neighbours, I swiped a bag of red apples for you one day and you made me take them back."

"Well I guess you must be Abe, he would be the only one to remember that." She released the security chain and beckoned him to enter.

"It's a longa time, Abe, what you doing now – you gotta family?"

"Yeah, a long time but talking to you seems like yesterday – why, you don't look a day older, Mrs Galento."

"Eh, you're a crazy, Abe – I'm a seventy-two – whatta you want with my Pepe?"

"I got something that might interest him – where can I find him?"

"He don't live here any more, he ain'ta married but he lives in a swell apartment close to 5th Avenue – he'sa done well for himself – it better be something big you got for him cos he's a big shot now."

"Does he come and see you, Mrs Galento?"

"Sure he comesa once now and again and gives me money – as you know, Bruno died a few years back."

"Could you give me his address – I'm sure he wouldn't mind – he can only say no to my job if he doesn't want it."

"Pepe tells me to not tell anyone where he lives but I guess you're not anyone – I'll get it for you but you must promise to keep it to yourself, he's a busy man and don't wanta be bothered by callers."

The lady went into another room and came back with the address which she asked Abe to write out on his own paper. Abe stayed for a short while talking over old times and then got the subway back to Manhattan and changing to the 5th Avenue subway got out at 72nd street and made his way to Pepe's apartment.

He pressed the bell and was asked to say who it was.

"It's Abe Slyberger, would you please tell the tenant that I used to be a friend of his brother?"

Abe was sure he would have to give a further explanation but the door was opened and he was told to come up in the elevator to the eighth floor. The elevator opened into a room which was empty. Abe stepped out of the elevator and was immediately confronted by two heavies who frisked him.

"He's clean boss."

"Hullo, Abe, sorry for the slight inconvenience but you can never be too sure these days, there's a lot of crooks around now. What can I do for you Abe, and how did you get my address? Don't tell me, I know, Ma gave it you."

"Yeah, you're right – she said she thought it would be all right as I was an old friend. Anyway to answer your question, I got a problem which I'm not sure how to deal with and wondered if you knew of anyone who might help me."

"What kind of a problem?"

"There's a guy who bothers me and I want to get him off my back."

"What kind of guy is this… is he well known, rich or a nothing?"

"He's well known and rich."

"Well I might be able to find someone to help but it'll be two grand up front and another grand when the job is done."

"Yeah, I can manage that."

"Where's this guy live?"

"He lives up in New England – a town called Primrose – ever heard of it?"

"If he's out of town that'll be another grand."

Abe was taken by surprise but did not object but said he would be willing to go along with whoever although he himself had never been up to Primrose. He was given a day to get the two grand in used twenty-dollar bills and told to be outside this apartment at nine o'clock on Friday morning.

Abe duly arrived with the money in an envelope and waited –
a car drew up and the driver beckoned him over.

"You got the money?"

"Sure, I got it."

"Then jump in, we're going off to New England."

The driver had obviously studied a map prior to arriving
as the journey up north caused no problems and in the
darkness they arrived in the car park of the Lake Hotel in
Primrose.

It was gone ten at night and they asked for two rooms
which Jake was eager to supply, it not being the tourist
season. They had eaten hamburgers from a town back down
the road and were ready for bed after a tiring journey, most of
which had been on minor roads. They agreed to meet in the
morning at breakfast.

Next morning Abe was down to breakfast first and Jake
Ramsden showed him to a table in the dining room.

"You up here on business?" Jake asked.

"Yeah, sort of."

"What kinda business you in?" Jake was always keen to
know as any sort of business done in the area usually had an
effect on the hotel and in recent times most of the effect had
been good.

"Well, we're in the movie business – we're looking for a
small town which we can feature in a film we're making in
the summer – got anything interesting that happens around
this town?" Abe enquired, just as his companion joined him
for breakfast.

"Good morning, sir, your friend has just been telling me
you're in the movie business," Jake said and turning to Abe
continued, "Why yes, we got quite a bit that happens around
here since Mr Steinberg came to live here."

"Who's Steinberg?" Abe lied.

"Julius Steinberg that is, you know the big oil magnate – a
lot of people come to town just to see where he lives and
perhaps catch a glimpse of him when he's in town – then

there's the lake and the annual regatta. It's really a nice town. Well gentlemen, what would you like for breakfast?"

"I'll just have coffee and some flapjacks," Abe said.

"I'll have the same," his companion added.

"Before you go, where's this guy Steinberg live? Perhaps we could have a look at his place – we'd go to the house and ask him," Abe asked.

"Oh he lives just out of town, a swell place he has – but you're be unlucky seeing him – he was going to leave for New York early this morning so his driver told me last night."

Jake never noticed the annoyance on his guests' faces and went off to pass their order to the kitchen.

"Goddam it! I felt sure he'd be here for a few days after Thanksgiving, I never expected the sonofabitch would go back to New York so soon. What do we do now?" Abe almost exploded.

"You're paying for this – you tell me," his companion looked unperturbed. "I suggest we better take a look at the f****** house and then think again – I'll have to talk to Pepe and see what he can do for me."

XLII

Joe Miller spent hours in the local library either writing letters or just sitting and thinking. He began to wonder if his trip to Primrose had been worthwhile. Had he the courage to do the man harm, or should he just scare him? Perhaps he should get someone to do it for him. But that was not easy. How do you meet someone who is prepared to murder for you – and wasn't that risky anyway? Was there a way in which he could arrange an accident – a car accident? But what guarantee would there be that he would be hurt and what about others in the car? How could he live with perhaps the death of others on his hands? Joe would go through these thoughts most every day and gradually his wife noticed that he was getting depressed once more.

"What's bothering you, Joe?" she asked, when he returned one morning looking particularly worried.

"It's nothing, dear – I just feel a bit down – I can't figure something out."

"You were much better a while back – you didn't seem to worry so much that job interviews just didn't come your way – you need a holiday – why don't we go down to Miami like we used to? We've still got some money and with winter almost upon us the sunshine will do you good. What do you say?"

Joe was in no mood to argue. He could see that it might make him feel better and perhaps while they were down there he would be able to further his plans.

Mrs Miller telephoned their usual hotel and was able to arrange a room for two weeks starting the next Saturday.

XLIII

Julius Steinberg flew down to Miami and stayed in a large five star hotel where he was able to have a penthouse suite to himself, with a beautiful sun lounge and balcony overlooking the sea. He had made sure his secretary also had a room in the hotel as it would be most unusual not to have business interruptions whilst there. He liked the food they served in the hotel and he liked to sit on the balcony and look out to sea but he found it difficult to rest for long – he was after all a man of action and he had to be involved in some deal or other to be really happy. He had said to Mac before he left that he did not want to be disturbed but here he was two days into his holiday and wondering what was happening up in New York and Chicago. His secretary, Miss Ruby Steers, had spent two days sunning herself on the beach and was disappointed to get a message when she returned on the second day that her boss wanted to see her.

"Good evening, Mr Steinberg, you wanted to see me."

"Yeah, Ruby, get through to New York and ask them what's happening on the Gulf job. Mac hasn't been through to me since we arrived."

"OK, Mr Steinberg, I'll see what I can find out."

Ruby returned to her room and straightaway got through to New York and asked to speak to MacDonald.

MacDonald happened to be engaged on a telephone call to the elevator contractors complaining at the lack of service they were getting on their ancient elevators, which once again had broken down.

"We'll send someone along tomorrow morning and do our best to fix it."

"Well, I hope you manage to get it working, the old man likes it and won't change it. Do your best, Tiny."

"OK, Mac, we'll see what we can do but the elevator should have been retired years ago, if it wasn't for the fact we keep repairing and issuing a fit for use certificate it would have been condemned years ago. Anyway, we'll see what we can do."

MacDonald was given a message to ring Ruby in Miami. "What can I do for you, Ruby?"

"Hi Mac, the old man wants to know what's happening on the Gulf deal."

"I might have known he would be through to me soon – he told me he wanted a real holiday and that I wasn't to bother him unless urgent. I'll find out about the Gulf deal and ring you back."

The Gulf deal was the takeover of a small prospecting company operating in the Gulf of Mexico. The company had managed to fend off offers from larger companies for many years but the prospecting had cost more than their management had allowed for and there was still no oil. One of Steinberg's agents on the lookout for companies ripe for takeover had heard of this company and had been watching their progress. He had also been busy with other contacts in the Gulf, trying to find out the chances of the company successfully finding oil where they were currently drilling – and by a healthy bribe to a relatively unimportant employee for one of the large oil companies he had determined that, although it was not generally known, the small company was on the edge of a big discovery. He had passed this information on to Steinberg's office.

MacDonald was given this information and immediately telephoned Miami. "Hullo, Ruby, I got some hot news for the boss, can I speak with him?"

"I'm not sure if he's still in his room, I'll check and ring you back." Ruby had given instructions to the operator that no calls were to be put through to the Steinberg suite without first going through her – Julius never liked to be bothered unnecessarily.

Five minutes later she rang New York and told Mac that Steinberg would speak with him.

"What's the hot news, Mac?"

"Piper tells me that Turners is ripe for the picking – they got it good but don't know it."

"When did Piper get the dope, Mac – how do we know we're not too late?"

"He told me that it was given to him only yesterday and that he was unable to get through then as he was on the rig – he was trying to get me at about the time I got through after your question. He says it seems that Turners are just about to fold on the drill."

"We gotta act quick, Mac – I want that you should fly down and make that offer we talked about a week or two back. You better take Maurice with you – he's the best lawyer we got in New York – I'd prefer Alberto in Chicago but I know he's away in Europe – Maurice should be OK. I want no slip-ups and when we got the company I want drilling to stop."

"You want drilling to stop – did I hear you right, boss?" Mac was puzzled.

"Yeah, I want it to stop and change the team. I don't want them to get oil the day after I take over – it's gotta look legit, understand?"

MacDonald understood and knowing the urgency and importance that his boss placed on such deals he spent the next two hours on the telephone, making arrangements with lawyers and bankers who were to ensure the deal went through without a hitch.

XLIV

It was exactly a month after the last meeting of the redundants that Ray Holmes received the first letter from Tony. It was from New York, it seems that before returning to take up his post in Geneva he had been told to visit the main offices of the Group in the States and study their work methods. He had visited Chicago, Dallas, Los Angeles and Pittsburgh.

In his letter he said he had been told that his boss had a home in a small town in New Hampshire – Primrose. He went on to say it would be nice if someone unknown to any in Arkansas Oil took a trip to the area to see what the place and layout was like.

Ray read the letter, noting the town name, and then destroyed it as Tony had requested – included in with the letter were two return tickets to Boston, an automobile hire voucher for any two weeks in the next six months and dollars sufficient to contribute substantially to two people making a trip there.

Ray was now convinced that Tony meant business and he wondered who should go and what instructions they should be given. He did not sleep well that night but for some reason the name which kept coming to his mind was Ted Wilson. At first when the name came to him he could not remember who it was – at two o'clock in the morning one's mind is not always at its best – but when he awoke a second, or was it a third, time he remembered. This was the man Joe Thomas had said was willing to help if he were given something to do. Yes, Ted Wilson could be their man and he could go to the States without fear of any of the ex-WECO people in the south knowing anything about it.

Raymond considered carefully whether be should for the time being tell others of the redundants about the gesture made by Tony Bentley – he decided against it – he would tell only Ted Wilson. He would now have to think of a way of getting it across to Ted without his family knowing what it was all about. He hit on the idea of telling Ted he had won a draw which had been run for all ex-WECO employees. He would ask Ted to come down to London to pick up the prize at his house as soon as possible.

Prior to Tony's visit to the States, Raymond had been given a book containing the names and addresses of those who had come along to the meetings of redundants and next to Joe Thomas' name there had been added the name and address of Ted Wilson – there was no telephone number.

Ray Holmes wrote to Ted Wilson giving him his telephone number and asking him to ring.

Ted Wilson received the letter the next day. "We've won a prize in a draw," he said to his wife, on opening the letter.

"What draw, I don't remember us entering a draw – it's a catch, you'll see."

"No, it's no catch. This is a draw arranged through the redundants of WECO, no entry was necessary, all ex-WECO people were put into the draw and I won – I've got to ring Raymond Holmes. I'll go down to call box at the end of the street and see what it's all about."

"You'd better take plenty of change with you, it'll be an expensive call down to London."

Ted duly armed himself with as much change as he could muster and proceeded to the call box at the corner. His call to Ray Holmes was short and to the point – Ray told him briefly what he had won and that he wanted to have a word with him privately before he went – if possible this weekend, on Sunday.

"Well, was it worth the telephone call?" Ted's wife enquired when he returned from the call to London.

"You wouldn't believe it but we've won a trip to Boston with some money to spend."

"Boston? Why would we want to go to Boston? There's not much to do there. I had an aunt who used to live in Boston, can't say she ever recommended it for a holiday though."

"No, not that Boston, we've won a trip to Boston in America and we've been given cash to make a holiday of it – Ray Holmes wants to see me when he gives me the tickets, he's coming up to Sheffield on Sunday. I've given him directions to the house, he said he won't stay long."

"I still don't see why Boston – I've never heard of anyone going there for a holiday, seems funny to me," his wife, naturally of a suspicious nature, said somewhat puzzled.

"Well, it'll be a break and I'm sure it's been done with the best intentions – anyway Ray will tell us all about it on Sunday."

XLV

Joe Miller and his wife had enjoyed a few days in the sunshine away from the cold up north. Joe had relaxed and the things that had been worrying him at home were gradually assuming less importance, and once or twice his wife said she even saw him smile.

Over the many years they had come to Miami for a break the town had changed, no longer was it safe to walk in certain parts and the influx of immigrants had made sections almost unrecognisable from the days Joe remembered as a child. He, however, liked to walk and although avoiding the areas he had been warned had changed he was nevertheless mugged in broad daylight and hit over the head with something heavy. It happened outside one of the best hotels in town and first on the scene was the doorkeeper, who with the help of a stranger escorted the victim into the hotel lobby, sat him down and called for the hotel doctor.

The injury was only superficial and with a small plaster over the cut Joe was pronounced fit to return to his hotel.

It was while he was thanking the doorkeeper and the doctor for their help that he saw a familiar face coming through the hotel entrance. The lady he saw was middle-aged and he was sure he knew who she was. As she approached near to where he was standing he spoke, "Hullo, Ruby, fancy seeing you here."

Ruby, taken by surprise, took a few seconds to recover her composure and then said, "It's Joe Miller, isn't it? What have you been doing to yourself."

Joe gave a brief explanation and then asked, "Are you down here on holiday?"

"No, not exactly. Although he's left me alone a good deal over the past few days, but it can't last – it never does, he always finds something to spoil it all."

"Is Steinberg in the hotel now?" Joe asked, almost shaking with anger. Ruby looked at him with a worried expression on her face. "Are you all right?" she asked. "You don't look at all well – it's the shock of the mugging, I expect, you should go and sit down for a while until it's worn off. I'll stay with you."

"I'll be all right – is he in?"

"I'm not sure, he was when I left but that was a couple of hours ago – you really don't look in a fit state to go visiting. Why don't you do as I say and sit down? Maybe you could see him tomorrow – I'll tell him I saw you."

Joe realised that he did not feel too good and took Ruby's advice and sat down – Ruby came and sat opposite him.

"Did you want to see Julius for anything special – I seem to remember you were not happy when you left?" Ruby asked.

"No, nothing special, except to tell him to his face that I have not found any work since he threw me out," Joe said angrily. "That man is a menace, goodness knows how many lives he has ruined – and what for? What does he get out of it? He's got so much money he can't know what to do with it."

Ruby said nothing at first; she was surprised by the outburst and didn't know how to reply.

"Sorry, Ruby, it's nothing to do with you – you're doing a job and it's not your fault if your boss is a ruthless, heartless individual. No, I guess I'll go back to my hotel in a while and try to forget that bastard is in the same town."

Joe changed the conversation, realising it wasn't fair to bring the secretary into his affair. He asked her about her own life and why she hadn't married. Half an hour later he said he felt well enough to leave and said his farewells to Ruby, suggesting it was not worth mentioning she had seen him. "I think after all," he said, "it would be better we both forgot we had ever met – enjoy the rest of your time in Miami – and thanks for your shoulder, I appreciate it."

XLVI

Joe Mancini and Mac now knew Steinberg's little secret and although Mac played it down when Joe had asked him what he thought he should do, nevertheless, it was beginning to play on his mind. Even while working on getting the small Gulf oil company into the Steinberg fold, his mind frequently wandered and he tried to think what would be best to do. Of course, he reasoned, Peter Bronson could be Steinberg's son but then again it was all supposition. Supposing Bronson had already found out who his father was – that would settle it. He resolved to think some more and perhaps see if it were possible to discover whether Bronson knew who his old man was.

As has been said earlier, Mac was known by many in the less salubrious parts of Brooklyn, he had many friends who operated within the law but he had many who operated dangerously close to being outside. He would go down to his haunts and see if any of the guys knew this Peter Bronson.

It was December and Christmas was but two days away. The old market was decorated with coloured lights and paper chains and as he walked past the stalls he was wished a Happy Christmas by all and sundry.

Coming up to one stall he saw an old friend unpacking boxes at the rear.

"What do yer know, Marty?"

"Goddam it, Mac, you old sonofabitch – nice to see you. What are you doing around these parts – come to see how the poor live at Christmas?" The two men shook hands. "Hey Mac, you remember how we used to swipe toys at Christmas and how your ma nearly always made us take them back – seems like yesterday – I was only saying to Dutch yesterday – you remember Dutch?" Mac nodded, "he should not put those toys at the front of his stall as someone like Mac and me might have taken 'em – he laughed and swore."

"Dutch still around these parts? He must be nearly eighty now," Mac said.

"It sure is nice to see you, Mac – come in and have a drink," and then calling over to the young lad at the front of the stall, "Look out for me, Charlie, while I have a drink with old Mac here."

They crossed the road to a small bar. "I'm glad I met up with you, Marty, I got a question for you."

"Go ahead, what is it?"

"You been around a bit, Marty – ever heard of a guy called Bronson, Peter Bronson?"

"Where you been, Mac? Everyone knows Bronson – he's some tough hombre. What do yer want to know about him?

I'd be very careful with that guy, he's bad business, Mac – you stay away."

"Yeah, I don't keep in touch much now – never go to the joints, too busy I guess." Mac smiled.

"Too busy making a lot of dough – you look after yer ma, I see her sometimes, Mac – she don't change much. What is it wid this guy Bronson?"

"Someone I know knew a gal way back – way back just after World War I – and a friend trying to locate the gal for him but without him knowing discovered the lady had died years back, but she had a son – the son we think is this guy Bronson."

"I know, your guy is the father – right, Mac?"

Mac who thought he had worded his explanation without revealing anything was a little shaken by Marty's quick response.

"You catch on quick – well actually we're guessing – all we know is that the husband left his wife before the baby was born and rumour had it that the husband was not the father – we know nothing about the old lady but we know our friend had met the mother some months before the baby was born. We're just guessing but we were told that Bronson's mother would not tell him who his father was – she promised to tell him when he was twenty-one but she died before he reached that age. We just wanted to find out whether Bronson has ever found his old man."

"What are you going to do if you find out he still doesn't know who he is? You surely ain't just going to tell him?"

Mac had not thought that far ahead and hesitated before he could answer. "No, we wouldn't do nothing like that – it could have been anybody – we have no means of knowing. I guess I'm curious – my friend is an old man now, been married but had no children – I wouldn't know whether he would want to know anyways."

"Bronson's plenty rich, could do your friend a lot of good – or he could just kill him – he's plenty mean. What do you want that I should do, Mac?"

"Do you know anyone who knows Bronson well?" Mac enquired.

"Bronson set up in New York first and there are several guys who used to knock around with him before he moved his operation to Vegas – he comes back on occasions, I understand. Do you remember Mickey O'Brien? – Lived on the block – well he certainly was close to Bronson at one time. Mickey's in the big time now. Lives in one of those swell hotels by the park. I believe he still does jobs for Bronson. Mickey might know – I'll ring his ma for you to get his address before you go. Now tell me about yourself and what are you doing now?"

Mac and Marty brought each other up to date and left the bar a few hours later, after the latter had used the bar phone to get Mickey O'Brien's address.

XLVII

Ray Holmes left early on Sunday morning and was in Sheffield before lunch. He had eaten at one of the service stations on the way up and felt he could arrive at Ted Wilson's house without feeling embarrassed about arriving at lunchtime. It was not easy finding the road as he had mislaid the directions given but he got there and knocked on the door.

Mrs Wilson opened the door. "You must be Mr Holmes – please come in, we haven't had dinner yet, would you like to eat with us?"

Ray explained that he had already eaten but that they should not delay their meal for him.

"Oh, it's not quite ready yet – the boy is playing football this morning, he won't be back for half an hour or so yet – I'll just go in kitchen and carry on while you talk with Ted."

Ray was pleased to have the opportunity to talk to Ted on his own and quickly explained what it was really all about but asked him to not tell his wife.

"We want you to go to Primrose and look around and if you can get to see the house where Steinberg lives that would be a real bonus – make a note of the layout of the place if you do get inside. I know it's not going to be easy but we want someone to go there who is totally unknown to Arkansas Oil and we don't want anyone other than Tony Bentley and myself to know anything about it."

"I understand, I remember I told Joe Thomas to tell you all that I was willing to help – I can assure you I'll treat it as being a holiday. But of course my wife is not stupid and if we go to the town and seek out where Steinberg lives she's bound to cotton on to what it is all about. I just don't want to know what you intend doing afterwards."

"As a matter of fact we have no idea of what we are going to do so there is no need for you or your wife to worry – in any case you will not be connected in any way – take my word."

Mrs Wilson came in from the kitchen.

"Well, tell us all about it – why New England?"

Ray answered before Ted could say anything.

"I've just been telling Ted – New England is a lovely part of the States and there are many places to visit and enjoy. Why did we pick New England? Well, as a matter of fact we didn't – it was Tony Bentley. For the next two years he is working for Arkansas Oil in Europe but for the present is over in the States and he got hold of these tickets at a bargain price so we thought what better way to use them than to give them to an ex-WECO man. He also got this very special deal on the hire car you can use. I'm sure you'll enjoy it."

Ray could see that Mrs Wilson was not entirely convinced by what he had said and bearing in mind that Ted could envisage a problem at the time he and his wife arrived in Primrose, with him having to try to look over the Steinberg property, he decided to come clean – just why he had not imagined there would likely be a problem he did not know – he obviously had not thought it through.

"I have a confession, Mrs Wilson," Ray continued, "I can see you are too intelligent a lady to be taken in by what I have been saying. We have another motive and it was unfair of me to try to deceive you." Ray looked at Ted for reassurance and Ted nodded. "Tony Bentley, who was a director in WECO, now works for one of the Steinberg companies and he has found out that the big man has a large house in a small town in a part of the States known as New England. As you know none of the ex-WECO employees are very fond of this man and we have decided that he should be taught a lesson. The problem has been how to carry out anything when he is in the States. Well, now we have a man over there for a while and he thinks it would be a good idea to find out a little about the Steinberg mansion so that when something is decided upon we at least have a location to carry it through. Primrose being a small town we obviously did not want anyone known by Steinberg or connected with him to survey the house and we also saw no reason to involve, at least at this stage, any other of the WECO men down south – the fewer who know about this the better – I believed your husband would do the job for us. I assure you he will not be further involved and this is all we would expect him to do – he has said he will do it."

"I'm glad you have told me. I don't like it – but from what I have heard this man Steinberg is not a nice person and I know Ted feels strongly that something should be done to stop him, and others like him, from acting in the way they do – providing you can assure me Ted has only to try and look over the house then we will have a go. It's quite exciting really." Mrs Wilson glanced at her husband. "You are sure you want to do this, Ted?"

"Of course I'm sure, luv – it's the least I can do, although how it is going to help I just do not know. Anyway we'll have a holiday," and then turning to Ray, "I'll do my best to get what you want – but supposing I don't get any information."

"Oh, don't worry – I'm sure you'll find out something, at present we know nothing about Primrose or where Steinberg lives. Don't mention ever working with any company associated with him – just be a tourist who read about the man when he came over to the UK and met the Prime Minister. You know what I mean – pretend you have quite by chance arrived at this town while touring and discover this is the town this man lives in."

Ted said he understood.

After handing over the tickets and the map of New England, then giving instructions on how to book their flight and where to collect the hire car Tony had arranged for them, Ray gave them a cheque drawn on his account to cover the expenses of the trip. He advised them to get travellers cheques and dollars after the cheque had been cleared and finally asked them to let him know when they were about to leave and to ring again when they had returned.

"But don't mention Primrose in any telephone call – I'll contact you later and perhaps come and see you again," he added before leaving.

XLVIII

Mac did not bother asking anyone else in the neighbourhood about Bronson and, after calling in to see his mother, returned to Manhattan.

Armed with Mickey O'Brien's telephone number he arrived at the Wall Street office from which he had been operating while his boss was in Miami He wanted to know about Bronson and yet he was hesitant to proceed any further. On arriving on the fourteenth floor, the first person he met was Joe Mancini.

"Hi, Mac – I hoped I might see you. Have you got a minute?" Joe Mancini said.

"Yeah, come in the office. What's on yer mind?"

They entered the office and Joe closed the door behind him. Mac seated himself behind his desk and motioned Joe to sit opposite.

"I've been thinking about what I told you concerning this guy Bronson and I figure it's worth a try to find out if he knows his old man. You never know it could be doing him a favour, there ain't many guys as rich as Julius Steinberg."

Mac did not answer at once, inwardly he had hoped that he had played it down sufficiently so that Joe would take no precipitate action but it was obvious the man was eager to go ahead.

"I can see what you're getting at, Joe, but I warn you to be careful. As a matter of fact I bumped into a guy only today who knew Bronson. It's like when someone points out an advert or someone you've never seen before and then suddenly you see it or them all the time. This guy told me Bronson is one of the mob and a pretty mean guy – you gotta play this one cool unless you want to end up at the bottom of the East River. My friend told me that an old buddy of mine knows Bronson and that he might be the one to ask about Bronson's old man. I was just wondering whether to bother but since it seems you just gotta find out, I better try and see what this guy knows."

"I figured your playing it down was only an act – Joe Mancini is not stupid, Mac – I know when I got something," Joe said, almost triumphantly.

"Hold your horses, Joe – I ain't saying it ain't important to find out but we gotta play it cool, this could be dynamite. I'll ring my old buddy and see what I can find out but in the meanwhile you do nothing and say nothing to nobody." Mac got out of his chair and made his way to the door, holding it open and inviting Joe to leave.

"When you going to contact your buddy, Mac? – And when do I see you?" Joe asked, making sure that Mac knew that he did not want to be left out, after all, he thought, it was my idea.

"Don't worry, Joe, I'll try and get him tonight and see what he knows – if I find out anything I'll let you know. I'll be away for a few days; Julius wants me down in Houston. I'll see you when I get back."

XLIX

Tony Bentley, having made the rounds of most of the major subsidiaries of Steinberg's empire, was now ready to return to Europe. They expected him in Geneva in the New Year so he had travelled back to England to spend Christmas at home before going to Switzerland. He telephoned Ray Holmes before leaving for Geneva and they met at The Queen's in Weybridge. Tony explained the set-up in Arkansas Oil and the ideas he had had for getting their revenge.

"Are you sure you still want to go through with this, Tony?" Ray asked.

"Too bloody right I do – someone has to stop him and we agreed that we would all do our best to help," Tony replied.

"I know all that but now you have a job back with them you surely must feel different – please don't feel you have to go through with it."

Tony smiled and took another swig of his whisky. "What do you take me for? If I let the boys down now what would they all think? No, I keep my word. As I told you, Steinberg won't keep me longer than my two years and then what? At least I will have earned myself a fair bit of cash. No, I owe it to all who were sacked at WECO to try and get back at the bastard."

Ray agreed to keep Tony informed as to what Ted Wilson found out when he eventually arrived back from the States.

"I don't think Ted would be wise to go for a couple of months until the weather improves," Tony said, "there's an awful lot of snow up there right now. It'll delay things I know but it's no good sending him out of season, not before the end of March anyway."

Ray duly telephoned Ted Wilson the following morning.

L

Abe Slyberger's investment in the uncompleted contract would of course increase now that they had had the wasted journey up to Primrose but by how much he could only guess. Did he want to spend more money? Was it worth it? What good would it do him? These questions kept running through his mind. Perhaps he would call it off – maybe Pepe would give him some of his money back. He soon dismissed the latter thought from his mind. Pepe was no fool and apart from actually firing a shot, the hired man had gone all the way as agreed; they had even got access to Steinberg's house on the pretence of being a film company – the housekeeper, who was promised a small part in the film when they returned in the summer, was only too pleased to let the two men have a good look around.

Back at his office Abe put a call through to Pepe Galento and was lucky to find him at home.

"Pepe, it's Abe Slyberger, I'm sure you know we were unable to conclude the contract, how do I stand?"

"Yeah, I heard – I guess we could do business again but it'll cost another two grand up front and of course the grand when the job is done. You let me know if you should want to go ahead and I'll try to accommodate."

"Another two grand – Jesus, I'll just have to think about it – I'll let you know." Slyberger had known it was going to be something like this but he had hoped it would be less. Perhaps there was some other way.

LI

Mac waited for Joe Mancini to leave his office and returned to his desk. He lifted the telephone and dialled the number he had been given by Marty. The call was answered by the hotel receptionist.

"What can I do for you, sir?"

"I am told you have a Mickey O'Brien who has a suite in your hotel, can you put me through to him?"

"Mr O'Brien does not accept calls without first knowing who it is calling. Can you give me your name and I will see if he is in?"

"Tell him it's a personal matter and it's an old friend from the block – tell him it's Mac – he'll know."

Mac waited and finally the receptionist came back on the line.

"Mr O'Brien is in and he says he will speak with you – hold the line I'll put you through."

"Mickey O'Brien speaking – long time no see, Mac – what's your problem?"

"Hullo Mickey, climbed any good walls lately? Sure remember the way you went over – we got lucky that night. I'm looking for some information, Mickey and Marty tells me you may be able to help – you know Marty Goldstein?"

"Sure I remember Marty, ain't seen him for a while – how's he doing?"

"Marty's fine, Mickey. He told me you know Peter Bronson."

"Yeah, I know him – what's on your mind?"

"Can I come over and see you, Mickey? It's only a small matter but I'd rather talk to you direct, if that's OK with you."

There was a few seconds' silence and then, "OK, if you can come over in the next hour, I gotta go down town soon – this matter, it won't take long will it? I'm a busy man, Mac."

"Thanks, Mickey, no, it won't take more than five minutes, I promise – I'll get a cab and be right over."

Fifteen minutes later, Mac was in the hotel and made his way to reception. He had hardly said who he wanted to see when a dark man standing nearby came up to his shoulder and said, "You MacDonald?"

"Yeah, that's me."

"Follow me."

Mac was hurried over to an elevator and whisked up to the twentieth floor. He followed the big man down a corridor and to a door at the end. Three knocks and the door was opened and Mac followed him into a room with several large and comfortable-looking seats, most of which were occupied by smartly-dressed men.

Mac hesitated as he came through the door and spotting Mickey seated behind a grand desk near the window said, "I'll come back some other time, Mickey." He raised his hands and turned towards the door.

Mickey spoke. "Come in, Mac – meet some of the boys," and then addressing the seated men, "Mac and I go way back – we lived on the same block – went to school together, that's when we bothered to turn up – eh Mac?" He laughed and Mac smiled back. "What's this all about, Mac, you can talk in front of the boys."

Mac felt decidedly uncomfortable, he was not sure if he should give this bit of personal information about Bronson to all and sundry. He would have to be very careful what he said.

"Well, it seems such a little thing to interrupt a meeting with these gentlemen. I hardly think I should bother you at this time."

"It ain't no bother, Mac – shoot, what's on yet mind?"

"I met a guy recently up New England way," Mac started and continued, "who used to know Peter Bronson's ma – way back in the twenties – it seems she died many years ago but the guy only recently found this out. He asked where the father was and discovered her old man had left her before the baby was born. He was told that young Bronson was never told who his father was and he was curious to know whether the man ever did get to know his old man."

"Why so interested after all these years – it seems as if the guy you met thinks he might be the father. After Bronson's money I guess."

"No, it's not like that, Mickey."

Mac began to wish he had never heard of Bronson. What was he doing this for anyway? He should have left it to Joe Mancini to sort out.

"Well, if it ain't like that, Mac, what is it like?"

"I can assure you the guy ain't after no money, he's got plenty – he's an old man and I guess he wants to be young again, so he thinks of time gone by and asks questions and not getting the answers he gets curious and wants to find out more – he's a real old guy, Mickey. He just wants to know if this Peter Bronson ever did find his old man."

One of the men sitting in a chair to Mac's right interrupted before Mickey could say any more.

"Pete told me once he never knew who was his old man – he also told me that his old man left his ma before he was born – he traced him to a small town up in Canada but it seems he had died there in the 1950s."

"There you are, Mac – there's your answer – his old man was traced but he was already dead when Peter Bronson came to the end of his trail." Mickey hesitated as if he was going to say something else, which those present sensed. "Of course he could have been wrong. I figure he traced his mother's husband – but from what you have said, Mac, he was not necessarily his father."

"I never said that – all I know is this old guy wanted to know if Bronson ever found his old man. Thanks, Mickey, for the help. I think I can safely tell my friend what you have told me – I don't know anything about what you think – I have to leave that to the old guy."

MacDonald walked to the door which was guarded and blocked by two heavies. For a moment it seemed he was going to be stopped leaving but on a nod from O'Brien the men moved aside and opened the door.

"So long, Mac, tell your friend he should watch out for himself – Pete don't like people snooping around. For you, Mac, it's different, we're old buddies, but be warned, the man is tough, I mean real tough. Watch out for yourself and remember me to Marty when you see him."

Mac left, not convinced that he had fooled anyone there – but then he thought no one is going to bother telling Bronson – Mickey would see to that.

LII

The rest of the Millers' time in Miami passed all too quickly. Joe almost forgot that just down the road in a hotel overlooking the sea Steinberg was also on holiday – or was he, did that man ever relax, and what new scheme was running through his mind and what more damage to lives would he now be doing? These thoughts passed through Joe Miller's mind on more than one occasion but for the most part he was content and happy.

When they returned from Miami, Joe once again began the routine of visiting the library and listing the job possibilities. Then began the letter writing and the expectations when the post came with the replies. He knew he would not get an interview but he now became intrigued with the replies themselves. The format of the letter became important and he would get very angry when the letter suggested they wanted someone with more experience or more suitable for the position for which he had applied. He enjoyed reading the letter which thanked him for applying and was sure that he would have been quite capable of doing the job but unfortunately the client insisted on someone under forty. He hated the four-page forms he was often required to complete – none of which were standard but in the end asked all the same questions, all the answers to which had already been given in his CV, sent with the original application.

His attention taken by letters, it seemed he was losing his obsession to do harm to Steinberg. His wife was sure it was the holiday that had made him more content but little did she know that the apparent small knock on his head when mugged in Miami had in fact caused some damage to his brain. He became giddy and was sent by his wife to the doctor who prescribed anti-giddiness tablets, which didn't work, and then when Miller returned for a further examination sent him to have a brain scan.

Joe Miller had great difficulty in coping with the scanner, as he was required to lie flat which immediately made him giddy and want to sit up. Then when finally he overcame the sensation and was slid into the scanner, he had to be removed as the disorientation he felt overcame him. However, they were able to take sufficient pictures to determine that he had had a blow to the skull which had caused some minor damage within. His wife was warned that he could suddenly change if he received any further shock to the system but they did say that the giddiness might disappear at any time – and keep taking the tablets!

LIII

There is no end to man's ingenuity, at least that is what Abe Slyberger had heard people say many times. Why, if this were so, could he not think of some way of getting his own back on Steinberg – there surely must be a way other than hiring a contract killer he could not now afford.

He had gained access to the house, and the housekeeper, having been promised a role in the film they would be making, would be expecting them to return. However, if something happened to Steinberg a second visit would surely place him under suspicion and although unlikely that the housekeeper would connect with the film company immediately she would undoubtedly recall the first visit and advise the police – it was most unlikely she would be able to give a description of any value after the first visit but a second visit would make it so much easier for her. No, a second visit by him was out, it would be far too risky; he would have to get someone else to do it for him – but who? Someone going to the house with the intention of causing harm to the owner would require paying and who could say the cost would not be equally as great as that he had been asked to pay by Pepe Galento.

For days he pondered the situation but did not come up with a satisfactory solution. Maybe he could get to the old man some other way, not at his home but let's say at his office. Abe began to think of ways he could finish off Steinberg in his office – he thought of a shot of arsenic in his coffee, pushing him out of his window, stabbing him with a paper knife – accidentally of course – but dismissed them all as being totally impracticable for him to accomplish without being discovered for sure. Goddam it, he thought, there must be some way of getting rid of this bastard. It was at this stage that he remembered the Brooklyn office was Steinberg's favourite – he pictured the office in his mind's eye. One entered by those early-century doors, passed the reception desk and then down the stone corridor to the first cage elevator, which was for Steinberg's use only, and so to a second used by staff. Jesus, he thought, why did old Steinberg put up with such an antiquated elevator? He remembered having to climb the stairs on more than one occasion and men were nearly always working on the elevators.

He stopped in his thoughts and a wry smile came to his face – not a pretty sight an onlooker would say – that was it, supposing the elevator happened to fail with old man Steinberg aboard? And supposing, just supposing it fell all the way to the ground? Why did he not think of it before? It was, he thought, the perfect solution. But there was one snag, he knew nothing about elevators and even if he did were there not stringent safety checks to ensure an elevator could not ever fall all the way down? But surely he had seen it on films and there must have been occasions, however rare, when such a thing had happened. Who did he know in the elevator business who might be prepared to fix an elevator for him?

There were hundreds of elevators in New York and there were many corporations operating in this field. He wanted to check the corporation that serviced Steinberg's Brooklyn office. Knowing Steinberg was down in Miami he took a cab over to Brooklyn and casually entered the building and crossed to the elevator, which he could see was somewhere up above. He pressed the button and whilst waiting for the cage to come down he looked for the maker's name. There it was on a metal plate attached to the outer cage. He noted the name and reference number and before the cage reached the ground floor he turned around and walked out of the office. Returning to his office he spent the next ten minutes ringing around to find out who serviced this particular type of elevator. He found three who had this ancient elevator on their books and one obligingly told him they were a real pain in the butt and should all be scrapped.

"No, mister, I would have nothing to do with a building having that type of elevator – don't take it on unless the landlord agrees to change to a modern one. We have one over in Brooklyn, it causes us so much trouble it is just not true – it breaks down regularly and we have warned the owners it should be changed but the guy who owns the building is a nutcase and keeps it because he wants the office to be how it was when he first moved there. I guarantee that if you go to that office each day in one week you'll find the elevator broken down at least on one day or else you'll find our engineers working on it. No, mister, stay away from it."

"Thanks for the advice, I'll remember that," Abe said.

"We're a small operation and that means we have no choice but to put up with all the trouble – this guy is powerful and could soon put us out of business. If you ever get the opportunity to put business our way it would be much appreciated – but keep away from the elevator we have talked about."

The first step had been taken it was now up to him to try and see if he could get them to fix it.

LIV

It took MacDonald four hours to get down to Houston and arrange to go down by helicopter to the Turner rig. The weather for the flight was clear and the OK was given for the helicopter to land on the nearby Texaco platform from whence they would take a boat over to the Turner rig, two miles to the south. Amos Turner had reached this amicable agreement with Big Red Thomson who owned the boat which ferried crew and gear either from the shore or from the platform owned by the giant oil company.

The sea which had looked calm from the helicopter was less so when they boarded the boat from the steps of the rig and it proved to be quite a feat ending up in the boat and not in the sea – Mac was anything but happy with the experience and had wished he had arranged to meet the boss man on dry land.

Getting off the boat proved equally hazardous but Red Thomson was adept at judging when it was time to jump and Mac made a safe landing. He was met by Amos Turner himself.

"Howdy, friend, I guess you're Steinberg's right-hand man – I'm Amos Turner."

"Pleased to meet you, Amos – I'm MacDonald but everyone calls me Mac. I don't know about Steinberg's right-hand man but I certainly jump when he tells me."

"Come aboard, it's better up top – we can have a drink and discuss matters." The lawyer who had accompanied Mac was introduced to Amos and they climbed the steps to the platform above; the lawyer was particularly glad to be on something that was not moving although it had at first seemed to him the whole rig was moving – he was feeling quite unwell and wished this platform had heliport facilities.

They were shown into a small office and given a drink.

"My understanding is that your boss is prepared to cover my debts and pay twenty dollars a share for my business." Amos opened the meeting proper. "The shares are owned mainly by my family and then there are those held by my manager and his deputy – but they don't amount to many. Does your boss want the lot or just a controlling interest?" he added.

"He really wants the lot but would settle for a few employees hanging on to their shares if they really thought it worth while," Mac replied.

"What about my employees?" Amos asked.

"Mr Steinberg intends to give all of them, except any skeleton crew needed to maintain the rig, twenty-one days' leave on full pay. He's having some of his own men come over and have a look around and take some more samples. He says he'll keep on your manager and any other key employees as well as the gang you presently use. He cannot, however, guarantee that he will not have to make some changes; after all you are selling, we understand, because you have not yet struck oil in this area. If we do no better then we can hardly be expected to carry on for ever," the lawyer said.

Amos Turner did his best to get some assurances for his key employees but nothing positive was forthcoming and since he was really in no position to argue he could only make token objections but finally agreed to the almost unconditional surrender of the business.

Amos Turner knew it was time to get out and he was agreeably surprised to get away so lightly – all his business debts paid and twenty dollars a share. The family, he thought, would be pleased now the big burden was about to be lifted from their shoulders.

After the lawyer had obtained the necessary signature, duly witnessed, on the agreement to sell, and celebration drinks had been consumed, the manager was invited in and told of what had just taken place. He was not surprised as Amos had kept him informed of the situation – he was, however, surprised to be told all drilling was to stop and that all, except, say, three men, were to be allowed off the rig on full pay for twenty-one days. He was told to take action right away and arrange for staff movement to shore.

Mac and the lawyer said their farewells and started the hazardous journey back to the heliport.

Back in Houston Mac rang Miami to tell Steinberg that the deal had been done.

LV

Tony Bentley, having made himself felt in Geneva and travelled around the various European subsidiaries, decided to spend a weekend at home. He arranged to meet Ray Holmes to discuss further action of the redundants; their meeting place was once again the Queen's at Weybridge.

Ray confirmed that the police had not been able to trace the originators of the letters written to the press but that judging by the mail received by the press on this matter, there was indeed quite a deal of support for some means being found to stop these individuals operating in the way they so often did. There had even been a programme on television in which the letters were referred to, and from which a lively discussion followed.

"We have at least made some people think but I don't imagine it will make any difference to some of the more unscrupulous bastards," said Ray. "There would have to be a code of conduct drawn up that takeover merchants would be required to adhere to."

Tony agreed but could not see anything like that being adopted.

"There are too many in high places who have been involved in companies who have operated in just this way – no, the only hope is to scare the living daylights out of anyone who contravenes the code of the redundants that we should devise," Tony added.

The two men began then and there to draw up the basis for a code of conduct which they decided should be sent to newspapers, perhaps anonymously, when in an acceptable format.

"Have you heard anything further from Ted Wilson – do you know when they are going?" Tony asked.

"Ted said he had arranged a flight for 6th April – I had told him it would not be much use going earlier. I know it's a good way ahead but if we believe it necessary to find out about the place we can only do it in what is likely to be a time for tourists – it would be too suspicious asking questions otherwise."

Tony said he would keep in contact with Ray whilst in Geneva and that he would probably see him in a couple of months' time.

LVI

MacDonald returned to New York from Houston and left the tidying up of the takeover of Turners to the lawyers and bankers – he was not keen to have to go out to that rig again.

He reported to Steinberg that he had stopped all drilling and that the crew had been given twenty-one days' leave on full pay as instructed.

"Nice work, Mac. We'll play this one cool. Get the Dallas boys to send men down to the rig to take samples but no more drilling until I give the OK – understand?"

"Yeah, boss, whatever you say. What happens when their men return?"

"They ain't gonna return. You gotta get rid of them. Make sure you don't do it until near to the end of their leave and make sure they are given the appropriate leaving pay, I don't want no mess up with any state or federal authorities. Tell them, if any ask, that Arkansas Oil are going to do exhaustive tests before proceeding, and that Steinberg knows he has taken a gamble but just can't afford to keep rig-men on when there is no drilling. You get the idea."

"What about the manager and his deputy, boss?" Mac asked.

"Pay 'em off too, we got our own organisation."

"But, Julius, we told Turner we would keep them on – the manager has been working for Turner for twenty-five years, he's in his fifties."

"Did you put anything in writing?"

"Jesus, no, boss, you know you always tell us not to put nothing in writing."

"Then we're OK – get rid of them – give 'em six months pay and say bye bye."

Mac should have been used to the way Steinberg operated but even he thought the sacking of the manager was a bit unnecessary – they would have to have someone eventually in charge and he would have liked to have kept this man in work, he seemed a good sort. But Steinberg's word was law, he knew that if he tried to change the mind of his boss he would be accused of being soft and would stand a good chance of losing his own job. Julius will do this once too often, he thought, someone will one day stand up for himself and sort the old man out – I reckon he's been lucky so far.

LVII

Abe Slyberger, in the weeks to follow, made contact several times with the elevator company who serviced the Brooklyn elevator and on most occasions was able to speak to the man to whom he had first spoken. He was gradually learning more about elevators than he had ever thought possible, but the more he learnt the more he began to doubt if his scheme would be possible.

* * *

Tony Bentley had settled in Geneva and had already started to change that office and made visits to all of the major subsidiaries in Europe and collected information on their methods of work. He could see where things could be improved. It then became a dilemma with his conscience as to whether he should implement the changes he could see were necessary. It hurt him to help Steinberg make more money but he also understood that the better he performed the less likely that any suspicion would fall on him should the redundants actually pull off some action against Steinberg. He was not, however, averse to seeing the back of one or two of the Geneva staff who had lorded it over him and others at WECO when first the latter had fallen to the Steinberg empire.

* * *

Joe Mancini for his part could hardly wait to find out whether the guesses he had made about Peter Bronson were true. Mac told him of his meeting with Mickey O'Brien, but without revealing who he was, and told Joe that he wondered whether either of them should pursue the matter further. Joe was obviously not impressed – it was a big matter to him that he had this particular piece of information and he was not going to let it drop so easily.

* * *

Joe Miller on the other hand seemed to have quietly forgotten his anger against Steinberg and concentrated his thoughts to the job applications and how they were answered. His giddiness on some days made him feel decidedly ill but on days when the giddiness was not around he was well and almost happy. His wife told her friends that Joe was getting back to his old self for the first time for some years.

* * *

Jake Ramsden had plans drawn up for his hotel extension but was still unsure if he should go ahead with the actual building. "Maybe I give it another season before I decide – it's nearly April and the tourists will be coming soon, then we will see if it grows more this year," he had said one night in the bar to a ready listener.

* * *

Mickey O'Brien himself was curious over the enquiry made by his friend Mac and pondered whether to pursue the matter with Bronson. He thought it could be worth something but was unsure and wondered if it would rebound – he would think it over and see how he felt when next he made his annual visit to Las Vegas in April when he would meet up with Bronson.

* * *

Ted Wilson and his wife had booked their flight to Boston and would be flying on the first Monday in April. They had studied the map of New England and read up about the places to visit and were looking forward to their adventure. They had notified Ray Holmes of the date of their departure.

* * *

Steinberg returned to New York and subsequently to Primrose late in March. He expressed to Joe Mancini, who met him at the airport, that he was glad to be back. He asked to be returned to his favourite office in Brooklyn and not surprisingly found the elevator service engineers just leaving, having once again managed to remedy a fault. After calls to various offices and a session with Mac he got Joe Mancini to drive him up to Primrose.

LVIII

Mac had acted upon Steinberg's instructions and with the help of the Turner Corporation office staff had ensured that proper notice and pay was given to all the sacked employees – a carefully worded letter, approved by the Arkansas Oil legal department, was sent to each person explaining the reason why their employment had to be terminated. It then fell upon him to speak with the manager, Lee Crocket, and his deputy, to tell them that their employment was also terminated.

Lee Crocket and Kevan Brown were met at the Turner's old office in Houston and Mac gave them the sad news and each a cheque for six months' pay, as instructed. It came as a considerable surprise to both men.

"I was told by my boss that my job would be secure – who has given you orders to release me? What has happened to change the situation?" Lee Crocket asked.

"I can't really say – I'm acting on instructions – probably head office have made a few more calculations and can't see how we can possibly keep you on whilst no drilling is taking place. It may be that our company will move the rig to another area as the present one seems to be dry and you can hardly expect them to carry on paying you both whilst no work is being done. I'm very sorry but that's the way it is."

Crocket looked angry. "Bullshit, you never had any intentions of keeping us on – you knew that Turner would never have sold out had he known his men were going to be treated in this way."

Mac was clearly embarrassed as he sympathised with the two men but had to pretend to see what had been done as being reasonable. He couldn't wait to get away from Houston and back to New York. Steinberg, he thought, as the cab drove him back to the airport, has definitely made two more enemies.

LIX

The Wilsons arrived in Boston after a seven-hour flight from Manchester. It was not their first flight as they had once saved up and taken a package holiday in Majorca but this was something different. Ted had been given the name and directions to a small motel outside Boston and all they had to do when cleared of customs was to pick up the car arranged for them by Tony. Ted held a driving licence although he had no car of his own, having sold it to supplement money on the dole and to save the not-inconsiderable expenditure necessary when running a car.

The hired car was far superior to the old Ford Consul Ted had once driven back home and he took a while trying out all the gadgets before leaving the car hire premises. The instructions given to the motel were duly followed and they were soon safely installed in a small cabin near to the parked car. That evening Ted and his wife studied once again the map on which places of interest had been marked and the next morning after breakfast they set off, intent on getting the most out of this holiday but at the same time remembering the final object of their visit.

They had decided that Primrose would be their first objective so that they could get as much information as possible before relaxing and hopefully enjoying the holiday. They estimated it would take them about four hours to reach Primrose. However, they had not reckoned on the small country roads and the general lack of directions when they were quite close by. It was therefore early evening before they pulled up outside the Primrose Lake Hotel. "We'd better go inside and see if we can get a meal and a bed for the night," Ted said. "I shouldn't think it would be too expensive."

Alice was only too pleased to agree, she was not only hungry but tired after trying to help her husband navigate through the winding roads.

Jake Ramsden soon came to reception when the new visitors rang the bell. "Good evening to you, what can I do for you?" he said.

"First of all we're hungry and would like something to eat, and secondly, have you a room for the night?" Ted asked.

"I can get you a meal very quickly, we've just started serving dinner in the restaurant, and, yes, I have a nice room vacant overlooking the lake."

"We'll take the room," Alice said before Ted had time to answer. "I would like to have a quick wash and then come down to a meal."

Jake looked pleased, business in the last few days had really began to grow. "You're English, aren't you? – Over here on holiday?" he said, as he beckoned that they follow him up to the first floor.

"Yes, we had been told how nice New England was in the spring so we thought we would come here for a complete change – we don't like noisy places."

"Well you won't find Primrose noisy – it's very quiet, the only time we get any noise is when one of the motor cruisers on the lake passes close to the hotel and that's only once or twice a day. You won't get any noise at night – ah, here's your room, number twelve. I hope you like it. Are you thinking of staying long?"

"We're taking it easy and if we like a place we'll stay a while, we will see," Alice said. "This is a lovely room, look at that view, Ted."

"I'll save you a nice table also overlooking the lake. Come down when you're ready."

Ten minutes later Jake showed them to their table and introduced the waiter who would look after them. There were three other tables occupied in the small restaurant. Once they had placed their order Jake came over with the intention of making sure they understood what an important tourist attraction Primrose now was.

"Our little town has become very popular in the past few years – of course it's very pretty by the lake as you will see tomorrow, but that's not the only attraction, a lot of people like to come here because they hope they might see our important resident, or at least to see where the man lives."

"And who may that be?" asked Ted.

"Have you ever heard of Julius Steinberg back in England?"

"Why, yes," said Ted, "is that not the man who runs an oil company and gives pictures to royalty?"

"That's the one, so he is getting that well known is he?" Jake replied. "He built a mansion here a few years ago and is often to be seen in town I've spoken to him a couple of times," Jake said proudly.

"Is there any chance of seeing where he lives, my wife just loves visiting houses – we do it a lot back home. Of course the houses there are generally old houses of historical importance."

"Well, I can sure show you where the mansion is but as for getting in to look around I guess that would be difficult. You see, the old man himself lives there a good deal of the time. As a matter of fact he came back from down south only two weeks ago. Of course he sometimes goes to New York and other places – even overseas – but as for getting in his house, I wouldn't know. I see his chauffeur sometimes, he comes into the bar – when next he's around I'll ask him what the chances are."

"Can you direct us to where the house is and then we can at least take a look from the outside," Alice said.

"Sure, I can show you but you can't even see the house from the main gate. I guess you get the best view from high up. Folks tell me that from the side of Hanover Heights you get a good view – I reckon that'll be about half a mile back."

Jake was interrupted by the waiter arriving with their order.

"Come and see me when you've finished your meal and I'll tell you how to get to the main gate and then how to get up to Hanover Heights."

Jake was not about to lose two potential customers for the sights of Primrose and was waiting by reception when Alice and Ted came out of the restaurant. They, for their part, also wanted to know the directions but had agreed at the table that they should not appear to be too interested in the house in case suspicions may be aroused later. They, therefore, walked as if to pass reception and climb the stairs – but as they had hoped Jake called them over and gave them precise instructions on the Steinberg mansion. "Of course we have a lot more in Primrose besides the house and you cannot leave this area without visiting the lake and if possible taking a boat to the other side and round to the falls – it's quite a sight, especially this time of the year when we have been having quite a lot of rain. Anyway, I guess you'll see in the morning – we haven't much nightlife in town but you'll find the company in our bar most interesting. You may even see Steinberg's chauffeur."

The English couple thanked Jake and went up to their room – it was still only eight o'clock but getting quite dark and although they were both tired they decided they would get changed and go down to the bar to see if they could gather any more information about Steinberg and the house.

The bar had only a few people when they arrived. They were surprised to see it had been made to look a little like an English pub and they learnt later that Jake had been guided in furbishing it by an ex-brewer's architect from Bishop Auckland who having visited Primrose a few summers back had offered to draw up plans for Jake to follow. Jake had never regretted agreeing to the re-design as most of the tourists appeared to like the atmosphere of the place.

One of the persons in the bar was Mayor O'Reilly, who, with his wife, ran the only ladies' fashion store in town. He was talking to John Butler, who last year had helped Steinberg's chauffeur, Joe Mancini, get the information on Zoë, the young lady Steinberg had met in the First World War. Two others in the bar were salesmen who were passing through and staying over for the night in what had become known as a good place for food, a drink, and a good bed at a reasonable price.

As the Wilsons entered, those in the bar looked up and carried on talking. The barman asked what they would like to drink and the couple went over to a table near the window. Mayor O'Reilly and his companion noticed the English accent and ever one for promoting his town and at the same time encouraging business informed John Butler that he was going over to introduce himself.

He approached the couple, who were conscious that they had been noticed. "Hello there, I'm Patrick O'Reilly and mayor of this town. Welcome, are you going to stay long?"

The Wilsons explained that they had been told how beautiful and peaceful the New England countryside was and they had came to see for themselves They said they had no definite plans and were quite prepared to stay wherever they were enjoying themselves.

The mayor then proceeded to state the merits of Primrose and of course referred to Steinberg and his mansion, the lake, the falls and Hanover Heights, etc. – he also managed to put in a word about his store, which he claimed was the best in the county and as good as any in Boston, as he had all the best makes and not the overheads the big city guys had to cover and therefore his prices were very competitive. Mrs Wilson, who had promised herself a new outfit one day, listened with interest whilst Ted tried to get O'Reilly onto another subject.

"Do come along and see what we have to offer, I know tourists from Europe think our prices are very good compared with what you have to pay back home."

Only two or three more people entered the bar whilst the Wilsons stayed but they both agreed the company was very friendly. Tomorrow they would make their first foray into the Steinberg domain – or at least if not into then close by.

LX

The last meeting of the redundants had been in September, now it was April and although Tony was away in Geneva, Ray Holmes considered it necessary to keep the group alive. In any case he felt sure that most were keen to know how others had fared since they last met. He therefore called another meeting and once again they would meet in the Queen's.

Those who said they would attend were Joe Delaney Joe Thomas, Jake Wint, and Jim Johnson, all who had previously attended, and there were two new additions who said they would like to come along, these were David Tibble and Tom Wright.

All duly arrived at the Queen's and once again each were asked to tell what had happened since the last meeting, or if new to the meeting what had happened to them since they had left WECO.

Joe Thomas still had not found work after what was now nearly five years. Joe could not understand why he alone had not managed to find anything but the truth was that his degree of skill was only required by fairly large companies, most of whom had for some time used the telephone number that would tell them whether the person concerned was a communist, and poor Joe was now paying for his politics. Ray knew Joe to be an honest, hardworking individual but he had unwisely made it known to all and sundry that he wanted England to have the same type of government as that of the Soviet Union.

"Why don't you try something completely different, Joe?" Ray said. "I don't think you stand a chance applying for the type of work you were doing."

"I was bloody good at what I did – why do you think I can't get anywhere?"

"To put it bluntly – I imagine you've been blacklisted."

Ray felt uncomfortable having to say this but it was time he was told or the poor man would never get any more work and he was still in his fifties and had a good few years to go before retirement.

"What do you mean? What makes you say that?" Joe asked.

Ray then told him, without revealing how firms got their information, that his politics and strike record were generally known and available to those interested. Joe was visibly shaken and protested that he had always worked hard and that not once had he called his men out without good reason. Ray agreed but said it was the only answer to his complete lack of success in getting employment when he was such a skilled worker.

The others present, not knowing the source of Ray's information, laughingly wondered which of them had equally been blacklisted.

Jim Johnson had long since given up looking for work – age was definitely against him and he was now living on his old-age pension and some government assistance. "If the government hadn't allowed the takeover to go the way it did I would still be working today, and I'd be paying tax and not having to ask for government assistance. It's crazy," he added.

David Tibble had suffered in an unusual way. He decided soon after he could see he was having no luck to try what he had often wished he could do. He would try his hand at farming. Within three months of searching for a suitable business he had found a smallholding which looked to his inexperienced eye just the job. However, although breaking even in the first year things began to go terribly wrong soon after and the writing was on the wall – the subsidies he had reckoned on were not forthcoming and he realised that it was virtually impossible to make a profit from the operation he had set himself. He had managed finally to dispose of the land to a big landowner nearby but the price he obtained was much less than he had paid and this, together with the money he had paid out to the previous small holder plus the losses sustained in trading, had meant that he was virtually bankrupt. He was, however, still a chemist and by all accounts a good chemist but being well over forty he would not find it easy to find employment. He told the meeting that he had written for half a dozen vacancies but to date had had no success at getting an interview.

Joe Tooley was still working at Heathrow for one of the smaller airlines and Jake Wint, smiling as always, had continued working for the company who had employed him soon after he had been made redundant – but, as he said, at a ridiculous salary and a journey that took him nearly two hours each way.

Tom Wright, who previously had worked for David Tibble in WECO, had also been forced to give up looking for employment as a chemist and instead had found a position in a well-known charitable organisation. Not a terribly well-paid job but one which Ray believed suited the man who, by nature, was a caring man and a local lay preacher.

All present at the meeting added their own particular story and at the same time told other stories of those they knew about who were not present.

Of course not all the meeting was gloom and doom – how could it be with Jake Wint present? – but the meeting showed a cross section of the tragedy caused by what the papers would simply report as a takeover. The only person they knew of who had improved his life had been Tom Delaney, who all knew had built up a successful small business from his love of nature and the countryside.

Ray Holmes reported to the meeting that Tony Bentley, although working for Steinberg, had promised he would help wherever possible to bring about rules that would not only govern takeovers from the share point of view but from the point of view of the effect on the economy and above all how such a takeover would affect the employees of the victim company. He asked those present to think about what should be included in a code of conduct which it was hoped the group would draw up for presentation to any MP interested in employee rights and the economy of the country. Any ideas, he said, should be written down and sent to his home address, which he then gave them.

They agreed to meet in six months' time.

LXI

Mickey O'Brien looked forward to his annual visit to Vegas, partly because he enjoyed trains and although there were now faster ways of getting there he chose to travel by train. However, since the virtual demise of many of the crack trains of the thirties and forties his journey was long and slow. Mickey did not seem to mind at all, he just loved railways.

It was thus three days before his journey ended and he entered the unreal world of Las Vegas. Of course over the last twenty years this town had changed beyond belief – and now in the seventies Las Vegas had become one of the fastest growing tourist towns. Whilst previously it had been a place for the glamorous and wealthy of Los Angeles, it now catered for those with less wealth.

Mickey had to attend the usual meeting of those who had control of gambling throughout North America, a meeting which on the surface was friendly but which underneath often hid much animosity. He was loosely tied up with Peter Bronson and thus he first called Bronson and arranged to meet him on the day before the meeting. Mickey could not decide whether to mention the meeting with MacDonald but decided in the end to play it by ear, if the proper opportunity arose he would bring it forth.

"What's the situation in Queens?" Bronson asked.

Mickey had known that he would be asked this question since they had had some trouble with certain of the local operators whom he had managed to deal with to everyone's satisfaction.

"It's OK now, Pete – I sorted out that bastard Italian kid – I think he'll stay in line in the future."

"What's his old man have to say about it? You teaching him a lesson?"

"He ain't got an old man, his ma brought him up," Mickey replied.

Bronson's attitude changed almost immediately and he said, "Take it easy on the kid – I don't want that he should be hurt any more."

"Whatever you say, Pete, but I think he knows now who is the boss."

Bronson could not help but think of his own childhood and how difficult it was for his ma to bring him up. "How's his old lady managing?"

"I guess she finds it tough but the kid should soon be able to bring in some dough to help – if he does as he is told," Mickey said.

"Give the old lady a couple of grand from me," Bronson added.

"Sure, Pete, but why?"

"I never knew my old man and my ma struggled to keep me – I spent three years in the Pen trying to get some money to help her – I should not want it should happen to another young kid."

This was the opening Mickey had been waiting for, it was as if someone had planned he should say it.

"Strange you should say that, Pete, someone was asking recently if you had ever found your old man."

"Yeah, I found him but he was dead – never knew him though – he left my ma before I was born. Neighbours told me he had left her because he believed he was not the father. It's always bothered me, I'm still not sure that the guy I found was my true pa although he's the one on my birth certificate."

"Guess you done all right though, Pete, without knowing your old man – couldn't have done much better for yourself, I reckon," Mickey said.

"It's difficult to explain, you feel cheated – I suppose it's possible my true old man never knew I was born – Ma never let on, said she'd tell me all about it when I was twenty-one – she died before then and I was still in the Pen. Guess I'll never know the truth now." Bronson paused, thinking back to his childhood, he could see his mother scrubbing the step at the front of their little terraced home and he could see the kids playing baseball in the street outside his house. Suddenly he was aware of Mickey O'Brien looking at him and it brought him back to the present.

"What was that you said about a guy asking whether I ever found my old man?" Mickey was not a good liar and knew it, he realised that he would now have to came clean and give at least part of the story to Bronson. "An old buddy of mine I hadn't seen for some years was sent by Marty Goldstein – you know Marty, did a job for us once way back – to see me. It seems someone had asked this guy if he knew if you had found your old man – I suggested that someone was trying to muscle in on your money but Mac, that's my buddy, said the guy was already loaded. He said it was an old guy who it seems knew your ma one time and learning that her old man had left her before you were born wondered if you had ever met him. That's all it was, Pete."

"This Mac, did he say who the guy was?"

"No, he seemed to want to keep it close – I myself wondered who the old guy might have been."

"Christ, Mickey, I've always wondered about my old man, didn't you know? You should have found out more – this old guy could be the reason my old man left my ma."

"You know me, Pete, I don't poke my nose in other people's business. I sure didn't know whether you had a pa or not. One of the guys in the room at the time said he knew you had looked for him – that was the first time I knew about it."

LXII

Ted Wilson and his wife went down to breakfast quite early, but already seated at the table next to them were a middle-aged couple who greeted them as they entered the small dining room.

"Good morning – it is a lovely spring morning," the female of the couple said. She was a lady in her fifties, who spoke with a southern accent that Ted recognised from films he had seen at the cinema and on television; the gentlemen with her had a rather flash bow tie and sported a grey moustache.

"Yes, we were thinking the same," Alice replied.

"I think you must be from England but I don't quite recognise the accent."

"Yes we're from England, our home is in Yorkshire – I think we know you come from one of the southern states – I've heard people speak as you do in lots of films," Ted said.

"My, fancy you recognising the way we talk and coming from all that way from South Carolina. Yes we live in Charleston. We had heard such a lot about New England that we thought we would come up and see what those Yankees have to offer. It sure is nice. I guess you folks are up here an holiday – are you staying long?" the man said.

"We're not sure – it all depends, if we like a place we will stay a while," Alice answered.

"We heard there were some interesting places to see around here and we'll certainly stay to see those. My wife likes looking at country houses but I understand there is not much, if any, of that sort of thing over here – not like back home. I'm told there are some fine houses to be seen but since people arc living in them there is not much chance to see any unless invited," Ted added.

"Have you heard of Julius Steinberg?" the southern lady asked.

"Yes, the proprietor was telling us about him last evening – I believe he has a rather grand house near here. My wife and I were going to try to see what we could of it. Mr Ramsden has told us that you get a good view of the house and the grounds from Hanover Heights which is close by the lake – we'll probably go along there this morning."

The southern lady looked at her companion and spoke to him in a quiet voice before turning to the Wilsons, and said, "My husband, Cyrus, is a business acquaintance of Julius Steinberg and we came here particularly to see where he lived. We were curious to see why a man with all his wealth should choose to live in such an out of the way place. It is charming of course but why he would want to spend the rest of his life in such a place is hard to understand. We thought we would call in to see him – he's not expecting us, we're not great friends of his but he did tell us to call in and see him if ever we were up this way. Cyrus is going to give him a call after breakfast and if it's all right we'll go along. Would you like to come with us – I'm sure Julius won't mind, he'll just think you are up here travelling with us."

Ted and Alice exchanged glances and could hardly believe their luck. Now they would not have to ask awkward questions and try to think of ways of gaining access. It would be a huge weight off their minds. Although Ted had not confided in his wife she knew he was worried about the whole thing. Not because he was frightened but simply because he felt obligated to do a good job for the redundants. Now, providing the new friends came up trumps, their worries would be over and they could actually enjoy the holiday. "We would love to come, it's very kind of you to think of us – by the way I'm Ted Wilson and this is my wife Alice."

"I'm Jenny Arkwright and this is my husband, Cyrus. Cyrus is in chemicals."

Cyrus asked to be excused just as the waiter brought their breakfast. "I'll only be a minute, Jenny. I'll make the call to Julius now before he gets other ideas as to how to spend his day."

He returned in a few minutes and announced that he had fixed it. "Julius says he'll even give us a cup of coffee. I told him our guests liked looking over swell houses and he said he would get someone to show us all around, if that's what we would like."

"Where shall we meet you and at what time?" Ted asked.

"Meet us in reception at ten o'clock, I'll get directions from the hotel manager and we ought to be there in good time for coffee."

LXIII

Joe Miller's wife just knew her husband was getting along fine. He never now seemed to mention Steinberg or Arkansas Oil and on his return from his daily visits to the library he was generally smiling and seemed to be more settled with his position. He continued to write letters but he was becoming more and more obsessed with the way they had been written. His morning routine consisted of a slow walk down to the town centre and after looking at a few of the shops but buying nothing he would enter the library and seat himself in a familiar chair next to the same table. If others were occupying "his" chair he would look at them as if they should know it was really his and that he had only been gone for a few minutes and they should not be so inconsiderate.

After seating himself he would take all the newspapers he could get his hands on and go through the job vacancy columns carefully, making notes and writing down addresses. This routine over, he would leave the library and make his way back to his home where he would sit down and write his letters of application. Of course he knew he would not get an interview or a job but he was interested in how they replied. He had, he thought, become an expert on the way letters should be written and indeed additionally wrote critical letters to those who he believed needed to be told how their letter was wrong.

Unfortunately, he did from time to time find himself becoming giddy but he tried to avoid telling his wife as he knew it would worry her. Sometimes, he had difficulty in getting out of bed as the room began to revolve around him. However, he did not let these spells of giddiness interfere with his work of correcting letters. He had told many of his less fortunate employment consultants or prospective employers in no uncertain terms that we are here in our houses waiting for your letters and it is important that you know how to write.

It was when these thoughts came to Joe's mind that he would suddenly feel strange, almost as if he was not there and in a dream. A few moments later and he would feel giddy and try to stand but unless he put his legs wide apart he knew he would fall. This was Steinberg's fault, he said to himself one day – he never gave me a letter when I left, perhaps it was necessary to teach him how to write real letters – Joe smiled, he would have to do something about it. Now, where was it the man lived – Joe thought hard but the name would not come to him – perhaps the doctor would know, he would ask him.

He got up from his chair and was about to walk out of the library when he was greeted by a neighbour. "Hullo Joe – how you feeling now? Bessy tells me you've been a lot better lately. Got to look after yourself. Remember me to your family."

Joe stopped as soon as the neighbour spoke, he listened to what the man said and then said, "No one seems to know how to write nowadays – goddam it, when I was young we learnt how to be polite in letters but today all them manners we learnt are gone. Did you know Steinberg, Mr ... I've forgotten your name."

"It's Fred, your next-door neighbour – what'sa matter, Joe, don't you feel well?"

Joe looked at the neighbour but there was obviously no recognition – here comes the giddiness, Joe said to himself, why does the room go round in circles? The doctor could tell me, I guess. Who did that guy say he was? Perhaps he writes bad letters too. Why are all these people looking at me? Joe steadied himself against the bookshelf next to him and slowly slid to the floor. He was still conscious.

He heard someone say, "Get an ambulance, someone's fainted," and then the giddiness disappeared and he slowly rose to his feet.

"Why, hullo, Fred, what are you doing here, I didn't know you read books," Joe jokingly said to the worried man close by. What's all the panic, someone in trouble?" Joe continued as if he was unaware of what had just happened.

The call had not been put through for the ambulance and as Joe now seemed to be quite OK, no one thought an ambulance necessary.

"Do you mind if I walk along with you, Joe? You acted a bit strange in there. You sure you're OK?"

Fred walked along with Joe to his home and left him at his gate. A few minutes later Fred was relating to his wife what had happened. "I got worried when he obviously did not know me – asked me about someone with a Jewish sounding name – I've never heard of him. I think Joe must have had some sort of attack – perhaps we should tell Joan."

His wife was standing behind the ironing board and deftly ironed a shirt before replying.

"I'll have a word with Joan when I see her – but I mustn't worry her. She was only telling me the other day how well Joe was getting along. The poor dear has had a lot to put up with what with Joe not finding a job, then getting mugged in Miami, and now this. I hope Joe will soon be well."

LXIV

For MacDonald it was the usual type of day – Julius telephoning about five times in the morning with instructions to do those things that become part of the job of a senior person's right-hand man. Then there was that phone call from Las Vegas.

"It's Mickey O'Brien, Mac – I'm in Vegas and I've just seen Bronson. He wants to see you, Mac."

"Jesus, Mickey, what have you been telling him?" Mac said.

"I'm sorry that it happened this way, I had no idea he was so keen to know about his old man – it seems he has suspected all along that the man on his birth certificate might not be his father and now with this opening he can't wait to know about the guy you told me about."

Mac was not sure what to say – he should have known that once he started asking about Peter Bronson he could be stirring up a hornet's nest.

"I gotta level with you, Mickey. The guy who was supposed to be asking about Peter Bronson doesn't even know of the existence of him. It's purely guesswork on someone's part who knows this guy. It seems this guy mentioned a dame he knew way back and we know that he met her once after she had married. Someone I know thought it would be nice for the old boy if he located the dame for him, and without saying anything about it to him started making enquiries. In these enquiries he discovered that it was rumoured that the husband left before a baby was born because he believed it was not his. The enquirer also found out that the old guy he knew had met the dame several months before the babe was born – and, well, he put two and two together, but really it is purely guessing and he's sure the old guy knew nothing about it."

"OK, Mac, I understand and I'll pass the information on to Bronson but I know he's going to want to know who the old guy is, so you better make sure the one who told you better make up his mind to spill the beans – Pete Bronson isn't a guy to mess with. I'll be in touch."

Mac wished he had never got involved – he could end up losing his job. Why had he allowed himself to get caught up in this? He called out for his secretary. "Julie, as soon as you can get hold of Joe Mancini, get him to come and see me or if he is still up in Primrose get him to give me a ring when the boss is not around. I've got to speak to him without Julius knowing."

LXV

Lee Crocket, after collecting his pay in Houston, went around the employment agencies to see what jobs were on offer. He soon realised that there were many men in a similar position and that there was no doubt his age would work against him. Oil from the Gulf was still flowing but there was a surfeit of gangs looking for work and Lee knew he would be wasting his time to stay. The only work on offer was overseas on rigs being built for further North Sea exploration. He decided he would return home to Memphis.

Before leaving, however, he went around to see Kevan Brown, who had been his deputy for the last ten years. Kevan lived with his wife and two young children in a nice apartment in the suburbs. The children were at school and Kevan's wife was just leaving to collect them when Lee arrived. "Why, hullo, Lee, didn't expect to see you, Kevan's inside, probably watching TV. I'm off to meet the kids – be back soon."

"Nice to see you, Betty – I'm not stopping long, I'm going back to Memphis."

"Oh, that's too bad – we'll miss you – hope you're still here when we get back. Walk in, the door's open."

Lee did just that after pressing the bell. Kevan had got up from his seat in front of the TV when Lee tapped on the kitchen door and entered.

"Hullo, Lee, what can I do for you?"

"I'm going back home – there's nothing around here for me. I'm too old."

"Have a seat, Lee – goddam it, you too old? Not on your life, there's plenty of mileage left in you yet – you shouldn't think like that."

Kevan walked to the refrigerator. "Can I get you a beer? Here you are, I got one of your favourites – catch." The can was hurled across the room and the seated Lee deftly caught it in one hand over his head.

"I see you haven't lost your touch as catcher – you too old, that's nonsense."

"Well, I tried a few agencies but I could see they just didn't want to know. I'm not going to stick around where I know I'm not wanted – there are too many young guys out there looking for work. How you getting along?"

Kevan, opening a beer for himself, took a big swig before he answered. "I've had no luck so far – there's not a lot going at this time, but I shall get something before long. I got fifteen years on my side so they can't say I'm too old. Still, I guess I'll be lucky to get the same sort of job as I had with Turners – those jobs don't grow on trees."

Turners had been good employers and both Lee Crocker and Kevan Brown had been very well satisfied with their lot and had been devastated when old man Turner had decided he could carry on no longer.

Lee nodded agreement. "Yeah, we worked hard but it was a good job. You know, I just couldn't understand why we hadn't hit oil – I was sure everything was right for there to be plenty. I guess I was wrong but it was the first time in twenty years."

"No one has proved you wrong, Turner just ran out of money. I understand the new owners are going to move the rig – anyway, as you know, they've stopped work on it for the time being. So we'll never know if you were right or not. You know that Portuguese who works on the Texaco rig?" Lee nodded. "Well, he's going to keep a watch on where they move the rig – he lives just round the corner from here – his kids play with mine too."

"Not much use to us now – it's too late."

Lee and Kevan carried on with their talk on the job situation and whether there was oil and to where the rig would be moved. Soon Betty and the children came home and Lee took his leave, saying he would keep in touch.

LXVI

Ted Wilson and his wife were in reception at the hotel just before ten and were joined shortly after by Cyrus Arkwright and wife, who suggested they all go in their car to the Steinberg's.

Jake Ramsden was pleased to give detailed instructions as to how to get to the house, which it turned out was a little over a mile from the hotel. Ted took note of the high brick wall surrounding the property and that there were two gates along the road. The first, Jake had told them, was not the main entrance and led directly to the back of the house which he had been up to during construction. The second gate was most impressive and was locked. Cyrus got out of the car and pressed the bell and a female voice asked who it was. "Cyrus Arkwright to see Mr Steinberg," Cyrus announced in his deep southern accent.

Almost immediately the gates began to open and they were soon driving along a wide gravelled road which curved between rhododendron bushes for about a quarter of a mile until the house came into view.

"I could imagine I was driving up to see some old friends down south. There unfortunately aren't too many left like this but there are a few," Cyrus said, as they approached the house built in the colonial style. "Mind you the ones I know down south don't look so new as this one – it looks as if it was a part of a set from *Gone with the Wind*," he continued. They were met at the entrance by the housekeeper and taken inside and into a grand drawing room overlooking a wide patio with grounds falling away towards the lake in the distance, on the other side of which were hills rising to about a thousand feet. It was a most beautiful vista and all the visitors were so enchanted by the view through the enormous doors that they almost forgot to notice their host standing by the open fireplace, above which was a huge painting depicting a landscape of similar dimensions to that through the glass doors.

"How are you, Julius? You're looking well – what a beautiful view – it's fabulous. You know Jenny, and these are two friends of ours from England, Ted Wilson and his wife Alice, they're from a place called Yorkshire and they would be most interested, as indeed we are, to see your wonderful house."

Steinberg, who had only entertained guests in an evening when it was dark, was pleased the view from his drawing room had impressed his visitors. "I'll be pleased to get my housekeeper to show you around after we've had a cup of coffee. How is business, Cyrus?"

The conversation over coffee was friendly and Cyrus and his wife brought Ted and Alice into the conversation as much as possible. After about half an hour Steinberg called his housekeeper and asked her to take his guests on a tour of the building and grounds.

Downstairs, apart from the wonderful drawing room, there was a dining room with a table that could seat about twenty guests, two studies and a superb kitchen with quarters for staff adjoining. The entrance hall, which was entered from the front by two sets of doors, was spacious with a wide staircase sweeping to the floor above, where, they were told, there were nine bedrooms, each en suite. Four of the bedrooms overlooked the rear gardens, having balconies wide enough to comfortably seat four persons. The huge patio with numerous pot plants led down to a beautifully-kept lawn by means of fifteen wide steps. Around the patio was a finely-built decorative wall about two feet high, on which stood a number of neo-classical figures.

Ted Wilson mentally noted all that they were told about the place and since he and wife had previously decided that they would both try and draw a plan of the building when they returned to the hotel, they both could be seen taking in everything they were told.

Alice, who had visited a number of stately homes back home, could not help but mentally make comparisons. There was of course really no comparison, for not only was this house small compared with old English mansions but it was so new. Nevertheless, she thought it lovely and certainly the aspect from the drawing room was as good as anything she had seen. Yes, she had not only enjoyed the tour but would love to have lived there, which is more than she could say for any of those magnificent homes she had visited in England.

The tour complete, they returned to say their farewells to the owner and congratulate him on having the vision to build such a lovely house.

"I only wish my father could have seen this place – if you had seen the place I was brought up in! I can hardly believe I was ever in such a hovel; it's like a dream. Then, my father was an immigrant and he never earned much money when he was in work and later none after becoming ill from working below water on the Brooklyn Bridge construction. He died soon after I was born, some eight years after the bridge was opened. My mother brought me up and earned money by taking in washing from houses out of our neighbourhood – she used to carry the washing on an old baby carriage and when I was old enough I had to help do it with her. She could never have imagined a place like this."

The guests listened with interest to this man telling of the hard childhood. The two southerners were inwardly not impressed. They had both been brought up in families with an aristocratic background – families that had suffered terribly during the civil war but had managed by the time these two were born to have returned almost to the status they had reached before that war. They, unfortunately, due to their upbringing, still found it difficult to recognise inwardly those who had came from humble backgrounds. It was likely that they believed that no one could have risen to such wealth in so relatively short a time without having done something that in the best circles would have been frowned upon. In the case of Steinberg, they were not far from wrong although they had really never given it any thought as to how he had made his money; all they believed was that quick wealth came from no good.

On the other hand, Ted and Alice, who themselves had come from humble backgrounds – although unlike Steinberg had not made it to the top – were impressed with what he had achieved and listening to the hard life he had had as a child began to soften the feelings they had built up against him over the past years since Ted lost his job.

Steinberg, when asked by Cyrus why he had come to Primrose, even told them of the lady he had met in the First World War and how he had returned to find she had married. This again drew sympathy from Alice, who was a bit of a romantic.

They left the house after having been there about two hours and returned to the Lake Hotel. Ted and Alice on getting to their room decided they should both have a try at sketching plans independently and then comparing them to see how they differed.

When they compared them they were pleased to see that both agreed on the main points. Both had drawn the patio roughly to scale and noted the number of steps down to the lawn. They had also put in balconies and noted the two sets of doors at the main entrance. All in all they were sure the redundants would be well pleased with their work even if they wondered what on earth use it would be to them in the end.

LXVII

It is surprising how quickly one learns when one has an incentive to learn. Abe Slyberger, although inwardly having doubts as to whether he could possibly succeed in getting the elevator to fall and with Steinberg inside, nevertheless pressed on with gaining more and more information on elevators. He even got a book out from a library and was amazed at how much there was to be learnt. He now knew all the safety measures on the Brooklyn office elevator and knew that he could, in theory, eliminate them, given the time and access to the machinery. However, how to gain access bothered him and even if he did, how could he cope with the other things he might be required to do... could he climb on top of the cage or underneath if necessary, or would he be too big to get through the trap-doors or agile enough to hang on whilst working, or would it only be necessary to get to the engine housing on the roof? He finally resolved to try and restrict his activities to the engine house and from then on concentrated his studies to the elevator mechanism in this area. Having acquired what he considered was an adequate knowledge of how he could eliminate the safety devices in this area, he was ready to go into action.

He decided he would have to pretend to be an engineer from the elevator company and should therefore dress accordingly.

Thus, on a fine bright Monday in May '76 he left his home as an elevator engineer bound for the Brooklyn office of Julius Steinberg. He had determined the day before that Steinberg would be in the office on this day and thus it was just possible if he could make the necessary changes that before the day was out the elevator would fall to the floor with Steinberg inside. He took public transport to Brooklyn and arrived there at 7 a.m., which he thought would be a good time for engineers to start work, well before office staff were due to arrive.

As expected the main office door was locked but he knew there would be a side door open, which was used by the office cleaners. He walked round to the side of the building, down a small passageway, carrying his bag of tools and found the door there unlocked. He entered, made his way to the staff elevator, opened the cage door, got inside and made his way to the top floor. He then located and climbed the iron staircase to the roof and walked over to the small building housing the elevator mechanism. His heart sank when he saw the lock on the door and realised that he had quite forgotten that the door was probably locked. He tried the handle and much to his relief it opened. He remembered, when young, he and another man had had to go into one of these elevator buildings in order to wind down an elevator car which had got stuck between floors. The mechanism he had seen in the books, and when young, came to life before his eyes – he knew where most parts were located and with the aid of his tools was able to release the Steinberg elevator from the safety controls. The elevator would continue to work but after a few uses would suddenly slip and fall to the ground.

There was nothing further he could do and so he climbed back down from the roof and walked down the stairs to the ground floor. He left the building at 8 a.m. and had only been seen by one cleaning lady, who he passed on the sixth floor. He took public transport back to his home, changed into his usual office wear and drove his car to his office where he arrived at nine thirty. All he could do now was wait.

LXVIII

Joan Miller was disturbed when her next-door neighbour Bessie told her about the episode at the library. Although she had believed Joe was better, not continually getting depressed over losing his job and not being able to find any suitable work, she had once or twice felt a little concerned over the giddiness her husband experienced from time to time. She had been told by the doctor that the giddiness was not uncommon in older people but that it was possible the blow on the head when he had been mugged had made things worse – but he also wondered whether Joe had been worrying a good deal. Joan had repeated the story she knew she had told him a few years back and said that this was obviously the main source of worry. Now his collapse at the library made things worse and she began to wonder what might happen next.

"Fred said he just didn't know him – he collapsed and then suddenly was quite normal and didn't even know he had collapsed. Fred said it was weird," Bessie said again, to emphasise the point.

"He hasn't done that before – at least not that I know. It's worrying. It all started when his company was taken over by that awful man, Julius Steinberg. I really thought Joe was going to do the man some harm at one time, he was so angry. Thankfully he seems to have calmed down over the past few years. Imagine, it's years now that he has been seeking work – the time just flies," Joan said.

"I can't advise you what to do but I do think you should get Joe to go and see his doctor again – collapsing in the street could be quite dangerous. It's almost as if he were becoming epileptic." Bessie was the ordinary type of neighbour, it took a lot for her to even tell Joan about what had happened and to advise took extra courage from this quiet lady.

"Thanks for the advice, I think you are right but it's not going to be easy to get Joe to go and he'll not necessarily tell the whole story. I reckon I should have a word with the doctor before he goes – Joe will never know."

LXIX

Mickey O'Brien was an important man to those who operated with him in the Bronx and Harlem districts of New York. However, he knew his limitations and on a countrywide basis he was small-time whereas Bronson was respected all over. Although Mickey feared no one, he was not going to jeopardise his operation in order to cover for an old and really long-forgotten acquaintance. Peter Bronson was a big man and Mickey knew that he could so easily upset the whole works for him if he felt he had been crossed. Mickey would certainly come clean on all he knew – which really wasn't much, but once he had given Bronson Mac's telephone number he would feel more secure. Mac may be stubborn about revealing who the old guy was but he would warn him that in everyone's interest he should spill the beans.

Bronson was alone when Mickey arrived at the Bronson hotel suite. "What news you got, Mickey? Have you found out where your buddy can be contacted?"

"Yeah, Pete, I've written down his work telephone number," Mickey said, passing over a piece of paper. "He travels around some of the time but is mostly found on that number in New York. Remember he says it's someone else who told him they knew someone who wanted to know if Peter Bronson had ever found his old man."

Mickey was pleased to get this off his chest but was apprehensive in case Bronson would not believe his story. however, it seems he must have convinced him for the time being at least.

"It's four o'clock now, I'll try New York but I bet the sonofabitch will have gone home by now – still he might be there."

He dialled the number and waited – Mickey stood by the window, wishing he had had the good sense not to have got himself involved in the first place.

"Who is that I'm speaking to? You got a guy named MacDonald on this number?" Bronson said impatiently. "What do you mean he's just had an accident – where is he? What's that, he is being taken to hospital? – OK, I'll ring tomorrow." Bronson put the telephone down angrily. "Have you been telling him what to say, Mickey, when I rang – they say he's in hospital – had an accident in the building. Are they pulling a fast one?"

"I shouldn't think so, Pete, if they say he's had an accident then I guess we better believe it – you'll soon find out tomorrow – you could always ring the hospital," Mickey said, hopeful that this would satisfy Bronson for today.

LXX

Steinberg sat in an easy chair, looking out across the patio and lawns to the lake and the mountains beyond. He had just said farewell to Cyrus Arkwright and companions – he was thinking back to when he was young. He had never seen anything so beautiful; he wondered whether his father and mother had ever seen anything like this. Perhaps they did in the old country, he said out loud, they certainly would not have seen anything after they came to live in America. There were no lakes like this one in New York – there was of course the East River and on the other side of New York he had been told when a kid that there was the Hudson, but until he left school he had never seen it. You stayed in your neighbourhood and you worked all hours – most of the kids where he lived had parents who worked in making clothes. The conditions in the factories, which were mostly tenement buildings, were dreadful and the pay very small – his mother had worked in one of these sweatshops for ten hours each day but when his old man got that job on the new bridge over the East River they had believed they would now be better off than most. Then his dad became ill… and then there was the washing his poor mother had to cope with… Steinberg stopped in his thoughts and gripped the side of his chair. Those bastards who employed him never helped – Papa was not the only one, he said to himself. You have got to be hard because people tread on you if you are soft. This had been his philosophy throughout his life and many had suffered on this count. He was a bitter man, who had never quite forgotten his childhood and wanted to make sure that society paid for the way they treated his parents. There was no one to tell him that there were good people in the world, no one dared tell Julius anything once he had became powerful and wealthy. He was, however, a different man whilst in Primrose. He had found a sort of peace – he was lonely but he never really thought of being lonely, he mostly kept busy by keeping in touch with his offices throughout the States and then there were those visits overseas where people now respected him. He had come a long way and been everywhere but somehow Primrose was the place he realised so late in his life that he liked the best. Maybe it was Zoë, he thought, that had made him like it so much, maybe it was a desire to capture his youth once more. His youth, when he had been accepted as a man by those he had met in the army – some had made uncomplimentary remarks about him being Jewish but they soon changed their tune when he had entered the army boxing tournament and came out winner of his weight – they then nicknamed him Caesar. He smiled to himself, Julius Caesar, yes, he was happy in the army, people were better there than when they got into civvy street. He was awakened from his reverie by the housekeeper entering the room.

"Your tea here, Mr Steinberg."

"Thanks, Molly. You ever been to England, Molly?"

"No, Mr Steinberg, I haven't been very far from here. I did go to Buffalo by train from New York once – that's the furthest I've been in my life. Never wanted to travel really. Why did you ask me if I had been to England?"

"Oh, it was only the connection with tea, great tea drinkers the English. That's where I got the idea of tea when I went over in '17 before we were shipped over to France."

"I didn't know you were ever in the army, Mr Steinberg."

"Oh yes, I was in the army for a while – as a matter of fact that's how I come to live here. I was stationed right over that hill. Was there for two months learning to be a soldier. Came over to Primrose a couple of times and fell in love with the place."

"Sounds strange to me, falling in love with a place – you sure there wasn't a girl in it? Oh, forgive me, I shouldn't have said that."

"That's all right, Molly – you're not so far from the truth. I was young then of course – and quite good-looking, though I say it meself. I came back after the war to find her but she had got herself married."

"Oh, that's too bad. Have you ever seen her since?" Molly asked.

Steinberg got out of his chair and walked across to the window and stared out into the distance. Molly moved as if to go to the door, then he spoke. "Yes, I did see her again when she told me she was married and then I saw her just once some years later."

Molly, who had never heard her boss speak about his personal feelings before, sensed that the man wanted to talk and so she stayed, when she could, at that moment, have left the room.

"How was that, Mr Steinberg?"

"Well, when she told me she was married I thought she still liked me and I wanted to meet her again so I persuaded her to meet me in the same place on the same day four years later, in case things were different. Neither of us knew if we would be there but we both turned up for the meeting and spent a lovely afternoon together.

"That was the last time I saw her – it was 23rd April, which I learnt later was the birthday of William Shakespeare. Whenever I see or hear a mention of Shakespeare I always have an image of Zoë – that was her name."

"That sounds very romantic, Mr Steinberg, but also very sad – I wonder what happened to her. Did you ever find out?"

"No, I never did. I got married and led my own life and the only time I was unfaithful to my wife was when I went up to Primrose and met that girl for our long-arranged date. I guess she would be old now, or perhaps even dead."

"Haven't you ever tried to find out, Mr Steinberg? It's such a pity and you living up here all these years – shame on you."

Molly was amazed at her boldness in speaking to this man in the way she had but Steinberg did not appear to mind. "Sure, I've thought about it once or twice but that was another world over half a century ago – it wouldn't do anyone any good to open up the past. It was so long ago it is almost as if it had never happened – perhaps it didn't. Thank you for the tea, Molly."

"Would you mind if I tried to locate the lady, Mr Steinberg? If she were a local lass, I'm sure someone will know something. Zoë, you said, wasn't it? What was her second name?"

Steinberg hesitated before speaking. Inwardly he wanted to know but yet he was afraid. Afraid of what she may think if she saw him now. Afraid that he would not like what he saw; afraid that his memories of years ago would be lost to him forever.

"I cannot remember her second name – I know it reminded me of a town but which one I have no idea. I guess you can try and find out but I trust you will not mention my name. Let me know if you find anything about her."

Molly had lived in the area all her life although not in Primrose, however, she nevertheless knew many people from the town and she would make some discreet enquiries.

LXXI

The Steinberg elevator going direct to his office on the twelfth floor was supposed to be for Steinberg's use only, since its door opened directly into the office. It was kept locked and only Steinberg, his secretary and MacDonald had keys. The latter would never use it if it were known the great man was in the office, in fact it was only occasionally used by the secretary when she was in his office and when he wanted her to get something from downstairs urgently.

MacDonald always used the other elevators down the corridor when going up to the twelfth, not because he was afraid to use it but simply because he could not be bothered to find his key and unlock the cage.

Steinberg had not been to New York for some weeks, he was too settled in his house in Primrose. However, there were the daily calls to his secretary in Brooklyn and often calls to Mac or other close associates either in their offices or more often than not at ungodly hours to their homes. One such call to Mac one May evening required him to return to the office that evening and collect a small package and forward it immediately to a company in Jersey City. Steinberg was insistent that it be delivered personally that night – it was in fact a birthday present he had purchased some weeks earlier whilst down in Miami – it was for his late wife's favourite niece, who Steinberg had helped from time to time – she was a lady in her fifties but it had become almost a ritual to remember her birthday and to send a small gift. It was in fact the only birthday he ever remembered, but this time he had forgotten to ask his secretary to post the package for him and it was only while in his favourite chair in the lounge at Primrose that it suddenly came to him that it was 12th May and the birthday of his niece.

Mac could have wished Steinberg somewhere else – fancy having to return to New York this time of night and then drive over to Jersey City and then all the way back to Bay Shore on Long Island.

He arrived at the Brooklyn Office at eight o'clock and unlocked the front office door and went down the corridor to the staff elevators and thus up to the twelfth floor and back to the Steinberg office. He soon found the package and seeing the Steinberg personal elevator cage door open and knowing he had the key for exit on the same key ring as that key which had opened the front door, he went inside, closed the cage door and pressed the button to descend. The cage started and then fell away, being brought to a sudden halt which shot Mac to the roof and knocked him unconscious. He was found next morning by the early morning cleaners and as soon as the fire brigade could move the elevator and prise open the cage doors he was taken to the nearest hospital. The package he had been carrying in his hand was later found and handed to Steinberg's secretary, who, after speaking to Steinberg, had it delivered and an explanation given to the lady as to why the present had not been delivered on her birthday.

Mac had received concussion, a broken arm and abrasions to his legs. He would be in hospital for about two weeks.

LXXII

Ted Wilson and his wife returned to the UK at the end of April and soon after arriving home Ted contacted Ray Holmes. The latter arranged to drive up to Sheffield and they met at Ted's house on the second Saturday in May.

"We were lucky," Ted told him and then proceeded to relate the meeting with the couple from Charleston and how they had been shown over the Steinberg mansion. Ted produced the sketches he and his wife had made of the house and additionally gave a drawing showing what they considered was the extent of the estate showing the lakeside and entrances from the road from Primrose.

"There didn't appear to be any guard dogs and I would guess the easiest access to the building would be from the lake and then up on the patio with a not-too-difficult climb to any of four balconies outside the bedrooms. But really I cannot see any of our people doing such a thing and in any case we were agreeably surprised by the man himself. We had built up an image of a real nasty piece of work but found to the contrary that he was a solitary individual who had had a humble upbringing and had worked hard all his life. He was not at all the man we had envisaged." Ted was clearly not of the same opinion as he had been before he had left for America and seemed to have forgotten the hardship the man had caused to himself and his family.

"I can see your feelings towards Steinberg arc different from those you had before you went to America," Ray replied, "but you have to remember that although he may seem a nice guy he appears to have no scruples in the way he operates. He has caused enough trouble for us ex-WECO employees and we know we are not alone. There must be scores of others throughout the States and elsewhere who curse the name of Steinberg. He has to be stopped and if we could stop him without injuring him I would myself be most happy – I certainly have no wish to do the man physical injury – but how else do we stop such people operating? I am sure many of the same type of people give the impression of being nice respectable people – some of them are excellent family men. Then there were those who thought Hitler a nice man."

"Yes, I do understand – but I wish we could think of some way of scaring the living daylights out of him so that he never acted in the same way. Couldn't some warning be given, spelling out the hardships he had caused to the many people?"

"Yes, we could but in order to give specific instances we would really be disclosing who were giving the warnings," Ray replied and continued, "Our plans have not yet been made but you can be sure that we will try every way possible to stop the man without resorting to physical violence."

LXXIII

Ray Holmes returned to his home in Surrey and the following day put a call through to Geneva.

"Is that you, Tony, it's Ray."

"Hullo, Ray, to what do I owe this honour? It must be important for you to clock up your telephone bill with a long distance call."

"I thought I should let you know as soon as possible that the Wilsons are back and I went up to see them. They had a successful holiday. When are you next coming over so that we can sort out our next move?"

"Did they manage to get much information on the house?"

"They not only got some information on the house but they actually had a tour around it – I'll tell you more when I next see you."

"I was planning on coming over for a couple of days at the end of May, I'll try and push it forward a bit and let you know when I get it organised."

"How's the work going, Tony?"

"I think I'm getting it sorted out, boy but what a mess it was in – those clowns had really run it down, such a pity after all the work we put in back home – it makes me very angry. I saw Otto in Vienna, you remember Otto? He is now working for a small company and seems to be getting along – but regrets very much the demise of WECO, with whom he was associated for so many years. He too knows what unhappiness the Arkansas Oil takeover has caused. He wished to be remembered to anyone who knew him in WECO."

"Oh yes, I remember Otto – he told me when I was over there all about how he was with the German army outside Leningrad – he reckoned they could have taken it early on but for the hesitancy of the High Command. It's funny what things stick in your mind – Otto always reminds me of that."

"I'll see you later this month, Ray."

Ray would not call a meeting of the redundants at this time as it will be remembered that none other than the Wilsons and Tony knew anything about the trip to New England. The next full meeting had already been scheduled for September.

LXXIV

Steinberg, following his disclosures to Molly, had for the next few days gone about the house as in a dream. The revelation of his obvious love for Zoë had come back to him more strongly than it had at any time in recent years. He wandered in the grounds, sat by the lake in town and on one day even walked into the Lake Hotel and talked to the receptionist as if seeking company, and then walked all the way back to his house, leaving his driver sitting in the car near the lake.

But on Tuesday in the last week in May he at last got in touch with his office. Mac was out of hospital but was home on the sick list. Steinberg spoke to his secretary.

"Is there any news on Mac? When is he coming back to work?"

Ruby, who over the past several days had been catching up on filing and generally getting her untidy office shipshape, felt aggrieved that her boss had once again started to ring her. She felt this was the end of the nice quiet comfortable period she had been enjoying and she was sorry. It is of course a common trait that the less work one has to do the less one wants to do – it is like a sales assistant in a shop who having not seen a customer for hours almost resents one daring to come into her shop. "Mac's getting on fine but it'll be a couple of weeks before he is back, Mr Steinberg."

"Get Weimer to find out the latest from the Turner rig – it's about time I had a report."

"Mr Weimer is out of town – gone to Denver – I'll get Houston to give me a report and I'll be back to you as soon as possible."

Ruby contacted Houston who said they would telex a report on the following day.

LXXV

Mickey O'Brien was surprised to receive a call from Peter Bronson on the day he was due to catch the train back to New York. In fact he had packed and was waiting for his cab to take him to the station.

"I was just about to leave for the train, Pete – what can I do for you?"

"This guy Mac, I want that you should see him when you get back to New York and persuade him that I really want to see him or at least find out who the guy is who wants to know whether I found my old man. You know how to persuade him. I shall look upon it as a very helpful gesture on your part. I shall be in Vegas for the next month."

Mickey told Bronson that he understood and would certainly do his best to make Mac spill the beans or come to Vegas to talk.

Mickey was still on the telephone when the hotel porter came to advise him his cab had arrived. He left the hotel and headed for the station. The first part of his journey to New York would be ruined as he would, he knew, be thinking of how to persuade Mac to reveal who was the old boy in question.

It would take him three days to get back and he guessed that in that time he ought to be able to think of some way to make Mac come clean – he had no wish to get heavy with someone he had grown up with in the same neighbourhood.

He arrived back at Grand Central station on 27th May and went straight to his apartment and, going over to the telephone, switched on the answerphone to listen to the messages left for him. He carried on unpacking and appeared to be taking hardly any interest in the voices coming over to him until one said, "This is Spike, I got that number you wanted it's ..." Mickey had rung Spike from Kansas City on a stopover and told him he wanted Mac's telephone number, it was urgent.

Mickey played the tape back to be sure of the number and then dialled. "Arkansas Oil – Aileen speaking."

"I believe you have a Mr MacDonald working for you, can I have a word with him?" Mickey said.

"I'm sorry, Mr MacDonald is not at work today, he is off sick at home."

"I'm an old buddy of Mac from way back – we used to go to the same school together – I suppose there is no chance of you giving me his address, honey."

"I'm sorry we are not allowed to give private addresses without the permission of the person concerned. I can't even give you his telephone number. I understand he will be back at work next week, you could see him then."

Mickey was agitated; this young girl could screw it up for him. He would try another angle.

"How about you ringing him at home and telling him I want to speak to him, and if I give you my number you could ring me back and tell me what he said. How about that, honey?"

"OK, give me your number and I'll do what you say."

Mickey put the phone down and waited. Five minutes later the telephone rang and on the line was MacDonald.

"Mickey, it's Mac. I understand you want to speak to me quite urgently. What's it all about? As if I didn't know!"

"Yeah, it's Bronson, goddam it, Mac, that guy's all screwed up about his old man. He wants that you speak with him or tell him who the old guy is who was asking the questions. I'm sorry, Mac but you asked the question, you should have guessed where it might have led."

"Damn it, Mickey, it's not easy to tell you who told me. In any case the chances of the old guy being Bronson's father is pretty small, it was just a guy I know putting two and two together and probably making five."

"I understand what you say, Mac but Bronson ain't going to stop asking and I'm telling you he ain't the guy who will take kindly to being told no dice."

There was a hush on the line as Mac tried to recover his composure. He was angry, angry with himself for being so stupid as to get involved in the affair. Now he would have to reveal who it was, or at least who had told him, and then let Joe Mancini do the worrying as to whether to come clean and how.

"Are you still there, Mac?"

"Yeah, I'm still here. Give me time to make contact with the guy who told me and I'll be back."

"Bronson is not a very patient man – how long you going to be?"

"Give me forty-eight hours."

"OK, but don't let me down."

LXXVI

"Mr Steinberg, I got that report from Houston on the Turner rig – I'll fax it through to you right away."

Steinberg was still up at Primrose and had just rung his Brooklyn office to get an update on business.

He had been thinking a good deal about times gone by. It was not something he did very often, in fact it was usually only when making an after dinner speech that he referred to his early past and he did this without any nostalgia but simply to impress others with the way he had climbed and became so successful. Now it was different. Somehow, things always seemed different when up in Primrose and since revealing some of his past to Molly, the housekeeper, he had thought a great deal, more than he could ever recall in the past. It was not only the thoughts of Zoë and his period in the army but he found his mind wandering to other parts of his life and he remembered faces of people he had met and people he had sacked. However, his thoughts of his past except for those early years were not pleasant thoughts. He began to question for the first time some of the things he had done and tried hard to convince himself that he had been right. Of course he had been right from his point of view – the only view any in his position could afford to take – but for the first time he began to recognise that there were others involved in many of his activities and they must have had points of view too. It worried him. Was he becoming soft? What was happening to this hard case, this man who gave no thought to others where money was concerned? He argued that what he had done had really been for the good of many and that if he had not done it someone else would. Somehow he did not convince himself. Why was it he was thinking this way? He must get out of it – you can't afford to be soft or let anyone know you have any feelings, he thought.

The fax came through on the Turner rig and as he read it his eyes sparkled. He had done it again. The thoughts he had been harbouring a few minutes ago disappeared and he was once again the ruthless takeover man he had been for much of his working life. I'll get them drilling again shortly and then we'll show them, he said to himself.

LXXVII

Abe Slyberger had waited patiently for some news of an accident at the Brooklyn offices but nothing came. Either the work he had done had been useless or something had happened but had not made the papers. He had not wanted to ring the Steinberg offices in case there was some investigation going on but he thought that after three weeks it would be safe to see what he could find out. He did not want his secretary involved but he had to have something plausible to ring about.

"Could you put me through to your payroll department."

"Just a minute, sir – I'll put you through."

Straightway the ear was treated to a John Philip Souza March whilst Payroll found someone who would answer the call. Slyberger started tapping his feet to the music when it stopped abruptly.

"Payroll. Susan speaking, how can I help you?"

Slyberger gritted his teeth, if there was something he disliked it was the way in which staff were now trained to answer the telephone – he was not interested that he was speaking to Susie or whatever her name was, he just wanted to speak to Payroll. He was now agitated and it made him forget how he had planned to speak.

"I want some information on my pay – or rather the Government want it."

"What is your name, sir?"

"John Johnson – I left some years back, but you know those guys after federal tax they never let up. Tell me, girlie, is Julius Steinberg in today?"

"I'm sorry, I don't know that name – Julius who?"

"Steinberg, he's your boss. Let me speak to the manager of the department," Slyberger said in the most authoritative voice he could muster.

"I'll see if he is free – I'm new here."

Slyberger waited, more Souza music and then a male voice, "You wanted to speak with me."

"Yeah, I just asked the chick if she knew if Julius Steinberg was in today and she didn't know who I was talking about – I guess you do though."

"Why yes, sir, I think they must have put you through to the wrong department, we are Payroll, you, I imagine, want his secretary, I'll get you transferred."

"No, don't bother. I reckon you know if he is in – most guys working for the great man know when he is around – bush telegraph, don't they call it?" Slyberger laughed.

"As a matter of fact I do know. I understand he is up at his home in New England. We don't see so much of him lately."

"I trust he is quite well?" Slyberger asked.

"Well, as far as I know he is." The manager stalled a little.

"You don't sound too sure, bud."

"Oh – I was just thinking of that accident and how near he was to not being well."

"What accident was that?" Slyberger asked.

"His private elevator in the office fell four floors but as luck would have it, he was not aboard."

"Was anyone hurt?"

"Yes, one of the personal assistants to Mr Steinberg was injured but he's out of hospital now – good job it wasn't Mr Steinberg, at his age it could have been fatal."

Slyberger did not ask any more questions about the accident in case it aroused suspicion. Instead he thanked the man for his help and said he would probably ring Steinberg at his home.

Abe was angry that his plan had misfired and yet he was pleased and somewhat proud that he had managed to fix the elevator. Yes, there were no flies on Abe Slyberger, he said to himself.

LXXVIII

Joan Miller arranged an appointment to see her husband's doctor without Joe knowing and she went to see him whilst she knew Joe was in the library. The doctor, a man in his fifties, had been known to the family for many years and whenever he called to see Joan she always offered him a glass of whisky to which she knew he was very partial. However, on his home ground the doctor acted a good deal more professionally with not the slightest sign of any drink at all in spite of the fact that there was talk among his patients that the man had a problem.

"What can I do for you, Joan?"

"It's Joe I've come about – he's not well – at least from time to time he is unwell. I expect you heard he collapsed in the library the other day. Well, he doesn't remember it at all and our neighbour, who was there at the time, says he looked really ill and didn't even recognise him."

"Yes, I know all about it, Joe did come and see me. I'm afraid there is not much I could tell him. I guess he's been overdoing it – what has he been up to lately?"

"Overdoing it! He hasn't done a day's work for years now. He does nothing at home except read and write letters – it certainly isn't physical overwork."

The doctor shuffled uneasily, he really did not know quite what to say. He knew Joe Miller had been out of work for years and he was sorry for him. He remembered Joe as the big executive who was going places, and indeed went. But this loss of his job had undoubtedly unsettled the man. The doctor knew only too well that the man was heading for a complete breakdown but how could he tell Joan without worrying her.

"Yes, silly of me to say that, I meant his brain has probably been overworked. Goodness knows what has been going on inside his head but my guess is that he has been putting it to a great deal of work and because it has not always produced the right answer for him he has worried a lot. Worrying is not good but you simply cannot tell people not to worry and expect them to take notice, it doesn't work that way. The man is sick and unless he can somehow relax more he could end up with a complete breakdown. Of course we don't know what the knock on the head did to his brain, but I would have thought that by now he would be feeling better than when I first saw him after the mugging. Can't you get away somewhere and stop him always trying to get a job? I would have thought that by now he would have accepted the inevitable that he may never work again – certainly not in the way he used to work."

Joan listened, twisting her hands in her lap and looking more worried the more the doctor said.

"Yes, I can see what is happening but I don't know what to do. He has seemed quite all right when at home. Of course I used to get fed up with his continually reading and writing letters but he has been doing it for such a long time that I have now got used to it. We don't talk as much as we used to. Still I suppose when you live in each others pockets day in and day out you run out of what to say – if he were at work it would be different."

Joan Miller left the doctor and returned home, arriving before Joe came back from the library. She looked at him as he entered the room – he hardly looked at her but went straight into his study and sat at his desk. Joan poured him a coffee and took it in to him. He thanked her but again had nothing more to say.

"Joe, are you feeling all right?" she said.

Joe looked around and smiled weakly as if he were smiling at someone he hardly knew. He turned back to the papers in front of them on the desk and went on reading as if she were not there and had said nothing.

"Joe, I wish you would stop looking for a job – I think you should rest for a while. Perhaps we could go away. You were better down in Miami."

Joe stopped reading and looked up at his wife. "You know there are so many bad letters that if someone doesn't do something about it, the art of letter writing will be lost. I must try and help. I haven't got the time to go away."

Joan, almost in tears, left the room. She knew now for sure that Joe was ill, ill in his mind and needed some help, help which his local doctor would be unable to give. She would have to consult a specialist. Why did it have to happen to someone like Joe? she thought... someone had a lot to answer for and yet what could she do, she knew only too well that takeovers were happening all the time. Perhaps it was always like this. Maybe Steinberg was no different from many others, but what if he were? That did not make it right. Something should be done to give some form of protection to employees – but what?

She certainly did not have the answer, although she remembered Joe saying that if a successful company became victim of a takeover it would not be unreasonable for those instituting the takeover to be made to offer some form of protection for the key employees of that company, particularly those who had served it well for many years – they should not be allowed to throw these people on the scrap-heap. It was all too much for her but she understood what Joe meant. She sat down and looked out of the window onto the small lawn at the rear of the house and wiped the tears from her eyes. What could she do?

LXXIX

At the end of May Tony came over to England as he had promised and on the same day he arrived back, telephoned Ray Holmes and arranged to meet. The bar of the Queen's Hotel was almost empty when they arrived and thus they were able to choose where to sit; they chose a quiet corner so there was little chance of them being disturbed.

Ray explained exactly what the Wilsons had found out about the Steinberg mansion and at the same time produced the plans of the building they had prepared.

"It's pretty obvious that Ted Wilson was right, the best place to enter the estate is from the lake. Whoever was chosen to do the job would have to hire a boat and wade or swim ashore," Ray added.

"I suppose he wasn't able to find out how deep the water was close in which is a pity – we ought to find this out before anyone attempts to get in. How about coming over with me, Ray and we'll get a boat and try it out?"

"I thought we agreed it would be too dangerous for any of us to go there in case we could in any way be connected," Ray said.

"Yes, I know we did but we are only going to literally test the water and we could easily be on holiday – who's to connect us?" Tony said.

Ray was astounded by Tony's apparent indifference to the possibility of someone recognising them and later relating them to the happening.

"Half a minute, Tony, what about Steinberg and any others that work for him? You told me you met Steinberg and I most certainly did, although it's doubtful if he would remember me."

"I happen to know Steinberg is going to the Philippines in June – I know because he wants to see me in July when his secretary said he would be back from there. If we arranged to go in mid June we are sure to be OK. From what I gather practically no one goes up to Primrose at any time and certainly not when he is away. He has a driver who will take him down to New York and then after seeing the old man off at the airport he will report back to the New York office and work from there until his boss returns. No, we would be on our own up there. Anyway it'll do you good."

Ray looked pensive – they had sent the Wilsons to avoid any connection and it seemed wrong that they should change in midstream and start thinking differently. But – here he hesitated in his thoughts – had they not sent the Wilsons because they wanted to keep what they were doing from as many of the other redundants as possible – the fewer who knew exactly what was going on the better.

"Well, I can see what you mean, Tony, I could do with a break but frankly I haven't the money, nor am I likely to have in the job I am now doing. No, you'll have to go on your own. But what about Geneva – won't you be missed?"

"You're coming, Ray, my fare will be paid by the company – I'm getting very good money and I will put up the cash – I will need company, I think I would stick out like a sore thumb if I poodled around up there on my own. I'd be bound to be drawn into talking to others who would think I was lonely and the less we talk the less people are likely to remember, no I definitely need company. What do you say – can you get the time off for, say, ten days?"

Ray was persuaded, he would enjoy the break, the first he had had since his wife had died.

"OK, I'll come."

LXXX

Ruby, Steinberg's secretary, faxed a follow-up on the first Turner report to Primrose. Steinberg took the document from the machine and read:

Special gang led by Tim Magee spent five days on the Turner platform and carried out drilling for four of those days. The samples produced on day four indicated that it was almost certain that oil would be reached within two further days of drilling. Magee awaits head office order to proceed or continue to hold. Gang have returned to Houston and been advised not to disclose what happened on their visit. Magee confirms gang understand and is sure they can be trusted

Steinberg smiled to himself. His gamble had succeeded; the question was, should he tell them to hold or should he get them to bring in the oil? He realised that if he held on, someone would sooner or later let it slip that Steinberg was holding and then the questions would be asked. Why was he holding? Had he been given some inside information before he bought them out and was holding back so that it did not look so obvious? On the other hand, if he drilled and succeeded in getting oil they may either think he did indeed have some inside information or he was simply a lucky bastard.

He chose to drill and informed Brooklyn to get Houston to "go for it". Within a week a new gang had taken over on the ex-Turner platform and had succeeded in reaching and capping the oil.

The news quickly spread among the drilling fraternity and there was much muttering and sympathy shown to the Turner family and the many men who had worked on their platform.

Kevan telephoned Lee Crocket in Memphis to let him know that his prediction that oil was near had proved to be correct.

"I think someone knowing how far we had drilled and what we were bringing up compared it with the depth of drilling and strata on the successful adjoining rig and put two and two together. One of our gang must have been talking to someone on the other rig when shipping back to shore, someone who was well informed on that rig. I reckon whoever he was working for – and my guess is Arkansas Oil

– was told of the situation and took a gamble on a buyout. We've been taken for a ride, Kevan," Lee said angrily.

"Well, you told old Turner you thought we were near but he didn't hang on. He had the same chance as Arkansas Oil," Kevan replied.

"Not quite, he only had my word that I thought we were near – I could have been wrong – he didn't have the knowledge of how far down the adjoining rig had struck it. I suppose if he had really tried he could have found out but he didn't have the money to carry on – the bank had had enough. In a way he was glad to get out and get something for the company. It's us who were hard hit. If I ever find out there was a plant by Arkansas Oil to spy out our progress, I'll not rest until I nail whoever set us up."

Lee had not found work in Memphis and was beginning to get depressed about it – this bit of news had not helped.

"It's no use worrying about it, Lee – it's just our bad luck. If I see any of the gang I'll try and find out if they have any idea who the sonofabitch might have been." Kevan was obviously less concerned than Lee appeared to be, in spite of having a family to look after.

LXXXI

Abe Slyberger, having failed twice in his attempts to get rid of Steinberg, was now not a happy man. He still hated paying over those royalties and he resented Steinberg treating him the way he had after he had done his dirty work in closing the WECO operation. He knew he could not think of using the elevator again as his executioner and he therefore started to think once more of other ways he could get this man eliminated.

If he went back to the house in Primrose he could see he would more readily be identified in the future should something happen to Steinberg in suspicious circumstances.

No, if he did anything it would have to be anywhere but in that town.

Back at his house in Yonkers, Abe Slyberger was able to relax to some extent and the thoughts he had whilst in his office about how he could deal with Steinberg practically vanished. His housekeeper had prepared his supper and he was now enjoying a coffee while sitting in his favourite chair in front of the television. He was not taking much notice of what was showing – the adverts ended and the news started. He was half watching and looking at a paper at the same time when something attracted his attention. The newsreader was talking and pictures were being shown of how home-made bombs were being used by Animal Rights activists in Europe. A detailed diagram was displayed showing how easy it was for these crude devices to be made. Abe took in the detail and resolved to tune to another station where he knew the same news would be shown in half an hour's time. He set the video to record the programme and waited. Sure enough the news was repeated and once again the diagram and explanation as to how to make a bomb were shown.

Abe studied the video and knew that given the material, he too could make a bomb.

LXXXII

Mac returned to work in June just after Steinberg had gone on his trip to the Philippines. Although fully recovered, he was still shaken by what had happened and on entering the Brooklyn office he made a point of not being alone in the elevator on his first ride to the upper floors – he realised of course that it was stupid to be worried and that others in the elevator would make no difference if it should fall, nevertheless he felt more comfortable He met Steinberg's secretary near her office and after formal pleasantries asked her if they had discovered what had gone wrong with the elevator when he had had his accident.

"They didn't seem to be sure, Mac, the elevator people said they had told Arkansas Oil that the elevator should be changed as it was so old and always breaking down – but they considered it had always been serviced properly and most certainly they considered there was no chance it would have been able to fall from the way they left it after the last repair job. Since no one said they knew anything about the running of the elevator or had been near the engine housing on the roof, it was assumed that the elevator company must have overlooked something when servicing. Since, however, they had so often warned the company about the age of the elevator the police could not see how any charges of negligence could be brought. The man who ran the elevator company was right to the end of the investigation convinced that someone had tampered with the mechanism – but no one took much notice." She paused and opened her office door and then, "I guess you'll be making a claim on the company's insurance, Mac."

"Well, I guess I should but I think I'll wait for Julius to return or else he might get upset. Insurance companies generally try to reclaim what they pay out in the next premium and I don't think Julius would like that."

Ruby smiled a knowing smile and went into her office. Mac walked down to his office, limping slightly. He went straight to the telephone and got through to reception.

"This is MacDonald, have you seen anything of Mancini this morning?"

"Yes, sir, he was about somewhere ten minutes or so ago. Shall I tell him you want him if I see him? He's probably gone round the corner for a coffee. He often goes there when not wanted."

It was half an hour before Mancini arrived in Mac's office.

"You wanted to see me, Mac?"

"Yeah, it's important we talk. I had a call from Peter Bronson, he wants to know who the guy is who is asking after him." Mac got up from his seat and limped to the window and looked out towards Manhattan.

"I thought you said we gotta play it cool, how the hell Bronson wants to know who the guy is? I didn't even know he knew anything about it."

"It's a long story, Joe, it all got ballsed up – I tried to get something from an old acquaintance and he blurted it out to Bronson and the guy hasn't let up since. He wants to know the guy or the one who spoke to me about it – that's you." Mac turned round to see Mancini's reaction. The Italian's face was a mixture of anger and disbelief.

"What are you going to do? You ain't gonna tell him, are you?" he said hopefully. "We're going to be in big trouble if the old man finds out."

"We could be in even bigger trouble if we don't come clean – this guy Bronson means business. My friend tells me we had better tell him what he wants to know," Mac said firmly. "I've told him I will be seeing you shortly and he seemed to be satisfied to wait providing you are able to tell him what he wants to know."

"Me?" Mancini said in an incredulous tone of voice. "You know who it is. Why me?"

"I was really stalling for time so that we could decide the best way to play it. Have you got any ideas?"

Mancini looked blank. "Jesus Christ, Mac, what do you expect me to come up with? You've really loused it up for us."

"Now steady on, Joe. You were the one who wanted to carry on when I was for playing it cool. You even said it might do the guy a favour as there aren't many as rich as our Julius. No, Joe, you're the one to tell him."

"I suggest we take a couple of days to think about it and you come to my office at the same time on Wednesday and we'll sort out what we are going to say – at least you won't be bothered by Julius in the next couple of days."

LXXXIII

Ray Holmes and Tony Bentley left Heathrow on the morning of 12th June and arrived in Boston two hours later on the clock. By the time they had cleared the airport and picked up a hired car it was two o'clock and thus on a beautiful sunny June day they headed towards New Hampshire and Primrose. Ted Wilson had given them rough instructions on the way to go and, with the aid of a cheap map, they were soon eating up the miles. The countryside was lush as there had recently been a sustained period of rain and on the narrow roads near to Primrose the water was still running from the fields onto the road.

It was dusk when they drew up outside the Lake Hotel – both had taken turns at the wheel and both were tired and hungry. Ray felt as if he had been there before, it was just as it had been described to him by Ted Wilson and his wife. They entered the reception area and rang the brass bell on the desk. The receptionist came through from the office behind and offered assistance.

"Good evening, welcome to the Lake Hotel – how can I help you?"

"We've come a long way and are hungry – we'd like a meal first and then we'd like a couple of rooms if you have them," Tony said.

"We can fix you up with a meal, we have just started serving dinner – two rooms may be a little difficult. You see, this is the tourist season and we have had a number of people stop over. Anyway while you are eating I'll have a word with the proprietor and we will see what we can do. If you would like a brush up before eating you can use room twelve on the ground floor just round the corner. I'll get you to sign the register when we see if we can find rooms for you. The restaurant is straight ahead."

Tony and Ray felt less tired after a wash and made their way to the restaurant where Jake Ramsden met them at the door.

"I'm Jake Ramsden, the proprietor, I think we will be able to find space for you tonight – my receptionist thinks you are English. Is she right?"

"Yes, we work for a travel company and are checking out places to stay and see in this part of the States – we might be around for a few days," Tony confidently said.

"You'll be made very welcome, you can be sure," Jake said, and then added, "as indeed are all our guests."

The meal they both thought was very good and they were about to go to reception to see what accommodation they were to be offered when Jake Ramsden came over to their table.

"Hope you enjoyed the meal?"

They assured him it was very good.

"Do you know anything about Primrose?" Jake asked.

"No, nothing much really," Ray said.

"Well, tomorrow you must go and see the lake – take a boat out and you'll see the countryside at its best. We have a lot of people from the cities who have built houses and come up here to live in the summer. We also have some important people who live here permanently. The Malloy family have a big place here. You probably would not know them but they were big in railways. Then there is our prize tourist attraction – Julius Steinberg, I reckon you heard of him, we've had several people come over here from your country who have heard of him. Then there's the waterfall – you must see that and of course the gardens by the lake – old Steinberg sometimes goes down there and just sits and looks across the lake."

"Sounds very nice," Ray said. "Yes, we know of Steinberg. We understand he has a big house near here."

"He sure has. It's a new place he had built a while back. Very grand – plenty of land but it's surrounded by a ten-foot wall so you can't see much from the road. The best place is from the lake or Hanover Heights. Take a boat and go left past the hotel, you'll come to the Steinberg estate about a mile along – you can't miss it. You'll have a clear view of the house from there – but of course you can't go in. We had a man and his wife from England last month who were lucky enough to get to see the place as they got talking to two people who knew Julius and who were calling in to see him – they asked them along. I saw the place when it was being built but haven't been up there since."

Jake had really got the bit between his teeth and was doing his best to project the merits of coming to a place like Primrose. He continued, "Of course not everyone is interested in houses or indeed old Steinberg, but the place itself is so peaceful and quiet and the countryside so lovely that now it's been discovered I'm sure more and more people will come up here."

"That'll do your business no harm," Tony remarked.

"No, you're quite right – I have been thinking of extending my hotel for some time – but it's a big decision. But you have to gamble sometimes in this life, don't you?" Ray and Tony nodded agreement.

"Would you like me to show you where we have fixed you up – I'm afraid you'll have to share a room as we are full but it's a good size room with two beds. I'm sure you will be comfortable. You can sign the register later. We have a popular bar just over there."

Tony and Ray collected their bags from the car and followed Jake to the room. After registering they went to the bar, it was now pitch dark outside and any proposed activity in Primrose would have to wait for the following day.

LXXXIV

Joe Miller sat in the library looking at the daily papers but today he was not taking notes in his usual fashion. He sat still turning the pages almost as if he were a machine. He did not seem to be reading them, in fact he was not – he was thinking.

He remembered his childhood and how he had tried so hard at school but not until the sixth grade did it all suddenly click. Then there was old Mrs Garby, the old lady who always smiled and waved at him when he passed her house on his way to school. Funny the things you remember – little things like walking to the park with Matty Jones and taking that ride on the lake for a nickel and then knocking at houses on the way home on a hot day and asking for a drink of water – sometimes being given a glass of lemonade. Then there was Christine – she was a nice little girl. Waiting outside her school when aged about twelve and hoping to see her. Then there was the cinema – Clark Gable, Lana Turner, Betty Grable, Edward G., and what was that guy's name who played small parts in gangster films? Joe thought hard, it bothered him not to remember – he was, I remember, Ed Brophy. That was a long while ago – then came the war and Guadalcanal, that was a bad time but I survived. Then there was all the studying and hard work in Burnside Chemicals – and the promotion. I became a big shot then – made it right to the top. Look at me now – reading newspapers in a library pretending to look for a job when all I am doing is playing a game. Nobody wants me now – that bastard Steinberg is still around and look at me.

Joe Miller became conscious of people looking at him – had he expressed some of his thoughts out loud? He looked down at the paper in front of him again but immediately his mind started racing through past events until nothing made sense and he heard voices but could not understand what they were saying. His mind began to clear.

"Are you all right, sir?"

He looked up to see two people standing next to him, one leaning down and looking directly into his face.

"Yes… why? What's the matter?" Joe stumbled out.

"We thought you might be ill," one of the onlookers said.

"No, I'm all right, thank you."

Joe thought it must be time to go and picking up his glasses case he walked unsteadily to the door.

It was only a short walk to his house and Joe Miller walked as if he were very tired. He stopped to look in the window of a shop in Main Street and saw next to his reflection in the window two other people looking too. They seemed to be looking at him. Why would they look at him? He would ask them what they wanted. He turned around to face them.

"What do you want with me?" he asked.

The man looked surprised and pulled his lady companion's arm and walked away. Joe continued to walk slowly home. I wonder what they wanted, he thought, it was strange that people were beginning to take an interest in him; perhaps he had changed. He walked on, and around the corner by the bank he turned into his street and was soon walking up the garden path to his house. He let himself in the front door with his key and walked straight to the kitchen where his wife was sitting, peeling an onion.

"Hullo, dear," she said. "Would you like a coffee, lunch will be a little while yet. You're earlier than usual today, are you all right?"

Joe nodded and sat down in a chair on the opposite side of the table to his wife.

"Have you any idea why people are looking at me and talking to me? I was looking in a shop window when a man and woman stood behind me and looked at me in the window."

"Perhaps they were just looking in the window and you thought they were looking at you, dear – I think you must be imagining things. Come on, have a cup of coffee and you'll soon feel better – have you got that headache again, dear?" Mrs Miller tried to calm him although she could see he was not his old self – he had a strange look about him. There was almost a smile coming from his lips and yet he did not really seem to be there – what was he thinking? she thought.

"I don't seem to be much use now, do I?" he suddenly said. "I was once though – I was a big shot once. I used to be the boss – do you remember that time?" He looked at his wife and a tear came to his eye. "I'm a failure – I'm so sorry – I don't seem to be able to cope any more. Things are beginning to get on top of me – I can't stand nobody wanting me and now everyone looks at me and talks about me behind my back – why do they do it?" Joe was not looking at his wife now; he was staring over her shoulder out onto the lawn behind the house. His face had a faraway expression. "Do you remember Harry King? Corporal Harry King he was – we were buddies. I told him not to do it, but you know Harry. I can see him now – he made it halfway up the beach and threw the grenade and then they got him. Poor old Harry, he was only twenty-two."

His wife did not know quite what to say – his mind was obviously wandering. She hadn't met Joe until after the war, so how could she know Harry King? "Why don't you go and put your feet up for a bit, I'll give you a call when lunch is ready."

Joe got up from his chair and walked from the room.

Over the next few days Joe became very depressed and his wife became more and more worried. The doctor called and after a second visit recommended that Joe went away for a while in a home where he would get good treatment to help him recover from what was obviously a breakdown.

LXXXV

Tony Bentley and Ray Holmes were well pleased with their night's sleep and came down to breakfast feeling refreshed. It was a beautiful day with hardly a cloud in the sky. A few early birds had already finished breakfast and were in reception paying their bills and taking luggage to their cars.

Jake Ramsden was fussing around and seeing the two English guests coming down the stairs made a point of greeting them as they walked to the dining room.

"You'll be going on the lake today, I guess – it'll be lovely out there, you couldn't choose a better day."

"Yes, I expect we will – if we can get a boat."

"Oh, you'll have no trouble getting a boat – do you know anything about boats?" Jake asked.

"My friend here was a sailor in the last war and had a boat of his own back in England – I think we can manage, thank you."

"I'll book you a good one if you would like – I know the best people to give you a good boat – I'll have them make ready if you say the word," Jake eagerly said.

Ray and Tony exchanged glances and agreed they would let Jake get them fixed up.

An hour later they were out on the lake, heading for the other side of the water. They had decided to make sure that all could see they were only people interested in the lake and would in no way arouse any suspicion that they were most interested in the Steinberg residence.

After going as far as the waterfall and sailing along the opposite shore they gradually made their way round towards where they had been told they would find the Steinberg mansion.

The lake was over a mile wide and about three miles in length and although deep in the centre was shallow inshore on the south side on which stood the hotel and the Steinberg residence.

Tony steered the boat inshore and as they came round from the west side of the lake they saw the house which was obviously the mansion they were seeking. It had been built about five hundred yards from the lake and they could see the lawns sloping down to the lake edge. About fifty yards from the lake there was a low open fence with bushes behind and beyond that they could just see what appeared to be a fault in the ground running parallel with the fence.

"No wonder he has such a low fence near the lake to protect the property. I bet he has some sort of a moat a few yards back – do you see that break in the ground?" Ray said. "He wanted to have an unrestricted view of the lake so instead of carrying on his ten-foot wall he has built some other obstruction. What do you think, Tony?"

Tony had been looking whilst steering closer in to the shore. It was not easy to see what the fault in the ground was hiding but it certainly looked as if there could be something.

"I can't see what it is but what you said makes sense – I suppose it did seem strange having a ten-foot wall round the grounds and then giving easy access over a low fence by the lake – you're probably right. But I suppose we ought to make sure – not much good trying to gain access from the lake if there is something built to stop us."

They were now as close in as they dare take the boat but still were not able to see what was hidden in the ground.

"I think we should go back now and perhaps if we are clever we can find out from some of the locals who may know. Alternatively we look for a volunteer to try to get past it in the dark," Tony added with a smile.

Back at the hotel they met Jake Ramsden in the bar. "Did you have a good trip on the lake?" he asked.

"Yes, we thought it was very lovely – especially close by the waterfall – that is something worth seeing, a truly lovely spot," Ray answered.

"What about the mansion, Steinberg's I mean, did you manage to see it?" This was the opportunity they had hoped they would get and Tony didn't intend to let it slip.

"Oh yes, we think we must have seen it – but of course it is a long way back from the lake. We were surprised he had such a low fence guarding the house from the lake – seemed silly after having gone to the trouble of building a ten-foot wall elsewhere."

"That's where you are wrong," said Jake triumphantly. "He's no fool – no, not Julius Steinberg – he's built a moat right along the lakeside which goes right under the wall at both ends so that you have to cross it in order to get in to the grounds."

"How ingenious – we couldn't see it from the lake – but suppose he wants to go down to the lakeside himself, how does he get there?" Tony asked.

"Well, I haven't seen it myself, but I am told he has a bridge which moves out from the bank – it's electrically operated by remote control. Can't be seen from either side until you are actually up to the moat. Thus his view of the lake is not marred by anything as unsightly as a modern bridge."

"That's most interesting – he certainly seems determined to keep out unwelcome visitors – I suppose he hasn't got crocodiles or piranhas in the moat?" Ray asked jokingly.

"I have no idea what he has in the moat but nothing would surprise me," Jake said and continued, "Do you think you'll be staying any longer?"

Tony answered, "We have a number of places to visit so we will be off tomorrow but I can assure you we will place Primrose high on our list of places to visit when we arrange holidays for people to come to see New England."

The next day Ray and Tony left for Boston, having managed to book a suitable flight to Heathrow. Their journey had been satisfactory, they now knew that if someone thought the lake entrance was the easy route into the Steinberg estate they would be wrong – the wall might be an easier bet.

LXXXVI

Joe Mancini duly arrived at Mac's office as agreed. With Steinberg not yet due back from Luzon it was not difficult for him to find time, especially if he had the excuse of seeing the man, who most in the know recognised as the great man's right hand.

Mac was on the telephone when Mancini arrived being ushered in by the blonde relief secretary who eyed the big handsome Italian.

Mac put the telephone down and got out of his chair, at the same time motioning Joe Mancini to sit.

"I've just been talking to Julius – he's coming back today," Mac said.

"Christ, Mac, I didn't expect him for a few days, what time will he be at the airport?"

"Hold your horses, Joe, he won't be here today, he's leaving Naga on Luzon today. He's got an overland journey to Manila and will be flying out from there tomorrow if he can get booked – I shouldn't think he will be here until Saturday."

"That's a relief, I thought I'd got to tear over to the airport." Mancini paused. "Well, Mac, what have you decided we do?" he added. Mac looked thoughtful and walked over to the window.

"I thought we agreed you would be the one to talk to Bronson," he said.

"I agreed to nothing, we said we would think about it and come up with ideas – at least that's what I thought was how we ended it. Why don't we both speak to him?" Mancini said.

"The guy's in Vegas – how we both going to speak to him. Perhaps we should ask him to come over to New York?" Mac said sarcastically. "Jesus, Joe, we have to speak to him on the telephone – at least at first."

It was at that moment that the door of Mac's office opened and his relief secretary entered with coffee for the two men.

"Thanks, er... what do they call you, honey?" Mac asked.

"My name is Patricia but you can call me Pat." She smiled and winked at the seated Italian as she walked to the door.

"Oh, by the way, whilst you were out yesterday," she said turning to Mac, "a man by the name of Peter Bronson telephoned for you twice. He seemed annoyed on the second call and said I should tell you that he wanted an answer."

"Did he leave a number?"

"Yeah, he did, I think I've got it somewhere, I'll let you have it when I find it." She passed a further look at Joe and left the office.

"Jesus, I've been in the office all morning and she suddenly remembers to tell me Bronson rang – some of these agency dames!" Mac raised his arms in disgust. "Well, now you know this guy means business," he added.

"I think the only way now is for us to come clean and try and get Bronson not to reveal the source of his information. That's all I could come up with, Mac."

"I was thinking on the same lines – I suppose I had better speak with him since he is calling me, but you had better be ready to talk to him if he wants to know more, after all you are the one who started it all. We just have to hope Julius has told the story to others so that it doesn't point directly to you," Mac said, and added, "I'll ring the number if my secretary finds it – or perhaps he'll ring again."

LXXXVII

Steinberg's housekeeper, Molly, was a discreet individual and she determined not to allow anyone to know what her boss had revealed to her concerning his distant past in Primrose. However, she was, as most humans, curious and could not wait to find a suitable opportunity to see if she could find out about the girl Zoë.

Molly made regular visits to town to order and buy food for the household. When Joe Mancini was around she would get him to take her to the shops but when he was away with his boss or in New York whilst Julius was abroad, she would ride in on her bicycle.

She knew all the shopkeepers, after all, the town had only a few shops, and on this particular day she would make a point of visiting them all and tactfully ask the question.

Her first call was to the one and only butcher in town. Jeremy Tucker had lived most of his life in and around Primrose and was as likely to know most people who had lived there in his lifetime.

"Morning, Mr Tucker – fine day."

"Good morning, Molly – sure is. What can I do for you?"

"Well, Mr Julius is away at present so I only want a couple of nice chops and a piece of steak for Saturday."

"You sure like your special on Saturday, Molly. I'll cut you off a nice piece." Molly moved around the shop and looking out the window and trying to give an air of indifference she said, "You've been around these parts for a long time, Mr Tucker. Did you ever hear of a lady with the name of Zoë?"

"Sure ain't a common name – I guess I would have known her if she had lived around here since I was alive. No, can't say I have ever known anyone with that name. Why do you ask?"

"Weren't important – someone I know thought a friend of theirs had once lived around here. Guess they were mistaken." Molly turned to face the butcher. "I'll call in to collect my meat on my way back – got a few calls to make first."

She left the shop and passing the newsagent, where she could see a number of people waiting to be served, made her way to the ladies' fashion shop which was the pride of John O'Reilly, the Mayor of Primrose. She entered the shop and started looking at the rails nearest the door.

"Good morning, Molly – it's nice to see you, can I help?"

"No, that's all right, Mr O'Reilly. I'm just looking – got to get something for my holidays."

"Where are you going?" O'Reilly asked.

"I'm going down to New York and stay in one of those big hotels and I'm going to see three or four shows – it's all included in the package. I'm looking forward to it. I've never been to New York before."

O'Reilly looked up from the stock book he had been marking off. "I went there once during the war – saw *Oklahoma* at the James Theatre. They had a special matinee for the forces – other folks had to wait months to get a ticket. I enjoyed New York then – I was young, I guess. I've no wish to go there again. But I guess everyone should try to go once in their life especially if you live on the east coast."

"You been around a long time. I didn't know you were in the army."

"Sure I was in for three years – made top sergeant too."

"Did you ever know anyone around these parts called Zoë?" Molly asked.

"No, can't say I did – never knew anyone with that name. Any special reason for asking?"

"Well it was just you saying you was in the last war – and I remember my daddy saying he knew a girl called Zoë – thought she might have come from these parts," Molly lied, keeping her fingers crossed.

"Seen anything you like?" O'Reilly asked.

"There are so many nice things in your shop, Mr O'Reilly – I think I'll come back when I have more time." She moved towards the door. "I'll be back soon," she added.

O'Reilly returned to his stock book. He was used to people coming in and saying they would be coming back, he knew it was generally an excuse to get out. He reckoned he could tell the genuine ones from the time wasters.

Molly walked on up Main Street until she came to the biggest shop in town – John Butler's General Store. She pushed open the double doors and walked inside. The round stove in the centre of the shop looked unwanted at this time of the year whereas she knew that in the winter one would nearly always find a small group seated round the black metal container which would be giving off its welcome heat. Around the walls of the shop were articles of all descriptions and jars and tins of food on shelves. John Butler was talking to a customer who had just purchased, as far as Molly could see, a new spade.

"I guess this one should see me out," the man said as he walked out of the shop.

"Morning, Molly, what can I get you?"

"Good morning, Mr Butler. I got my list written down but I can't take it with me as I'm on my bicycle. Could you deliver it to me when you are up that way? There is no hurry." She handed him the list which he glanced at before replying.

"Sure, Tony is going up that way tomorrow – he'll drop it by. Julius away, is he?"

"Yep, he's gone to the Philippines – should be back soon. He's getting old to keep travelling around the world. But I guess he would be lost without it – he seems to live for his work."

"He's sure a busy man, must be nigh on eighty, I wouldn't wonder."

"He's more than that," Molly added.

Molly walked as if to go to the door. "Oh, send your account up to the house – I'll pay you then if that is all right?"

"Sure, I think I can trust that Julius has got enough to clear what he owes," he said with a twinkle in his eye.

As she reached the door, Molly hesitated. "Mr Butler, you and your ma have been around here a long time, did you ever hear of a lady with the name Zoë?"

"Why sure, Molly…" He paused. "Why do you want to know?"

"Well, Mr Butler, I don't really think I'm at liberty to say – I could tell you some story but I guess I can't tell a lie."

"Don't worry, Molly, I'll tell you who it is," John Butler said. "You are not the only one to ask me the same question –

but like you I had better not say who asked me. I do know that it was something to do with your boss."

Molly was taken completely by surprise. She shuffled uneasily and taking her hand off the door she had been about to exit walked across to the proprietor.

"Of course you are right, Mr Butler. I was quite unaware that anyone else knew anything about it – foolish of me to think I was the only person he had told. However, if you did give the other person an answer they certainly have not passed it on to Julius, I know because he would have told me and he offered no objection to me trying to find out what happened to the lady."

At that moment another person entered the shop and John Butler stopped his conversation – he looked at the new customer and offered his help and asked Molly to take a seat and wait a moment.

As soon as the customer had left he once again took up his position behind the counter and prepared to carry on the conversation.

"I believe I know why Julius hasn't been told," he said.

"Why was that, Mr Butler?"

"Well, I don't think Julius knew the person concerned was making enquiries and then when he found the lady had almost certainly died many years ago, I guess he decided it wasn't worth telling the old man. I also told him not to get involved with the son – a big shot gambler living in Las Vegas, not a very nice man according to Jake Ramsden."

"Jake Ramsden – does he know too?" Molly gasped. "And I thought he'd just told me."

"No, you're wrong there, Molly. Jake don't know nothing – I just asked him if he knew a Peter Bronson – that's the name of the son. He did as it happens – indeed had met him. But I didn't say anything about the kid's mother."

John Butler then related what he had found out from his mother.

"I think I'll tell Mr Steinberg at a suitable time that the lady he once knew has been dead many years. Thanks for telling me, Mr Butler – that clears it up anyway." She now had no further need to go to any other shops. "That will save me going round the town trying to be casual when asking if anyone knew a lady with the name of Zoë." They both laughed as she left the shop.

LXXXVIII

September '76 came around all too quickly – where had the summer gone? Ray Holmes, after his short visit to the States, had returned to his work in Guildford. Although he was not being paid anywhere near his salary of a few years back he at least had a job. It was indeed quite a good job and gave him a deal of satisfaction without the undue worries associated with the high-powered job he had lost at WECO.

He had not heard from Tony since their joint visit to Primrose but they had agreed that they would meet again at the next meeting of the redundants.

Ray wondered who would bother to attend the next meeting. It was now five years since he had first been sacked and it had been over the following twelve months that most of the others who had attended previous meetings had also been set aside. Years had passed, there had been one death, at least one not yet in employment although actively seeking work, another who had not bothered to look for work knowing his age would eliminate him from having a chance, and many in work but who still bore resentment that they had suffered financially and would never get back to where they had been previously. This was of course the story of those known to Ray Holmes but he knew only too well that there were many hundreds who had at the same time lost their jobs but of whose circumstances he was unaware. He had not forgotten that being made redundant for one man had changed his life completely for the better – and although he was not financially much better off, he was doing something for the first time in his life that he enjoyed – he was truly the exception.

Ray thought of all these people but wondered more than ever if there were still any who felt so strongly that they would be prepared to take action against the man who had been the cause of their troubles. Ray knew that although he still felt strongly about the type of action taken by Steinberg, he knew that as the years went by that the anger began to subside. If it did for him, who had perhaps lost, if not more, then certainly as much as anyone, then it probably did the same for others. Indeed, he wondered whether the meeting would become nothing more than a meeting to let off steam or simply a reunion which perhaps each hoped that no drastic action would be taken. MPs had not listened and the threat made to the newspapers had now died a death without there being any noticeable effect on takeovers.

It was with these thoughts in his mind that he started ringing around to see who would be attending the meeting.

He was surprised at the response – yes, people were still interested in attending but he noticed that any questions raised related to who would be coming rather than what it was they hoped to achieve, it had become a reunion and was no longer a protest meeting.

I.XXXIX

Kevan Brown wondered whether he should tell his old friend, Lee Crocket, what he had learnt from the Portuguese who lived in the next block. He knew how angry Lee would be and he could not see it would do any of them any good. He was younger than Lee and had managed to pick up another job after three months so he was once again in harness and although he had obviously lost out due to the takeover he was now earning as much as he had at any time. He missed the old gang but life goes on and he knew that changes would occur in time in any job. No, he was not even angry any more but he was sensible enough to know that Lee, a much older man, would hold on to anger. Should he tell him or just say nothing?

Kevan was at the end of three days' leave from the rig and was due to return the next day. He sat looking at the television and had just seen a picture of Julius Steinberg, handing over a painting to some foreign museum. It was only on the screen a few seconds but it started a train of thought. This was the man who had taken over the Turner rig and had then sacked the supposed key staff after his agent had promised old man Turner that they would be retained. For a few seconds Kevan felt a surge of anger but then it was gone – it did, however, make him think of Lee. He had not spoken to his old friend since he had told him that their old rig was now flowing. He decided to have a word with him and see whether he had yet got a job.

"Hi, Lee, I thought you might be around. How are things?"

"Nice to hear from you, Kevan. How's the family?"

The pleasantries were soon finished and it did not take long to realise that Lee was not a happy man.

"Have you heard any more from the Portuguese?" Lee asked.

Kevan was taken by surprise at getting the question so direct and was not sure what to say. "Eh, why yes, I did have a word with him the other day when he brought Johnny back home," he stumbled out.

"Did he have anything to say about what we talked about – has he found out anything?"

Kevan was not good at telling lies and knew he would now have to tell Lee what he had been told.

"Yes, he said that Wayne Tinson – you remember Wayne, the guy we got when Lennie Wye was taken ill? – had been friendly with Charlie on the Texaco rig, they used to go to bars together, and had pumped Charlie over several months without Charlie thinking there was anything to it. Well, soon after our rig was taken over, Wayne was no longer around and when Charlie made enquiries as to where Wayne had gone he discovered that he was working with Arkansas Oil. He also found that Wayne had worked with them before coming to Turner – and we know he never mentioned this when you took him on because I remember you asking where he had previously worked, I was there."

"The bastard must have been in the pay of Steinberg – there's no other answer – I bet he did nicely out of it. So it was a fix – I've heard of this sort of thing in films but never come across it in real life. Guess it happens."

Kevan could sense how angry Lee was and wished he had not rung him. "Well, it's in the past now, Lee – there is nothing we can do about it. It's best to forget it."

"Forget it! It's all right for you, you are young and got a job. I've got no work and as far as I can see I will be lucky to pick up anything – forget it – not on your life. I'll do something about it – someone is responsible for this, someone set it up and my bet is it was this guy Steinberg we keep hearing about – a national hero is he, everyone proud that he is an American? He's no better than those in the rackets."

Kevan listened and more than ever wished he had said nothing.

"Wished I hadn't told you, Lee – it's really upset you – I'd try and not let it get you. You'll find something soon. I must go now – the family have just come in and want me for something. Take it easy."

XC

MacDonald sat in his office and rehearsed what he would say to Peter Bronson when he talked to him again. Joe Mancini had left the office wishing Mac the best of luck and said he would be in the building for an hour or so and of course would be interested to know what Bronson said.

Mac finally resolved to make the call and asked the temporary secretary to get the number she had taken from Bronson. At least, Mac thought, she had had the good sense to take down the number even if she had forgotten to tell him of the call for some time.

"Your number, Mr MacDonald."

"Thanks – put them through." There was a short pause and then a voice at the other end of the line said, "Bronson Amusements, Sylvia speaking. Can I help you?"

"Yeah, I hope so, I would like to speak to Peter Bronson – tell him it's Mac."

"Hold the line, I'll see if he will speak with you."

A long pause filled with tape music came to a sudden halt.

"Bronson. What you got for me?" Bronson's abrupt manner took Mac a little by surprise and he took what seemed to him a long while to gather his thoughts before he replied.

"Before I give you what I have found out, I would like you to know that the person to be named is important to my colleague and me as he happens to be our boss. I can assure you he knows nothing of this and it would be appreciated if you did not tell him where you got your information. He may of course guess but we're hoping my friend is not the only one who he has told."

"OK, Mac, cut the crap – I ain't interested in telling him about you guys."

"Ever heard of Julius Steinberg?" Mac said.

"Why sure, I guess there ain't many who haven't heard of him – what's he got to do with this – Jesus, is he the guy?"

Mac felt he was not doing very well. He had hoped to do a little more explaining before revealing the name but Bronson's manner was a bit off-putting. "Yes, he's the guy. It seems he told his driver one day that he had known a girl in Primrose when he was in the army in World War One. He told the driver, my friend I have spoken about, that the girl's name was Zoë – no second name, that's all."

"If that's all, how come you ask someone about me – someone must have known I had a ma whose name was Zoë – give me the full story."

Mac explained how his friend had taken it upon himself to see if he could locate the lady named Zoë and he discreetly asked around in Primrose if anyone had known a lady with that name. He found out that Zoë had died many years back and that she had left a son. "Since my friend was told that Zoë's husband had left her before the baby was born because, it was rumoured, he felt the baby was not his – he made the wild assumption that perhaps, just perhaps, the baby might be Steinberg's. Well. Here we are."

XCI

Some people can easily forget and even forgive but some find it difficult to forget and have no intention of forgiving. One such was Abe Slyberger, he meant to get Steinberg – not to rid the world of someone who continually brought unhappiness to so many people, about that he could not care less, but simply because Steinberg had, in his eyes, treated him badly and in any case it was about time that he stopped paying those phoney royalties over to him.

Abe was doing quite nicely, he was not like the many who had been sacked and years afterwards were still suffering – Abe Slyberger was not a wealthy man compared to his now-sworn enemy, Steinberg, but he was a man of means. His business was going along smoothly and he went into his office daily as much from habit than anything else. If he decided to pack it all in and retire he could sell his business and live in comparative luxury for the rest of his life. But he knew he could not retire until he had got even with f****** Steinberg as he always referred to him. How to fix Steinberg had become an obsession.

His secretary was unaware of what he was up to, even when she was asked to go out and buy items for him which she had never done before – wire, batteries, a clock, a box, etc. She remarked one day to another colleague in the building that she thought her boss was going mad. "He spends his time playing with a clock and some wires..." she had said.

Finally Slyberger's bomb was ready – had played his video over many times and had checked that he had done everything necessary to make sure that when he set the alarm on the clock the bomb would explode. He of course had no idea what sort of an explosion it would be but he felt sure it would be enough to polish off old man Steinberg, if set in the right place.

Ah, but that was it. Where indeed was the right place?

XCII

The lapses into what was almost a state of unconsciousness plagued Joe Miller and his behaviour in that state began to worry his wife, Joan, so much that in the end she agreed that her husband would have to go away for treatment. Joe's lucid moments had became few and far between and indeed it was whilst in one of his bouts of unusual behaviour that he was whisked by ambulance to a home twenty miles outside Pittsburgh.

He was placed in a ward with other patients suffering varying degrees of stress and depression. He was given injections which calmed him down but was spared electro-convulsive therapy, which had been stopped in the hospital the previous year. His wife was able to visit him almost at any time but found it difficult to make the journey as she did not drive and the buses to the hospital were unreliable and infrequent.

On one of her early visits she had an interview with the doctor looking after her husband. He questioned her deeply as to probable causes of the illness suffered by Joe. He asked about his work and Joan gave him the full story of how Joe had been a very senior executive until his company had been taken over and how he had at first been given another senior post in the takeover company only to find in less than a year that he was pushed aside and sacked. She explained that from then on he had gradually sunk into depression, relieved by a short while when he had finally obtained a job in Canada, only to find a few months later that he had once again been thrown on the scrap heap by the same man, purely coincidental but nevertheless true. She thought her husband from then on had increased his hate for this man who had ruined his life. She told the doctor the man was Steinberg. She said how pictures of this man in newspapers seemed to make her husband get very angry. She explained how for over two years he had gone down to the local library to read the papers for jobs and how he had become obsessed with writing and correcting letters, without the hope of getting a favourable response from any. She told him of how he had been mugged in Miami and how her neighbour had one day brought him home from the local library after he had suffered what was likely a fit.

She was assured that he would get better but that other upsets would likely result in the same depression and consequential illness. They thought he might have to stay in the home for about six months.

XCIII

Once again the meeting of the redundants was held in the Queen's at Weybridge. Tony had arranged a London visit from Geneva so as to coincide with the meeting, and he and Ray were the first to arrive. Tony had spent nearly a year with the European branch of the company previously looked after by Abe Slyberger and he told Ray that he believed he had begun to pull the business out of the mess into which it had sunk. He said he knew this would not go down well with the old, UK ex-WECO employees but he needed to gain the confidence of Steinberg if he were to be beyond suspicion when whatever was planned as action against the man was carried out; he also reminded Ray that there were still a number of their old friends and associates from Europe who having been taken over themselves were now Steinberg employees and at least he might save their jobs. Ray and Tony agreed that Tony's success would not be relayed to the meeting as it would only likely cause resentment as the others were unaware of the contribution made by Tony in seeking revenge on Steinberg.

Five others turned up at the meeting. All had been previously and all but one had settled into a new way of life and their previous WECO life was beginning to slip into the past. However, poor Joe Thomas had only succeeded in getting part-time work in garages, having many years earlier served an apprenticeship in a London bus garage. The work was better than spending his time doing nothing but he was an angry man and found it difficult to accept that it was due to his politics that he had found it so difficult to get full-time employment in the work he had been engaged in for so many years and in which he was particularly skilled.

After the initial salutations Ray gave a resume of what he knew of the latest happenings to the ex-WECO employees – others added further information.

The meeting was little more than a get-together of old colleagues, most of those present, although not saying as much, did not appear to have any great desire to carry on any crusade against those who were in the business of takeovers. The conversation was mainly about their own jobs and of other ex-colleagues from whom they had heard. No one asked questions as to whether anyone had any ideas for stopping takeovers, indeed it was almost as if the purpose of the meeting had been forgotten. Neither Ray nor Tony, who had talked aside, said anything which would have given any hint to a stranger attending the meeting that this was anything but a meeting of old friends having a get-together away from their wives.

It was near to closing time when Joe Thomas, who had begun to wonder exactly what he was doing there, spoke up.

"Comrades," he said with a twinkle in his eye, "Comrades, I've enjoyed very much having a drink with you all and I've enjoyed the jokes but I have begun to wonder what the bloody hell I am doing here. I thought this meeting was called to further our quest for a solution to the takeover problem but instead all we have talked about is our jobs, or lack of them, and what Tom Dick and Harry are doing now. It's great to know we have all kept in touch and that most of us have found jobs but what about the anger we all had a few years back and how we believed it was up to us to try to do something about these guys who mastermind takeovers? What has happened? Have we all forgotten or have we once again settled back into our little holes and hope to forget all about it? Well, comrades, you may be all right, but I for one am not. I haven't had a steady job since I was sacked and I can't forget – I seem to be pretty helpless on my own, but at least I thought I knew some who were trying to do the right thing, which although it might not help me, at least it could help other poor sods who otherwise might find themselves in the same situation we were all in some years back."

There was a stunned silence – Ray and Tony looked at each other but said nothing – both wanted to tell the meeting what they had done, how they had got the Wilsons to go to Primrose and later they themselves had made a short but valuable trip there also, but they had resolved that the fewer who knew what they had done and guessed what they might be intending to do, the better.

Jim Johnson was the first to speak – he had listened and knew exactly what Joe meant and to some extent he felt uneasy, in fact most there felt the same. "We all know and agree with what you say, Joe, no, we haven't forgotten but, yes, we have gone into our little sheltered lives and tried to forget. I figured a long while ago that although we talked a lot at first, I doubted whether any of us could ever change anything. Sure we shot our mouths off and I bet it made most of us feel a little better inside, just as if we were really doing something. But it was all talk – there was nothing we could do and most of us knew it. We all feel sorry for you, Joe and I know we wished there was something we could do to help but it's as much as most of us can do to look after ourselves. Sure, we come to the meetings and at first we thought we were part of a crusade but latterly I am sure we came because it's good to talk and extra good to be able to talk to people who have been in the same position. We all know that unless you have been made redundant you have no idea what it feels like – we are indeed your comrades, Joe, but we are not about to start the revolution – I'm too old in the tooth anyway."

Ray was the next to speak – he measured his words carefully, wishing he could say that one had done something but knowing that to do so was not wise. He would have to wait – wait until some positive action had been taken and then providing it was not such that he might cause the law to come down on either he or Tony he might be able to say something. Anyway he thought it was not a case of trying to show one had done something, much rather to do something that would help others in the future and stop this foolish waste of manpower, jobs and time.

"I think Jim has said what we all feel. There comes a time when one has to decide to get on with life – sure we would like to have seen the downfall of such as Steinberg and all would-be takeover specialists whose only desire is more and more power and more wealth and self-aggrandisement, but we failed to make our mark, but we did give it a go – we did write to MPs and although most of you don't know it the letters to newspapers from Redundants' Revenge a couple of years back was the brainchild of someone known to us – more, I cannot say, but don't think that because nothing happens that that means that we have all gone to ground – you should of course keep this under your hat, especially as you all attended the meetings."

The announcement made by Ray came as a surprise and somewhat of a shock to the more timid of those present. It was pretty certain from the reaction of those who did not know that there would be no more said about it.

The meeting broke up but no date was set for a further meeting and Ray guessed that those who were against what had been revealed would hardly want to involve themselves in other actions which might at some time bring them into conflict with the law.

XCIV

Of the million or so inhabitants of Memphis, Tennessee, going about their daily lives whether working in pharmaceuticals, cotton, river transport or the many other varied activities of this city, Lee Crocket was unaware as he sat on a seat overlooking the great river. He was deep in thought. His mind travelled to Texas and his first time in oil as a young man. He remembered the excitement of his first gusher and the celebrations which followed and later, much later, his first sight of the sea when he was transferred to work on one of the new rigs in the Gulf of Mexico. Old Turner was a good and fair man and Lee had enjoyed the years he had worked for the family. It was a pity the oil ran out on the inland field he had operated with Mike Turner and even more a pity that it had taken them so long to drill at sea so that this time the money ran out. If only Mike had believed him when he had said that he was sure they were near to hitting it big – goddam that bank and goddam that bastard double-crossing the old man – double-crossing me too, he thought.

It was near dusk when Lee slowly got up from his seat and made his way back to his apartment. He had made his mind up – some of these guys think they can do anything and nobody can touch them – well, he thought, there is one guy they can't mess with, no, not Lee Crocket.

In his apartment he watched television for a while but most of the time his mind was elsewhere. He was trying to figure out how he could find out where this big shot Steinberg lived. He knew Arkansas Oil had offices in Houston and he thought it would be a good idea to put a call through and find out more about the corporation. It was too late to ring that evening but he resolved to ring first thing the next day.

At nine thirty the following morning he duly telephoned Houston and after much trouble was able to discover that most of the work was now done by the corporation in New York. He also managed to find out that the big boss, Steinberg, had a home somewhere up in New England.

Lee had earned good money on the rig and he had managed to put by several thousand dollars, enough to last him, providing he lived carefully, for a few years without earning at all. He had never been to New York but knew that if he wanted to find out more about the man, he would almost certainly have to go to there. Therefore he withdrew some of his savings and bought an air ticket to New York.

Arriving at La Guardia in the late afternoon he was soon in a taxi and being driven to a small hotel which the taxi driver had assured him was both comfortable and reasonably priced.

Armed with the addresses given to him by Houston he had decided to take a taxi first to the Brooklyn office where he would try to get Steinberg's home address and if unsuccessful then take a taxi to the offices on Manhattan.

It was ten o'clock the following morning when he entered the Brooklyn office and going straight to Reception asked whether it were possible to see Steinberg.

"Mr Steinberg is not in the office today – can I leave a message for him? Who shall I say called?"

"He wouldn't know my name but if you see him you can tell him a representative from his rig in the Gulf called to see him," Lee replied and added, "is he likely to be in today?"

"I am sorry I have no information on that point but I could put you through to his secretary, she may be able to help you."

Lee thought, for a moment, "OK, put me through if you can."

The receptionist managed to get the secretary. "Pick up the telephone over there, I have Mr Steinberg's secretary on the line."

"Hullo, I understand you are Mr Steinberg's secretary – could you tell me if he is likely to be in the office today?"

"No, he won't be in today – how can I help you?"

"I worked for your boss for a short time – I'm up from Memphis – I wanted to have a word with him, it's a personal matter."

"I'm afraid Mr Steinberg will only see people by appointment and I can tell you he will only see a small proportion of those who wish to see him – he's a very busy man. Would you like me to see if he will see you? Can you tell me what it is about?" Ruby knew that it was most unlikely her boss would see this man but nevertheless she would go through the motions.

"As I said it's a personal matter – you can tell him it concerns some oil." Ruby had made some notes on their conversation and was about to reply when Lee continued, "Is he at his home in New England?"

"He was this morning – in fact he will be there for a few more days – I am required to go up there today – I'll pass your message on to him. Have you a card? I'll pick it up on my way down, I'm just about to leave."

"No, I guess I haven't – just tell him Lee Crocker wants to see him – I'll be in New York for another week and I could visit him in his home if he would prefer that – I'll give details of my hotel to the receptionist."

The conversation ended and Lee duly passed his hotel details to the receptionist. "So as I know her again, would you be a doll and point out to me the lady I have just been speaking to? I understand she'll be down very soon." The receptionist, a lady near to Lee's own age, looked at him suspiciously and he smiled nicely at her.

"She's usually in a hurry, but I'll point her out to you – but don't you tell her, it would be more than my job was worth. I've been told not to let strangers know who are those who work on the twelfth floor – that's the management floor. But I heard you say you've come all the way from Memphis to see him – my grandfather came from Memphis, so I feel I ought to help you a little."

Lee thanked her and took a seat opposite the receptionist desk. Ten minutes went by and then just down the corridor the cage door of the old personal elevator was opened and the receptionist immediately signalled to Lee that this would be Steinberg's secretary.

The cage door was closed and brisk footsteps along the corridor announced the arrival of the secretary. She walked over to the reception desk. "I believe you have a hotel and room number of a gentleman I spoke to a short while ago." Lee Crocket listened but after looking up at the lady as she passed kept his head down, only taking occasional glances over his newspaper to make sure he would be able to recognise her again.

As she left he got off his chair, thanked the receptionist and went out of the building not many steps behind Ruby, who he saw ahead walking towards the subway. Lee followed. However, close to the subway entrance she hesitated as if she had changed her mind, turning round towards Lee she hailed a passing cab. Lee at the same time looked anxiously behind him and luckily he too attracted the attention of a cab following close behind.

"Could you see if you can catch and follow that cab which just pulled out in front?" Lee breathlessly said to the driver.

"OK, bud, I'll see what I can do. Do you want that I should stop them?"

"No. I would just like you to follow – I have been asked to follow the lady."

The roads were busy but not too crowded and Lee's driver had little difficulty in catching the cab and following at a respectable distance. Both cabs were soon crossing the Brooklyn Bridge and then left into Park Row right onto Broadway. Travelling north and crossing traffic lights quite close together until 33rd Street where they turned left and shortly drove into the bus depot opposite the Penn station. Lee's cab pulled up close behind just as Steinberg's secretary walked away from her cab. The cab driver paid, Lee walked casually towards the ticket desk where the lady he was following had stopped. Having made her purchase she walked away towards a bus parked nearby.

Lee went up to the ticket office.

He produced a badge he had in his pocket and flashed it at the clerk issuing tickets – the badge was one used for identification when making a boat crossing to a rig.

"I'm Memphis police and following the lady who just bought a ticket from you. Can you tell me what ticket she bought?" Lee said, returning the badge to his pocket.

"Gee, police – I ain't never had occasion to help the police – what has she done? Gee, you wait till I tell Martha."

Lee looked impatient and expressed his feelings.

"Come on, friend, I've followed her halfway across the country, I can't lose her now – tell me quickly where she is going."

"Sorry, officer, the lady bought a ticket to a little place up in New England called Primrose – it's up north – New Hampshire or Maine or somewheres."

"Thanks, what time does the bus go?"

"It goes at noon – that's twenty minutes from now – do you want a return ticket?"

"Why sure – how much is that – and is there a later bus?"

The young clerk looked at him incredulously. "Why no, sir, there is only one bus a day on that route, not many folks use the buses up there – guess there aren't many up there anyways." He smiled. "That'll be fifty dollars."

Ruby had got onto the bus and seated herself near the front behind the driver's cab. Lee, armed with his ticket, did not get onto the bus straight away but walked across to a bookstall and bought himself something to read on the journey.

Just before noon when he had seen the driver climb up into his cab Lee walked smartly to the bus and boarded just before the driver closed the door and drove off.

Drivers were changed at Albany and Claremont and the bus finally pulled into Primrose at eight o'clock that evening with only six passengers aboard. Lee had read his book for most of the journey but had fallen asleep and was awakened by the bus driver calling out "Primrose". The lady he was following was already climbing down from the bus when he dragged himself, half-asleep, from his seat.

On getting off the bus he could see they had stopped right outside an hotel well lit by lights shining on the building and a hanging sign which read "Lake Hotel".

He followed his prey into the hotel at a respectable distance. She walked straight to the reception desk and was met by Jake Ramsden, who was holding the fort whilst his receptionist had a break.

"Good evening, Miss Steers – we got your message and have kept a room for you. Mr Steinberg's chauffeur will pick you up at nine tomorrow. I expect you would like to go to your room before dinner – we have put you in room seven, second on the right at the top of the stairs – here's your key. I have reserved a table for you."

Ruby took the key and, carrying her small bag, disappeared up the stairs. Lee, who had been standing behind the lady, moved forward to the desk. "Can I help you, sir?" Jake said.

"I hope you have a spare room for tonight."

"I think we can manage that – would you like dinner? It is still being served."

Lee said he would and was shown to his room on the first floor.

ACTION

XCV

BOMBS ARE NOT easy things to carry, especially if they
have been made by an amateur. Abe Slyberger had a bomb –
at least he was pretty certain it was – but he had made it
rather big and thus would easily be detected if carried on
one's person, he needed to find something to carry it in. Of
course he could take it to his car but at both ends of the
journey, wherever that may be, he would be obliged to
portage.

Abe was not someone who carried a briefcase or indeed
an attaché-case, the only case he possessed was one he took
with him when he went away from home for a long stay. He
decided he would need to invest in another as his one and
only was far too big. Thus armed with the appropriate
measurements he went searching for a case. It struck him that
he would be better to buy his case at a big store where they
were unlikely to remember him if the case were found near or
at the scene of the crime. He also decided that he would pay
cash as no one would then be able to trace who bought the
item – yes, he had to buy in Macey's or Bloomingdale's.

He eventually bought his case in Bloomingdale's and
since he took so little time in buying, and paid for the item in
cash he convinced himself that no one would ever be able to
trace the case back to him.

Slyberger was now ready to go into action – but where?

XCVI

Steinberg sat in an easy chair in his well-furnished study. It was evening but still quite light outside although the sun had sunk below Hanover Heights, which he could see from his window. He had some paperwork he should look at but he was not in the mood for writing – he was getting old, he thought. But actually he had had a strange feeling come over him that made him sit and think. Being in Primrose it was not unnatural for his thoughts to be turned to long ago. I wonder whatever happened to Sergeant Stowski and that creep Johnson, he mused – and his mind went back to the parade ground just over the hill and to the time he and his buddy, Jem Hood, went AWOL to get over to Primrose to see girls they had met. A contented smile came to his face. Suddenly he remembered Molly and he wondered whether she had found anything out about Zoë.

He pressed the bell next to the chair to call his housekeeper, who appeared shortly after.

"Yes, sir, can I get you anything?"

"Oh Molly, I was wondering if you remembered our conversation a while back and whether you managed to find out anything."

Molly came further into the room before answering, almost as if she did not want anyone else to hear what she was going to say. She had turned the matter over and over in her mind and had wondered whether perhaps it would be better if he were not told the truth but finally she had decided she would tell him but only if he raised the matter first.

"Yes, I did make some very discreet enquiries and I have found that the lady who was probably the one you recall died many years ago." Steinberg visibly shuddered; it was something he had expected but somehow he had begun to hope that perhaps she was still alive.

Molly, who had noticed the reaction of her boss, hesitated before continuing. "As far as I can make out she had a son who is still alive but she died many years ago."

Steinberg was silent for a while and Molly stood by, not knowing what else to say. It began to make her wonder if it would not have been better for her not to have told the old man.

"Would you like a cup of tea, sir – I remember you said you liked one now and again."

"Yes, that would be nice, Molly – it's such a long while ago I can't even remember the girl's face – I know I thought she was beautiful and she probably was, but beauty is in the eye of the beholder as my old mother used to tell me. Bring a cup in for yourself, I feel I need a bit of company for a while."

Molly turned to leave the room and as she turned, she noticed Steinberg's eyes had filled with water.

She returned with the tea on a large tray, which she placed on the study desk and poured the tea into the delicate cups from a china pot.

"I'm a very wealthy man, Molly – I think I would like to help her son if he can be found."

Molly was thoughtful for a moment. Should she tell him what she had been told about the son or should she let him find out for himself. It was a difficult decision for her to make but she was sure her boss would not wish to become involved with a big-shot gambler who, she had been told, was not a very nice person to know. It would do Steinberg's image no good at all coming at a time when from what she had read in the papers he was a highly respected business man who people seemed to admire.

"I think I should tell you Mr Steinberg that although I have little information concerning the son, I was told that he is not a nice person to know. It seems he is a big shot gambler who lives in Las Vegas – his name is, I think, Bronson – Peter Bronson."

XCVII

"Get me Mickey O'Brien. I want to speak to him," Bronson called to the secretary in the next office. It was usual for a secretary to be on hand when the top men returned from the clubs, even though it was now near to midnight.

The secretary tapped out the name on the keyboard in front of her and very soon the telephone number and the address appeared on the screen. She saw it was a New York number and got up from her desk and walked to the next office. "That number you asked me to get is a New York number and as you know it's the middle of the night there – shall I leave it to the relief secretary to ring first thing in the morning?"

"Lady, when I say I want to speak to someone now, I mean now – I don't give a damn if he's fast asleep, I want to speak to him."

The secretary was almost out of the door before Bronson finished speaking. She could see how angry the man was and being new at the job was keen to please. She picked up the phone and tapped the number. It rang for a while and then a male voice answered.

"Yeah, who's that?"

"I have a call from Las Vegas for Mr O'Brien."

"Christ, do you know the time – what sonofabitch rings me at this time of night?" Almost as soon as he had said it, his tired mind realised the only person who would have the nerve to ring him in the middle of the night. "It's Mr Bronson."

"OK, put him through."

"Your call to Mr O'Brien."

"Mickey, I want that you do a job for me. I want you to find out all you can about a guy called Steinberg – Julius Steinberg. You no doubt have heard of him, he's a big man in oil. He operates from New York."

"Yeah, I know of the guy – he's loaded."

"I want that you should find out where he lives. What kind of a guy he is. If he's married, if he has any family. You know the stuff – a complete rundown on the man, his life history if you like. But I don't want him or any of his close associates to know who is asking and what it is all about. Can you do that for me?"

"Sure I'll do it, but you'll have to give me a little time, these big guys usually keep their private lives very private – it won't be that easy, Pete."

"I want that you should do it for me and I'll of course remember you kindly."

"OK, Pete, I'll start on it right away – that is in the morning – Jesus, Pete, it's three o'clock in the morning here – I'm back to bed now – Goodnight."

Mickey replaced the receiver next to his bed and put his head on the pillow and tried to go to sleep but all the time his mind kept thinking of Steinberg. It was gone five o'clock before he eventually settled to sleep, after having guessed why Bronson wanted to know all about Steinberg and planning how he would begin his enquiries.

XCVIII

Some weeks had passed since the last meeting of the redundants had been held and Ray Holmes, who had not really discussed with Tony the events of that meeting, thought it was time they decided what if anything they were going to do. Tony had returned to Geneva and Ray put a call through to him one evening.

Tony agreed that they should meet and said he would arrange to come over to London the following weekend. Once again they would meet in the Queen's.

It transpired that only that week Tony had heard that now he had put this European operation on its feet Steinberg had decided to sell and having found a French company keen to buy, Tony's time with the company was coming to an end.

He had been told that he would be paid for the remainder of his contract but apart from handing over to the new French owner he was no longer required. Thus after a further visit to Geneva he would once again be on his own.

Asked what he thought should happen concerning the Steinberg affair, Tony stated he did not want to let the matter drop. Ray for his part had lost a great deal of his anger but it seemed that Tony, in spite of having worked again for Steinberg, still wanted to do something. The recent action by the big man had reminded Tony in no uncertain way that Steinberg had little or no thought for others. Tony had a contract but most of the other employees in Geneva would lose their jobs as the French company would undoubtedly bring in their own staff.

"OK, Tony, you think we should do something. What exactly do you think we should do? Do you intend killing the man or just scaring him? Do you think we should do it ourselves or have you got someone in mind to do it for us?" Ray said, half in jest, but soon realising Tony was far from jesting.

"I've got one more visit to Geneva and then I have a ticket to the States to hand over some very confidential documents to the parent company. I thought about sending them by courier but since they offered me a ticket I thought I would go. In any case I can clear up my own personal paperwork concerned with my contract. I'd like you to come with me."

"Tony, I've got a job to go to. It is not going to be easy for me to get more time off."

"This is our one opportunity to do what we decided to do some years back, you must come. I'm sure you can find some excuse to take some leave."

Ray was obviously not happy about taking more leave but Tony had put it in such a way that he felt obliged not to let his friend down."

"OK, supposing I do manage to get the leave, what then?"

"I reckon we go to the States and find an hotel in New York where we stay until I have settled my paperwork and then we head north to Primrose – perhaps we stay somewhere nearby rather than actually in the town. Then we sort out our problem – anyway, we play it by ear."

"Yes, but what are we going to do? I have got to be frank, I don't think I could kill the man in cold blood – as I said at an earlier meeting a lot of the anger has gone."

"Your anger might have gone but the fact that the man has once again taken action without any concern for the people who worked for him has made me very angry, I certainly could strangle him ... I mean it."

Ray could see that Tony meant what he said. He had no wish to get involved in a murder but lacked the courage to say no – after all, he had suffered as much as Tony. Perhaps his anger would rise again so that he could help carry out the deed or perhaps he could persuade Tony over the next week or so that it just was not worth the risk. Maybe if he tagged along he could make it all go away!

"I'll come with you but I may try and talk you out of killing him. Perhaps we could rough him up a bit."

"You'll help for old times' sake – the bastard does not deserve to live when he keeps creating so much unhappiness."

Tony told Ray that he would book the flight and let him know the dates arranged in good time. If there were a problem on getting his leave Ray promised to let Tony know so that the dates could be changed.

XCIX

After two months in the mental institution Joe Miller was feeling better. He had undergone insulin treatment and for much of the time he was almost his old self. As has been said earlier his wife did not find it easy to visit him and at one visit the doctor in charge of her husband's case told her that he could go home for a visit providing she would make sure he returned for further treatment after the weekend.

Joe was duly allowed out and indeed was so well at home that weekend that he said he would like to return on his own, particularly as it would save his wife a return journey on the infrequent bus route. His wife rang the hospital to see what the doctor's reaction would be and received a favourable reply. Joe duly returned on the Monday under his own steam.

The following weekend he again went home and returned on the Monday. He was now feeling very well. However, he told his wife that he would not come home the next weekend as he had promised to spend some time with one of the male patients with whom he had befriended and a man who needed to regain his confidence and Joe felt sure he could be of help.

The weekend arrived and Joe booked in to say he would be leaving the hospital to return on the Monday. It was now Friday afternoon and Joe took the bus from the hospital to Pittsburgh and then a cab to the airport where he collected $1000 from the bank. He then booked a return ticket to New York by credit card and later that evening found himself a small hotel off Lexington Avenue on the east side.

During the night something happened and he awoke and tried desperately to remember where he was and what it was all about. He had great difficulty in recalling what he had done the previous day but he knew it was something important. He had been in hospital, he knew that, but why was he there and indeed where was he, and more importantly – who was he?

The next morning he washed and dressed, packed his bag and went down to reception. He was greeted by the clerk behind the desk as he handed in his key. "May I have my bill, please?" he said.

"Why, don't you remember, Mr Milne? You insisted on paying last night as you were only going to stay one night. I booked that bus ticket for you," he added.

Joe Miller looked puzzled.

"Oh yes, the bus ticket. How much do I owe you?"

"You don't owe me nuthin', you gave me cash and here's the ticket which Tony collected for me this morning."

"Thanks very much and thank Tony for me. What time is the bus?"

"Gee, Mr Milne, you must have had a good night – don't you remember? You asked me to ring the bus station before you gave me the cash. They told us there was only one bus and it leaves at twelve noon."

"Oh of course – how stupid of me. So I've got a bit of time to spare as it's only ten thirty now. By the way, where is the bus station?"

"I did tell you last night but I guess you were tuned in somewhere else. If I was you, Mr Milne, I'd take a cab and ask him to drop you at the bus station opposite the Penn Station. Would you like me to come along and make sure you get the right bus? I clock off soon and gotta go to the Penn."

"Thanks, that would be good of you. I seem to have forgotten where I am and where I'm going."

The receptionist smiled, "Yeah, I thought you had a problem. You seemed to be fine last evening, I guess you got a slight attack of amnesia – I remember seeing it in a film not long ago. This dame – oh well, anyways she got her memory back after being hit on the head. Guess you wouldn't want nothing like that, eh Mr Milne?" He laughed. "Don't worry, I'll see you're OK. You go in the dining room and I'll get someone to bring you a coffee – you'll get your bus all right, I'll call you when it's time to go."

Joe Miller thanked the man and walked into the dining room and sat down. He was on his own. He sat thinking – he knew he was Mr Milne as the receptionist had just told him, but he could not yet remember anything else. The receptionist had said he would be all right so he should not worry – yet if he had asked for a ticket last night it must be to his home, wherever that was, and if he arrived home he was sure he would soon recognise it and recover his memory.

C

Mickey O'Brien's obvious contact to find out all he could about Steinberg was MacDonald. Therefore, soon after breakfast on the day he had been so rudely awakened by the call from Las Vegas, he telephoned the Arkansas Oil offices in Brooklyn.

"I'd like to speak to MacDonald – is he around today?"

"Who is it speaking?"

"Tell him it's Mickey – he'll know me, I'm an old buddy of his."

Mac was not in his office but the operator put out a call for him and he answered on another line.

"Hullo, Mac here – it's Mickey, isn't it? I'm not in my own office. Can I call you back?"

"Hi, Mac – there's no need for that. I'd like to meet you, we should talk, you know about what. Can you decide a place and I'll come over?"

Mac thought for a moment and then said, "I go to a small Italian restaurant around the corner – I could see you there at twelve thirty, if that's OK. It's right round the corner from this office on Fulton Street – it's called Luigi's."

"OK, see you there at twelve thirty."

Mac left his office at twelve fifteen and made his way round to Luigi's and got a table for two. Soon after twelve thirty, Mickey O'Brien entered the restaurant with two heavies and made his way across to Mac's table.

"What's with the heavies, Mickey? I thought we were going to talk."

"Hi, Mac – the boys follow me around – guess I must be popular. I see you're on your own, I'll tell 'em to come back in an hour."

Mickey spoke to his guards, who looked suspiciously at Mac and they turned round and left the restaurant.

"You know me, Mickey – you know there was no need to show me you meant business. I'll be straight with you, if only for old times' sake."

"Well, you see, Mac, I get so used to guys trying to pull one over on me that I begin to trust no one."

"What can I get you to drink?" Mac asked.

They had been there ten minutes, in which time the preliminaries to getting food and drink had been gone through, when Mickey raised the matter for which he had called the meeting. Mac of course knew what it would be all about.

"Pete Bronson telephoned me last night – he wants the low-down on this guy Steinberg. I guess you told him who it was. Now he wants to know all he can about the guy and has given me the job since I first got the information and am near to the main place for his operations."

"What sort of information do you think he wants?"

"He wants to know everything I can get hold of – his age, where he comes from, where he lives. Is he married? Has he any children? What kind of a guy is he? You know the stuff – now come on, Mac, what do yer know?"

Mac had guessed this might be what Mickey wanted and whilst he had waited for him to arrive had recollected a few points on his boss.

"Well, he's a tough old bird. I'm not sure of his age but he's in his eighties, quite well along I would think. He's Jewish, but I guess you guessed that already. He's from New York – his father was an immigrant a hundred or so years back from Poland or somewhere in Europe. He often tells people about his old man working on the Brooklyn Bridge – in fact, his old man died after getting an illness due to working for long hours under water level when they were building the foundations. He was brought up in a tough neighbourhood. He joined the army in 1917 and went to France; I believe he was taken prisoner. He was stationed one time up in New Hampshire, not far from where he now lives.

That's where he met this girl. He told the story to a colleague of mine. Seems he returned after the war but found she had already married. He later got married himself, had no family and his wife has been dead for years. He now lives in a new mansion which he had built up in New Hampshire."

"What's the place called?"

"It's a small place called Primrose."

Mickey asked more questions which Mac did his best to answer. Almost exactly one hour after dismissing the heavies the door opened and the two big apes entered and came over to the table. Mickey put a small bundle of notes on the table, got up and followed by the two heavies left the restaurant. As he got to the door he turned round to look at Mac and out loud said, "I'll be in touch."

CI

The dining room at the Lake Hotel was nearly empty when Lee Crocket came down for breakfast. Lee chose a table near the window and Emile, a long-time waiter at the hotel came over to him.

"Good morning, sir. What can I get you?"

"I'd like two eggs, sunny side up, and some bacon. And have you got some hot rolls? I'm feeling hungry this morning."

"I'll see what I can do for you."

Emile took a glass of grapefruit juice from the tray he carried and placed it in front of Lee, who picked it up and swallowed it down.

"Could I have another?" And whilst Emile picked up another glass from his tray Lee continued, "Last night I came in from New York on the bus and another passenger, also from New York, got off here and came into the hotel – I guess she stayed here. Have you seen her this morning?"

"Oh, you mean Miss Steers, the middle-aged lady who works for old Steinberg."

"Do I?"

"Yeah, she was the only other person to come off the bus with you. No, I've not seen her this morning but I guess she'll be down right soon, as I heard Jake say her driver would be coming for her at nine this morning. Joe ain't usually late."

"Does she have to go far to this boss of hers?"

"No, I guess it's no more than a mile up the road to the Steinberg mansion. But then there's that long drive, guess that's why they send a car down for her."

Emile left the table and moved into the kitchen. At that moment Ruby came into the dining room, passed the time of the day with Lee and took a seat at the next table.

"I saw you on the New York bus. Do you come all this way often?" Lee said.

"Not very often, but occasionally my boss wants me up here when he does not feel like making the journey down to the big city. He's getting old."

"He must be an important man to get you to come all this way."

"Yes, I suppose he is. It's Julius Steinberg, the oil magnate – I think he is quite well known. No doubt you have heard of him."

"Oh yes, I know he comes on television sometimes."

"What are you doing up here? You don't sound like a local and certainly you're not from New York?"

"You are quite right, I come from the South – I'm from Memphis and I came up here for a break. I needed somewhere off the beaten track to just relax and think – I've had a few problems and I think it is necessary sometimes to take stock of one's life. Don't you agree?"

Emile arrived with Lee's breakfast and then turning to Ruby asked her what he could get her. She told him and then continued her conversation with Lee. "Yes, I know what you mean, never done it myself, always been too busy to think straight. Sometimes feel I could do with a break – but then coming up here is always a break for me. I enjoy the bus ride, the countryside up here is so beautiful – and it gives me time to think. Oh please, don't let me stop you eating your breakfast, it'll get cold."

"Why don't you join me at my table, it'll be easier on our necks," Lee said smiling. Ruby got out of her chair and moved to the seat opposite. She was a good-looking woman – perhaps forty-five years of age and very smartly dressed. Lee himself was a man in his fifties, well built, quite handsome and standing close to six feet.

"Do you know the area?" Lee asked.

"Not very well but I have been up here a few times and in odd moments I have managed to see some of the very local area. Of course the lake, the waterfall and Hanover Heights."

"Do you have any spare time on this visit. It's probably an awful cheek but I was wondering if you could show me around and then perhaps we could explore some more on our own."

Ruby was taken by surprise by Lee's advance but quite liked it. She had never seemed to have time for men since she had been let down almost a decade ago when she almost married. She had decided then to pursue her career and keep away from the opposite sex.

"Well, I don't get much spare time but it certainly sounds a nice idea. I don't even know your name."

Lee hesitated. "Oh, my name is John Davis."

"I'm Ruby Steers – nice to meet you."

"Will you be free this morning?" Lee asked.

"No, I'm sorry. I have to go out to my boss's house. He wants me for something – I have no idea what he wants but it must be important or he wouldn't have got me to come all this way up here. If I am finished early I might be able to come out for a while. But how would I get in touch with you – I expect you will be going out exploring?"

"Oh I shall certainly take a stroll along Main Street this morning and then go and see what the lake out there looks like, but I won't go far afield and I'll be back for lunch. You could ring the hotel if you are free and if I'm not there leave a number for me to return your call."

Ruby agreed this is what she would do. They continued their conversation right through an enjoyable breakfast and whilst drinking their third cup of coffee they were disturbed. Joe Mancini came into the dining room and said he was ready to take her up to the house.

"I'll perhaps see you later," she said, as she picked up her briefcase and left.

CII

Julius Steinberg now in his eighty-sixth year had been told by his housekeeper that his secretary had arrived from New York and was waiting in the office. Steinberg said he would call her when he had finished his breakfast. "I didn't have a very good night, Molly. I kept waking and going over my life, I guess it was sparked off by what you told me yesterday. Give her a coffee. I'll see her shortly."

Molly noticed that he looked tired and she was concerned that she had been the cause of his restlessness. She returned to the office and explained to Ruby that her boss was still having breakfast, having been late up after a restless night. She did not, however, say why she thought he had had a bad night.

Steinberg knew he had appeared vulnerable to his housekeeper and he knew that this was not how he had been through most of his life. He was aware that he could not show this side of his person if he was to remain on top – he firmly believed that it was a weakness which would only lead to disaster in business if one ever became soft. He told himself it was a temporary phase that he would soon come out of and he would soon be back to his old self. He had been a tough businessman all his working life and he knew he had upset many people over the years but what he did not know was that there were people out there who wanted revenge and that some were prepared to take action.

He certainly never considered that Abe Slyberger would be seeking to do him harm or that people from that Limey company had been for some years plotting some action against him and his kind. He also would have been surprised to know that a foreman from a drilling rig was even at this moment staying in the Lake Hotel close by and probably contemplating doing him no good. Neither did he know that the man he had employed for a time as his second in command had had an obsession to do him harm and was now in a mental institution. Nor did he know that the son of his ex-girlfriend of many years ago was about to contact him and perhaps may wish him harm also. No one in all his working life had ever really faced up to him and none certainly had ever openly threatened him, any adverse mail he had received from victims of past takeovers or past employees had been kept from him by well-paid staff who acted closely with sharp lawyers who would very quickly frighten off any who appeared too aggressive.

Thus protected for many years his only fear was from the possibility of break-ins and the loss of some of his treasures – he had no fear of a personal nature simply because he never ever contemplated anyone being interested in doing him harm.

Having finished his breakfast he picked up the telephone and rang the room where his secretary was waiting.

"Good morning, Mr Steinberg."

"Good morning, Ruby. I'll meet you in the lounge in five minutes, it's more comfortable in there."

They both arrived in the lounge at the same time and Steinberg directed where Ruby should sit.

"I guess we have a few routine matters to clear and no doubt papers for me to sign. Let's get these out of the way first – I've got something I want you to do for me when we've finished."

The routine paper work finished, Steinberg got up from his chair and walked across to the window and looked at the hills on the other side of the lake. "Did you know why I came up here to live?" he said, but before Ruby had a chance to gather her thoughts at such an unusual question, he continued. "No, I guess you wouldn't ..." he hesitated, as if trying to decide whether to tell her or not. Ruby said nothing.

"I first came up here during the war. No, not the last war, the 17–18 war, that's a hell of a long time ago. I was in the army."

"I didn't know you had been a soldier, Mr Steinberg."

"Well I was, although it could have been another world. I was stationed for a while right over that hill," he said, pointing to the hill to the left of the lake. Ruby got up from her chair and moved to the window to get a better view.

"Yes, we were in a camp on the other side and Primrose was the nearest habitation. Not that much different from what it is now in the centre but without all those new houses near the lake – and of course before this house was built."

"It's certainly a nice place, you must have some happy memories of it to make you want to move up here when you had the whole of the States to choose from."

"I never looked at it that way. I'm a New Yorker and like to go back from time to time. Guess I feel I am not too far away even though it probably takes just as long to get there by road from here as it would do by plane from way out."

Ruby had been up to Primrose a number of times before but her boss had never before spoken to her in this way. She was conscious that there was something he wanted to tell her but was not finding it easy. She certainly did not want to miss hearing what it was and felt it necessary to prompt him.

"What was it you wanted me to do for you, Mr Steinberg?"

Steinberg was still looking out of the window and did not reply. "Is there anything the matter, sir?"

"No, I was just thinking. You see I knew someone who lived here many years ago and I was told only yesterday that she was dead. Of course, since it was so many years since I had seen her I had known that it was a strong possibility but nevertheless when you are told it is as if it had just happened."

"I understand," Ruby almost whispered.

"I would like you to try and find out all you can about a man named Peter Bronson. It seems he resides in Las Vegas – he's a gambler, I am told. Also, I was informed that he is not a very nice person."

"May I ask why you want me to find out about this man?"

"He is the son of the lady I used to know and when I was first told I thought I might be able to help him – but it seems he may not need help, nevertheless I would like to know a little about him. Maybe he is not as bad as I was led to believe."

Ruby said she would do what she could but until she had thought about it for a while she would not know where to start. She asked if she could enlist the help of others who worked for Steinberg and was told that she could but that he would not wish her to reveal who wanted to know, nor would he want Bronson to know there were enquiries being made about him and particularly who was making these enquiries.

Before she left, Steinberg dictated several notes, which he asked her to send straightway to his lawyer.

"I hardly need remind you, Ruby, how confidential these notes are."

"Yes, of course I understand and …" she hesitated, "may I say thank you, thank you so very much."

CIII

Abe Slyberger was anxious to see if his bomb would work but could not decide where he should place it. In truth, he had been so obsessed with the idea of making the bomb that he had given little thought as to what he would do with it afterwards. All he hoped was that it would give a big bang and dispose of Steinberg.

He was aware that Steinberg spent most of his time up in Primrose and therefore if the bomb were to be placed in the Brooklyn office it could only be done when it was known that Steinberg would be there. Exactly how he would be able to find out Steinberg's movements had not been worked out. He was certainly no friend of MacDonald so that avenue was closed to him, and he knew that if he asked Mac his boss's movements he would immediately become suspicious. No, there would have to be some other way.

He remembered that on his one visit to Primrose with Pepe Galento's contract man that they had told the housekeeper that they were from a film company and even suggested that she might be given a small part in the film when they returned. Maybe, he thought, she would be able to tell me when her boss would be in New York.

Abe, who had noted Steinberg's telephone number when being shown over the house by the housekeeper, now decided to use it.

It was early afternoon when he rang and he figured Steinberg might be having a rest after his lunch as he had been known to do when in New York.

"Hullo, Miss Steers speaking."

"Are you the housekeeper, lady?"

"No, you have Mr Steinberg's secretary – you should ring the same number but change the last digit to eight, you should then get Molly, I think she is in."

"Thanks, lady."

Abe redialled and after a considerable pause the receiver was lifted at the other end.

"Housekeeper."

"Hullo. is that Molly?"

"Yes. Who is that?"

"I called at the house some time back, we were thinking of making a film, do you remember?"

"Why yes – I remember – I thought you must have changed your mind."

"Well, these things sometimes take longer to set up than you first think. It finally got the go ahead and we will of course need to have the place virtually to ourselves when we film. We wouldn't want to worry your boss – anyways he might object to the idea – so if it's OK by you we would want to come when he is out of the way. I understand he goes down to New York from time to time and if you could let us know when he is down there for a few days, we could soon get ourselves set up."

"How exciting. How shall I contact you to let you know when he will be away?"

"Unfortunately, in this job we are always on the move so it's best that I ring you from time to time. That's if you don't mind me ringing too often. I think it's the easiest way for us to operate."

Molly agreed that it would not bother her in the least and it was left at that. Abe now had the means of knowing when his enemy would be in New York and all he had to do was to figure a way of getting into the Steinberg office without anyone of the staff knowing who he was.

* * *

Mickey O'Brien having got the information he required from MacDonald wondered whether it was worth making any further enquiries before passing what he had over to Bronson. He decided he would ring that night.

Bronson was out at a club and a message was left on his answerphone telling him that O'Brien had something to tell him.

On his return Bronson rang New York and of course once again got Mickey in the middle of the night.

"I know the place this guy lives. It must have been my ma he knew, she used to live there before I was born. I think I'll take a trip over there when I get time, I'd like to meet this guy. Try and find out his movements but don't let on I want to see him and if you find out any more let me know."

CIV

Ruby was puzzled where she should start to gather information on this man Peter Bronson. When she had arrived that morning she was happy and could not help thinking of the man she had had breakfast with in the hotel. Now she had been given this job to do and it had spoilt her morning. Of course she was interested in what her boss had told her and she would like to help him but it was not the sort of work she had ever done before and she wondered if she could do it. She sat for a while on her own to contemplate her position and apart from coming to the conclusion that Steinberg would have been much better giving the job to an agency which specialised in finding persons, she was no further forward. She thought of people with whom she worked and the worldliest man of all those she knew was MacDonald. Perhaps he could help but she was worried lest he should reveal why she was being asked to do the job and so she prepared a story which she would tell if asked. She put a call through to the Brooklyn office and asked if Mac was around. When she found he was out she asked if he would ring her back on his return.

Just after lunch he returned her call.

"What can I do for you, Ruby?"

"I wondered if you would be able to give me some advice. Julius has given me a job to do and frankly I just do not know where to start. How would you go about finding out about a person who lives on the other side of the States?"

"What sort of person is it? Are they well known in entertainment or business? You know the sort of thing – or arc they unknown and just an ordinary John Doe? That's what I would sort out first."

"Yes, but then what do I do?"

"Give me a clue as to the sort of person you are looking for and I might then be able to help. I have several friends who have contacts throughout the States."

"This man I have never heard of before but I understand he is from Las Vegas or at least now lives there. He's a man probably in his fifties."

Mac could not help guessing who it might be since he had so recently been involved with such a man.

"Would he be a gambler, Ruby?" Mac asked.

"Well as a matter of fact he is." Mac's question had shaken her at first but then she realised that it was an obvious question to ask since when that town was mentioned it immediately conjured up gambling joints.

"Would his name be Peter Bronson?"

Ruby was stunned.

"How did you know, Mac?"

"I just guessed since I too have become an unwilling party to Julius's long-lost friend."

"I don't understand. How did you get into this – has Julius asked you to look for this man?"

"No, he certainly has not – he knows nothing of my involvement and I would not wish him to know."

"Then how on earth did you get involved?"

"It's a long story but take it from me, Julius has told me nothing. All I know is that this man is the son of a lady Julius knew over half a century ago. He is a tough individual who himself wants to know about Julius. It seems they are destined to meet soon, I wouldn't mind betting."

"Can you tell me anything more, Mac?"

"I guess Julius has told you about the girl he knew whose name was Zoë. Well, it seems Zoë married whilst Julius was away in the war – she lived in Primrose – he had been a prisoner in Germany and had been in hospital a long while after the Armistice and she thought he was never coming back. They agreed to meet in four years to see how their lives had gone. They met just before Zoë was due to move away from Primrose and it seems her husband left her soon after. It was rumoured he left her because he said the child she was carrying was not his. Now, could it be that young Bronson is the son of our Julius? Intriguing isn't it?"

"Can you tell me any more about the man?"

"Well, I have been told that he is not a very nice person to know. He served a sentence in the State Pen many years ago, that we do know. In fact he was in prison when his mother died. She had promised to tell him who his father was when he reached twenty-one but she died before that."

"Sounds a sad story – poor lady. I rather hope Julius doesn't find out but I expect if he digs deep he will. Thanks, Mac, I don't know quite what to say to Julius. "

"I think he would become suspicious if you find all this out so quickly and for Christ sake don't tell him who gave you the information."

"Before I ring off – how did you get involved, Mac? Would you mind telling me?"

There was silence for a moment.

"I suggest you have a quiet word with Joe Mancini. He's up there, isn't he?"

"OK, Mac. Thanks again, I'll speak to Joe."

CV

Peter Bronson did not wait to hear further from O'Brien, he had enough information to go and see Steinberg and perhaps discover if he was in fact his real father. He had appointments in Vegas but as he said to one of the secretaries, "Tell them I got important business to deal with on the east coast and that I'll see them when I get back."

He got one of the girls to book him on a flight to New York the following day. The knowledge that after all these years he might be able to find his real father had completely changed his normal life pattern. He never figured that the chance, however small, of meeting his old man would have such an effect. Why the hell should he bother to seek out the old guy and what would he do if he met him?

It was while driving to the airport that he started thinking about his life. It had been anything but easy, certainly not in his early years, but then most kids without a father and no money could say this. There had undoubtedly been excitement, too much sometimes he thought. "I reckon I could write a book," he had once said to an old acquaintance. But no, he could never write book, English and writing had never been his strong point – and what about spelling? He smiled to himself, remembering the trouble he had at school.

He remembered how he had been the butt of one of the teachers at school, simply because he had difficulty in spelling. Joe Spedding, or One Lung Spud as he was known to the boys, took great pleasure at frequently humiliating him by picking on him to spell – the teacher would sweep into the room, his gown flowing behind, and swinging his arm to the left without looking or stopping as he made his way to his desk, would point straight at Bronson huddled in the farthest corner and shout, "Bronson, spell..." He remembered the laughing faces of the other pupils turning towards him as he rose to his feet and desperately tried to spell the word. No, he could never write a book. Bronson smiled as he remembered the time when One Lung had swept into the room and asked him to spell when he was at home sick, or so the boys told him.

Bronson boarded the plane in Las Vegas and soon after take-off his mind again wandered back through the years. He could not recollect at any time having been so concerned with his past – he was not the man for the past. He lived life and made life live for him but the idea of actually meeting his old man had somehow prompted this thinking back over which he seemed to have no control.

School was not all bad, he did have one or two friends but none of those who lived in the better side of town seemed to want to know him – maybe it was their folks who influenced them not to mix with any who lived on the wrong side of town, or maybe it was just him. He knew his ma had to work hard and he of course had to do his share to help earn some money – a butcher's round, a milk round and a paper round. He left school at fourteen and went to work in a tool factory – at first sweeping floors, taking rubbish to the furnaces, running to get tools for the adults and making sure the clocking-in cards were taken promptly up to the Payroll Section. It was in this section that he first met Olive – he could still remember the smile she gave him when he dropped the cards as he entered the office. She must have been the office junior at the time and was very friendly. However, he knew that office girls seldom went out with boys from the factory – at least he had been told by the foreman that those girls in the office were not for the likes of him. But he was not one who worried too much about authority and handing over the cards one day when he was barely fifteen he asked if he could take her out. That was how it began – her name was Olive, Olive Larkin.

But he had little money left by which to take her out after giving most of his small wage packet to his ma – he had to get more money – or how else could he impress the girl? Of course it was pool that got him money and also into trouble. It had been whilst he was still at school that a neighbour, taking pity on him because he had no father, had often taken him down to the local pool hall. The neighbour taught him the game and before long he was able to give a good game to any of those who regularly attended the place. When he left school he began going to the hall more frequently, seeking a game with any person who had no one to play with, just so long as they paid for the table. He began to get very good but not having any spare dollars did not at first play for money as most of the men did, although he was sure he could beat most of them who played there.

But now he had a girl he needed money and figured the only way he could get some was to play pool. He started in a small way, winning, and occasionally losing, one or two dollars but on balance made enough to take Olive to a dance or to the movies.

Thus he carried on for some two years, in which time he became engaged to the girl, who lived on the other side of town. Then in 1941, when he had managed to get enough money to buy an old automobile and found many of the locals would not play him for money, he decided to move further afield. He gave up his job in the tool factory and at seventeen started to play small towns in Vermont, New Hampshire and Maine, travelling in his broken-down old Cadillac. He stayed generally only one night and if he made a winning made sure not to return the next day but moved on to the next town. He used the pretence of being a salesman, looking for a game and some action, he was just passing through. He had become a hustler.

It was when he moved down to Boston that he met his match and was tempted into a game with another hustler who was better at that time than he was. He ended up in debt to two guys who said they were prepared to wipe out the debt if he did a job with them. It seems they had a foolproof scheme for robbing a small town bank which they assured him would give them easy pickings. The town was Primrose, New Hampshire.

However, everything went wrong and a bank employee was badly injured and no money was taken. They ended up behind bars. He, being the youngest and having no previous convictions, which the other two had, received a five-year sentence. Whilst he was in prison his mother died and two years later he was released on parole; he was twenty-one and had served almost four years.

His fiancée had stood by him when he was convicted and said she would wait. It was 1942 and America had been at war almost a year. Early the following year Olive joined the marines but continued to visit him whenever she got the chance, that is until in 1945 when she was shipped out to the Pacific. After that he received just one letter, written whilst on board ship, and then came that terrible day when he was told she had been killed in an airfield on Okinawa. It was just a few months before he was due for release and he was devastated and although over the years to follow he had become a hard man, he could never hear her name without his stomach turning and feeling sick within. It was of course Toni Felati who really changed his life – he owed much to Toni. It had been a chance meeting with Toni Felati on the pool table in the Pen which changed things for him and indeed helped to make his life in prison more bearable. Felati was a man twice his age, who took a liking to the youngster, especially admiring his skill on the pool table. Toni was a big-shot among the prisoners and was able to see that no one messed with his young friend, although in truth Peter Bronson was able to look after himself.

It was Felati who gave him his start after leaving prison just one week after the Japanese surrender following the dropping of two atom bombs. He was introduced to members of the Felati gang, who were about to move their operations out west, where they figured the big money would be. The men he met were mostly heavies, the exceptions being Otto Felshein and big Jim Booker. Both of these accepted the new man and he was soon being told of how most of the east coast operations were to be closed and how with the money cleared they would be going legit, out west. They were to make the up and coming town of Las Vegas in Nevada, the state which had favourable gambling laws, their headquarters. They opened a gambling house and soon were having an hotel and a new gaming palace built to their own specifications. Felati, who left prison in 1947, put him in charge of the remaining east coast operations which had been made more acceptable to the law by scaling down and closing the more dubious activities, and of course always making sure those in power were kept informed and looked after.

After three years Felati made Bronson his second man when his two lieutenants were killed in a car crash – Bronson then moved out west.

A further five years and Felati died leaving Bronson in charge. All the gang accepted the new boss, now a millionaire, and in any case who would have wished to do otherwise since Bronson had become a real tough hombre, feared by most who were not on his side? He now ran three hotels in Las Vegas and two gaming houses; he also had the major interest in two other hotels, one in Chicago another in New York.

He had indeed come a long way since the failed bank raid in Primrose. However, he was a somewhat lonely man, he had never married and for many years had only lived for his work, showing little interest in women – he had never quite got over the death of his fiancée so many years ago.

* * *

He arrived at the Hilton late afternoon and immediately asked one of the clerks on reception to locate a telephone number for him and get the call transferred to his room. It was a call to Arkansas Oil. Bronson expected service and usually got it, not only did he have that look which makes people not question what he said but he also knew how to tip and that it was expected in the Big Apple.

Soon after arriving in his room the call came through. "Arkansas Oil – how can I help you?"

"Are you able to tell me if Mr Julius Steinberg is in New York or up at his home in New Hampshire?"

"I'm sorry, sir. I cannot tell you, as Mr Steinberg seldom visits this office. If you hold the line I'll put you through to

Brooklyn and they should be able to tell you." There was a short pause until the operator in Brooklyn answered.

"I understand you want to know if Mr Steinberg is in the office or at home. I can tell you he is not in the office and as his secretary went up there only yesterday I am pretty certain he will be at home, for a few days at least."

Armed with this information he decided he would pay Steinberg a visit, an unannounced visit. First he had to find the best route up to the town of Primrose. Again he sought the services of the clerk on reception and asked him to bring him up a map of New England and charge it to his bill.

Ten minutes later he received the map and began deciding on the best route to Primrose. He had not been there for more years than he cared to remember and of course the place and the roads would be changed. He arranged for a hire car to be made available for the morrow.

He left the Hilton at ten thirty the following morning and covered the first hundred miles in just over two hours, which he considered good, allowing for the much slower traffic when leaving the built-up area of New York. He pulled up for a meal in Albany, setting off for Claremont just after two o'clock in the afternoon. He had not quite made up his mind how he would confront Steinberg or when he would do it, he just knew he had to do it. Although there was no evidence to show that this man was his real father, he had it firmly fixed in his mind that he was and he was angry. He never even considered that even if he were the son that his father may not be aware that he had a son. In his mind Steinberg must have known and must have deliberately done nothing to help his mother and the more he thought as the miles passed by, his anger grew.

He stopped again at Claremont and the break seemed to calm him and he began to think more rationally. The next section of the road was on quiet and almost mountainous roads and he switched on his radio to take his mind off his mission. A local radio station was advertising the Lake Hotel in Primrose and mentioned how many tourists were making this little town a must when touring New England. By the time he reached Primrose and pulled up outside the Lake Hotel, it was six thirty and he was tired. He got out of his car and his heart gave a jump as he looked across the road to the bank that many years ago had been the cause of his visit to the Penitentiary. It was his first visit to the town since then.

He walked into the hotel and to reception where Jake Ramsden was standing behind the desk.

"Good evening, sir, can I help you?"

"Yes, I want a room for the night and a meal."

"We have one room only left so you are lucky but I think there are empty tables in the restaurant across there. Are you likely to want to stay long?"

Bronson ignored the last remark and replied, "I'll take the room. I've left my car outside, get someone to put it away for me. I'll have dinner after I've washed up in my room."

"Would you mind signing the register, sir?" Jake passed him the book and watched him sign, *Paul Brown.*

Jake handed him his room key and asked for his car key.

"Don't I know you from somewhere? I seem to have met you before."

"No, I doubt if you know me. I ain't been around these parts in forty years."

"I'm sorry, I guess I must be mistaking you for someone else. I hope you enjoy your stay."

As Bronson walked up the stairs to his room, Jake was trying to think where he might have seen him. Jake prided himself on his memory for faces and he felt sure he had seen this man somewhere before.

Bronson came down a little later and Jake, still puzzling, followed him into the dining room. Emile seated Bronson at a table near the lake and took his order. Jake busied himself near the kitchen, passing furtive glances towards the man. He was convinced he knew him. He then took the wine list to him. "Can I get you any wine?"

"I'll have a glass of white wine, dry," Bronson abruptly answered.

Jake brought him the wine. "Are you up here on business or touring?" Jake expected an abrupt answer again but instead Bronson said it was a bit of both.

"I want to meet someone who lives up here, you may be able to help me. I got some business for Julius Steinberg. Do you know him?"

"Why, everyone knows Julius Steinberg. He is one of our main tourist attractions although those who come to see where he lives seldom ever see him – but they still come."

"Does he live far from here?"

"Oh, no, he lives no more than a mile from the hotel but he does not see visitors unless they have an appointment. He has to do this or else he would be for ever having people going to his house."

"How does one get an appointment – can you fix it? I'll make it worth your while."

"Oh no, sir, I can't fix an appointment – it would have to be with the housekeeper or his secretary when she is there. Joe Mancini sometimes comes into the bar in the evening, he's his chauffeur, perhaps he would be worth talking to."

"Can you tell me where the house is – I might just call there. I'm sure he would want to see me if he knew my business."

Jake went on to explain where the house was situated and how it would be difficult to get past the gate but the new guest did not seem to care. "Let me know if this Mancini guy comes into the bar tonight – I'd like to meet him. In any case, I'll try my luck tomorrow."

CVI

After putting the telephone down on MacDonald, Ruby went downstairs to the kitchen where she knew she would find Molly the housekeeper and perhaps Joe Mancini.

"Hullo, Molly. Have you seen anything of Joe lately?"

"He was here a short time ago, does Julius want him? I think he went to the garage, said he'd better polish up the car after that run out yesterday."

"I'll go round to the garage. If I miss him would you tell him I would like a word with him?"

Ruby walked out of the kitchen door and over the paved side area to the garage tucked behind two large oak trees.

"Anybody at home?" she called.

"Hi, Ruby. What brings you down here – does the old man want me?"

"No, it's you I've come to see, Joe."

"What is it then?"

"Two things. First, would you mind running me into town sometime this afternoon, and second, I've just had a word with Mac up at headquarters. He says you know all about this Peter Bronson business."

Joe looked surprised and at first said nothing. "What's Mac been saying?"

"Nothing much, except to say I should speak to you."

"What do you know?"

"All I know is that Julius has asked me to find out about this man called Bronson and Mac has told me a few things, but I was intrigued to know how Mac got involved. He said to ask you."

"Jesus, why did Mac tell you about the affair – he knows it could put our jobs on the line."

"From what I understand, you are both concerned that Julius does not find out that you have been making your own investigations. However, now I know through Julius himself I guess you are nearly off the hook. I certainly won't tell him anything about you and Mac but I would like to know how this all started."

Joe then related how he had taken Steinberg over to the other side of the lake and how he had been told of the girl Julius had known in the First World War. He then told her how he had made enquiries to see if the lady was still around and how one of the locals had found out about the girl from his mother. There was also mention of a son and when the local had told him that the husband had left the wife believing the son not to be his, he, Joe, put two and two together and wondered if perhaps Julius was the father. Their further enquiries had come to the ears of the son, who had never known his real father and they had been forced to reveal who this man was who once knew his mother. Joe told Ruby that this Peter Bronson was a tough egg and not one to mess with.

"Well, I can guess that Julius knows nothing of your actions in this. I think he has only recently found out about Bronson and has asked me if I will try and find out something about him. I didn't know where to start and thought of ringing Mac to ask him if he had any ideas. It was when I mentioned the person I was to find out about was from Las Vegas that he straightway guessed I was to find out about Bronson."

"Actually we don't know much about the guy, except we've been told to steer clear of him, or at least Mac has. The local who found out about him for me said Jake Ramsden had met him once."

"You mean the hotel proprietor? Does he know about Julius?"

"As far as I know he knows nothing. I think he thinks Julius might want him to do a job for him. I suppose he might be able to fill you in a bit more about the man."

Ruby again assured Joe that she would not mention him when reporting back to their boss.

"I've got to make a call and if everything is all right I'll get you to take me into Primrose."

Ruby returned to the house and picked up the telephone and dialled a number.

"Hullo, Lake Hotel."

"Could you put me through to Mr John Davis, a guest at your hotel?"

"Just hold the line a moment, I think he went into the dining room."

A moment's pause whilst Lee was fetched and then: "John Davis here – is that Ruby?"

"Yes. How did you know it would be me?"

"As far as I know you're the only one who knows I am here. Are you able to come and show me around?"

"Yes, I'll be over in about half an hour. My boss's chauffeur will bring me in. I'll see you in the hotel. Bye."

Thirty minutes or so later Ruby came into the hotel and seeing Jake Ramsden near the foot of the stairs went over to him.

"Excuse me, Mr Ramsden. Do you mind if I ask you a question?" she said.

"Why, hullo, Miss Steers. Ask me a question? Why sure, as long as it won't incriminate me," he replied with a smile.

"I understand that you once met a man called Peter Bronson. I am wondering if you could tell me a little about him."

"Peter Bronson?" he said, and as if thinking what next to say he hesitated before continuing. "Peter Bronson," he repeated, "by jiminy, that's who it is. Or if it ain't it's someone mighty like him. Sorry, lady, I have had something on my mind that's been worrying me since last night and I think I've got the answer."

"Did you understand my question, Mr Ramsden?"

"Why, sure I did, it was just that the name bothered me. You see, I saw someone last night who I was convinced I had seen before but he said he had never met me. But I couldn't think of a name and now you've given it to me. Now I know who he is or who he reminds me of."

"Where did you see this man?"

"Right here in the hotel. He booked in here last night."

"Did you check the register and see what he signed?"

"Why sure, I saw him sign. He signed Paul Brown." He paused. "Why, that's it PB, them's his initials, Peter Bronson alias Paul Brown. Now I'm certain it's the guy."

"Do you know what he is doing in this hotel?"

"Well, he said last night that he wanted an appointment with Julius. I told him it was not easy and he said he would go along and try himself. Now you're asking after him. Why would he change his name and why are you wanting to know about him? Now I remember, your boss's chauffeur was, according to John Butler, asking after Bronson some time back. I told John that I had once met him – I thought Julius perhaps wanted him to do a job for him. Now you're asking, I guess I'm not far wrong."

"Yes, I do want to know about Bronson but am surprised as you that the man is here under an assumed name. That's if you've got it right."

"I pride myself that I never forget a face. I know I'm right," Jake said indignantly.

Just then Lee Crocker came out of the lounge and greeted Ruby.

"John, something has come up. I think I had better get back to the house."

"Is there anything I can do?" Lee asked.

"You could drive me back, as my driver has no doubt returned."

"It'll be a pleasure. Do you want to go now?"

"Yes, but I think I should make a call first. I won't be long." She walked over to the public telephone and dialled the house.

CVII

Paul Brown, alias Peter Bronson, had stayed around the hotel the morning following his arrival as he had several calls to make to Las Vegas and he knew it would be useless to ring before lunch.

He had left the hotel once to take a casual walk down Main Street but otherwise he had stayed in the lounge. After lunch he picked up his car and drove towards the Steinberg mansion. He soon came upon the high brick wall and passed the tradesman's gate he had been told about. Another quarter of a mile and there was the main gate, set back off the road with room to park either side. Bronson drove to one side of the gate and left the car. He pushed the gate in the hope it might be open but it was not. On the left-hand side of the gate there was fitted a button, which he pressed.

"Who is it?"

"I have come to see Mr Steinberg, my name is Brown – I have something to discuss with him."

"Have you an appointment?"

"No, I haven't but I am sure he will want to see me."

"I am sorry I have strict instructions to open the gate to no one unless they have an appointment."

There followed a silence as the line went dead. Bronson, obviously angry, got back in his car and drove back towards Primrose but stopped by the second gate and got out of his car.

He pressed the button by the gate and the same voice answered. "Who is it?"

Bronson assumed a different voice and answered.

"I have a package for a Mr Julius Steinberg – does he live here?"

"Yes he does. Are you in a car?"

"Yes ma'am."

"Then would you drive it up to the side of the house and someone will take the package from you."

"I want it signed for, ma'am."

"They will sign it for you."

Bronson went back to his car and the gates slowly opened. He drove through and up towards the house. He was in.

The drive curved to the left, hidden from the house and land on either side by trees and thick undergrowth. As the road straightened, Bronson saw a building ahead and as he approached slowly he could see it was a garage with three doors. He stopped the car before the buildings were reached and got out and walked the remaining few paces. A paved area to the left went up to the side building of the house where he could see a door and windows on the ground floor. He made his way to the door and as he approached it opened and a lady appeared.

"Where is the package, have you left it in your car?"

"I haven't got a package," Bronson said. "I tried to get in to see Mr Steinberg at the other gate but was refused entry, so I thought I would come in this way," he continued, and smiled.

"I am afraid Mr Steinberg only sees people by appointment, you are trespassing. I shall have to call his guards if you do not leave." This was the first time Molly had been faced with this situation and it was all she could think of to say to him.

"Now, lady, I don't want to cause no trouble but I would not recommend you call them. I just want to have a talk with your boss." Bronson spoke in an authoritative way and Molly was not sure what to do next. She knew Ruby had gone to town and she hadn't seen Joe since he left to drive to town. He could be back, she thought, but she really did not know. There were two gardeners somewhere in the grounds but she could not see them and Steinberg was on his own.

"If you wait here I'll see if Mr Steinberg will see you." Molly started to go back into the house and close the door. Bronson stepped forward and placed his foot in the door to stop it being closed. Molly jumped in fright. "Lady, I mean to see him. I've come all the way from Las Vegas just to see him and I ain't going back without."

The mention of Las Vegas immediately rang a bell with Molly and she wondered.

"Would you give me your name, please?"

"I gave it you before when I tried to get in by the other gate. Paul Brown, it is."

"May I ask what is your business with Mr Steinberg?"

"My business is with Steinberg and not you, so go get him – or perhaps I should come with you."

Bronson stepped inside the house. He looked menacing and Molly wondered what would happen next.

"You can follow me if you would like."

She led the way along a corridor and up a back staircase to the ground floor, which had been raised from ground level to allow there to be twelve impressive steps to the main entrance. Along a wide passage, opening to the very spacious hall from which most ground floor rooms were reached. "If you would like to take a seat over there, Mr Brown, I will see if Mr Steinberg is awake."

Bronson looked around and made his way to a seat near the main door. Molly walked hurriedly over to one of the doors leading from the hall and knocked gently on it, waited a few seconds and then opened it and went inside. Steinberg was seated in a chair, reading a book when Molly appeared.

"What is it, Molly? You look agitated."

"I'm sorry, Mr Steinberg but I am afraid a gentleman has got into the house under false pretences and he wants to see you."

"What do you mean, 'under false pretences'?"

"He pretended he was to deliver a package but that was simply a ruse to gain entrance. He says he has come all the way from Las Vegas to see you and he means to see you. I can see he will not take no for an answer. What shall I do, sir? He's outside in the hall."

Steinberg too picked up on Las Vegas and wondered whether it could be the man he had asked Ruby to investigate.

"I know what you are thinking, sir, but he says his name is Paul Brown."

"I suppose we better let him in. Would you bring us some tea, Molly?"

Molly went back into the hall and asked Bronson to follow her. She spoke as they walked to the door. "Remember he is not a young man, Mr Brown."

"OK, lady, I ain't gonna do him no harm."

They walked through the doorway.

"This is Mr Paul Brown."

"Come in, Mr Brown. What is so important that you have to trick your way into my house?"

"Someone tells me you used to know a lady who many years ago lived in this town. I am trying to find out how well you knew her."

Steinberg was not surprised that the man had come about Zoë but he was surprised that this man assumed they both knew who the lady was and that the only question was how well he knew her.

"How do you know I knew a lady here and assuming I did know someone, what makes you ask how well I knew her? You don't even know if we are likely to be talking about the same person."

"Oh, we're talking about the same lady, all right," Bronson interjected. "The lady you knew was Zoë, wasn't it?"

"Yes, as a matter of fact it was but how do you know the lady I knew is the same Zoë."

"This is a small town and I guess there ain't too many dames with the name Zoë. My friend's mother was called Zoë and he is trying to trace his old man."

"Your friend, what is his name?"

"Peter Bronson."

"Sit down, Mr... er... Brown, wasn't it?"

Bronson walked across to the chair Steinberg had pointed to and sat down. "How is it that your friend believes that I would have any idea where his father might be? It was over fifty years ago when I last saw this lady and I never met your friend's father."

"Ah well, you see, the husband of my friend's mother left her before my friend was born and he left because he said the child was not his. His mother promised to tell her son who was his real father but sadly she died before she had told him. It seems he found the grave of his mother's husband but he is naturally curious to know who was his real father."

The fact that this man had entered the house seeking information, which it seemed had not been prompted, as Steinberg had originally thought, by the investigation being carried out by his secretary, came as a complete shock and he asked himself how could this man know about him?

"That's all very interesting but even supposing I did know your friend's mother, how am I expected to help in tracing the father of her child?"

"I said at the beginning I was trying to find out how well you knew the lady. You see, so far my friend has only been able to trace one man other than her husband who knew his mother near to the time he was born."

Steinberg could see clearly what was in the man's mind. Could it possibly be that he was indeed the father of her child? His mind went back to that afternoon all those years ago. Why did she not try to get in touch with him? Perhaps there was someone else – that's it, there must have been another man that he did not know about.

"The fact that your friend has only traced one man other than her husband is certainly no reason to suppose there were not others. After all, it was half a century ago."

"My friend has always kept a photograph, which his mother had placed in an envelope and which he found at the bottom of a drawer when he returned to his home after being away when his mother had died. The photograph is of a soldier, no name and nothing else. This, he has often wondered, might be his father."

Steinberg did not want to ask the obvious question – he felt sure the photograph would be of him. He had no recollection of giving her any photograph but everything was pointing to this being what he would find if he asked the question.

"Have you by any chance seen the photograph your friend talks about?"

"I can do better than that." Bronson paused. "I have the photograph here." He put his hand inside his coat and as he did so Steinberg could not help but catch a glimpse of a gun holster. Bronson quickly pulled his coat together when he saw the look on Steinberg's face and withdrew his hand, in which he was holding a dark envelope. He lifted the flap of the envelope and drew out what looked like a piece of cardboard and when he turned it over Steinberg could see it was a photograph of a soldier. "This is my friend's photograph," he said as he passed it face up to Steinberg. "Do you know the man?"

Steinberg knew immediately it was a photograph of himself. He had not seen it since he must have given it to Zoë. It had faded little but there he was, standing next to an aspidistra perched on a tall wooden stand, all in sepia. "That is me."

CVIII

Lee left the hotel with Ruby and picked up his car from the lot at the side of the hotel. It was only a short drive to the house and when they arrived at the first gate, the one used by tradesmen, Ruby got out of the car and pressing the button at the side of the gate replied to the question, "Who are you?"

"It's me, Molly. I got a gentleman at the hotel to drive me down. Is everything all right?"

"Oh, I'm sure glad you came back. Yep, as far as I know we are all all right. Our visitor is still in with Mr Steinberg, I'm speaking from next to the main entrance hall and all is quiet. I'll open up for you." With that, the gate slowly swung open and Lee drove through and continued up the drive towards the house. Reaching the open paved area near to the garage, Ruby told him to stop and then thanking him went to walk towards the side of the house.

"One moment, Ruby – I thought you said there might be a problem. Would you like me to accompany you?" Lee shouted through the car window.

"Well, Molly said everything was all right but it would be nice, if you don't mind."

Lee got out of the car and walked over to Ruby's side and as they walked to the door leading to the kitchen area Lee thought how lucky he had been to get into the Steinberg estate so easily.

"Let me go in the house first, just in case things are not right – I wouldn't want to lose you before you've shown me round Primrose," he said. "Are you likely to come back with me if you find all's well?" he asked. Ruby opened the door and Lee went inside – there was no one about. "There's no one here," he said, as Ruby followed him.

"You'd better let me go first now, we'll go to the entrance hall – I'll show you the way."

Moving down the corridor and climbing the steps to the hall they met Molly. She looked pleased to see them.

"They're in there," she said, pointing to one of the doors. "I can just hear them talking so I think they are both OK."

"I think I would like you to stay with us, John, if you don't mind. For a while, at least until the man in with my boss has left. I am sorry about this but after what the hotel proprietor said I think it best I stay anyway."

Lee, who had been given a brief rundown in the car, said he would stay. He knew he could not have hoped for a better opportunity to see Steinberg than to be given an invitation to stay. He had come to Primrose with the intention of facing up to Steinberg but he had never had any real idea of what he would do. All he knew was that he had been very angry but somehow after the long journey north and meeting Ruby his anger, although still there, was less. In a way, he pondered, he was being asked to stay to see that no harm came to the old man... no, that could not be, how could he act as a minder to Steinberg...? However, he consoled himself by saying he was not acting as protector to the man but rather to the lady. He now felt better about the situation in which he found himself.

After ten minutes or so waiting near the door to the room, it opened and the uninvited visitor came out, leaving the door ajar. Ruby looked into the room and saw her boss standing by the window. She turned to Bronson, who was talking to Molly.

"I am Mr Steinberg's secretary. Is there anything I can do for you before you leave?"

"No, I think I've sorted it out with him."

"Will you be coming back?"

"It's possible – I ain't leaving Primrose just yet."

"May I have your name please, so I can put it in my diary?"

"It's Brown, Paul Brown."

CIX

Steinberg looked across the vast expanse of lawn leading down to the moat and lake. He had seen a man who had once again brought back his memories of his first time in Primrose. The man called himself Brown but to Steinberg it somehow did not ring true, neither did the story of doing all this for a friend. Could it be possible, he thought, that he, Julius Steinberg, had had a son all these years? Why, oh why, if it were so had it been destined that he would be denied this knowledge until he had reached old age? What would he do now, should he deny it, or should he embrace it? If only Zoë had told him, things could have been so different for her and the boy. The boy, he mused… my God, he would be well into middle age!

At that moment his secretary knocked on the door left ajar and entered. "Are you all right, sir?"

Steinberg looked back into the room but did not answer immediately; he seemed somewhat dazed, almost as if his mind were somewhere else. Ruby walked across the room to where her boss was standing and repeated the question.

Steinberg looked back at the window.

"I've had a bit of a shock, Ruby."

"Oh dear, I was worried when I learnt from Molly that someone had tricked their way into the house – I came back from Primrose at once… can I help in any way?"

Again Steinberg did not answer but walked back to his favourite chair and sat down.

"I think you had better sit down too, Ruby."

Ruby seated herself in a chair opposite the old man.

"The other day I asked you to investigate a man called Bronson and today that man, who has just left this room, who says he is a friend of Bronson, has produced an old photograph of me which he says was undoubtedly treasured by Bronson's mother. And it is obvious that he considers me a candidate for his friend's father."

Ruby shifted uneasily in her chair. She now had no doubts that this man who called himself Brown was Bronson, Jake Ramsden was right. Her only doubt had been if the man had wanted to speak to her boss on something entirely different. The fact that he had come to speak about Steinberg's relationship with a lady many years ago had clinched it. Now what should she say?

"Mr Steinberg, it is really no business of mine but I think you should know that that man is probably Peter Bronson and not Paul Brown. At the hotel in Primrose the proprietor, you know Jake Ramsden, said he thought he had met the man when he booked in last night but was put off by the name and couldn't remember where he had seen him before. Then this morning having been told that Jake had met Bronson I decided to ask him what he knew about him. Then as soon as I mentioned the name it immediately reminded him where he had previously seen the man who now called himself Brown – he was Bronson. Also the initials matched – Paul Brown… Peter Bronson."

Steinberg did not look surprised; he had himself been suspicious but had not had the courage to speak up whilst in the man's presence.

"That means that if I were the father of the lady's child, then I have been speaking to my son. What a strange world we live in. Why, if he was almost convinced I was the father, did he not say who he was? Why would he come from Las Vegas, virtually break in my house, ask me how well I knew his mother and then not reveal who he was? Did he think maybe that I would react differently had I known who he was?"

"Did he say what he was going to do next?" Ruby asked.

"He simply said he would report back to his friend. He did say he would be staying in Primrose for a few days."

"I don't wish to alarm you, Mr Steinberg but I really think you should get yourself some protection. I'm not suggesting this man will do you any harm but if you look at it from his point of view he would not likely be over-friendly, particularly if he thought his mother had been deserted in her hour of need by this man. It seems from what I have learnt that he and his mother did not have an easy life – after all her husband left her and she had to bring up the child without any male support. Young Bronson spent time in the State Penitentiary and was there when his mother died. She never told him who his real father was. I really think you should get some bodyguards over here."

Steinberg did not say anything but a picture of the revolver holster when Bronson opened his coat to bring out the photograph came to his mind. "You may be right, Ruby. I'll get Mac to fix something for me."

"I'll arrange it through him if you would like – I'll do it right after I leave this room. You must be careful."

Ruby left the room and returning to the study picked up the telephone, dialled the direct fine through to Brooklyn and asked to speak to Mac.

"Hullo, Mac, I've got something that Julius wants you to get onto right away. He wants you to fix up some bodyguards for him – pronto."

"Why, what's happened?"

Ruby told him and wanted him to make sure he got some men up there as soon as possible.

"OK, Ruby I'll get things moving. In the meanwhile I'll come up there myself. I ain't got a lot on at the moment. I'm sure the old man won't mind me coming."

"That's fine, Mac – I reckon he'll be pleased. Although, you know him, you'll probably have done it all wrong!"

CX

After making her call to MacDonald, Ruby returned to Lee, who had been sitting in the entrance hall talking to the housekeeper.

"I am sorry to have left you so long, John, but I had to do something for my boss. You know he is an important and very rich man and yet he does not really have anyone around whose job it is to protect him. That man who just left almost forced his way into the house and could have done anything. There is just no one around to see he is all right. I have been trying to put that right."

"I know I will feel a lot happier to have someone around to look after us – that man really scared me," Molly said.

"Is your boss OK?" Lee asked.

"He seems fine – just a little shaken. He is no longer young and he has had quite a shock."

"Did the man burst into the room or something?" Lee asked.

"Oh no," Molly said, "I introduced him to Mr Steinberg. It was just that he had got into the house by a trick."

"Surely a man coming to see him and being shown in the proper way should hardly be anything to shock him."

"No, it was not that which shocked him, it was what the man said to him," Ruby said. "I can't say what it was but you can take it from me it upset him."

The three of them walked down to the kitchen. Lee was curious to know what it was that had so shocked Steinberg but thought he would let it rest for the time being and bring it up later when, as he hoped, he would be alone with Ruby.

"I'm going back to Primrose with John here. I won't be too long. You'll be all right?"

"Oh yes, I'll be fine. I'll have a word with Joe Mancini to keep his eye open for any intruders," she said, with a smile. "I think I'll make Julius a nice cup of tea. He's fond of tea, you know."

Lee and Ruby left the house by the side door and drove back towards Primrose. Lee felt comfortable with this lady and looked forward to spending a few hours with her.

"Now, you had better tell me which way to go. You are going to act as my guide, remember?"

"I think it would be nice to drive around the lake and on the way I'll show you the falls. They are very popular, you know. Then later if there is time we could take a boat out on the lake. Do you like boats, John?"

"That all sounds good to me. Sure I like boats. I guess it'll be great on the lake."

"You've never told me what you do, John. I've been trying to figure out your occupation."

Lee was not sure what to say but thought he had lied enough and could get himself really tied up if he told her some other occupation.

"I guess we turn this way," he said. "I'm in oil, leastwise I was."

"Well, that's a coincidence. Of course you know my boss is an oilman and that makes me in oil too. Who do you work for?"

"I did work for a small oil company known as Turners."

The name meant something to Ruby – no, it couldn't be the same company, she thought, that would be too much of a coincidence.

"I'm sure Julius had some contact with a small oil company of that name. In fact we took them over – they had a rig in the Gulf which Julius was keen to get."

"Yeah, that's us. We were victims of your boss's greed." Having said it he could have bitten his tongue. He had no wish to be rude to his companion and he had not planned to tell her for whom he had worked, but it just came out.

"That's a little unfair, isn't it? He paid a fair price for it."

"There is more to paying a fair price. I was assured my job would be safe. I was head man – we were paid off."

"You came up here to see if you could have a word with Julius. You then cottoned on to me in order to get close to him. I thought you were interested in me and all the time you were using me to get at him."

Lee slowed down, drove the car onto the grass verge and stopped.

"You have got it all wrong. Yes, I did want to meet up with Steinberg and let him know a few home truths but you are quite wrong on the other score. Yes, I started out with the idea of getting to know you but I quickly discovered you were a lady I would like to know a lot more about. In fact I began to think less of my problems with Steinberg and more about you. I like you very much and hope that this will not spoil our friendship."

Ruby was clearly upset and did not know whether to believe her companion or not. He looked an honest man and she liked him too but this had shaken her confidence in him.

"What had you intended doing if you managed to meet him?" she asked.

"Frankly I am not at all sure. I guess the way I was feeling a while back I could have done most anything. That man must have ruined so many peoples' lives. Have you ever thought what happens to all those people who work for the companies he takes over? How do you think they feel? Many of them are pushed out, some are too old to find alternative employment, some never manage to find work, some have breakdowns and some kill themselves. Oh yes, it happens. One day someone is going to show these guys that they should watch what they are doing – someone is going to get hurt – there's a lot of angry people out there. I know cos I'm one of them."

Ruby could see the anger rise in her companion and was worried.

"I've been with Julius for getting on for ten years and no one has ever expressed such anger to him. I'm sure if he knew how angry some people were with him he would not have carried on. He's a tough individual but he still provides employment for thousands of people throughout the world, that can't be bad, can it?"

"Sure, he has thousands working for him but there must be equally as many out there who have suffered in some way from his takeovers. I would be most surprised to learn I was the only person who took exception to the way he operates. It's not just the fact of taking over companies that annoys, it is the underhanded method he uses to get control. He employed spies on our rig and took the rig on knowing reasonably certain that oil would come in, in a very short while. In fact only a matter of weeks after he got rid of the original crew he brought in a gusher – we know now how he knew what was going on. He is unscrupulous in the way he works and he ought to be stopped and I came up here to do just that."

Ruby was not sure what to say. She liked the man but how could she trust him when he had treated her in this way? If the truth were known she had never really thought of what her boss was perhaps doing to scores of people. She read the papers and they seemed to rate him as a great businessman and indeed more recently he had been raised higher on a pedestal by the many gifts he had given to charity and the pictures he had bought for museums. The media certainly looked upon him as the tops in the business world. But was it true that he had been the cause of so much unhappiness and how in any event could she know it was true?

"What evidence have you got that so many people have been made unhappy by the actions of Mr Steinberg?"

"Ruby, it doesn't take much to know that if a company is taken over, there are usually people asked to leave – of course there are exceptions but these are all too rare.

"The news of a takeover, if it is ever known by the public, and small ones such as Turners never make the news, usually centres on how much the shareholders are likely to get both now and in the future. Sometimes there is a mention that jobs may be lost but that is usually the last occasion the public hear about it. The man at the head of the takeover is just as likely to be feted for his vision in this country whilst in England he's likely to get a knighthood." He paused in order to calm down a little and then continued, "I am sorry I have bothered you with this. You can see how angry I am. I really do not know what I should now do. My original intention of facing Steinberg is now secondary to not wishing to offend you. I like you too much. I think I can say in all honesty that your boss is now safe from me – entirely thanks to you."

Ruby did not answer at once; she was not sure how to reply. It was not worth pursuing a defence of her boss as it would just evoke more anger from the man she was now sure she could love.

CXI

Following the phone call from Ruby, Mac got in touch with an agency who undertook guard duties for important people.

They assessed the situation from what Mac told them and said they would do their best to get two men up to Primrose by Sunday night. Mac told them that he would be there to show them around as he was going up that day (Saturday).

Mac telephoned Primrose and left a message with Molly to tell Ruby, who was out with Lee, that he had arranged everything and that he would be up there later that day and asked that Molly have a room prepared for him.

Having informed all concerned at the Brooklyn office and at home he set off on his journey north. Mac made good time and was at the main gate of the Steinberg house not long after dark. The gate was opened by Molly after he identified himself and he drove up to the house, which had at that time several lights on in rooms at the front. He was met by Molly, who showed him to his room and said she would get him something to eat if he came down to the kitchen. Mac said he would like to have a word with Julius to tell him he was around but Molly said the old man had already gone to bed and it was best he saw him in the morning.

Mac told Molly that he would like to have a guided tour about the house and the immediate grounds if she would take him. He had been up there before but on this occasion if he was going to be of any help in an emergency he would like to familiarise himself with the layout. Molly showed him around the house and, after having switched on all the lights she could, then walked with him around the house pointing out who slept in which room.

When they returned to the house Joe Mancini, who had been to the bar in the Lake Hotel had been trying to get an answer to his call from the gate, and judging by the way he spoke was getting pretty angry. He calmed down when he learnt that Mac was at the house.

"What are you doing up here, Mac?"

Mac told him of the call he had had from Ruby and was surprised that she had not asked him to stay around this evening if she had been so worried. "Where is Ruby?" Mac asked.

"She went out earlier this afternoon with a new guest she met at the hotel. I saw them at the hotel, they were just finishing dinner when I left. Ruby seems as if she's found a man."

"You going to stay up here for a while, Mac?"

"That all depends, I shall certainly stay until the guards arrive."

"Guards?"

Yeah, I've organised some guards to look after Julius."

"I guess there must have been a reason. It looks as if I've been missing something. What's going on around here?"

Mac related what Ruby had told him and made the point that it was almost certainly Bronson who had tricked his way into the house. Mancini needed no reminder from Mac that he should be vigilant. They agreed that if either heard a disturbance in the night they would immediately call the other. Joe Mancini retired to his room but Mac remained downstairs and waited for Ruby to return. He told Molly he would open the gate and she could also retire if she wished.

It was nearly midnight when Ruby finally returned via the tradesman's gate as was the usual practice.

CXII

Joe Miller drank his coffee and waited for the young man behind the hotel desk to come for him and take him to the bus station. He was a worried man and tried hard to remember who he was and what he was doing in this hotel. He felt in his pocket and pulled out a wallet. Opening it and taking a credit card from one of the partitions he read the name, *JA Miller*. He was now even more puzzled but realised he must have given a false name for a reason – or perhaps the wallet was not his. He looked further in the wallet and pulled out a piece of paper that again mentioned the name Miller.

The name, however, still did not mean anything to him but on the back was a sketch. The sketch was obviously of a house but was very crudely drawn with only one or two rooms shown plus two protrusions from the rear of the house with two arrows pointing to the word, *"balcony"*. Also behind one balcony was written – *"the bedroom"*. A note underneath in almost unreadable scribble said, *"loosen bricks under"*.

Joe was now even more puzzled and tried to think what this might mean. It was obvious to him that if the bricks beneath a balcony were loosened then there was a good chance the balcony would fall, particularly if the occupant of the bedroom behind happened to tread on the balcony without knowing the bricks had been tampered with.

He was a killer, perhaps a contract killer, he thought.

It was while he was going through the possibilities to himself that the dining room door opened and the young receptionist appeared.

"I think we ought to go now, Mr Milne. I'm free now and have a train to catch."

Somewhat as if in a dream, Joe Miller got up from his seat and walked to the door, carrying his small case.

"We'll pick a cab up outside – of course I usually go by the subway but I guess you won't mind me sharing a cab with you," the youngster said, planting a huge grin on his face.

"No, of course not, I'm relying on you to make sure I get the right bus." Up until then Joe had not looked at his ticket and had no idea where he was going, but in the cab he felt in his pocket to make sure the ticket given to him was still there. He withdrew from his pocket and read the destination – Primrose!

It took the cab barely fifteen minutes to the bus station and in that time his companion did not stop talking about the film he had seen where this dame had amnesia.

"Where is this place called Primrose?" Joe asked his companion.

"Sorry, I ain't never heard of it – even the booking clerk had to look it up – sure not the most popular place. It's somewhere up in the sticks, but I can assure you the bus goes there. You'll no doubt recognise it when you get there. I'll ask when we get you to the bus how long the journey will be. You'll be all right, 'specially if your wife hits you with the frying pan – a blow to the head usually does the trick. Well at least at the cinema it does."

Locating the bus to Primrose was no easy matter since no one seemed to know where the town was situated. Eventually it was found with a quarter of an hour to spare. Joe thanked the hotel employee, whilst giving him some compensation for his trouble, and boarded the bus. The young lad hung around until the bus left, seeing his charge safely on his way.

Joe Miller looked out of the window of the bus and was not conscious of the other passengers who filled the bus. There were many stops en route but when they finally got to Claremont, where drivers were once again to be changed, there was a hold up. It seemed the relief driver had not arrived and there was an argument between the bus company representative and the driver, who was being asked if he would continue the journey. After a delay of nearly half an hour the bus was again on its way with the unrelieved driver, who had insisted on having something to eat and drink before carrying on.

It was now getting dark and most of the passengers had already left the bus. There were about fifteen people remaining on board and at the first stop after Claremont, two more alighted. It was now quite dark and the roads on which they were now travelling had no lighting. There was hardly any traffic coming in the opposite direction. Joe Miller was dozing and dreaming in his mind he was back in the war. He was taking shelter in a foxhole on a beach and there was his buddy a few yards in front of him, being mown down as he charged up the beach. He was then near a building and climbing a wall beneath a balcony – he knew he was there to surprise someone but he could not remember who it was. Suddenly the balcony began to break away above him and was crashing down on top of him.

He opened his eyes and there was darkness around and silence. He lifted his head and saw the wheels of a vehicle on its side, with the wheels spinning gently. He heard a moan from nearby. In his mind it was his friend Corporal Harry King. He tried to move but found his legs were trapped by something. They must have got a direct hit on our truck or we hit a mine, he thought. Suddenly the moon came from behind the clouds and lit the terrain in front of him. He was outside a huge iron gate attached to two high brick pillars. The gate was closed. This must be Jap headquarters, he thought, but where are the sentries? Perhaps they've evacuated the place – but it doesn't look as if there has been much action here. He turned and moved the obstruction to his legs, which was a man's body – he was dead.

Joe Miller summed up the situation. He seemed to be the only one alive and there was still that job to do. He was not clear exactly what it was but he knew he had to damage a balcony. It must be the balcony to the Jap commander's bedroom. It was obviously an important assignment. He moved over to the side of the gate and hid in the bushes. He felt in his pocket and produced his wallet, from which he took the piece of paper showing the balconies of the house. It was much too dark to see anything and he hadn't a torch but very soon the moon appeared again and he could quite clearly see the sketch. Yes, that was it – he knew he had to get into the grounds beyond the gate. He looked next to the gate but was faced with a ten-foot wall – he would have to climb the gate.

He grabbed the ironwork of the gate and began to climb – it was not at all easy but he reached the top and was soon climbing down the other side. When he reached the ground he darted off the road, moving away from the gate. He realised he had no rifle and nothing with which to carry out his task but he nevertheless carried on. I've got to do it for Harry, he said to himself.

CXIII

Joe Miller worked his way through the bushes until he arrived at the side of the house. Here he waited and looked around. There appeared to be no guards that he could see. He made his way carefully to the back of the house, stopping once to look again at the sketch he had in his wallet when the moon came out of the clouds.

There were lights in two rooms at the back of the house, one on the first floor and the other from a room on the ground floor. It puzzled him why there was no blackout but he guessed they must have thought they were too far from the nearest American-occupied island to worry about it.

He studied the rear wall of the house from some bushes near to the wall rising from the lawn to the patio above. He waited for the moon to disappear behind the clouds and moved forward to the steps leading up to the patio. Keeping close to the side of the steps, he climbed them and then moved across to the wall of the building. He ducked down as be went past the window showing a light on the ground floor and placed himself directly under the balcony in front of the window from which the light was shining. Next to the balcony a wisteria climbed the wall and some of its branches had grown remarkably thick. Joe looked at them and wondered if they would support his weight. The plant had been tied back to the wall with heavy spikes, reminding Joe of crampons he had used when he had gone climbing in the Appalachians. He braced himself for the climb but after grabbing his first branch he found it very difficult to lift himself off the ground. He could not understand it as it had not been long ago when he had won that schoolboy climbing competition. That last action had undoubtedly taken it out of him and he would have to take it easy. Somehow he would have to get up there. He pulled on his arms again, they felt weak but he managed to get up onto one of the spikes and edged up to the next.

He could now touch the balcony but he had not been quiet and he realised the noise he had made could easily have awakened the Japanese commander. He climbed one step further and heard the door onto the balcony being opened. He remained still and a figure came out of the room and walked to the wall around the balcony and looked over. Joe made a grab at the body, pulled it over and sent it crashing to the ground. Joe quickly stepped down from the wall and hurried across the patio and down the steps onto the lawn. He did not look back as he hurried through the undergrowth and made his way to the gate, which he climbed with some difficulty and perched himself on the top. As he sat there he saw the lights of a vehicle approaching and in his haste to get down the other side of the gate he slipped and fell head first onto the road below. He was out cold.

CXIV

Tony telephoned Ray at his home on a Sunday, he was ringing from Geneva. "I've booked a flight from Heathrow on the twenty-seventh. I finish here next week, that'll give you two weeks to make your arrangements at your office."

"OK, Tony. I think it will be all right. So you will be back in Weybridge a week from today. I'll give you a call then."

Two weeks later the two men left Heathrow bound for New York, one with the avowed intention of getting rid of Steinberg and the other hoping there would be some way other than murder to prevent him ruining yet more lives.

They arrived at their destination early evening and took a cab to their hotel, the St James on Sixth Avenue.

It was agreed that on the morrow Tony would clear up his affairs with Arkansas Oil, where he would check that Steinberg was at his home in New Hampshire, and providing he was there would hire a car and drive up state as soon as possible.

That evening they did the town! First they strolled down to Times Square and passing the Met casually asked if there were any seats for the evening's performance of *La Traviata* and much to Ray's surprise they were in. After the opera they found a number of bars and ended back at their hotel about two in the morning.

Tony left the hotel after breakfast to visit the Brooklyn office and arranged to see Ray in the hotel lounge at twelve thirty. Ray took the opportunity to go window-shopping on Fifth Avenue, returning to the hotel just in time to meet Tony, who had finished his paperwork without a hitch. They were now ready to go.

The hotel arranged for a hire car and right after lunch they were on their way to Primrose where Tony had confirmed Steinberg would be.

They stopped twice for refreshments and took it in turns to drive and by the time they were through Claremont it was dark. The last part of the journey in the dark was not easy on the country roads leading to Primrose but every now and again the clouds would clear from the full moon and the countryside became alight.

"Almost there," Ray said, as they turned a big right-hand bend that he remembered was immediately before the lake came into view. "What's that ahead on the road?"

The car's headlights had picked up something. Tony jammed on the brakes as they came up to what was obviously a wreckage.

"Christ! It's an accident, looks as if a coach has turned over."

Ray got out of the car and could see that some people had been thrown from the coach and he guessed others may still be inside.

"Tony," he called, "can you turn the car a little this way so I can see if anyone needs help."

Tony duly reversed and came forward at a different angle and lit up the scene on the bank at the side of the road where the coach was lying on its side. Ray ran up the bank so that he could see inside and yelled back to Tony that there were people still inside but no one appeared to be moving.

"I don't think there is much we can do here, I think it is best we get through to Primrose as soon as possible and alert them of the accident. Ray got back in the car and Tony carefully drove around the wreckage and on to the town. He stopped outside the hotel and both of them ran in. "There's been a nasty accident about a mile outside town. A coach, I mean a bus," he hurriedly corrected himself, "has turned over. Would you please alert the police or whoever to get help there? It's on the road south of here."

The receptionist picked up the telephone and less than a minute later was telling the highway patrol the problem. By this time Jake Ramsden had arrived in reception and started asking questions.

"Ambulances and the fire brigade will be needed as there are people still inside the bus and some on the ground outside. It was too dark to see how many and whether they were unconscious or dead."

"It's going to take some time for rescue services to get here as they have got to come from Berlin," Jake said.

"Berlin!" Tony said. "No wonder it'll take a long time."

"This part of New Hampshire is pretty remote with not too many towns and fortunately not too many large scale accidents to deal with. I reckon it'll take them at least half an hour to get here from Berlin. I'll have a word with some of the guests in the dining room and bar and see if we have any medical people who might be prepared to go out there to give some first aid until the services arrive." Jake rushed into the dining room and came back with a nurse and her husband, who said he would drive her out there. Then in the bar he was lucky enough to get a doctor, who said he would go out if someone would drive him. Jake asked for two other drivers who would be prepared to use their cars to help give some light to the disaster area.

Within fifteen minutes the Lake Hotel "rescue party" were on their way. Tony and Ray were part of the team.

They counted twelve passengers and the driver. Four were dead and others were either unconscious or in shock, unable to speak. First aid was given where it could be of help and about half an hour later the rescue services arrived and took over.

Back at the hotel Jake thanked all concerned and then turned to Tony and Ray.

"It was lucky you came along when you did, there are so few cars using that road at night that it could have been hours before it was discovered. It was right outside Julius Steinberg's house – I guess his house is too far off the road for those inside to hear any disturbance. I noticed his gates were still locked." Jake moved behind the reception desk as he spoke. "Were you wanting a room?"

"Yes, we've come up from New York. Took us a little longer than we anticipated."

"I seem to recognise you two gentlemen – you're from England and work for a travel company. Guess you must have thought we were worth visiting to come back again."

CXV

The dead from the crash were taken to a garage behind the hotel but the medics in the team decided that two of the injured needed special treatment, which could only properly be provided in Portland and thus four of the more serious were to be taken down the mountains to the coast some 125 miles away and a three-hour drive. Two other passengers and the driver were taken to Berlin whilst the other three were off-loaded at the Lake Hotel and were attended by Doc Wise, the only doctor in Primrose.

One of the three left in the Lake Hotel was Joe Miller, who had regained consciousness and apart from a hefty bump to the side of his head seemed to be all right. He was examined by Doc Wise in the hotel lounge which had been cleared on Jake Ramsden's instructions.

"How do you feel, Mr…?"

"My name is Miller, doctor. I think I am all right but I can't remember what happened and indeed where I am."

"That's not unusual, you have been in a road accident just outside of town. You were luckier than some. I guess if old Jake can find you a room you'll stay overnight, last bus is gone anyways. I'll come and see you in the morning. Where you from, Mr Miller? Guess you oughta tell your family where you are."

"I'm from Pittsburgh – I'll leave it until the morning. They are not expecting me back tonight."

"I'll see you in the morning."

"Thanks, Doc – goodnight. Oh just a minute, Doc. Where am I?"

"You're in the Lake Hotel in Primrose. Goodnight."

Joe Miller thought back. Now he remembered. He had asked to go home for the weekend and instead got to New York and then took a bus. Yes, he had intended coming to Primrose but what for he wasn't sure.

CXVI

The Lake Hotel, Primrose, was unusually alive considering it was a Sunday. Jake Ramsden had made sure that he was up bright and early; in fact he had had hardly any sleep as he had not been able to get to bed until almost three when he had closed the door on Doc Wise.

"Anything further happened after I went to my room, Jeremiah?"

Jeremiah, a young man, tall like a beanpole, stood up from behind the desk. "No, nothing happened, boss, 'cept number nine wanted some coffee at about four. It sure seemed creepy with those dead bodies out in the garage. I'll sure be glad when they collect them."

Jake ignored the remark and made his way into the dining room to make sure that all had been tidied up after all the helpers, firemen and medics, who could be spared, had had cups of tea and coffee.

It was a bright sunny day and the first of the hotel guests to rise had already passed through the reception area and walked out into the street. Ray had always been an early riser and the fact that he had been so late to bed did not make any difference to his uncanny ability to awake usually in time to be the first into breakfast. Today he had seen from his bedroom window that the day was so beautiful that he just had to go out for a walk before he sat down to the morning meal.

As he walked towards where the boats were moored by the lake he was desperately trying to think how he could possibly stop Tony from doing anything they would both regret. Although they had for some years thought and talked how they would like to take action against Steinberg and conspired in some way to get into the man's home, now it was close to the point where their thoughts were to be acted upon, all Ray could do was to think how he might persuade Tony not to take the ultimate action as his choice.

He returned to the hotel and went straight to the dining room and was soon joined by Tony. Other guests had taken tables and amongst these was Joe Miller, who sat by himself at a table opposite to the two Limeys. Most guests passed the time of day to their near neighbours as they seated themselves but even though Ray, and later Tony when he arrived, nodded to Joe Miller as he was passed, there was no recognition by either of them. It had been several years since Joe had come over to England to negotiate the purchase of WECO and in that time he had through illness and worry got old and the two Englishmen would never have been expected to recognise him. As for Joe, he hardly knew where he was or why and he most certainly would never have thought of seeing anyone he had known from Europe.

The breakfast topic of conversation was all about the accident. Everyone was full of it. Some were telling how they helped, some were listening intently and feeling part of it, whilst one or two were actually in the bus and told what they remembered. That is, all except Joe Miller. "Excuse me, sir," said one man sitting at the table next to Joe Miller, "I believe you were in the crash. Are you feeling well enough to give us your version of what happened?"

Joe Miller looked up in surprise.

"Yes, I was in the bus, so they tell me, but I'm afraid I do not remember anything. I suppose I have temporary amnesia."

"What a pity – I hope you soon remember – or should I say I hope you are soon better?"

The conversation gradually flagged after nearly all those present had added their particular experience or contributed their ideas of what caused the accident.

Lee Crocker came into the dining room after the accident conversation had died; in fact he had slept soundly through all the action in the night. Jake brought him over to the two Englishmen's table and asked whether they minded him sharing their table as with all the extra people who had stayed that night the dining room was a little full.

"That's OK, we'll have to go soon anyway," Tony said.

"I'm sorry to have to interrupt your meal but the proprietor tells me there was a bus crash out of town and as a consequence things are a bit upside down."

"You obviously were not staying in the hotel last night."

"Oh yes I was. I went to my room about eleven and went straight to sleep. Must have slept like a log. Probably got used to noise when drilling."

"You're not from around these parts, even though I'm English I still recognise a southern accent – I'm right, aren't I?"

Lee confirmed he was indeed from the south and was up here to see what it was like in Yankee land.

"What are two Englishmen doing in this part of the world?" Lee asked.

Ray gave him the same story that had been given to Jake Ramsden. They were working for a UK travel firm to find out the right places to stay in New England.

They were deep in conversation when Jake Ramsden came over to the table.

"There is a telephone call for you, Mr Davis – you can take it in reception." Lee excused himself and left the table.

"Hullo, John Davis here."

"John, it's Ruby. There has been a terrible tragedy out here. I'm afraid my boss is dead. Of course I won't be able to come in to town this morning."

"Jesus, how did that happen?"

"Well we don't know for sure. He was found a little while ago, lying on the patio. Looks as if he fell from his balcony."

"Would you like me to come out? Do the police know yet?"

"Yes, I rang the police, they'll be out here any minute now and yes, I would like you to come out later. I imagine I'll be tied up for a while so leave it for an hour or so."

Lee returned to his table where Ray and Tony were still seated.

"Just heard, that the man behind much of the tourist trade in this town has just died."

"Who do you mean?"

"A man called Steinberg. He's quite a celebrity round here."

"Yes we do know of him. How did he die?"

"My contact doesn't know for sure. She simply says he was found lying on his patio a short while ago. Could have fallen from a balcony she thinks."

The two Englishmen looked at each other. It had happened. What they had talked about for years had really happened. Not as they imagined it would but it was now all over. Steinberg was dead.

"I'm going out there shortly so I may know more then."

"What is your connection with the Steinberg household, if you don't mind me asking?"

"Oh, only a loose connection. I met a lady in the hotel a few days ago and she agreed to show me round the area. She happens to be the dead man's secretary.

"My goodness this is going to make a real difference to this town – the hotel proprietor will not like it one bit."

CXVII

It had been MacDonald who had found his boss on the patio. Mac had begun a walk round the house after having had breakfast, when he found Steinberg. He felt his boss's pulse and knew he was dead. He also knew enough not to touch anything but returned inside the house and reported the news to Ruby. "You'd better call the police."

It was some fifteen minutes later when the chief of police, accompanied by one officer and Doc Wise, who they had dragged from his surgery, arrived.

"Nothing has been touched, officer – we only found him a short while ago."

Doc Wise examined the body and came to the conclusion that the old man had had a heart attack from which he had died, but bruising showed that he had fallen heavily, probably from the balcony above.

"I would like all those in the house last night to meet me in the hall," the police chief told Ruby who straightway got

Molly, Joe Mancini and MacDonald to accompany her to the entrance hall.

The police chief arrived soon after with the doctor, having left the officer looking around the patio to see if there was anything suspicious. "The doc here says the old man died of a heart attack but I have to know if anything caused the heart attack other than natural causes. So I would like you all to tell me, one at a time, what are your duties and what you were doing last night. OK, you first," he said, pointing to Molly.

Molly explained she was the housekeeper and that she had gone to bed and left Mac up to answer the call from Ruby and open the gate when she returned from Primrose.

Ruby confirmed that she had returned at about eleven thirty and that Mac had let her in to the grounds. She went to bed soon after.

MacDonald told the chief his story, which tied in with what had been said. "What are your duties up here?" he asked Mac.

"I came up here after a call from Steinberg's secretary that the old man was very vulnerable to an attack and that he was worried about a man who had tricked his way into the house. In fact I have organised for two men to come up from New York to guard the house. They should arrive tonight."

"Who was this guy who got into the house?" the chief asked, turning to Ruby.

"He is someone who is staying at the Lake Hotel, or at least I think he is. His name is Paul Brown but we have reason to believe he is really a Peter Bronson, who now lives in Las Vegas."

"Did anyone hear anything in the night?" asked the chief.

They all said they heard nothing and Joe and Mac told of the arrangement that if they did hear anything one would immediately contact the other.

"Could anyone get through those gates to the grounds or come in from the back of the house?" the chief asked.

Ruby, Molly and Joe Mancini confirmed that it was impossible for the gates to be opened without setting off the alarm and as for coming from the lake they considered this would have been most unlikely, as the moat would have to be crossed.

"Of course the wall or gates could be climbed but someone would have needed a ladder to scale those walls," Mac added.

The police chief, who was obviously revelling in his questioning, then told them he wanted them not to leave town until he had finished his investigations. Primrose had had nothing like this since way back as far as anyone could remember. Oh yes, there had been one or two motoring offences and then there was the time when old Butler's store had been broken into, but nothing so important as this. Although it had been said that way back the bank had been robbed.

"You come with me, Doc. We're going back to town to question the hotel people. Put a call through to warn them not to leave until I've cleared them," he said, addressing the officer who had just returned from outside.

* * *

Back at the hotel the news of the death of Steinberg travelled fast. Jake Ramsden was standing near the door of the dining room when into hotel reception came Jane Worple, the lady whose job it was to keep the police station clean. She almost ran to the reception desk and Jake, seeing her agitated look, hurried there too, to hear what she had to say.

"I've just heard Julius Steinberg is dead," she breathlessly said.

"How did you hear that, Jane?" Jake asked.

"The chief called Doc Wise and told Abel Johnson to be ready to go to the Steinberg house as old man Steinberg had just been killed."

"Killed you say, Jane? They said he's been killed?" Jake asked.

"Well, no, I can't rightly say they said killed but they did say he was dead and the fact they were all rushing out there looked mighty suspicious to me. I reckon he's been a killed," Jane said triumphantly.

"You hadn't oughta say such things, Jane, lessen you sure. He's a mighty important man and they are sure to make a show of things when such an important man dies," Jake said, whilst inwardly thinking what such a thing could do to his business. Mind you, if he had been killed it would be better for business than if he had just died, he thought.

Jake, whose whole success in business over recent years had been geared to the goodwill created for Primrose by the fact that Steinberg had come to live there, was conscious that most of his guests were there because of a Steinberg connection, however remote. He thought he should make a brief announcement to those in the dining room.

"Sorry to interrupt your meal, ladies and gentlemen, but I know a lot of you are up here because Julius Steinberg has a house here. I have to tell you that we have just heard that the great man died this morning."

A murmur went up around the tables, with the exception of the table that had already had the news through the telephone call direct from the house. Speculation as to how he died started right away. Joe Miller, hearing the announcement, paled – now he remembered why he was in this town. He had came up there, he guessed, to kill Steinberg – now the man was dead. Was he involved?

Jake Ramsden came into the room a few minutes later and made the following announcement:

"I have been requested by the police that all persons in the hotel remain here until the police say they can go."

Further murmurs greeted this announcement and one person who had just entered the room asked Jake what it was all about.

"It seems Julius Steinberg died in the night and the police have called from the house as they want to interview my guests who were here last night." Peter Bronson was then shown to a table, which he had to share with Joe Miller.

Jake further announced that he would serve extra coffee if people would prefer to stay in the dining room rather than go to the lounge.

Bronson ordered his breakfast and then spoke to the man opposite. "This seems to be a big thing, the old guy dying."

"It's a big thing when anyone dies but I guess this town's prosperity is tied very closely to the man."

"Did you know him?" Bronson asked.

"No, I didn't," Miller lied.

"Strange thing, I met the old boy yesterday. It was the first time I had seen him. He certainly didn't live up to the reputation he had as a business tycoon."

"People are seldom what you expect them to be. He was just a man who had a ruthless bent for business and was prepared to tread on people to get what he wanted."

"Hey now. That's pretty strong stuff. I thought you said you didn't know him."

"One does not have to know these high flyers to know what they are like. They could not possibly be where they are without having a ruthless streak and have little thought for others. You mark my word, if anyone cares to really find out about the man now he is dead you will find many things that most of us would rate as downright dishonest."

"How come he is so revered by the locals and tourists if you reckon he's the guy you think he is?"

"Unless one has had experience of takeovers in any of their forms, one really has no idea of the effect they have on many of the victim employees of a takeover. Those who are not associated in this aspect and who benefit financially by the goodwill created in the town naturally only see good in the man. Also, whilst the media continues to report the gifts given to charity and/or the nation, the true image of the man is distorted. Such persons are cleverly concealing wrong doings by what is nothing other than bribery."

"Jesus Christ, you have got it in for these guys, or is it just this guy?"

Miller realised that he perhaps had gone a little too far. What if he had had something to do with Steinberg's death? It could now easily be said that he had a motive. He would have to keep quiet.

"Sorry, I guess I got carried away. I have been a victim of two takeovers and they ruined my life. I have been in a mental institution. You must excuse me."

The conversations in the dining room continued until about half an hour later when Jake Ramsden announced that the police chief now wanted to see everyone in the lounge. "Not all at once though. He asked if you would come in the parties in which you came to the hotel."

Two or three tables rose and walked to the door. Jake Ramsden motioned the first to arrive into the lounge. After about two minutes they were out and another sent in.

Tony and Ray went in and were asked to sit down. The chief of police and his subordinate sat opposite. The chief spoke. "Can you tell me why you are in Primrose and what you did last night?"

Ray explained that they were here to find good accommodation for prospective visitors from the UK. He said they had only arrived last night and were the ones who had first seen the bus crash and reported it in town. The chief thanked them for coming and said they could go.

Lee Crocket told the chief that he had taken Steinberg's secretary home later last night but had returned straightaway and had gone to bed. He said he had come up there from Memphis to see what New England was like.

"Please don't leave town, Mr Davis. I may have to ask you more about the man you say you saw at the Steinberg house."

Others passed through routinely and then it came to the turn of Joe Miller. "Why are you up here, Mr Miller?"

Miller hesitated as if he were not sure how to answer. He had guessed at the breakfast table why he must have come up there but he knew he would have to lie and pretend ignorance.

"Well frankly, officer, I don't know. It seems I was in the bus crash last night but I don't even remember that. I think the doctor who attended me will testify to that. He gave me strict instructions to go to bed and he would see me today."

"OK, Mr Miller, you can go. I won't need to check with the doc after seeing that bump on your head. By the way, where do you come from?"

"Pittsburgh, I think, but I believe I was in a hospital."

"OK, take it easy."

Peter Bronson was next.

"OK, Mr Brown. Where were you last night?"

"I was in the hotel."

"Have you anyone who can verify this?"

"Why no, I don't think I have. I would have to think carefully if anyone saw me."

"Why did you trick your way into the Steinberg house yesterday?"

Although Bronson had been expecting this question, he was not fully prepared as to what to say.

"I wanted to see the old man on personal business and that was the only way I could see him."

"You'll have to tell me the personal business. You must realise this is a possible murder enquiry."

"Murder, Jesus, no. No one said he'd been murdered."

"Nor did I. I merely said it is a possible murder enquiry. We have to look at all possibilities when someone dies in this way. Your forced entry into the house must make you a candidate for suspicion."

"OK, officer, I had better came clean. My name is not Brown; it is Bronson, Peter Bronson. I have come from Las

Vegas and I came with the purpose of meeting Steinberg, who I have reason to believe was my father. You can check my story with a man called MacDonald who works for Arkansas Oil. He operates from New York, they'll tell you up at the house how to get in touch with him."

"I've already met this man MacDonald, he's up at the house. He never said anything about you and Steinberg perhaps being father and son."

"I didn't even know he was in Primrose, he certainly wasn't at the house when I went there yesterday. You check with him and he'll tell you all about it."

"I most certainly will." Then turning to the accompanying officer, "Get a call put through to the Steinberg house and tell them I want to speak to Mr MacDonald now. In the meantime, Mr Bronson, I want you to remain in the hotel."

CXVIII

Lee Crocket had been told not to leave town but felt sure it would be all right to go out to the Steinberg house. He thus left in his car and drove to the tradesman's gate, pressed the button and was answered by Molly. He said he had come to see Ruby, who would be expecting him. The gate was opened.

Ruby, Mac and Joe Mancini were together in the lounge, having a coffee. Lee was taken to the lounge by Molly, who had obviously been crying. "Hi, John. Come in. I don't think you've met Mac and I think you met Joe yesterday. Would you like a coffee?"

"No thanks, we've been drinking coffee at the hotel, waiting to be interviewed by the cops."

Lee suddenly felt uncomfortable as he realised he knew the man Ruby had just introduced. Mac was looking at him.

"Don't I know you from some place?" Mac asked.

"Yeah, I guess you do. We met down in the Gulf on an oil rig," Lee said.

"Yeah. Now I remember, you were the foreman on the Turner rig. It was the name that threw me. How are you and what the hell you doing in this neck of the woods?"

Ruby flushed a little. Now she remembered. Of course Mac had been the one Julius had sent down to Houston. It would be extremely embarrassing for Mac to think that she did not know all about John so she came in quickly. "Yes, John has got some pretty hard things to say about Arkansas Oil. He thinks we gave him a raw deal. He came up here to talk to Julius about it but he never got the chance. I had arranged for him to see him today," she lied.

"Well, I must admit that I thought it tough the way you boys were finished off there, but that was the way with Julius. He had few scruples when doing business and he always liked to have men around of his own choosing. What are you doing now?"

"I haven't had any work since I left Turners. They say I'm too old."

"I should think we are all in a difficult position right now. Of course the company will continue but without Julius it ain't going to be the same. I don't know who can step into the old man's shoes." Then turning to Ruby, "Did Julius ever say anything about who was to take over when he packed up?"

"Yes, I did some notes for him only a day or two ago. He didn't actually say who would take his place but he made it very clear who of the people he knew well should stay. He also made sure of their continued interest in the company by arranging shares to be transferred to them in the event of his death. The letter was sent to his solicitor under his signature only last Thursday. I am of course not at liberty to tell you the contents of the letter. That'll be up to the solicitor."

"Has he yet been informed?" Mac asked.

Ruby said she had not yet done so as it was Sunday. She would try and get him at his home but if not she would ring his office in the morning.

CXIX

After being interrogated by the police, Ray and Tony decided that since rather fortuitously they had completed their mission they would stay over at the hotel for another day at least and take the opportunity of looking at the countryside around the lake. They first telephoned Boston and booked a return flight to Heathrow.

At first they said little to each other, the news of the death of Steinberg had come out of the blue and it would take a little time to sink in. Of course, over the past few years a great deal of their time had been spent considering what to do about this man and now he was no longer there. They should really celebrate but somehow neither was in a celebratory mood. A drive out into the country and perhaps a walk by the lake would make things seem different.

"I wonder how quickly the news will get back to the UK. I wouldn't mind betting one or two of 'the redundants' will soon be on the blower to you or me to share the news."

Ray said, "You're right, but what when they find we're both away in the States? That'll start them thinking."

They drove on the road which circled the lake and went on up the hill directly opposite the Steinberg mansion which could now be seen in all its glory. "That's quite a place. I wonder what will happen to it now?" Tony mused. They continued over the hill into unspoilt country, which looked as if it had seen no human for years. A short way down the other side they passed some open land where years earlier there must have been habitation. Tony slowed the car as they passed and where once there had been a gate there were the rotting remains of what had been a barrier or flagpole, whilst back from the road could be seen the foundations of old huts which had long since disappeared. Over to one side lay the rusty hulk of a lorry and close by a derelict car of model T Ford vintage. "Strange having a place way out here. Reckon it must have been an old army camp. That old car pre-dates the last war. Pity the poor sods who were stuck out here. It's a damn long walk to Primrose."

"And not much when you get there," Tony added.

CXX

MacDonald had never given much thought to what would happen to his job when Julius decided to retire or died in harness. He had lost someone he understood, someone who though often treating him almost as if he were dirt, nevertheless respected him in his own strange way. Mac knew Julius was a hard man but he accepted this and often gave as good as he got.

There was too much happening that Sunday morning for Mac at any time to think of what might happen to him. Now he had to go into Primrose to talk to the chief of police and it was only while driving the short distance from the house to the hotel that it hit him. What would he do? Would he still have a job with Arkansas Oil and would it be sufficient to support his wife and two children? The thoughts did not remain long in his mind as he reached the hotel and after parking the car went straight to reception, announced who he was and said he understood the police wanted to talk to him.

"I am told you know of this man Peter Bronson, who has been staying in this hotel under the name of Paul Brown."

"Sure I know of Peter Bronson but I ain't ever met the guy."

"He said you know about him likely being the son of the late Julius Steinberg."

"Yeah, that's true. I was the one who was responsible for the guy finding out about Steinberg. But understand we don't know for sure they were father and son – me and Joe Mancini, Steinberg's chauffeur, were only guessing."

"OK, Mr MacDonald, but would you believe that this guy Bronson would trick his way into the Steinberg mansion, get to see the old man, and knowing he might be his son, still say nothing?" The chief of police obviously found it difficult to understand and was equally surprised by Mac's answer.

"Yeah, I'll buy that. Sure I can understand he would go in cautiously, not claiming to be his son but trying to find out all he could about the relationship the guy had had with his ma. Yeah, I think I would do the same."

"Do you think it was possible for anyone to have got into the grounds last night?"

"Well, I had a good look around soon after I arrived and I would have thought it most unlikely. The walls are ten feet high and the gates can only be opened from the house. And as for coming from the lake, forget it, the moat Julius had built is almost impossible to cross. No, I don't think anyone came to the house last night – Joe and I would have heard them, I'm sure."

The chief thanked Mac for his help and said he was free to go. "Get the night porter, I want to have another word with him."

Officer Pyke left the lounge and returned with the night porter. "Did anyone leave the building after you locked up last night?"

"Well, we didn't finally lock up until almost three thirty. There were a lot of people in and out until then but after I locked the door no one went out until I unlocked the door at seven o'clock this morning."

The police chief walked across to the window which overlooked the lake. He wanted a little time to think. The night porter sat impassively in a chair on the other side of the room. The chief turned round and faced the porter. "How well do you know the guests in the hotel?"

"I'm not sure what you mean?"

"I mean do you recognise them and know them all for the time they are here."

"Sure I recognise them. I make a point of trying to remember their names. Jake says it's what a customer likes, it makes them feel important and then they might stay longer or come again. There ain't much work around these parts and this job is important to me so I do my best."

"I know you're not here all the time so how do you know those who arrive when you're not on duty?"

"Why, that's easy, chief. I always make a point of looking at the register when I come on duty and soon figure who the new guests are. Of course, if they only stay overnight I sometimes don't see them until they are leaving but there aren't many I miss altogether." The porter looked pleased with himself.

"There was a man by the name of Brown, who registered yesterday. I want to know if he left the hotel last night."

"Well, chief, as you know there was a lot of action last night but I can say for certain that that man never left the hotel."

"How can you be so certain?"

"As I said I always learn the faces of those that register and I sure didn't see his face until he came down to breakfast this morning. He must have signed in before I came on duty and had dinner and gone up to his room. No, I am certain he stayed in his room right through all the action last night."

"That's fine, Abel. You can go now."

Abel left the room.

"Well I guess that wraps it up. It looks as if the guy really did fall from his balcony. The doc said there was no sign of foul play but I had to be certain before I could accept that."

"Yep, chief, seems no one got in the place but what about those already inside the house?"

"All of those in the house worked for Steinberg and their jobs depended on him being alive. They all seemed genuinely upset. Their jobs must now be on the line. No, they were not involved, the old guy fell – he was nearly ninety, I guess he looked over for something… perhaps he heard a noise, a fox or something, and came out to look and lost his balance."

"Yep, guess you're right, chief."

"Tell that guy Brown or Bronson he can leave now."

EPILOGUE

CXXI

JOE MILLER WAITED in the hotel reception area as it was near the time he understood the doctor would return to the hotel. Whilst waiting, he checked on the bus back to New York and found that it was due at twelve thirty. It was, they told him, the only bus that day.

He desperately tried to remember back over the past few days but only little snippets came back to him. He had the recollection of being in a hotel and speaking to a young man. He remembered a taxi and being on a flight to New York, which he was able to confirm with the return flight ticket in his inside pocket. He remembered he was in a hospital outside Pittsburgh and that he had booked out to go home for the weekend. It was now Sunday and he was due back Monday morning, if he caught the bus at lunchtime he could perhaps find an hotel in New York and get an early flight out to Pittsburgh and be in the hospital by lunchtime, before they started ringing his home.

Doc Wise arrived at eleven and examined his head. He asked him a number of questions, including whether his memory had returned and was his vision satisfactory? Having received answers, he said Joe should take it easy and see his own doctor when he returned home.

"Do you know why you were up here yet?" doc asked.

"No. I have no idea but I think it best I return home," and then he added the lie, "I have left a message for my wife on the answerphone. She is away for the weekend and I can't get in touch with her, she'll be back by the time I get home. I'll be all right, doc – and thanks. How much do I owe you?"

"Shall we say ten dollars?"

Joe, whose wallet was fairly bulging with the notes he must have got with his card after he left the hospital, handed over the ten dollars. He then went over to the reception desk and asked for his bill, which he again paid for in cash.

Jake Ramsden took the money.

"OK, sir. I guess it's not worth you signing the register as you're leaving and only came here cos you were in the crash. Have you remembered where you were going?"

"No, I'm going home. I need to rest, the doc says – he reckons my memory will return. It's a nice hotel you have here. Next time I come up this way I certainly will make a point of staying. Thanks for the service, I'll get my things from the room and I'll catch the New York bus at twelve thirty. It stops outside, doesn't it?"

"Yep, right outside. The driver always comes in the hotel to make sure he don't miss any passengers. May not be so many soon now old man Steinberg has gone."

At twelve thirty on the dot the bus left Primrose with Joe on board. It arrived in New York at nine o'clock that night and Joe took a taxi to the hotel named on the bill he had found in his wallet.

The receptionist at the hotel immediately recognised the new arrival. "Hullo there, Mr Milne. Back again to see us? How's the amnesia? Did you remember what you were going up there for? What've you been doing to your head?"

Joe recognised the young man but could only vaguely remember part of what happened when he was last there.

"I was in a road accident. The bus I went up north on from here crashed. I was lucky but some were not."

"Gee, that's bad luck. How long you staying with us?"

"I'm only staying overnight. I want to get the first flight out of New York to Pittsburgh. Could you find out the time?"

Joe had forgotten he had given the wrong name but as soon as he realised this he made sure his return ticket with the name of Miller on it was not handed over to the receptionist. Joe would have to make the booking himself.

The night porter called him early and arranged for a taxi to take him to the airport in time to catch the Pittsburgh flight.

He arrived in Pittsburgh safely and took a taxi straight back to the hospital where his first job was to ring his wife. He was now back in familiar territory and he remembered why he was there and why he had felt so angry with Steinberg. He remembered that he had lied to his wife and the hospital authorities about the weekend but he could still not remember the bus crash or indeed much of his journey to Primrose.

Steinberg was dead and perhaps now he could carry on with his life without those continual bursts of anger and frustration. The doctor asked him about the bump on his head and Joe made some plausible excuse.

"Can I go home soon, doctor? I do feel much better."

The doctor looked at the notes in front of him and then at Joe.

"I reckon all being well that you will be able to go home soon. We will have to make a few tests after that bump on your head has gone down. No knowing what a bump like that can do – it so easily can cause amnesia. Still, who am I to tell you? Your army record, which we managed to persuade them to release some while back, says you suffered amnesia after being injured by mortar fire on Guadalcanal. You remember Guadalcanal, I guess?"

Joe sat for a while without saying anything. Guadalcanal, that was it, he remembered the beach and he remembered the big house and a balcony. Thank God for that. That's where it was!

CXXII

A week after the funeral, Steinberg's lawyer asked Ruby to call together certain people employed in Arkansas Oil as he had something of advantage to tell them. He asked that the meeting be held in the Steinberg house in Primrose.

Those to be present at this meeting, which it was understood was just one of three such meetings to be held in other parts of the country, were Ruby, MacDonald, Mancini and Molly.

"Thank you all for coming. Ruby knows already what I am about to tell you but it was at his request that you hear it in his house and in the town which he said he was most happy.

"You are each to receive your present salary until you reach sixty years of age, or if you so wish you can have a lump sum paid to you now, equivalent after discounting to the cost of providing that sum. In addition, you will each be given shares in the company to do with as you will. Shares are at present one dollar twenty-five each. Mr MacDonald, you get 50,000, Ruby 15,000, Mr Mancini 10,000 and Molly 7,000. That is all – thank you again for coming." Mac could hardly believe his good fortune.

"I'm sure he would never have done this if he hadn't come to live in Primrose. It's something to do with the place. You know we owe it to that dame he once knew." Mac looked out of the window across the lake to the hills beyond. "Thanks, Julius – and thank you, Zoë."

CXXIII

Lee Crocket had stayed up in Primrose until after Ruth had had her meeting with the lawyer. They saw each other every day and Lee had confessed to her that he, like Bronson, had given her a false name. She was at first annoyed but soon forgave him, particularly when he asked her if she would marry him when he had found a job.

She said she would.

"I guess I have Steinberg to thank for this. If he had not taken over my company and thrown me on the scrap heap, I would never have met you. Strange how things work out."

Peter Bronson, although told he could leave Primrose, nevertheless stayed and attended the funeral of Julius Steinberg. He later learnt from the Steinberg lawyer that Julius had left the sum of ten million dollars to the son of Zoë Bronson with a note which said simply:

In loving memory of Zoë and Primrose

CXXIV

Back in England Ray returned to his job and Tony, ever resourceful, was soon looking for someone to partner him in an enterprise he wanted to set up in the Midlands.

They had, as expected, to answer calls and questions from other ex-WECO colleagues concerning the death of Steinberg and now that one of the main objects of the redundants' meetings had been eliminated, they decided one further meeting should be held to see if anyone wished to carry on.

Several attended the meeting but although the death of Steinberg was mentioned the main topic of conversation concerned what had happened to each since the last meeting. The anger of redundancy had all but gone. Even Joe Thomas, who had found it so difficult to get work, had succeeded in getting employment, having taken the advice given to him by Ray to stop looking for the same work as he had been doing at WECO.

The scars of redundancy remain but time is a great healer.

CXXV

Ted Wilson had found employment as a storekeeper at a new factory which opened up outside Sheffield with the help of Government money.

He pointed out to his wife the small piece in the daily paper, which reported on the death of Steinberg.

"*...he was found lying on the patio below the balcony from which he had fallen.*"

"Looks as if what we did was a waste of money. Just as well," his wife said.

"I wonder," Ted replied.

CXXVI

Jake Ramsden had become a worried man. It was not that business had fallen; he was worried as to what would happen now that Steinberg was dead. He had heard what Mayor O'Reilly had said to Rube Malcolm, the police chief, immediately following the great man's death but he knew there was not much that could be done to keep the interest in the Steinberg legend alive without the old man's house. It would be difficult to get the townsfolk to come up with the money to buy it when the only real beneficiaries would likely be Jake Ramsden, the few shopkeepers and the people hiring boats.

It was lunchtime and Jake was standing in his usual place by the entrance to the dining room, greeting guests as they entered and showing them to their tables, when John Butler entered and walked straight over to Jake.

"Have you heard the news?"

"What's that?"

"That big New York lawyer rang O'Reilly just a short while ago and told him that the Steinberg place has been left to the town – the house, the grounds and even the big stretch limousine, in fact the whole shebang. 'Course the town's got to keep it looking good and there are certain other things we gotta do. Anyways, the town's got it if they want it. The lawyer wants an answer and is coming up here next week."

"Jesus, John, you've made my day. Now we can really do something."